RUNAWAY HEART

BOOK 2 IN THE RUNAWAY ROCKSTAR SERIES

ANNE ELIOT

For Skyler!
Hope you like this one too!
xo
Anne Eliot

BUTTERFLY BOOKS, LLC

Runaway Heart, Book 2 in the Runaway Rockstar Series.

ISBN PRINT: 978-1937815-12-7 - - ISBN eBook: 978-1937815-13-4

Cover art by Chiara MacFarlane.

Cataloging Information:

A teen runaway is saved from putting her brother in foster care when a famous rockstar agrees to a fake marriage, all while they help search for her missing father; but as they go on world tour in London, Paris and on to Berlin while lying to the public and the press —the way the couple feels for each other becomes anything but fake.

1.__Teen Fiction Romance, 2. __Women's Fiction and College, 3.__Rockstars New Adult, 4.__Military Family Life and ARMY families, 5.__Coming of Age, 6.__ Modern Fairy Tale Love Story, 7.__Teen Runaways, 8.__European Tours, 9.__International Teens: London, Paris, Berlin, New York City

A NOTE FROM THE AUTHOR...

Hello, and welcome (or welcome back) to the Runaway Rockstar Series.

This is a reminder note that I hope will bring you back up to speed on what happened back in book one, as well as serve as a *fast-track* for those who didn't read book one but who want to read out of order.

I decided to write this note because I always wish every author would do this for me. I read too many books, too fast. Often life, families, kids, pets and that part where I need to cook, do dishes, laundry and vacuum endlessly sucks out my mind—to the point that I can't remember even where I've parked my car sometimes, I think reminder notes like this are necessary!

If you don't think so, or don't need it—STOP HERE. Skip this chatter, head to Chapter One, and get reading! Either way, know that I love you like crazy for being inside this book at all. Forever grateful. ~xoxo AE

So here goes. My re-cap of Runaway Girl with very *few spoilers. (Please know, once you start reading Runaway Heart, I can't avoid them from creeping in, so you've been warned!)*

Runaway Girl, book one, is the story of main character, Robin Love, as she runs away with her younger brother, Sage. Their father is US ARMY, Special Forces, but has been missing in action for over a year. Robin's guardian doesn't want to keep the teens long term and is sending her little brother, Sage to foster care when Robin goes off to university. Robin has refused to let that happen so they runaway. At nearly eighteen, Robin thinks she can raise her brother by herself. Only, after one week of being on their own, she and Sage wind up broke and homeless. They accept temporary shelter from this amazing family (The Perinos) who sense Robin and Sage need help. Robin also lands a temporary, cash paying job, working with the famous band, *Guarderobe* as a nanny.

The band is hiding a baby girl, one who was left, apparently abandoned by her mom, in the Rock-band's top floor hotel suites. They need short-term childcare while they search for the mom all while they try to hide the baby from the press. Robin is hired, signs papers that keeps their secrets all while she keeps her own secrets about being a runaway. The members of Guarderobe keep even more secrets from Robin, too, but they also become very curious about this hard-working girl they've all begun to like very much.

Royce Devlin, the resident bad-boy and the *dirt-bag-baby-daddy* of the baby, becomes a guy Robin can't stand. First because he's a jerk, and second, because he hardly looks at his own baby daughter. He won't claim her as his own, though everyone knows he's the father. Robin, who misses her own father too much, takes this all personally, vowing to inspire Royce to become a *good* father.

Royce, while trying to avoid Robin's annoying as hell *parenting-tips,* develops a secret crush on the nanny-girl. He's never met anyone who pushes him to be/create/reach for something bigger than just a being a musician. Despite his promises to leave the charming nanny alone, he's also attracted to her. Her smile, her laugh, her outlook on life and how she sees *him,* the real him, becomes his addiction. (So…yeah…400 pages of attraction, friendships, learning how to adult. love-hate—worry about the future—the baby is adorable—and this rockstar-life is *crazy* happens, all while *searching-for-the baby's-mom* stuff ensues.)

And then, there's this day—this one day—where Royce kisses Robin. When he should not have touched her (duh). And Robin—because she's only human and Royce is this super-hot silver-eyed rockstar—she kisses him back. This one kiss makes everyone's 'secret' dominoes all fall down. The paparazzi already has questionable photos, and they write a big story, hinting incorrectly that Robin's job up in the rockstar-hotel suite is…inappropriate. (okay, that was a big book one spoiler—so sorry, but I am trying.) Then, BAM. Poof. Trouble. Robin's also been outed to the police back home as a runaway, and now she is a possible *kidnapper* of her own brother! She risks losing custody of Sage forever. The new family (the Perinos) who sheltered them and whom

Robin now loves, nearly gets exposed by the press for their own sad and secret pasts—all because Robin let this family help her. Worse, if people believe the Rumors about Robin, Guarderobe will be breach of contract —for keeping 'working girls' on staff! It's all rumors and lies of course, but people—fans—*the world*—they love lies. Especially if it means careers and futures are getting ruined. And these are the kind of stories no one would ever forget—so Robin and the Perinos would be ruined forever.

There. How's that for telling 'all' with 'very few spoilers'? This little note has taken me days of fretting. *Days!*

So…if you are curious about book one, go read it now. Turn back here. Anything past this spot including the first chapters of Runaway Heart is filled with the big spoilers. Last chance! I WARNED YOU. :)

Book Two, Runaway Heart, begins moments after Runaway Girl ends, just after Royce has *proposed*, and Robin has quickly agreed, because the marriage appears to fix everything that's going wrong. There's going to be a super-fast wedding. Bigger lies will be told. More secrets will need to be kept.

Like secrets about Royce and his runaway heart…

Sending all my love from Colorado, USA, to you and your dreamy, fairy-tale-loving, rockstar romance-reading, awesome big hearts.

Xo Anne Eliot

DEDICATION

For all who dream of kissing a beautiful rockstar on a stage…
and in London….
and in Paris…
and in New York City…

1

ROYCE

Name: Royce Devlin
Age: 21
Job: Singer/Songwriter for Guarderobe
Facebook: 10,987,698
Instagram: 63,495,605
Snapchat: 48,000,847
College Degree: maybe later
Long Term Relationships: 0
Future fake wives: 1

I'm losing it. Because it's my wedding day. My fake wedding day.

Because I'm not prepared to have a fake wedding day, and that's because I'm only twenty-one and too young to be getting married--even *if it is, all for show.*

But, *damn-me,* if speeding along in a dark limo crammed in next to your silent, dressed-up family, your best friends, and the breathtakingly beautiful girl who is about to sacrifice her life and freedom, all because you're a complete screw-up, makes one hell of a *no-going-back* impression.

I figure a wedding day could make anyone feel queasy—feel like bolting—feel like they might be doing the wrong thing. I also wonder if Robin Love, the girl who's squished in next to me right now and trembling slightly—the girl who is my fiancé as of one hour ago—I wonder if *she's* losing her shit underneath her passive expression as well?

Of course she is. She's heading to her fake wedding, too.

Because…Robin? She's just *eighteen.* Today's her birthday!

So, if twenty-one is too young to get married, then getting married at eighteen is fucking unheard of, considering this is not Medieval times nor is it the backwoods where this kind of shit might still go down, *right?*

Hell, aside from the kiss that ruined our lives and the kiss that sealed this engagement, we haven't even officially dated.

Oh, and worse, my fake-bride just graduated high school a few weeks ago.

High school. That's right. Meaning still knows her locker combination by heart, was in the school musical last month, prom just happened, *high-school*!

Which is why I'm going straight to hell.

Because no one should be marrying an innocent girl who's *fresh-out-of-high-school,* right?

I try to tell myself this could be worse. Like she could be pregnant and her daddy could have a shotgun pointed at my head. So, yeah, at least it's not *that* kind of wedding.

Though…shit again!

I'm sure the press is going to speculate that Robin is pregnant.

My eyes flick wild glances at my bandmates Adam Marcus and Hunter Kennedy, and then to my grandmother, the esteemed Mrs. Greta Felix, then to my uncle Gregory.

None of them will meet my gaze. They're avoiding it on purpose.

A situation that is fine by me for now, because if I catch any of their gazes, they're going to read my mind. Or, I'm going to read theirs. We will all have to acknowledge that we've hit sheer insanity with this new plan.

But crap again. And again!

Quickly, I take out my phone and type into the group message that my uncle set up: *Has anyone thought about the ramifications of the 'Robin-being-pregnant' rumor that's going to fly once we say our 'I-do' lines? It's going to take months of paparazzi stalking, along with published photos of Robin's flat stomach to disprove that rumor. Months! Poor Robin.*

I wait and watch Adam and Hunter read my message, then instead of replying, they pocket the phones and turn their faces farther away from mine like there's nothing they can do. Because…yeah, there's nothing they can do about my worries.

As for Robin's dad holding a shotgun at my head? *Hell.* I actually wish the guy could be here to do that right now. If he knew what I'd done to his sweet daughter's reputation, he probably *would* shoot me. And…maybe I'd welcome that. If he could only *poof,* miraculously appear and put a smile on Robin's pale face. But he can't. He's some sort of Army, Special Forces trainer who has been missing in action for over a year.

He won't be at this wedding.

Worse, my uncle Gregory, a man who's retired Special Forces himself, told me that it's possible I may never get to meet Robin's father. Ever. Because SF soldiers never go missing for this long.

Not if they're alive.

That's a fact Robin and I have never spoken about, maybe because we don't know each other well enough to talk about things that hurt. Or maybe because that topic is unthinkable. Unspeakable. Yeah. I'll go for the latter.

My head grows lead-weight-heavy with guilt, sadness and fear, as I ponder how much Robin and Sage have been through since their father went missing before we met. I also can't help but think how they're about to go through so much more—*because* we met.

Because my grandmother and uncle never should have hired her as a nanny in the first place, and because I kissed her when I should have left her alone.

It's so overwhelming. Robin's past and our colliding *insta-future* as a 'married couple' is supposed to help her. But, hell. What she's about to enter into with me, could actually crush her. So much so, that I'm finding it hard to breathe, because it's up to me to make sure that doesn't happen. Only… I don't know if I have what it takes to pull it off —to keep her safe how she deserves.

For Robin's sake, though, and because Sage, Robin's thirteen-year-old brother, is sitting across from me, smiling at me like I'm some sort of hero-guy to him already, I pull in a slow and steady breath, and toss the kid a small smile.

Because…I'm going to try my best.

And because, *God-help-us-all,* the damn kid is the only one in this limo who thinks all of this is actually real. We'd all decided he couldn't handle the truth—and even if he could he's so young he'd probably mess up in front of of the press, so we need to keep him believing that Robin and are are truly a couple and madly in love.

Which is why we're all so quiet, and why none of us can talk about the plans we need to go through, *or* rehearse how any of this fake-wedding shit is going to go, and why texts are blowing up my phone non-stop, instead.

If Robin's holding steady and my own Grandmother is contemplating the Orlando skyline as it zooms past us while sporting a little smile that matches the Mona Lisa's, then I've got zero right to freak out about, no matter how badly I want to, and no matter how badly my insides feel like I'm about to puke-up six-hundred live snakes as we get closer and closer to the sports arena where it's all going to happen.

We're going to do this. We're having a wedding after our concert.

The plan is already in play, and once we cross this threshold there is going to be no going back. For a long, long time.

It's a wedding in name only, not the first and not the last of its kind.

And my girl, Robin? If I can even call her that—because I'm pretty sure I've got no real right to do so—she's the exact girl anyone would dream of marrying, even fake-marrying. The press is going to pick up on that straight away and fall in love with her.

She's smart, all about family, not any sort of gold digger, that's for damn sure. I've met enough of *those* girls in my life to know the difference, too. Robin's the real deal. The genuine girl-next-door that any guy would be proud to take home to Mom.

If you had a mom. Which I don't. Just how she doesn't have a father…

Robin's also a way better person than I am. A creative artist in her own right, too. Not as a musician like I am, but as a fine artist. Painting, drawing. Told me once she wants to be a sculptor.

She has such talent that what I've seen of her stuff blows my mind. She also has a great career ahead. At our first press conference tonight I need to remember to mention how she's an artist. I think it will be interesting to the paparazzi, as well. They will love to hear how Robin has a legit scholarship to the best art school in NYC. That she means to start attending there in September, too. Once all of this newlywed-attention blows over.

If the press will ever let this story blow over, that is. But I try not to think about that, or about how crazy the press is going to be once this wedding is going off, because every time I do, the swirling-stomach-snakes crawl right up my throat and make me want to choke.

My PR guys swear that once we're married, we will turn into old news fast. They say as long as there's not cheating going on, no one gives a crap about married people.

Hell…until today, I sure didn't give a crap about married people. So it must be true.

I swallow hard, thinking…praying: *please. Please…let it be true.*

All I want is for the press and the fans to eat up the story of how our band met these two near-orphans, Robin and Sage. For them to record things like how we are now trying to save them from being separated. The goal is for the world to become our allies and worry over their missing father, just how we do.

We want Robin to be reported on as the brave girl who took care of her little brother at all costs. We want the story of how she ran away to Orlando so she wouldn't be separated from him, to really come out. Above all, I hope they see how she's generous, brave, kind, and incredibly strong.

The PR guys think this surprise wedding will hit the internet and world news networks by storm. It will cause utter mayhem for a while, which is just what we we are trying to create.

Curated mayhem. Mayhem and that's full of rumors and lies that *we create and control*—instead of the bad rumors that were started about Robin yesterday that, even now threaten to jeopardize her future.

Those rumors? They were started because I kissed her—hell made out with her—and then popped off at the mouth in front of this insane groupie person who'd witnessed some of our kissing. That girl blabbed all that she'd seen and heard to the press. Stories and lies which had Robin branded some sort of *groupie prostitute* who worked privately for our band. As a live-in, groupie prostitute.

And all of that was my fault. The kiss, the damn groupie misinterpreting shit, hell…the part where I couldn't keep my hands or my curiosity about what it would feel like to kiss a sweet girl like Robin Love… just once.

My fault.

My responsibility to fix it.

Our plan today, is that this insane wedding will create a full tsunami of new, *good clean legit* stories about Robin and I being in love. It should easily erase the rumors flying around about Guarderobe, especially the ones stating that we hired, and kept in-house, live-in, paid prostitutes up in our Orlando top floor penthouse where, Robin Love, was written about as our 'best employee'!

I shake my head, wishing I could unsee what I'd read about Robin online. Wishing I could turn off the whole damn Internet or at least delete every damn photo ever taken of her entering and exiting our private elevator to 'work'. Wishing I could turn back the clock and have never gone in for that kiss.

But…I can't. I can't do any of that looking back. So, going forward, the wedding has to create a new storm like no one has ever created. Inside of which, the whole band, and my grandmother and uncle will take the time to clarify the *real* truth to the press.

I run both hands through my hair, almost laughing at that, while thinking…*clarify the new fake truth, that is. The new pack of mega-lies.*

Once we're done, we'll simply step back and wait to see if it works. And if it does, we ride it out, then wait for the spotlight to go off of us and onto some bigger and brighter star with a better story than ours.

That always happens, eventually. We just need to be patient.

The current plan has us heading to NYC once our 'in-residence' Orlando parks concerts here are completed. There's the legal crap we're going to have to wade through to make sure Sage's custody is settled. We're also going to have to navigate through the part where Robin was a teen runaway, one who took her little brother across state lines, which is now being called *kidnapping*.

Once all that goes through, then there will be stuff like how I just found out that if I marry Robin, then I will also need to have a judge's permission to leave the state. Our entire band and my close family might need background checks done, too. My attorneys assured me and my grandmother that all of that will sort itself out, but possibly not before it nearly exhausts us all, that is.

Our legal team has been on this project for almost twenty-four hours straight. They're the best, and with them, my finances and my Grandmother's finances, plus her reputation and legal team backing us as well, it shouldn't take long to get it—*us*—our new married lives straight. Most importantly to get it all legalized where everyone is safe and happy.

After that, Robin and Sage will spend the summer getting settled into my penthouse apartment in NYC. Once autumn sets in, she will get to start her classes, on time, as a freshman university student. How she'd planned—dreamed about—long before she was forced to run away—forced to fake-marry me.

We think Sage will begin a day prep school that my grandmother has found nearby the penthouse. He'll have to test and interview to get in, of course. but the kid is smart and we think that won't be a problem. It's a school that will get him into any college he wants, and we've written in the contracts between Robin and myself, that Sage's school will be paid for, for the entire four years as part of this marriage deal—whether it works, or not—the kid will be set.

I even heard talk that my grandmother and Uncle will offer to serve as additional guardians to Sage along with Robin should her father not be found soon. This will help to prove to the courts that Robin has all the family, financial, and emotional support she needs to keep her brother by her side. Despite her young age, and the mistakes she made while trying to run away and parent him, we should be able to collectively show that she has the support needed to raise her teen brother just fine.

Robin and Sage will be settling in to NYC, all while the band and I have begun the Asia portion of our world tour. Provided we can stay on schedule. As the time passes, we've also promised Robin that we will help her search for her father's whereabouts.

I lie to myself. *And yeah—all should work out just—fine.* Overwhelmed by the huge tasks ahead, I shake my head and swallow down a hard lump, lying to myself again: *This should go off just fine. On time. And all…of this…will be very easy.*

We aren't sure yet how long Robin and I will have to 'stay married'. That's all up to the press and fan attention, but once it wanes, she and I will create some sort of quiet reason for a divorce. My guess? It will be sometime next spring. And my other guess is that I will fake-cheat on her so that it all looks like the split is my fault. Because she doesn't deserve any hate from the split, and because I am, after all Guarderobe's resident bad-boy, after all. I'm sure it won't surprise anyone that I can't keep a wife…not at my age, that's for damn sure.

Enter the lawyers and the paperwork again. Add in some new plans for Robin and I. Layer on some scheduled appearances where she and I appear to hate each other, stage some press conferences or a tantrum on a red carpet somewhere where one of says, 'I'm done.' And then she and I should be good to go on with our normal lives.

If any of us can remain even one-bit normal after this mad scheme plays out.

If the fans buy into this bullshit wedding.

If everything stays on track with the legal team as planned.

If not…well, shit…not much I can do about any of the above, but at least we tried, right?

At this point, none of us will let Robin and Sage face the possibility of being orphans alone. We owe them at least that. If it doesn't work out, we create a back-up plan that will be supported and funded by us.

She and Sage have a kind family here in Orlando, the Perino family, who are waiting for them. Should all of this blow up in our faces and we're exposed as frauds tonight, then Robin and Sage will probably go back there—though that will cause a new wave of problems we will have to wade through.

It's a family who befriended Robin and Sage a week ago, too. Actually, on the same day we all met Robin. It's a family who also now love them and treat them just like they could be their own family. Robin and Sage were thinking about starting their Orlando life with them before things—the rumors went out of control up in our penthouse. The Perinos even had a little furnished cottage in the back to rent out to Robin and Sage long term. And Robin had this plan of becoming a waitress after her nanny job was over. But once the rumors I'd accidentally created were all over the news and the Internet, the Perino option became instantly impossible.

This awesome family was in jeopardy of being flayed alive by the press, possibly even worse than Robin was because ten years ago, Angel Perino, Robin's friend killed the man who murdered his sister and put a second kid in a wheelchair. It was all for self defense, but it took a decade to get Angel off the news, and off of crime shows who'd made a ton of money featuring Angel's and his mother's sad story. They couldn't afford any negative limelight, because one glimmer that Robin was living with this very infamous family would have dragged out all of the old stories that they've worked so hard to forget. No one, especially Robin, because she loves this family, wanted the Perino's to be hurt, simply because they'd sheltered her while she was in her darkest hour of being a runaway.

That last fact, and the Perino family being fragile, is partly why Robin agreed to the plan to marry me so quickly. She'd wanted to pull the looming bright lights and attention as far away from this amazing family as she could. It's also why the Perinos aren't even attending the wedding with us tonight, and why my uncle is pissed off at me, because he's fallen in love with this Mrs. Perino woman! Seriously, the old guy told me he's *in love.*

Now he's got to wait a couple of months to formally start officially *courting her.* His words. Not mine. More annoying, he's actually pouting about this inconvenience. *Like I should feel sorry for him right now because he has to date her over video chat now. But I won't—can't! Because the only one I'm going to feel sorry for is Robin. She's the one who signed on to our—check-in-anytime-you-want-but-never-leave—*Hotel California life, and who has no clue what that means.

She's the one who needs us *all* to feel sorry *her.*

We all got Robin involved with Guarderobe's crazy—and so all of us, including my uncle who is responsible for hiring Robin in the first place after I told him not to do it, he can just help me suck it up and do what's right.

My lungs tighten as I drag my thoughts away from my own worries and I notice the way Robin's got her eyes closed too tight. Her breathing seems shallow and her hands are also fisted golf-ball-solid into her lap. This makes the ring I've placed on her left hand flash like a mini-warning light as we pass each street lamp.

I stare at it, unable to look away as a prickle of sweat breaks out on the edge of my forehead. The words my grandmother spoke to me as she'd handed over that ring come flooding in: *"In my day, Royce Devlin, when a wealthy, well-appointed man ruined a young lady's reputation, he would do the right thing and marry her. Most of the work will fall on you, dear boy, but I feel we have no other choice but to encourage you to make this right. This plan saves everyone, and darling Robin won't survive should she be forced to lose her little brother. And imagine the consequences to Sage if he's taken from Robin and placed with strangers? There's no other choice."*

No. Other. Choice.

The heartbeats slamming through my temples must have pounded bruises into the sides of my head from the inside out by now.

That's when I realize Robin's heart is beating just as fast as mine is, because I can visibly track her pulse right through the thin skin on her wrists.

My swirling thoughts won't quit: *Do the right thing. Save the girl. Save the band.*

No other choice.

Dress. A dress she's expected to wear but that she's never even seen! Isn't the wedding dress supposed to be an extra important choice for a bride?

Ring. An engagement ring given to this girl only an hour ago and a second ring, the wedding band, hiding in my pocket.

Bride. My bride.

No. Other. Choice.

I tear my eyes off the ring, deciding to catch up on 'the plans developments' which are still pouring in as texts. Adam and Hunter, and even my uncle and grandmother, seem to be breaking out of their stupors and doing the same.

I gently bump shoulders with Robin, and when she opens her eyes I place the phone low in my lap, signaling that she should read along with me.

The first one is from the stage manager that says how some sort of fancy, bleached, beach wood —*whatever the hell that means*—gazebo has been delivered. And that it's *gorgeous*. Another text reports it is now successfully set up with lights and silk fabric strung all over it.

A third confirms that the gazebo-tests worked, and it's ready to rise through the trapdoor we use under the stage for Adam and his drums. People will be in place to swap them out.

The next, informs us that we have enough dry ice *and* have added extra smoke machines to fog out the stage more than we ever have done. This fog should serve to hide some sort of red carpet they will lay down for us to walk on, and that the whole mess will stay hidden until they blow the fans. But that I'm to give the signal for all to go off when I'm ready.

I try not to roll my eyes at that last one, or stop breathing, because *who in the hell thinks I'm going to be ready*?

Another text says 40,000 LED, auto-light-up sticks and 40,000 color-changing LED wrist bands are ready to pass out to each audience member. Some will get to have both. These devices are always sold during the concert to accent our various songs with different auto-change colors. Tonight we are giving them all away.

We control them backstage, by network and it's a very cool effect when we can turn an entire stadium blue, or pink, or flash rainbow colors, all to the beat of Adam's drums whenever we want. With all of them passed out to fans for free, the effect will be huge, like a sea of stars going off when we decide to turn them into *bright-wedding-white.*

The next text says: *This white-light change will happen during Royce's speech. Which is why we will not use white for the entire concert so it will come on as a surprise—while Royce is saying what he needs to say.*

I almost choke and the head pounding increases. *Speech. Speech? WTF do I need to say? These people are expecting too much from me.*

We next read how the wardrobe and stylists are set up to get the girls and my grandmother ready first. *The bridal party.* Then, there's a back-up crew in place who will shove the rest of us—the grooms and groomsmen—into tuxes when we're done preforming.

But shit…even with all that pre-beta-data, I can't picture any of this.

I glance up at Adam, who at least looks apologetic, and quickly I text a quick reply to the group message, letting Robin read my response that says: *Awesome. Thanks for the rally, and thank the crew and roadies. So excited for you and them to meet my new wife.*

Then, I pull the phone away so Robin *can't* read my next text.

It's directed only to Adam, Hunter, my grandmother and my uncle: *Has anyone thought about what the hell I'm supposed to say at this 'speech' and what is going to happen tomorrow, or the next day? Shit. Guys. Gazebo and tux's aside. We are not ready to execute, are we? Are we?*

Adam shrugs, but at least has the grace to look even more apologetic, because he knows this situation is all his fault, as he replies to my text: *We will be, dude. We will be ready.*

I want to reply more. Remind them that they're not the ones getting hitched, and that maybe we should just murder Adam instead of having a *wedding.* Only, killing him would not help fix any of this, it would simply create more scandal.

I start to text questions like: *Has anyone but me thought of what in the hell is going to happen when I step on stage and rocks fall off my tongue instead of words? Forget about the speech that is supposed to come out of my ass, what if I can't remember even one of our hit singles when it's time to sing?*

What about that?

Instead of hitting send, I slowly delete each and every word, while I flick a dark glare at each of their perfect poker faces. I want to shout: *Have any of you worried about any of this bigger stuff?*

But I know the answer.

No. No they haven't worried about any of it.

Because enthusiasm, sappiness distracting the press and creating epic lying, smoke-screens are Adam's strengths, and cool-collected straight faced bullshit, despite huge inner turmoil, is Hunter's strength, my strength is worrying and fixing everything everyone else didn't think about.

I'm the one who *deals* during emergencies while the others cover for me and act like perfect rockstars while I'm dealing. I'm the one responsible for always righting the Guarderobe boat before it flips. That's why no one seems worried right now. I'm the groom. The one who is literally and figuratively driving this wedding boat right now, and they're just counting on me like they always do.

Which is why I'm going stop panicking from this point forward, and do what I do best.

Deal. Deal. And deal some more.

Everyone believes in me—from the band, to my family, to a thirteen-year-old boy who thinks everything is awesome right now, all the way to Robin whom—when we got engaged—I begged for her to *trust* me. I told this girl, straight to her face, that this was all going to work out fine.

Because, it will.

Over my dead body will I flip another boat when Robin Love is sitting inside of it—and she's more than inside of this boat. She's the bride. My copilot.

I already single-handedly sank this girl to the bottom of a very scary sea, all because of one selfish kiss. Now, I'm committed to dragging her back out of the deep. I will do all it takes to fix how I've ruined her good name, even if it means I have to lend her mine, and even if I'm the one who drowns while doing it.

Her result, her future…it's all up to me.

And, no matter what, I will not hurt her again.

2

ROYCE

As THE LIMO parks at the concert stadium in front of the back entrance where we go inside, I lock gazes with Adam and Hunter, and then with Vere. They're shifting in their seats, helping my uncle Gregory get my grandmother's wheelchair set up outside so she can exit first. Adam's unbuckling the little car-seat-baby-carrier thing that's holding his baby daughter, Apple, inside of it. Just like me, heck just like everyone besides the baby, he also seems to be freaking out about this plan.

I ponder the last time the baby came into the stadium.

It was the first day I'd ever met Robin. Hell, it was also the first day I'd met Adam's baby and wife in person, for that matter.

One week ago is when this all started—hell, let me rephrase that. One week and nine months, *plus* the months it took for Adam to fall in love, then derail our whole lives by lying to everyone he loves for over a year, and then appearing with a baby and a *wife*! That is when it started for *him*. Way back when we'd rented a castle in Wales to record the same album the band is now about to take on world tour. Way back when he ran away from that castle.

My part—or should I say my part *with Robin*—the part where we almost destroyed her entire future? That all started a week ago.

Everyone else, was also only ramped in to the real truth—about the baby—and the stupid 'first plan' that Adam and I had made to protect the baby, only a few days ago.

Meaning, Adam, Hunter, Vere and I only told my grandmother and uncle the truth about the baby when our stupid first plan spiraled out of control. But that's the problem with stupid plans. They require another plan to Band-Aid the stupidity. Often, the next plan is stupid as well, but eventually it all works out.

The baby appeared in our lives when Adam showed up to me and Hunter with a wife and a baby, and told me he wanted to out his family to the press and to the world, in a big surprise reveal. After we got over the shock of actually meeting them in person—*that's* the direction we were heading.

TA-DA, Adam is married and he's got a family.

Sadly, instead things going as Adam and Evie had planned, Evie had to turn around the day she arrived, and go tend to her very sick mom back in the UK.

Adam and I had thought, *no problem—we could just pause the plan.*

We figured the situation would only be for a few days, so we let people—my grandmother especially, assume the baby was *mine*. See, my grandmother talks too much. She would have slipped up and exposed the truth to the press too soon. We didn't want Evie getting mauled and stalked by paparazzi while she travelled back to Wales. That result is exactly what would have happened to the poor girl if her story had leaked—and the UK paparazzi—they are way more intense than the US paparazzi. Adam had worried they would have been all over the hospital.

All over Evie. But…Evie? She's got a messed up past of her own. She's really afraid of crowds, public attention, people—she's nearly claustrophobic. To top that off, she's kind of afraid of everything—unless Adam is by her side—so that's why we came up with the idea to lie, thinking…that she'd just be back. Really fast.

Only, of course we weren't thinking—about shit like Wales is really far to travel to and back from, and we weren't thinking about Evie's mom taking a turn for the worse, which—sadly, she had for awhile, delaying Evie's return to her baby. And…fine, this is the first baby we've ever involved in any of our schemes, so we didn't know what the hell we were doing.

On that first day, because no one knew their heads from their asses, my grandmother saw that the baby had blue eyes, and assumed the baby was mine—and so Adam and I just rolled with that assumption. Worse, my grandmother became like an insane granny-mamma-bear and she became hell bent on me being an instant-good-father, so she followed me to my concert along with the baby so my new family could *stay together*. Which is why we had to hide the poor kid that day. We'd placed her in a big box so we could sneak her inside without anyone catching on to the fact that we were hanging with a baby.

Tonight has the same feeling as that night had, one week ago.

Utter and complete madness.

Only, tonight, the world and our 'mission' with the baby has flipped upside down.

This baby is not going inside while hiding in a box.

She's about to be waved around like a little ginger-headed, toothless, adorable, *look-at-me,* press magnet. Adam, has stepped up to the plate and will finally do his big reveal, and her mom, Evie, despite how difficult this will be for her, will soon be asked to play along with this scheme, too. Because, thank God, she's back, and she's arriving to the stadium from the airport as we speak.

I can only hope that the press will love Adam, Evie and the baby as much as they fall for Robin and Sage. Have to just keep believing that this plan *and* this wedding party, one made up of my family and my closest friends is going to soar. Even *if* Robin and I crash and burn and no one buys into this fake relationship I'm not alone.

I. Am. Not. Alone.

As I repeat that, I look over at Robin and my chest twists with guilt and sadness, and hell even remorse. Worse, I also feel like I've just failed Robin, because—this girl is heading into this fake wedding completely alone, not counting her thirteen year old brother, that is.

I have to remember that Robin has me now, and though she doesn't quite know us all very well yet, it also means she's got every single person who comes along with me as well—and together we are quite a force.

If only she knew us better already…

As I look up, I almost laugh at everyone's expressions, including my grandmother's expression, because they're suddenly all acting fierce and glancing at Robin, as the bodyguards take their places around the limo. I swear it's as though these people just read my mind.

Everyone seems to be just where I am. Scared. Resolute. Protective —very protective of Robin.

Hoping my friends and family can read the gratitude inside my own stapled on smile, I signal to them that Robin and I need a moment alone as they help hand my grandmother out to my uncle and settle her into the waiting wheelchair.

I can't ask them out loud because of Sage's presence, so, as Hunter and Vere try to leave, I reach and tap their backs. When they turn back, I signal for them to make sure Sage is watched over.

I don't include Adam in this request, because he's got the baby to deal with and she is probably seconds from one of her *wake-and-wail diaper-needs-changing-feed-me* sessions. Adam will have to handle that mini-crisis and he will also be searching for his wife who is supposed to be hidden in the stadium somewhere. One he, and the baby, hardly survived one week living without.

Hunter tosses me a look that says Sage won't be left alone for a minute. Quickly he calls out to Sage before Sage hops out, "First thing's first, *Sage-little-bro.*" The kid smiles back at Hunter calling him 'little-bro' and the kid looks so happy Robin's worried expression slips into a happy smile. "We have to get you a backstage pass and clearance so you can go anywhere you want backstage. So, dude, stick right by me, no matter who is shoving us around."

"Or hold my hand, if you want," Vere adds.

I can't hear Sage's response as he darts out behind Hunter and Vere, but we watch as he's happily sandwiched between Hunter and Vere, and hell yes he's holding Vere's hand as they enter the stage door, because Robin told me he's got a crush on Vere. She's saying something into the kid's upturned, smiling face, and Sage is so star-struck as he glances at the crowd gone wild that's waiting outside, he has no clue he's left his sister behind.

ROBIN TRIES to follow but I whisper out, "Wait…I need to… talk. Sage will meet you in the dressing room."

"Just another minute," I call out to the bodyguards, then pull the limo doors closed again. They all nod, then escort everyone inside the stage door safely, and return to the limo to wait patiently outside the door for us to exit.

Robin pulls back so she can look up into my face, then speaks before I can get my words together. "I was wondering when you would come to your senses. You don't want to go through with it, and that's okay?"

"What?" I frown, shaking my head, distracted by the way her wide blue eyes pick up light, even in dark limos.

Like I did to her hand while we were driving, she reaches over and picks up mine, smoothing out the tense fist I've unconsciously made out of my hand. "Royce. I was thinking it over and playing out how it might go, today, tonight…week after week."

"You were?" I chuckle. "Shit. I couldn't even play out how it's going to go in the next hour. What did you come up with?"

"You'll be stuck for months—or longer. And I mean stuck. You—this is too much of a sacrifice. What if you don't want—?"

"But that's just it, Robin," I butt in. "I don't think you understand how much I *do* want—I mean—*shit.*"

I stop myself as my stomach drops like a lead-weight and then clenches when I realize I almost said things out loud that I haven't even said to myself yet—and I mean things about her, and things about those damn feelings I don't ever want to talk about.

Dude. Say something more.

You just told her that you do want…what? Tell her. What, exactly, do you want?

Should I just come clean. Tell her that I do want this wedding to happen, because all other options make her leave my life which is unacceptable.

Can I say that to her?

Can I?

"No. No," are the only words that come out of my mouth. Making it more awkward, I think I almost shouted them. Then, as she frowns up at me, like she's waiting for the rest of what isn't there, I shake my head and recover myself, finishing lamely with a half-chuckle and: "Uh—I don't know what I'm trying to say. It's not too much out of my life, and we've been over this, too. I agreed to this wedding so did you. Once the crazy part is over where they make us wear hellish, fancy outfits we wouldn't be caught dead in, it's maybe even going to be fun."

I tug at her veil, trying to bring some laughter and what I hope looks like a sparkling-twinkle into my eyes.

When she doesn't answer or even smile, I take my hand out of hers and press one finger into the deep creases forming between her eyes. "Are you really so worried about *me*? Really?"

"Yes." She nods her head once. "And 'fun' is not what your eyes are saying to me right now. You're worried, I see it, and…" The crease between her eyes deepens under my finger. "And you're…something else. What? What is that look on your face that I don't recognize?"

"You also have a look on your face that I don't recognize," I counter. "You tell me what yours means first." I add in a shrug, because—*holy shit*, why is she so damn perceptive?

"Okay." She blinks, and shrugs back. "I'm scared. My stomach feels like it's swishing around some bad soup I ate two weeks ago. And… I'm pondering how I need about twenty layers of new deodorant, because I think I sweated twice the normal amount, and for the entire limo ride. I'm also wondering in the back of my head if my little brother is meeting groupies right now, oh, and now I'm also kind of stressed about the bad outfits you mentioned. And… like I already said, I'm really worried about you going through with this for the long term. That's what the look on my face means. Now, you. Go."

She pulls back away from me and looks up again—*into* me how she does. So far I feel the hair on my forearms standing up as I get goose bumps all over my body.

"Okay. I'll go…I'm, uh... I'm scared, too. Same. All the way up to the need for some quality deodorant," I throw out, quickly hooding my gaze away from hers to make her stop staring into my eyes.

I'm suddenly embarrassed. Alarmed. Humbled. Because just like since the day we met, this amazing girl feels like she can be completely honest bear her heart, reveal all details stored in her head including crap like sweat and deodorant, all while I feel the need to hide my true self from her.

I am hardly even worthy of being friends with a girl who's so noble, generous…honest. Real. I also can't talk about whatever my face is revealing to her, because I suddenly think I know what it is she's seeing. My new expression might have something to do with how, in the last twenty-four hours, combined with how this very conversation is unfolding right now…each moment, leading to this very moment, I think it's all made me fall in love with her when I swore to God and the whole universe that I'd never love anyone again.

But here she is, being Robin—earnest, bossy, amazing—brave as usual despite the terrible odds stacked against her, and once again, she's trying to save me.

And…damn, I love her for it.

Love.

Is that what is going on?

Am I? Is this love? As in, I'm in love? Oh fuck, no. No I'm not.

I'm so undone by this idea that I have to lean back into the limo seat, because, damn... my head hurts, and my chest hurts, and all of my fucking skin... *hurts.* Only, it is not a bad hurt, it's just this unwinding of my very soul. A slightly scary feeling that's making very pore on me feels like some sort of invisible, micro-needle-prick is hitting it, over and over again. It's like I'm being electrocuted with a singular cat hair, or maybe pelted with tiny, warm snowflakes, if that could be a thing.

Which it isn't. Because just how warm snowflakes can't exist, I can't actually be 'in love' with anyone. Maybe I'm having a stroke or a full-on heart attack, or maybe this is a case of Poison Ivy setting in? Sadly, for me, I'm pretty sure it's not anything like that. It's coming from how my heart just cartoon-Grinch-style, *doubled in size,* combined with how I'm vowing inside never to touch her how I want to right now, and vowing to never to kiss her how I kissed her back in my closet a few days ago. And I mean, not ever again, while at the same time looking forward to how I will get to kiss her after we say 'I do.'

I am in so much trouble here. And now I can't stop, staring at her lips.

So, again, hell-no, I'm not going to talk to her about my current temporary breach of insanity. But I will try to breathe in and out, and get control of myself while I try to fix the expression on my face to one that will not make her question me or scare the shit out of her. Definitely I need to come up with one that makes her stop staring at me back like she's going to crawl inside of my head and start flipping the crazy-rocks that have replaced my brain during this lapse.

I realize I've placed my hand over the spot where my heart still won't let up, and for some reason that, plus how I'm acting, makes me laugh out loud.

Damn this runaway heart.

"*Robin...*" I utter out again, and pull my hand away from my chest, fast like it's been burned. "I'm sorry I can't stop my trash mouth, and I'm also sorry because I don't mean to laugh right now. But a guy can't expect to be exactly acting right or anywhere near who he's supposed to be on his surprise wedding day, huh?" I ask, acknowledging it's a question geared more to make myself feel better than for her.

"It's okay." She laughs, too. "I feel the same, and I know you suck at lying, and you're probably trying to sort out what to say to me because I don't know what to say to you, either, but I want to clarify that if you did change your mind during that limo ride, I want you to know I don't care, and that we're cool. And like…whatever happens, I will only think good things about you. Forever. This, I promise. Come on now. Answer me. What do *you* want to do right now. Really. Be as honest as possible."

I breathe out, contemplating her flushed face. Then I breathe in, because I'm not ready and I'm not good at this; and because I'm covering up the pin-pricks and the perplexing *feelings*, coursing back through me. I breathe out all over again, all while searching for whole sentences that don't begin with me cursing non-stop this time.

"Okay," I start finally, running both hands through my hair with the next breath. "Really, I want to marry you, but…" I chuckle again at her skeptical expression, "I do," I insist. "I *want* to, and this exact conversation between us is why. Because ever since the day you met me, and even when I was playing the part of a complete jackass and pushing you away so hard, you only ever did, somehow, think good thoughts about me."

She shakes her head once. "At the time, I didn't think good things, but I thought you had tons of *potential*."

"There. You see? Ever honest. That's more than anyone else ever thought about me and I like it."

I grin at her second head shake and small glower.

"To answer the rest of your question?" I sigh out, tracking the dark circles marring the skin under her eyes. "What do I want to *do right now*? Honestly? It's this. I honestly want to wrap you up in to in my arms like I did back in the garden when I first asked you to marry me and squelch your worries. I have this urge to hold you until that hunted exhausted look on your face disappears, and until you know me well enough to know that I am, very much, okay with this plan. Long enough for you to know me enough to understand that you don't have to step up to save me, at all *ever* again."

She wrinkles her nose like she hates that I've said those words, but quickly I press on, "Those shots of us kissing after I proposed are probably already hitting the Internet, adding fuel to the fire that has already scorched us all. We're on the razor's edge of our reputations here, remember? At the end of this day you will be permanently branded either as a proper respected *wife*, or as some kind of trashy *prostitute* with an irreparable scandal attached to your good name forever." I hold up my hands. "That last bit is made up of all of my grandmother's words, by the way. But she's right. We've got no other choice here."

I place both hands on her shoulders and give her a little shake.

When her eyes meet mine, I lock onto hers. "*We* chose *wife*. Remember? We chose for the press to report that our band doesn't pay underage girls to come up to our hotel suites for special 'work' nor do you participate in that kind of work and we won't let anyone say that you did. Once this wedding happens and my name is connected to your name legally, then Sage is beyond *safe*."

I jerk one thumb over my shoulder to the arena. "To boot, he's out of his mind *happy* right now, which is all you ever wanted for the kid, right? That he stays with you and happy, yes? That dream is all coming true if you could just hold steady."

She nods and looks away, as I continue, "I'm probably going to suck at the husband role, but I *want* to do this. I do," I insist again. "But if *you've* changed your mind, then of course, we don't have to go through with anything. Okay? But…please. Let me carry some of the weight and worries for you. I'm good at that, at least. I caused so much of your current problems, please let me fix what I can. It's not going to be difficult for me. I swear."

"But for this whole limo ride, you've looked different. I don't know…like you were tormented or something…and even now, you look…a mess."

"I am… a mess." I reach forward and let a finger twine into one of the long curls that's escaping the veil by her temples. "Don't you not know me even a little, yet? Worrying is my essence and my personal curse. I'm always a mess and always worried all the time about something or someone I care about. Right now, it's about how *you* looked so worried on the limo ride, too. Which is why I stopped you from going out there. We have to fix our faces."

She blinks, eyes back on mine but this time I'm ready for her to look inside. "You mean because we can't go out there if we don't match on our expressions?"

"Exactly." I point outside the limo. "If you get out of this limo and walk in there with me it's going to be under my arm, and we will both need to be smiling into each other's eyes. I'll be slinging an arm over your shoulder, or twining my hands even more into your beautiful curls, or running a finger along one of your cheeks because…*girl…*" I lower my voice and raise one brow. "I find that I love your curls, and hell-yes, I adore the shape of your face."

Finally she laughs, cheeks going fire-truck red. "Oh God. Wow. You say that so convincingly my heart actually started galloping."

She puts both hands up to hide the flush, and I have to smile.

"I say it because it's true. I love the curls. The shape of your face—hell your whole face is charming. I'm going to tell everyone that I think so, that's the easy part because it's true."

She shakes her head as I forge on with what she *needs* to remember when we step out of this car. "You need to get *used to me* saying it though. You also have to figure out some stuff to say about me that's true for you as well, because out there—it needs to come off the lips easy and sound real. It needs to happen while your hand must either be entwined into mine, or if that's too awkward, then find exactly where your arm fits best around my waist. Because out there, we are so insanely *in love,"* I wink. "That from this point forward, we can't keep our eyes from meeting with *real* smiles, not worried ones. We also can't keep our hands off each other," I add in a wicked grin. "And I mean, we simply can't get enough of exploring the heat coming off each other's skin, because… that's the way love looks and how newlyweds act." I toss her a small hopeful look. "You probably also *love* the shape of my face as much as I love yours?"

She laughs again, seeming to get control of her blushing as she processes the words I've said. "As a matter of fact, I actually do admire how you're made, or I wouldn't have been able to paint you so well today. You're a study of perfect angles." She points. "That chin alone—all square planes and intriguing textures. Your cheekbones, would have sent Picasso to the happy moon."

I shake my head and sigh. "You make me sound like an inanimate object. Not that I'm fishing for compliments or anything, but it's okay to add in normal words like *handsome* or…*hot*? If I'm not that to you then, charming or funny could work? Or, you could say you fell for my big heart. Heck, even use my OCD-worrying thing. Say that was your *fall-for-me* tipping point? Whatever—sounds believable to the press, and as long as it rings passionate and all kinds of *true-love* somehow?"

She nods. "Oh. Right. Yeah. Hot. I can say. And you're big hearted for sure. Because you are that, and again, very handsome and yeah. Yes. Of course I can do that." She taps at her temple. "Making note to turn off the artist inside of my head before speaking about your beauty. Check."

I shake my head, and frown because she's really far off of where she needs to be, but I can't press her because I know she'll feel sad about her lack of knowledge. I'm just going to need to be ready for her to falter and cover by camera-hogging or cracking random jokes or asking the reporters my own questions until she's used to how things work with the press.

She flushes again like she's read my mind, then swallows so hard I wince, wondering if that hurt her, as she adds, "I'll get it right. I promise."

I nod and lie, "Not worried. I know you will. I've already sent a snapshot of that painting you did of me off to the PR group. I told them that you made it as a *wedding present* for me. They went nuts. Hope you don't mind, but it's going on my Instagram in a few, meaning millions of people are going to see your art."

She swallows another time, again wincing but covering it with a nod.

"And, crap." I pull in a breath, thinking of where the painting will be posted. "I better *follow* you on Instagram. Do you know I haven't followed anyone for over a year. This will be oddly news worthy to the vultures, I'm sure," I say sarcastically. "You'll need to follow me back okay? And…shoot. I guess I'll need to get a wedding present for you, don't I?"

She shakes her head, but I hold up my hand, not letting her answer. "Details, so many details we've all forgotten and that I hope no one catches onto," I mutter scrolling through Instagram, showing her my feed. "I'm *@GarderobeDevil*. Later, if you have time, follow Vere and the others. 'Like' a bunch of their new posts. Comment some if you can. If you have time."

She takes her phone and opens Instagram. While she's scrolling through that, I quickly text Vere: *Tell someone I need a wedding present for Robin.*

I glance at Robing adding: "How about a small…very nice traveling watercolor kit. And an oil paint kit? Maybe a little folding easel?" I breathe out, looking at her again. *No. Hold on. That's not good enough. I want to build her a studio, a real art studio in the NYC apartment. That's what I'm getting her. What do you think? We need to hire a design team ASAP, and see if we can get it in place before we arrive next week? Is that too much? I'm thinking it's only a matter of getting the right furniture. She can take over the dining area over by the windows. What do you think? Ditch the table I never use anyhow and add in art studio stuff?*

Vere answers: *Aww. That's just perfectly sweet, Royce. How about I get the fancy traveling art kits anyhow—and we will use those and a card to announce the studio to her. I'll tell Mrs. Felix about the studio. She will know who to hire fast.*

I reply: *Perfect. thank you.*

"Found you." Robin says, unaware that I've just ordered an apartment remodel on her behalf. "I'm @RobinLove12. If the PR guys do post the painting, then I'm going to comment that I made it as a wedding present for *myself* so I can have my *handsome, sexy* husband hanging on the wall whenever you're on tour. How does that sound?" She looks up at me, eyes hopeful.

I nod approvingly, and wonder how she will feel after that post has twenty million likes but that two million replies will probably hate-speak because she married me. "Sounds perfect," I answer. "And remember. Why did you paint it? Not because my chin is square."

Quickly I answer for her, fluttering my lashes and making a girly voice. "Well, it's because Royce and I, are head-over-heels, desperately, utterly and irrevocably *in love*." I laugh. "Right? Can you be that? Can you do that?" I switch to a low, wedding officiant's voice. "From this point forward, Robin Love, will you be easily and naturally in love with Royce, and fake-attracted to him, and gush all about his accomplishments and also do it with abandon on *all* social media platforms, now and forever…or…until divorce—you- do-part?" My voice cracks suddenly, but I cover it with a grin and another laugh.

"Sure. Got you. I c-can absolutely do and be *irrevocably*—good word by the way—in love. Yes.…and all that stuff you just said, forever and ever or until divorce we-do-part. I do."

She's pulling a face and those cheeks have colored again.

Suddenly we're both laughing.

"Good that we talked about all of this?" I ask, turning my phone back on.

"Yes. Very."

"Good. Because we are going to need to take a selfie."

"Of course we are." She laughs again, scooting into my phone space. "Remember when I wondered who would ever want to take one of these with you?"

"I'll never forget that day. Or that comment." I laugh more, and snap the photo thinking of how we met in this same limo only a week ago.

Quickly I post the selfie to my Instagram while she watches me type #lovethisgirl, #love, and #Guarderobe.

"Oh wow," she whispers.

"Ready?" I ask her.

She nods, but I just tracked a flash of panic crossing her face. I drop my eyes to glance away, pretending I need to tap the window to signal the bodyguards that we're coming out, but really, it's because I'm scared as shit my face may have reverted back to whatever face I was making before—because the damn *pin-prick-my-soul* thing has started up with a vengeance again.

"We've got this, Robin Love, and I've got you," I add, waiting for security to clear a path.

She pulls in a last, long, shaking breath, answering, "And I've got you right back, Royce Devlin. I really do."

"I love that about you," I whisper going first out the door, then turn to her out. The fans who couldn't get tickets to our show, but who've come down to say hello anyhow, roar with cheers as they spot me.

Her small hand grips into mine so tightly the contact has made me suddenly feel fiercely protective of her. I smile and wave to the fog of faces, drawing another cheer, all while my worrying habits have my eyes tracking all around me. I track the crowd's movements, the faces of the bodyguards, the person holding the door for us as well as the movement of the limo pulling away behind us. Why does suddenly everything in the world seem threatening?

Robin smiles up at me like she's completely unafraid, but just in case, I've pulled her closer. Responding easily and trustingly to the adjustment of the space between us, she nestles right under my arm and settles her other hand around my waist just how we'd talked about moments before.

I'm cheering silently for her fearlessness, as the crowd simultaneously cheers for us to turn back and give them another wave. Accommodating them, we both turn and wave again, then I shout out, "Who's up for some free tickets? Anyone want to see the show tonight?"

The guy who's been tasked at every concert to choose a few lucky people to come inside and see the concert steps forward waving a thick stack of tickets high above his head. He announces that today, we've created a last minute, standing mosh pit for this very *special* concert, the small crowd goes nuts. It pulls the attention off of us some, as the those in the crowd try to get noticed and chosen.

I glance down at Robin, noting she's not shaking at all anymore, just as she glances up again. She's watching me as though waiting for signals for what to do next, but her face doesn't seem anything but calm, happy and, I pull in a breath. Calm, happy, and—*hell*—by the way her eyes are shining up at me, she really does look like she's in love.

In love with me.

It's cute as hell, it's also sort of mind-melting-hot. Because, damn. I raise my brows and grin down at her. She raises her brows high in response. then winks as if to say, *I told you I'd get it.*

I shake my head and actually laugh out loud, because I'm again flooded with too many overwhelming feelings for this amazing girl.

Her responding laugh makes me feel as though, suddenly she and I now speak a secret language—or like, she I have suddenly discovered the capacity to *fly* through the stage door instead of walk.

I'm not sure how it happened, but in one limo ride and these few short moments, Robin and I have transformed into this symbiotic, unconquerable, shiny-new, set of *two*.

And she and I, or wait—!

We. I mean, *we*.

We might be invincible.

3

ROBIN

THE FIRST THING they'd shoved me into after I was detached from Royce then ushered into the Guarderobe dressing rooms, was, *the dress.* The silk and lace, sophisticated, once white but now ivory, faded from age, antique wedding dress. The dress that matches the veil and that had belonged to Royce's grandmother.

It's also the same dress worn by Royce's mother on *her* wedding day along with this same exquisite ring. Both worn by a woman who has passed away, who was very loved and who I will never get to meet…

Mrs. Felix told me that it made her happy to see the family ring on my finger, but how could it? This ring has only been worn for the most sincere reasons—weddings that were about true love and soul mates. Yet, on my hand it's going to be the symbol that will remind everyone that I represent hundreds of lies.

What would my father think?

Swallowing, I try not to think about that or him, as they're tugging at the front and the back of this dress, with me bobbing around in it like a lifeless doll stuck in the middle. The distant roar of the crowd going nuts inside the arena flows over my guilt and my humming nerves, thankfully becoming louder than the dark voices inside my own head.

I confirm Guarderobe has finally hit the stage when I catch strands of Royce's muffled but amplified voice talking to the endlessly cheering crowd. Unintelligible words echo down to where we are, followed by Adam's and Hunter's voices, also pumping up the audience.

More and more elated cheers flow down to where we are, and the pounding of feet is so loud, the screams so intense, that I have to smile. I'm thinking of Sage somewhere up there, screaming his head off, too, and living his dream. At the sound of the first guitar riffs, pounding drums, more talking and then the responding screams from the crowd, I actually get goose bumps. Guarderobe has a way of creating live electricity.

When the side-zipper on the wedding dress catches and stops up the middle of my back, just past my waist, even *after* I pulled in the breath and held it like they ordered me to, the small crowd around me also applauded.

But…why would they applaud. The dress won't zip. Isn't that a failure?

There's more applause and even a sigh of relief when my feet, with a little toe-pinching, fit into the ivory silk slippers that had been boxed along with the dress.

"Half the battle is won," says a short haired, blonde woman in her forties, who's been circling around me since they'd shoved the dress over my head. "*This* we can work with. Thank God you're gorgeous, dear Robin. But of course you would be *that*, marrying Royce Devlin and all." She shoves her hands on my waist. "And thank goodness you're nearly as tiny as Mrs. Felix and her daughter were when they got married."

She tugs the zipper again and I wince as it catches on my skin, then she frowns over my shoulder into the mirror, glancing between me, the dress and her waiting stylist team. "Call whomever is doing the underwear run *right now*." Her voice is urgent. "They're to bring every corset the stores have. I want *boned* corsets, do you hear me? As stiff as they can find. We're shoving a modern woman into an eighty year old dress, which was designed for much body types and different underwear. Tell them to bring me *everything* they've got."

"Corset? Didn't she just call me tiny? If that's the case, why do I feel suddenly fat," I whisper to Vere, who's been hovering near, smiling at me with this awkward, cheerleader, *go-fight-win* expression on her face, or holding my hand this whole time.

"They just need to bring in your waist so it zips without breaking the dress. A corset will do the trick," she repeats the obvious in her cheery-over-cheery voice.

Vere skips around me, looking me up and down, how the stylist had done. "Besides, corsets? They're so very bride. And they're back in style. What's coming will be awesome. I heard it's straight from Paris like all of the other stuff will be. Only the best for this bride because later some magazine will feature what you wore. They always do stuff like that. It's also going to make you look *wedding-night-level-hot.*" She waggles her brows over her large, almond shaped, ever-happy expressive brown eyes. "So, yeah. Don't worry. Okay?"

"Vere." I blink at her, biting back a laugh. "You're seriously telling me not to worry right now? Like I'm about to…you know, get married with little notice, but I'm not supposed to *worry*?"

"Yes?" She scrunched her face at that comment, and together we both start to laugh, because all other options from me cracking my molars in half, to fainting, to running, to starting to ugly-cry are options that are not going to fly. Not with all of these people watching, anyhow.

Mrs. Felix, Royce's grandmother, wheels forward in her wheelchair, calling out, "Silence please. Everyone. I'd like to make a formal introduction to the girl you've already shoved into *my* wedding dress."

When the room grows quiet, she makes this strange dramatic game show host motion towards me. "This is Robin Love, and as you've heard, she's about to elope and marry my dear grandson, Royce Devlin. It's rather untraditional but it will happen tonight on stage with my blessing."

She claps her hands to her chest and beams up at me and I have to smile back because I adore this woman, and I always love how her high, eighty-year-old voice makes her sound like actress in an old movie. It's something that makes everyone stop and listen as she goes on, "I know it's all such a shock, my darlings. But we all know now impulsive *my Royce* always acts. You also know how difficult it is for these dear boys to have any semblance of a normal life. They also *do* adore staying one step ahead of the press, which is why Robin and Royce are doing this so quickly. We thought a surprise wedding would be marvelous and *fresh.* With every other movie star and rockstar doing these cliché, boring beach weddings, or trying those secretive weddings under giant rented tents with everything so over planned and disgusting." She shakes her head and frowns. "My Royce wanted this wedding to be different and completely unforgettable. Something that has never been done before, and so…here we are darlings, each and every one of us so very *surprised.*

Isn't it wonderfully exciting?" She smiles and claps her hands again. "It's up to all us to get our dear Robin, set up and looking right. I had my dress shipped from New York City, and now that we know it's going to work, it's up to all of you to put on the frosting on this gorgeous, wonderful *last-minute-bride*. Can we welcome Robin and her dear brother Sage into our family?"

After she'd said that word *family*, all I could think of again was my father, and then my thoughts stormed to the Perino family we'd left behind only ten minutes from this arena.

They were the family who had sheltered Sage and I when I'd run away. We had grown to love them so much. Mrs. Perino was like the mom Sage and I had never had, Angel, her son like the big brother I'd always wished for, and his two little cousins, Ana and Julia—the sweetest little girls. Ones who I want to be around while they grow up. That had been the plan, to stay with them. To live in the little cottage they'd offered Sage and I as a home of our own while Sage and I started our lives together.

But then, poof—in one short day, all of those dreams became impossible. When the press wrote that horrible story about me being a prostitute, the Perino's sad past and how Angel had killed a man in self-defense when he was a kid, a sensational story that took ten years for the public to forget, was about to be re-exposed in the press. And it was going to be all because of me.

The Perino family is one of the reasons I agreed to this wedding so fast. They are my heart, they became our real home—the one we'd always dreamed of having. As much as I wanted to stay, I didn't want them to be hurt for simply sheltering me and Sage when we most needed help. Which is why they can't be here. Be near me or Sage or any reporter who might remember just who the Perino's were ten years ago.

Suddenly the Perino's all feel as lost as my father. While I stand here inside this stadium, half dressed for my fake wedding to Royce, I wonder who I am and who I'm about to become and I wonder if I will ever see any of them again. I wonder if, should I be lucky and get to answer 'yes' to my own questions, will things feel the same between us when we are reunited?

Mrs. Felix zooms her wheelchair to my side and picks up one of my hands, giving it a squeeze. "Robin. Are you okay? Did I say something wrong?"

"No. I was only missing the Perino family. And my father," I answer honestly, because there's no hiding any lies from Mrs. Felix, but then because the stylists seemed to be eavesdropping, in a louder voice I add, "I'm also touched you called me part of your family which really does help. Thank you."

"Of course you're missing family. Poor dear, don't fret, all will be well." She squeezes my hand tight, a flicker of sadness going across the silver-bright eyes that nearly exactly match Royce's eyes. "Sincerely, Robin. Though the vows have not been said, I already *do* think of you as my own granddaughter. After meeting Sage today, I know it won't be long before he owns my whole heart, too. You're not alone, dear. Please know, that though your father is far away and your dear friends can't attend here today, that Gregory who has started a close relationship with your Mrs. Perino—he won't let them stay away for long. These weeks of summer will fly by, and we will see them all so very soon. Yes?"

"Yes," I answer, praying to God that statement also applies to my father. The sweet old woman looks so worried that I lean down and give her a hug, whispering, "Thanks. You made me feel so much better. It will go fast and I'm so happy to have you standing in for everyone who can't. It—this—all means so much. Don't worry about me, okay? I'll be fine." I lean away and smile, happy that she looks less worried about me.

She nods once, like she's satisfied, and she speeds her wheelchair away.

AFTER THAT, for me, all morphed into a dream-state-blur.

I remember everyone in the room started clapping more, and some were shouting congratulations to me. Some, rushing over to meet me. The very genuine excitement on their faces about how much they wanted to help me make this wedding *special* (even though they didn't know me at all) made my own smiles back to them not seem so fake.

Mrs. Felix, all business at this point, once again silenced the room. "Okay. People. Introductions and sentimentality are over now. It's time to get to it. *First.* I'm going to ask Robin to remain quiet during all of this and let us all do our jobs around her or this will never work. And *stylists,* I'm going to ask *you* not to ask this very nervous girl any questions or try to chit-chat. She was feeling very queasy in the limo, for good reason, so let's just feed her sips of sprite, make sure she has a well-balanced snack while she's getting ready, and you can all get to know her later. She will be around a lot from this day forward. Deal? Robin? Is that okay?"

I remember blinking and feeling floaty-and fuzzyheaded as I'd answered, "I can do that, providing I can thank everyone later, as well."

"Of course. Consider you've thanked everyone in advance, as of now, and *onward*." Mrs. Felix then changed her expression to what I could tell was mock impatience for the group gathered around. She came up with some teacher-style double hand claps and clipped out, "Now, not another word. Everyone. Chop. Chop. We've wasted valuable minutes and we all have too much work to do. We have only 60 minutes to make this dress look *newer* while I'd love to make the bride look a tad…*older*. Possibly more…sophisticated?" She flips to French, adding with a sigh, "If it is even possible with that young face."

I do remember the almost clinical-level scrutiny I was getting off of everyone in the room that happened after that remark. It had made me stop breathing for a moment, so much so that Vere's hand squeezing mine was the only thing that made me start up again.

An older blonde woman with very short hair, who seemed to be in charge of everyone else, took over the commands then and called out, "Okay. You've had time to look at the dress and look at the girl, let's have them. Suggestions. Who's got some ideas? Dress first. Now. Hurry."

"How about let *me* get in that wedding dress and marry Royce Devlin instead? That should solve the biggest problems." A tall, very model-looking brunette girl calls out, making everyone laugh, but the glance she gives me behind her snide smile feels slightly murderous.

"*Productive* suggestions, Clara," the short haired woman shakes her head at the girl. "You will have to forgive my daughter, Robin. She had big hopes and dreams that she'd get either Royce or Adam to fall in love with her during her summer internship but now that she's learned the truth about Adam's wife and baby, and she has seen the ring on your finger as well, you can imagine that my Clara thinks she's having a very bad day." The woman laughs at her own remarks, but it sounds as fake as her daughter's smile looks.

"Bad day?" Clara nearly shouts, unabashed by her mother's comments. "How about ruined life? My reaction is a snapshot of how the entire female population of the whole *world* is going to feel

tomorrow. Forgive me for being human, but I think I've *died* from this news." Clara frowns while everyone else laughs again. "I am broken hearted, but I'm also patient." Clara walks forward to hand her mom a clipboard then whispers so only those close can here, "Because rock star marriages never last long. Maybe I'll be around to pick up the pieces for whomever dumps their wives first, right?"

"Clara! Enough." Clara's mom pulls in a fast, shocked breath, and darts me an apologetic look. "Don't joke about such things, or you could lose your job."

"It's not like this internship is paying that well, mother." Clara's dark frown slides into a wolfish smile and her eyes flick between me and Vere. "Vere, tell her about my sense of humor, would you? I'm sorry if I offended you. I'm sure we'll be great friends eventually, because I'm going to get to tour with the band this summer. You'll see a lot of me which is lucky because..." Her eyes scan me up and down in this way that makes me feel like I'm missing limbs all over the place. "It sure looks like you could use a stylist. Like. *Badly.*"

Vere smiles, but it doesn't quite reach her eyes like it usually does. "Clara. You're crossing a line. Robin's natural fashion sense is adorable."

"Natural? Is that what you're calling her lack of...*everything*?"

"Clara. Wow. Really?" Vere turns to me with a grimace. "Ignore Clara for the most part. Her sense of humor *is* dark, today she's acting like some fool who's lost the big Lotto Jackpot when there were thirty million other payers." She whacks Clara in the arm lightly. "Snap out of it. You can't think you even had a chance with Royce Devlin anyhow. He already had a crush on Robin before you'd ever spoken once to him."

She rubs a hand against her heart. "Okay. Yeah. Maybe you're right, but it still hurts somewhere deep. Summer interns have huge hopes and dreams, you know?"

I almost smile at that and add, "If it helps, I will try to help you find a different rock star to marry."

"It doesn't help, but..." Clara pauses and starts looking at me up and down again how she did before, before adding. "Yeah. Okay. Maybe I'll let you find me a replacement. Maybe."

If this were the real world I could just tell Clara that this whole thing is made-up. That, *yes* she's gorgeous and sophisticated, and that she's obviously the better choice for a guy like Royce. To me, she's seems the exact kind of girl who would know about fancy stuff, fashion and makeup, plus, she does have model-level looks. If people had to vote, her against me, she'd come out on top as the one who *should* be standing up next to a rockstar in a white dress. Heck, in any dress. Because she probably actually owns dresses where, I currently… don't own…*any.*

And heck, maybe I'd even tell her that she can *have* Royce Devlin if she wants him, just as soon as our divorce *is* final. But I can't admit to any of that, so instead, I pretended to be sympathetic to Clara, while two sewing machines were wheeled in along with two worktables, also on wheels. These are loaded with tubes of glue called *Speed-Set,* plus what looked like a whole store of gorgeous, Swarovski crystals in every possible size.

Clara's mom sends her away on some errand while she and the seamstress approached me again, tugged at me, tugged at the dress again, then whispered some more. Then they examined my face (or maybe it was my pores) way too closely. One of them whisked the dress up and over my head, got me into a robe, then shoved me into a tall director's chairs waiting at the make-up mirrors.

My veil was removed and my hair dragged into every possible hair appliance, while more products than I had ever seen got spritzed on my curls. The only part I liked was when someone massaged my shoulders and whispered things like—*darling, you must relax or the photos will not be beautiful. It is your wedding day. Think. Relaxed and beautiful—that is what you are.*

They re-attached the veil (but not before my face was attacked with this crazy airbrush thing spraying foundation out of it) all while the massage lady kept saying: *luminous. Luminous. Yes. Perfect.*

I vaguely remember eye-pokes and being told to hold very still during the eyeliner, and I recall earrings being placed in my ears just as Sage who'd been *pre-outfitted* (the stylist's term) with black pants and a white tuxedo shirt, all hidden underneath a collector's edition Guarderobe Concert hoodie, had come in to be fitted for which tuxedo jacket he'd be asked to put on after the show

He'd grinned at me, asked if I was okay, which of course I assured him that, *I was.*

Satisfied with what he'd seen he ran back out, but not before flashing me the coolest looking VIP lanyard with a dangling gold pass on the end of it. A stylist had followed him out, and I discovered he'd also been assigned a personal bodyguard to hang out with him in some special chairs they'd set up side-stage so he could watch the concert up close, but, as he'd told me so he could, "*be ready to walk me down the aisle when it was time.*

As the back of his bright-blond head flashed by out in the hallway, all I could remember thinking then was: *Is there going to be an aisle? On stage? And when is it going to be time.*

Time. Time. Time…

I'd have panicked then, but that was when a rack of fancy lingerie in various sizes was pushed up to me and I think I blacked out instead.

I sort of came-to when Clara's mom appeared to sort through the rack when I had only just sat there gaping at it.

She'd pulled out three things right away while pointing her finger at the others, saying, "No. No and *Never.*" She shakes her head. "Some of these were a last-minute order from Royce. Royce told me you'd want something pretty. White. His exact word was: *Memorable.* So, I had them deliver *everything* in white that the boutique, *Belle Provocateur*, had in stock. Considering it's your wedding night, we shouldn't care over-much as to what we're choosing. Because…" She winks. "You brides don't wear this stuff for very long, now do you?"

She flashes me this knowing grin and I nod and blush a lot which is, I think the proper response she was waiting for anyhow, as she rushes on, holding up three options of what look like mini strait-jackets without arms. "Pick a corset first, because it has to fit so the dress zipper doesn't pop. It will feel a bit difficult to breathe at first, but I can imagine you're already having that feeling anyhow, aren't you dear?"

Nodding again, I'd whispered for her and Vere to choose, and ended up stuffed into a pretty, lacy and ribbons one that covered me in all of the right places but was sheer down my ribcage in-between where the corset had its seams and stiffening-bits sewn in to it.

Their admiring gushing as to how *voluptuous* it made me look had me dying even more of embarrassment, because no one had ever used that word to describe flat-chested-me before, ever.

I think it's because my waist was cinched in so tightly that all of my extra skin and possibly my whole diaphragm and maybe even one lung was suddenly, full-on, *water-falling* like Niagara falls out from the top of the corset. Whatever it had turned all that I didn't really have into something that looked like real-live porn star boobs!

Noting how I was trying to push everything back down while trying to yank the corset up as high as possible, one of the stylists who was helping to tie the ribbons slapped my hands away and assured me I was *gorgeous* and that *the dress would keep everything too scandalous down where it needed to be.*

Vere was pulled away and told to put on a strapless, silver–shimmering bridesmaid dress. Then, she left my side to have her own hair worked on while I was ushered into a changing room while carrying the panties that supposedly matched the corset. If you could call them panties, because there was not much to them.

I ALMOST PANIC ONCE they're on, because as I turn to see why things feel so breezy in the back, I discover the back is made up of layer after layer of what looks like see-through, silk, flower petals. They're pretty, despite the part where I'm nearly naked. Sexy even, if that matters—because it *doesn't.* But if I were a bit older, and a real bride, this whole ensemble would be the best wedding underwear I could ever imagine.

"And it's most certainly *memorable*," I mutter, staring at the tags still hanging off of the corset reading how it's written all in swirly French writing. I make out the word 'couture' and I'm not good at money conversions, but I do know that *five thousand* Euros is a lot of Euros for one skimpy corset. It's also worth six months rent to a girl like me!

Shaking my head and trying not to be pissed off or shocked, I carefully untie the silk bow that's holding the tag onto the corset and let it drop into my hand.

"No plastic tag-thingies on *couture*, I suppose?" I ask, talking to my reflection.

I know all of this has to look and feel real, and I'm sure real brides to rock stars have closets full of this fancy stuff; but considering how I had zero money to my name two weeks ago, this feels wrong. So wrong. And, aside from that, if anyone, especially my future-fake-husband sees me wearing this, I'm going to die. *Die.*

Thankfully, the stylist ladies were pushing more garments through the dressing room curtain and bossing me to 'put it all on'. I couldn't pull on the opaque silk stockings—or the thick half-slip that attached over my waist, fast enough. The stockings are weird, and the slip is even stranger, but, heck—maybe this is normal wedding-wear. I don't know. And besides, whatever it takes to cover the awkward underwear, right?

The last thing they gave me to put on was what Mrs. Felix called the original 'cage crinoline' that was created when the dress was originally made for Mrs. Felix's mother.

This was the strangest item of all. I told Mrs. Felix I loved the thing. Because, I actually did.

It was like a fancy, fabric-covered birdcage! It had actual whale bones sewn around and *into* it. Ones which created a series of hoops going ever wider all the way down. They crisscrossed along the back where it was supposed to support the wedding dress train. It took three people to tie the ribbons and laces that had been sewn on every side of it, until it hung comfortably on my hips, and it covered me and the corset and the underwear like a bodyguard. No one was going to make it through this thing.

Mrs. Felix, who seemed to be enjoying my transformation into an old fashioned bride assured me this final touch would make the dress sway and settle nicely when I moved while, all keeping it off of my feet so I wouldn't trip.

Problem was, it was so heavy I could hardly move in it, which everyone found very funny to watch, including me. After a few practice-walks back and forth, then a full circle around the room, I had it down. The antique dress that the seamstresses had been busily 'modifying to suit me' (Mrs. Felix's words) this entire time, was then laid over the top of this contraption. I stopped drinking water when I realized I'd not be able to go to the restroom for the foreseeable future.

The same three ladies took almost ten minutes to do up the tiny, silk, button loops that attached the endless row of round pearl buttons that extended from the bottom of my butt all the way up the back to my neck.

When they were done with those, the veil that two other women were holding off to the side because it had just been steamed, was let to drop around my bare shoulders and everyone stepped back and paused as the room grew silent.

The head stylist pulled both hands over her heart and beamed at me. "This will be over-the-top *Disney Princess* fabulous on stage. We've done Mrs. Felix, Robin, and the spirit of the Orlando parks very proud here."

Mrs. Felix was clapping again, but this time with sheer delight, causing everyone to erupt with applause. "The seamstresses have pulled off a miracle! My word, pulling off the lace insert and stealing lace from the train so you could re-make the dress so Robin's shoulders can be bare is such a modern touch. Oh…it's a wonderful effect. Robin, I hope you're pleased. The scalloped-edging of that old lace makes your ivory skin just glow, darling. What do you think."

"Yes. Pleased." I say pulling in a very tight breath. "I'm still trying to figure out how to breathe in this thing, that's all. Any tips?"

"Small breaths dear. Many, many small breaths." Mrs. Felix, who, somewhere along the way has changed her outfit to match an older-woman's version of what Vere is wearing, zooms her chair even closer. "They didn't succeed much on making you look much older, but Robin, you're a beautiful bride. Truly."

When they turn me to face the mirror I gasp because I don't recognize myself—I mean I do, because it's me, and it's my face, but they'd made me into some sort of magazine-flawless-version of me.

My hair had been improved with extensions of crystal-embedded, twisted blonde braids, here, there, and *everywhere*. They'd used some of the same braids to create height up top to which is where they'd re-attached the veil and the handmade flower headband so what I was wearing could match the photos the paparazzi had taken in the garden where Royce had proposed to me.

And my *eyes*…oh what they'd done to my eyes!

I flutter my lashes because they're so full and thick with some fake glued-on extra layers, and the eyeliner they did had those perfect drawn on wings. I've never been able to do those, no matter how steady I hold my hand. They'd also added a streak of silver glitter liner above the black which looked really cool, and over my eye lid, there were subtle smudges of dark greens, browns and purples as well as some iridescent white-pink just below my brows that only I could see up close. At a distance, the combined effect, made my eyes seem twice as big, twice as wide and fairy-tale luminous!

"Wow," I say, putting a hand up toward one of my highlighted cheekbones. "Would you look at…"

"Don't you touch one thing," Clara's mom admonished me, shoving my hands away. "No touching the dress, not your face, not one hair on your head." She shakes her head. "This is why the bride requires a bouquet. So she won't mess up the look. Here. Hold this tightly." Before I can even register what the bouquet that's been shoved in my hands looks like, Vere, skips up next to the head stylist, saying, "We are ready. Robin, we have to go."

They escort me to a side door marked with a flashing red sign that says: *Exit to Stage Left.*

I notice that Vere's hair has been strung through with crystal encrusted braids also, but hers match her darker blondish-brown hair color. The wild mass that usually riots around her head has been made over and curled just like mine to hang down her back and over her shoulders. Instead of a veil she has a few baby-white roses connected to a sparkling headband. Mrs. Felix is also wearing the same headband. Vere's makeup nearly matches mine on the eyeliner and the lashes. I think she looks like a model, and she's definitely much more comfortable in her dress than I am in mine.

I'm whispering, "little breaths, little deep breaths," as we reach the door.

Vere jumps behind me to gingerly pick up the long train just how a real maid of honor might and says, "The guys are on the last song before they head down here for the tuxes. This means it's time to get you positioned on the lift. Do you feel ready?"

Because Clara's mom has followed us, and is hovering where she can overhear me, I let my eyes scream out, *no-no-no*, but answer with a small smile, "Aside from not feeling ready to be hydraulically lifted up onto a giant stage in front of thousands of people?" Vere nods as shake my head. "Vere, does anyone ever feel ready to get married?"

"I'm going to take that as a yes," Vere laughs, shaking her head and pushes me out into the hall where everything seems to be in total chaos.

Vere and the stylists start acting like they're official wedding-dress-guards as they're shouting, "stand back" and, "do not mess up the bride —keep off the dress," while blocking the path of anyone who comes near me until they retreat and we can pass them by unscathed.

One frazzled looking dude with hipster rectangle glasses and short black hair pauses to smile and give me a little nod like he approves, then he moves on to shout over everyone's heads, "Don't *anyone* push the button on the gazebo lift until Royce is done with his speech. Got me? Speech first, then the button." He shouts even louder. "I said, speech first, and then the button. And someone had better fire the dammed extra fog machines *now.* We're going for twice as much fog as usual for the bride reveal. Let's go people. We're about to make rock band history. Did the Rock Weekly photographers make it?"

Some guy answers him, "They're here, along with all the top entertainment channels—as well as every damn person with a press identification card who showed up has been let inside. One dude said he was from some South Florida, Everglades *nature magazine*. I was like, are there even towns down in the Everglades, but he's inside, taking notes for the gators."

The guy with the glasses' expression switches from stressed to relieved. "Good. Good. Will someone make sure to tell Royce? He was worried there would not be enough press."

"Really? Royce? Worried?" Someone else calls out, adding a little ironic laugh."I'll tell him right now."

As we wait for Adam's drum set to be carted past me off of the lift and the Gazebo plus a strip of red carpet is getting shoved on, I glance back to the people back in the dressing room, but it's like they've already forgotten me.

The bride stuff has been shoved aside and the table that held the crystals is now loaded with black and silver tuxedo ties. A row of silk wrapped white rose buds that will be pinned on the lapels of the guys tuxedo jackets have been lined up, and what looks like two racks of every size of tuxedo and tuxedo pants are now waiting.

The stylists have dragged five director's chairs and long mirrors all into a line, with make-up stands and make-up artists already standing there at each one, waiting.

The thought that Royce, Adam, and Hunter are heading down makes me move my feet faster as they pull me up onto the lift, saying that '*this will be a faster and safer way to get me and the dress safely to the stage instead of going around*' so I can stand in the wings waiting for the wedding music. I'm good with any thing as long as I don't get stuck in an awkward conversations with any of them right now. Especially with my fake fiancé.

As I settle in with Vere on to the lift, Mrs. Felix calls out, "Robin, please remember that *none* of your past needs to be a *secret* anymore, dear. You and Sage…you're not *runaways* anymore. It's important we give the press the whole love story between you and Royce, as well as we need to be very open with what's happening with your father. It's all a bit much for you to be blurting out, but you need to try so we can gain public sympathy for you after the wedding."

I nod, working hard on my breathing as I answer, "Yes. I'll remember."

Thankfully, Vere squeezes my hand again. Like Mrs. Felix knows she needs to cover for the part where she's just stopped my heart from beating and maybe she can tell I've got nothing left to say to anyone, the old woman pulls in a long shaky breath that matches the ragged ones coming out of my over-corseted lungs, and she adds loudly so that everyone will hear, "Just think, Robin, in a few moments we're going to be *family*." She smiles brightly. "Isn't that wonderful?"

"For better or for worse," I squeak out, trying to joke.

"Only for better, dear. That's why we're doing this, for the *better*." She zooms up beside the platform.

"Yes," I say brightly, but when I swallow, it hurts like I've choked down a small VW bus and the bumper has lodged sideways in my throat.

Linking gazes with Mrs. Felix's again, I wish I could read her mind. But she's smiling at me so genuinely and with such an excited gleam in her eyes that most of my fear dissipates.

I think to myself how she's a level-headed, international business woman who is in full support of what's happening here today. She's been married herself. She's raised her own children, and I need to trust her that all is going to be well, just like she said. So, I try to copy the calm look on her face.

She flicks the edge of my dress that's hanging over the lift onto the red runner. "You look beautiful, Robin. Go on, now. The lift will take you and Vere up, and then you're to find your spot side stage. Look for little taped x's on the floor and wait for Sage to lead you out."

I have so much to say to her, so much gratitude for all that this wonderful woman is about to do to help me and Sage, but because I know any tears will ruin my make-up I take a whole bunch of new, little breaths and croak out only a whispered: "Thank you."

4

ROYCE

WHEN I WALK BACK on stage I'm alone.

The lighting keeps me in silhouette and the crowd cheers so loudly the sound almost knocks me back. Somehow, in under five minutes, the stylist team had me showered off and spritzed, dabbed me with all kinds of shit, then had shoved me, Adam, and Hunter (equally cleaned up) into these awesome Gatsby-style tuxedos.

If I weren't so nervous I'd say I love this outfit. All the way from my shiny shoes, to the pants (boasting a nearly imperceptible satin stripe down the sides of each leg) to the snowy white tux shirt, the long old-fashioned, very cool jacket with tails, to the solitary white rose pinned on my lapel, to my black-and-silver bow tie.

A convincing costume for a wedding, to be sure.

Without a glance at Adam and Hunter, I motion for the lights to go up, and when the spotlight hits me the crowd goes wild again.

All of the guitars, amps, drums—everything but one microphone has been stripped off stage. Now the crowd and the jumbo-screens have registered that I'm standing alone, wearing a tux and it looks as though I'm floating in a sea of ankle-deep, man-made fog the crew has been blowing into the stage space since the middle of our last song.

It's expected after the last set, that after waiting through first minutes of screams, applause, and chanting from the fans, that Guarderobe—hell *every* band does this—returns for an encore. Only, what an epic encore this is going to be.

Because I'm still out of breath from running back up here, I have no clue what is going to come out of my mouth when I step up to the microphone. To buy time, I hold my hands out in front of me, waiting for the audience to quiet.

When they grow silent, I become so nervous that I only smile, really, really, wide. That was a mistake, because that's made everyone start cheering all over again.

I use that second roar from the crowd to grip the microphone stand and pull in some full, deep breaths for courage. The spot lights are still close in, ultra-bright and only on me. My stage manager told me when I give the signal the hundreds of roses set in tall vases all around me will be lit next. Carefully, I eye exactly where the gazebo will come up behind me, and note that under the fog my feet are pressing into the thick red-carpet runner I was texted about. They'll cut half of the fog machine blasts when the roses light up so the center of the stage will clear to reveal the red carpet just as the Gazebo holding Hunter, will raise up and somewhere during that time wedding music will play.

"Everyone. Please. *Please*," I say over the endless cheering.

As the crowd quiets again, my eyes travel quickly to the edges of the stage where I've been told, Vere, Hunter and Sage have been all lined up and are ready to go. But instead of finding them, my eyes land on Robin's form located off stage at the end of this damn red carpet.

It's too dark to clearly see how they've dressed her up, but I can tell she's in the white dress my grandmother promised.

Convincing costume number two.

I wish I could see her face, analyze the expression inside of her wide eyes, but I can only see how she's nodding at me like she's trying to encourage me not to freak out.

I bite my lower lip, discouraging yet another smile because of course Robin Love is trying to make *me* feel better right now, and suddenly I know exactly how to start.

"Who here believes in love at first sight?" I call out, relaxing some as everyone cheers all over again.

"Okay. Okay. Good." I widen my arms and hold out my hands so the palms are flat and facing the audience, feeling oddly like a preacher on TV. "If you could please be quiet and let me talk, because I've got to explain this tux." I make a show of fingering my lapels, and then straightening the rose. "See, we've got some huge announcements to make here tonight, and some fancy, formal things to do here today. With your blessings, of course."

Knowing how to work the crowd, and knowing our fans can't ever contain a cheer, I'm forced to pause, waiting out another round of screaming. When they quiet again, I continue. "Rather than let you all find out what those announcements are by reading them in a magazine, or by guessing at which online rumors are true or false, we've decided to reveal everything here, with the people we love the best and with people we trust the most." I nod, looking slowly around the entire arena while pointing in a slow half circle. "That's you guys. Our fans. We love you."

The crowd blows up again. And again, I wait for the lull. "You've been carrying us since the beginning, and without you in our lives, we would have no reason to wake up each morning. So that's why we want you involved here today. You, the fans are part of our family, and..." The crowd roars again and this time I go on, shouting over their noise. "And everything I'm about to tell you involves these words. *Family*. And *Love*. And hell-yes." I grin wide again, adding, "*love at first sight*!"

After the next round of cheering I ask them again, "Please. Please hold the cheers and let me get through this. I'm nervous as hell."

When the crowd settles, I go in talking fast: "First, we need to talk about Adam. My life-brother and a dude who's been really busy keeping secrets from all of us last year. I'm going to let you in on what he's been up to, but you all need to stay quiet, because we've got something amazing to show you all." I search the dark recesses of the backstage opposite of where Adam, his wife Eve, and his little red-headed baby, Apple are waiting. "Shh. Please. People. Quiet."

The audience, completely and thankfully on board with my requests, grows even quieter, and when I think they're ready I wave to Adam. "Will you come out here and say what you need to say, so I can get on with *my* life?"

When Adam steps out clinging to Eve, who is doing her best attempt at making her face not look terrified while carrying the baby. The crowd, visibly surprised, gets quieter, like they've all taken a breath. Once the giant screens focus in on them—on the baby mostly—we're all hit with wave of at least twenty thousand collective people sighing that same breath out: "*Aww,*" at the same time.

Luckily, someone has thought to outfit the baby with these cute little head-phone looking, noise reduction things in case the crowd can't contain themselves. In typical, mellow, baby-Apple fashion, she's content in her mom's arms and blinking at her surroundings happily. The baby's a show-stopper, because one of the genius-stylists dressed her up like a mini-flower girl in this cute gauze-and-ribbons miniature white dress, all while Eve is dressed up in a strapless silver gown that matches Vere's.

Evie could go down in history as the only bridesmaid who'd never actually met the bride before the wedding. But she, like the rest of us in the inner circle—she *knows* how insane our lives are, so she will never tell that story to anyone.

"Thank you for holding quiet." Adam speaks into the microphone in a very soft voice. He points at Evie. "I'd like to introduce you to my wife, Evie."

The crowd gasps and some people applaud, but most of the fans are grappling with their cellphones that they're too preoccupied to make more noise.

Adam clears his throat, flicking a nervous glance over Evie and the baby before going on, "We—Eve—Evie, is what I call her. She and I—we were married over a year ago and I didn't tell anyone. Please. Please don't scare the baby—let me finish." He holds up his hands as the crowd starts to erupt in noise, then they stop. "Better, I managed to keep my life, my bride and all of the changes going on in my life and in my heart a secret. Kept them secret for a very long time." He motions to where I'm standing. "I didn't even tell my bandmates and my best friends here that I was in love because…first, my Evie is a really shy person. And, then I didn't know how to tell them I was married, because—well, because of this baby, of course, because of a thousand other reasons." He smiles. "Reasons which you all will hear about later. Just know, I loved having Evie and our relationship be a secret. Time passes fast when you're in love, and well, I don't have to tell you all how babies are made but that's what went down." He grins with that Adam-trademark-impish grin of his, while Evie's face flushes as red as the hair on top of her head.

The crowd starts to go wild again. Adam looks worried, panicked even and quickly calls out, "Please. Please don't scare her. Okay, guys? Please."

I watch Evie's face more than I watch the baby's face, knowing full well that Adam is hoping the audience doesn't scare his *wife*, not his baby—because she's the one who's skittish in crowds.

Terrified even.

She and her past, and the baggage she hauls around inside her head that she may never be able to unload, is the 'thousand other reasons' why Adam kept his relationship and marriage a secret from all of us.

It's also the reason he almost lost her for good. I know their whole story, and watching Evie now just humbles me. I'm also so moved and relieved that she's here with all of us today and helping us out right now. Her participation, is the biggest wedding gift anyone could ever give. I know for her to stand on stage with her baby in her arms is costing her some real shreds of her sanity and it's hurting her to do it somewhere deep inside, which in turn hurts my best friend Adam.

Adam's got the crowd under control again, and after a saying, "Shh. Shh, please quiet down," once more, he adds, "I want you all to meet our beautiful daughter."

He takes the baby out of Evie's arms and holds her up a little so the crowd can see her. I try really hard not to be immature and imagine the opening of the Lion King movie as the spotlights hit the baby when Adam holds her up high and adds, "We've named her Apple."

The cameras zoom in to catch the baby's pudgy face on the jumbo-screens and the crowd collectively gasps and says, "Aww…" all over again.

Apple, the little champ, drools and grins her toothless grin like someone prompted her to do it, and my hoof beat-heavy-heartbeats start to calm.

The fans are eating this up so hard, and how could they not? The baby has stolen the show.

Adam tucks Apple close to his chest before speaking again. "My baby daughter has been here all week with us in Orlando while we do these last concerts. To make things work while doing these in-residence shows for the parks this summer, we had to hire a nanny. That's because my wife had to leave town suddenly to see to her mother. A mother who was very sick and far away in Wales, located all the way in the UK. This nanny we hired saved our lives, and she turned out to be cool, and funny, and really, really nice. Bear with me, there's a point to this story. Hold on, let me get Apple off stage."

Adam grins, looking over at me, while he's handing the baby back to Evie. When Evie and Apple are safely off stage Adam grins and goes on, "Royce Devlin here." He points at me. "He fell in love with our nanny! I'm talking head over heels, out of his mind—fell in love with the nanny!"

As the crowd cheers, then cheers some more, I step up and take the microphone away from Adam.

"Hell yes I fell in love. Her name is Robin Love, and we're going to get married, right here. Right now." I grin, and pace the stage. "Who's down to go to a wedding? Anyone? It's why we're all wearing tuxedos."

The crowd's lost it. The foot stomping gets so loud I worry the floors under the bleachers are going to break. Smiling at everyone wider and wider, I walk the microphone back to the stand and then move the whole contraption to the side while I'm talking. "Okay. Okay. Listen up. Let's go back to my first question. When I asked you all," I raise my voice so it carries high above the cheers. "Who? Who here believes in love at first sight? I was talking about myself."

As the crowd roars louder in response I press ahead over the noise, "One week ago, I didn't believe any of that crap. But now, I do. Oh man, I do." I shake my head, wondering at how true my words ring inside my head. "And now that we don't need a nanny anymore, and now that I'm in love and about to leave on a world tour, I also don't believe in letting fate decide what's going to happen between me and this amazing, beautiful girl."

I nod and grin more, watching how the jumbo screens feature me out of the corner of my eyes. "I'm locking this girl I love down by putting a ring on her finger. When you know. You know, and I've learned from my man Adam, here, that in our business if you meet someone, and if it's real, you need to jump in and make your move. Go for it at all costs. The press has already caught on that I was seeing someone, but they got the story all wrong. They made up lies about Robin which are not true. We think that it's bullshit that we can't have any privacy, and that random people are allowed to tell lies about us and then spread them all over the internet. We wanted the real story to come out here. We also want the bad stories about my bride to go away. This is why we opted for this fast wedding in front of all of you guys. Because it's fucking real." I'm shouting now. "Because you aren't random people, and we want people who actually give a shit about us to spread the word about what is really happening here. We want our fans —all of you to tell the real story—because you're the ones we trust. No one else."

The crowd cheers again, so loudly I'm actually wishing for earplugs.

I motion to Hunter. "We know Adam's surprise wedding is going to bum some of you out, because we know you fans hate missing details of our lives. So tonight, to make it up to all of you, my man Hunter—a dude who got himself a special minister license off of the internet today—he is going to marry me and the love of my life, Robin, right here, right now, with all of you as our witnesses. Will that make it up to you? Will it?" I'm shouting louder and louder now.

The echoing cheers are so loud I can only wave my arms and shout into the microphone, hoping someone can hear what I'm saying, "I'm guessing you're all in, then?" I wave my arms and signal the lights to go on over the roses.

"Damn! Okay then." The laughter that comes off my lips next surprises me as the screams nearly break my eardrums, but I know it's a mixture of half wonder half relief that everyone is so on board. "Then how about you all light up the LED stuff we passed out? Who wants to hold up a cell phone and record this special moment along with us and post the real story online tonight? Let's break the internet with this love story. I'm asking you to help us out, *go live* if you can, or post parts of what we're doing to let the whole world be part of it."

Through a new wave of cheers, the lights in the stadium flash bright and then go to complete black for a moment. The crowd does what I've asked, and back stage, on cue, has lit the entire circumference outside of the stage area with thousands and thousands of white twinkling LED lights. Better, just as many cellphone screens are now pointed at us. When the lights go back up on me, they're dim to feature how the trap doors below-stage have opened, and the lift has already started pushing the pre-lit, covered in silk, made from twined together bleached wood branches, wedding gazebo up onto the stage. I'm shocked to realize how legit this thing looks, and when a loud recording of the traditional 'dum-dum-da-dum' wedding march begins firing over the stage speakers and the crowd goes from wild to insane, I have to smile and place a hand over my thundering heart because I'm caught up, just how they are in this excitement.

Roses wave. Light sticks wave and every cellphone in the house that still has charge and storage space is recording everything.

When the spotlights find me again, the fog has blown off revealing the red carpet perfectly. I work to calm my voice, forcing the crowd to also calm down or they won't be able to hear me. "We couldn't be happier that you're willing to take this journey with us today. One more thing. Listen carefully please. Please. *Everyone. Please.* This is important stuff I want you all to know. My fiancé, Robin, has a father who's

Special Forces, ARMY. He's been deployed and he should be here with us today, but sadly he's missing in action. MIA for over a year. His status is part of the reason we decided to speed up our engagement all the way to a wedding, and to trust the love we feel for each other. It's because she and her little brother needed some help. They needed a family and they needed some support, some legal help, and they needed it fast." I frown as people start to cheer again and I say again, "Please. This is a lot. Let me tell the story."

The stadium grows nearly silent again as the cameras zoom in on my face. "Robin's little brother is only thirteen—he will be the one giving her away tonight. Robin, the girl I'm about to marry, had put her dreams on hold and had run away so her brother wouldn't have to go to foster care. They were on the run when we wound up hiring her as a last-minute nanny. She was trying to create a family and a safe place for him to finish growing up with or without their dad. But because Robin is young, only eighteen today actually, the authorities think that's too young to be a parent. They were discussing taking her little brother away from her this week. They were also making Robin go back to North Carolina to face charges of *kidnapping* her own brother. Can you believe this sadness?"

The audience responds with boos and roars of displeasure.

"Well it's true." I nod my head, agreeing with their anger. "I thought if I stepped up and married Robin who is the bravest person I've ever met, and that if my grandmother and uncle also stepped up, then Robin and her brother would have the instant family they needed. Robin would also get to be my wife, and considering I'd vowed to marry this girl from the very first moment we met, I think it's a *win-win*, right? I get her, and she gets me, as well as a family that includes all of you guys supporting her and she and I get to protect her brother together."

I sweep my arm out to the attentive crowd as I cry out, "She's only done exactly what each and every one of us would have done to save our siblings, right? And I'm only doing what anyone else would do to save the girl *I love*."

The crowd, again, goes insane.

"Do you all understand where I'm coming from now? It's been only one week that I've known this girl, but *damn-me*, I'm so lost every time I see her face. I can't breathe when she laughs because she's lodged deep into my heart." I put my hand over my chest. "And anyone who has felt this feeling, I *know* you get me…I'm in love. So in love that the thought of her leaving my side even for a day to face what she needs to face all alone?" I shake my head. "Oh, hell no. The thought of her hurting or being sad even for one minute without me by her side? It nearly kills my soul. And I guess, that's what love is, right?" I blink at the crowd, quieting my voice. "My mom once told me I would know I was in love when I cared about someone's happiness more than I cared about my own. And…that's how it is between me and Robin. It's maybe only been one week, but it's real."

The crowd cheers, louder and louder, and I wait all over again for them to stop.

"Guys. I—I—" I shake my head, chuckling a little to myself. "I'm nervous as hell and I'll bet Robin is even more nervous. So…I think I've got nothing more to say," is what falls out of my mouth next. "So…let's just do this thing, okay? Let's have a wedding!"

Turning away from the new wave of cheers, but fully aware the cameras are still on me, I run my hands over my eyes to make sure I'm not going to cry or anything weird, because talking about my mom and then feeling all weak-kneed and churning guts right now, is about as much surprise public vulnerability that I can handle.

I adjust my tie, and check the rose that has been pinned to my jacket again, and as the rest of the wedding party takes their places, I give Robin one last glance and a nod.

I'm able to force a laugh, as the wedding music comes back on and the noise of the crowd becomes so deafening it nearly lifts me off my feet. It doubles when I walk into the gazebo and take my place beside Adam, my uncle Gregory and flick a glance at Hunter who is poker facing so hard in his center position as our 'minister'. He looks like he's made of stone. Vere, *thank-God-for-Vere*—she's the only one who's grinning naturally. She's lined up on the other side beside my grandmother, and Evie who's holding the now sleeping baby—and still wearing her little headphones, looks slightly panicked, but is holding her ground.

Sage, with Robin on his arm, steps out and together they walk slowly down the red carpet runner heading in my direction. The guys who are running the cameras step up to get them onto the jumbo screens so the entire stadium all can see the brave brother and sister I'd just described. Their saucer-wide blue eyes, and their shy almost matching smiles, fill up the screens and it's not lost on me how shy and beautiful Robin looks right now.

The entire audience cheers so loudly the stage below our feet shakes and the roof feels like it's almost about to fall in. It's so constant and so loud, no one at all can hear the wedding music anymore.

When Robin's tentative, sweet smile moves off the crowd and reaches me, I lock onto it and quickly step off the stage to take her arm from her brother's. I see my grandmother's expression go from nervous to genuine as I help Robin up the two raised steps then lead her, hand-in-hand to stand in front of the podium while Sage, like he's done this a million times, goes to stand next to Adam.

Suddenly the entire stadium goes quiet. Out of the corner of my eyes I can see the crowd going wild, but I can no longer feel the floor shaking beneath my feet or hear one drop of sound beyond the breaths of air Robin is taking next to me. I can only note how her hand feels perfect as it settles into mine.

In mere moments, Adam is stepping forward and handing me two gold bands. Though it's over a loud speaker, from far away, I hear Hunter ask Robin: "Do you, Robin Love, take Royce Devlin, to love, to honor, to protect, to keep and to support, to comfort and to tend, to shelter and to hold, for all the days of your life?"

She answers with her eyes locked on mine and a shy, but clear, "I do."

"Do you, Royce Devlin, take Robin Love, to love, to honor, to protect, to keep and to support, to comfort and to tend, to shelter and to hold, for all the days of your life?"

Unwavering in my own gaze, again, it's so easy for me to answer, "I do."

The cheering nearly blows the lid off this place when Hunter says: "I now pronounce you man and wife. Royce, you may kiss the bride."

She's trembling, nearly gasping for breath as my lips meet hers for one gentle kiss. I almost lose control and take the kiss up a notch, but I hold back, knowing there's simply too many smart phones pointed at the jumbo screens for that.

When I pull away, her trembling seems to have doubled, so while Hunter shouts out, "May I present to you, Mr. and Mrs. Devlin," I sweep her up into my arms. I've surprised her so much with that move she looks up into my eyes, with gratitude as she says, "Thanks. I was worried I wouldn't make it out of here. You can't believe how hard it is to walk in this thing."

I smile and pull her closer, carrying her down the two steps that have kept us elevated from the rest of the wedding party. I pause to smile at the way she's got her eyes downcast, loving how her long lashes curve and curl against her cheeks, and honestly, I don't know how I make it to the center of the stage. Nor do I remember Hunter, Adam and Sage, Vere, Evie and the baby crowding in behind us as we left the stage to be herded into what will be our first press conference.

As we face the press, I don't set Robin down. I'm waiting for someone to scream out *fraud* and to make it all stop, but when it doesn't happen, and Robin grins up at me with a secretive twinkle in her eyes, I'm simply excited to see what's going to happen next.

5

ROBIN

ROYCE CARRIES me all the way back to the same dressing room where I was dressed for the wedding. Only, as we enter he starts twirling me around, and shouting out, "Robin, you've made me the happiest man alive. We pulled this off. We just eloped along with thousands of people cheering us on, just how we wanted."

I know he's acting, but I feel like I can't breathe because the smile he's sending out is sincere and truly looks so happy that I almost believe him. The guy's face is also so beautiful to me, smiling into my eyes how he's doing, that I could swear it's increasingly harder to breathe.

When I force my gaze away to scan just who he's preforming for now, I can't help but notice he, I, and the entire wedding party are on a new kind of stage. And I get by the tension that seems to be setting into everyone's shoulders, despite the serene expressions they're all wearing, that this show might be more important than the one we just performed on stage.

He sets me down carefully, but positions me so my back is facing the press. Quickly he leans toward my face, first brushing a quick kiss on my lips, and then he goes for a second one, this time the kiss is long enough for the sound of two hundred camera clicks to fire off. "Sorry. Had to do that." He whispers against my ear. "Let's see your deliriously happy newlywed face before I turn you around." He runs his thumbs over both of my hot cheeks, and I'm wondering if he's hoping some of the color that has to be there will fade away.

"How's this?" I work to shove my jitters away, and grin as wide as possible because those sliver-blue eyes of his are twinkling down at me like he's not anything but happy while he's patiently waiting for me to settle into the over-crowded too-attentive vibe inside this room.

"Perfect." He places his forehead next to mine how he did after we had our first kiss and keeps his hands on my shoulders. "God, but you're a beautiful bride, Robin, do you know that?" he whispers down to me.

I frown up at him, whispering back, "Save that kind of comment for when people can hear you, would you? But…as a groom, you don't look so bad in a tuxedo either." I shrug, adding, "So you know."

"Thanks." He chuckles, pulling away to pretend-fix my veil, then he leans back to my ear to whisper, "Keep that glowing-face locked on. Don't answer anything directly unless I squeeze your hand like this." He pushes a thumb deep into my palm. "Otherwise, keep on smiling and, please don't let go of my hand. We need to let them ask all the questions possible before we talk, because these vultures are going to bring up all of the things we forgot to think about in this mad plan. My team needs to take notes so we can fill any holes we may not have thought of as quickly as possible. Ready?" He pushes his thumb deep into my hand like he wants me to answer.

I squeeze his hands back and only nod because there's no point in telling him that *hell-no, I'm not ready for this.*

Whatever *this* is going to be.

A line of bodyguards has kept the press at a decent distance, but as Royce turns us both to face the crunch of rolling video cameras, he straightens his shoulders like he's facing a firing squad and raises his voice. "Shout out your questions quickly, guys. This is our wedding day and we've got transportation waiting—so much to—*do*!" He wiggles his brows suggestively and everyone laughs, while I shake my head, and gain another laugh by rolling my eyes a little at him.

"Royce. When did you know—when did you know you wanted to *be* with Robin? Marry her?"

"Like I said on stage. From the first moment we met. At first there was this connection to her that felt like no other, and then…honestly, I swear I just knew she was the one. The way things came together that led up to marrying her today? It was like fate kept intervening. I was walking on this road and everything lined up so easily." He glances around and points at another reporter. "You, over there, the woman in the blue dress? Do you have a question?"

A woman steps up, camera also rolling. "Robin, I'll ask you the same. Was it love at first sight with you? I mean come on, it's only been a week—and like we know it's too soon for you to wonder if you're pregnant—but are you, are you pregnant?"

Royce presses his thumb into my palm.

I pull in a deep breath and answer being as truthful as possible. "No. Of course I'm not pregnant. And, no, I never expected to fall in love with Royce how I did, but it's happened." I smile and flash my wedding ring. "Obviously."

Everyone in the room goes silent, listening while I sort through more truths I can speak about. "The attraction was always there for me, of course because—well—you see him here, he's…wow." I feel my cheeks going hotter.

People in the room chuckle.

I go on, "So that part was easy, considering." I laugh again along with them, keeping my gaze as steady as I can. "But, I didn't fall for him because of his looks. I fell for him when I realized what an amazing friend and person he is."

"What do you mean?" A man in the back calls out.

"Everyone thinks Royce is the band's bad boy, only he's not."

"Oh, here we go. She's going to blow my cover," Royce jokes.

"Royce has so much honor and his kindness goes above-and-beyond anyone I've ever met, and cares deeply about everyone. We shared this one kiss, and…" I glance at Royce who's watching me intently. "And I know it sounds trite, but it was like I'd been struck by lightning. From that point forward he was simply part of my mind—inside if it. I agree with what Royce said. That what happened between us has to be fate, because all of the puzzle pieces between us that should have seemed difficult—like how we've only known each other a short time, how I'm just a girl from North Carolina—a girl who ran away to save my brother, and because of my age, too? Well instead of those things being obstacles, they actually helped us get married even faster." I motion around to the band. "Royce aside, suddenly I had these amazing people who cared about me pushing the decision as well. These are people who I actually do trust and love and who say they love me right back."

Mrs. Felix wheels her wheelchair over to pick up my other hand and smile up at me, I start to tear up. "When Royce asked me to marry him

I, at first told him *no*. Told him he was insane. But with his grandmother telling me to let go of doubts." I shrug. "Encouraging me to not pay attention to what *society does, and doesn't do* and to simply live my life." I motion to Mrs. Felix, Gregory and the rest of the band, "I decided to trust. Trust these amazing people who wanted to help me, and," I glance up at Royce. "And trust how my heart feels, and I've never felt like how I feel when I'm with Royce. It's like Royce says, it's real and even though it's really awkward to tell a whole room full of strangers about it, I'm—" My voice falters as my gaze catches on Royce's. "We. We are, very much, in love."

"You're doing beautifully, dear," Mrs. Felix whispers.

The press mob starts shouting out hundreds of questions then, about my age, about why we didn't wait, about how this whole thing is crazy.

This time Mrs. Felix is the one to silence them by letting go of my hand and pushing the control on her wheelchair forward like she's trying to create a shield between them and us.

"It's your fault they had to get married so quickly, you know?" She points at them, shaking her finger like they're naughty children. "All of you—you—the *press*. You caused this instant wedding for these poor dear young people."

"How can that be true?" A man shouts out from behind a camera.

She wheels forward more as they stop shouting to hear what she has to say. "I'm sure you all know, or maybe some of you horrid gossips even *wrote* the damaging stories, the ones that called this nice girl here unthinkable things." She points to me. "For those of you who are pretending to not know what I'm referring to, Robin was being labeled as a prostitute who worked for the band. A money-grubbing groupie! And worse, when in fact she was only ever employed as our hired *nanny*."

Mrs. Felix shakes her head sharply, then points at her grandson. "Royce is in *love* with this girl, and given different circumstances he would have wooed her, dated her, and taken a couple of years to grow his relationship with her. But once you all wrote that garbage about the young woman he loves, the steps we decided to take were obvious to all of us."

She shakes her head and does the very cute 'tsk-tsk' sound she always makes. "Many a marriage around this world involves a bride and a groom who don't know each other well. What about the arranged marriages that work out? I've even heard there's even a few TV shows that feature fast marriages. And, what about those with the bachelor or bachelorette picking a husband or wife very quickly. We've watched these people fall in love."

"Or out of love," one reporter calls out in a snide voice.

Mrs. Felix gifts that man her worst stare and zooms even closer to the press, forcing them all to step back. "Well, that's true of course, but once in a while these arrangements allow a good couple to be happy together and to stay in love. But this is more than a good couple. This is better than any of those arrangements. This is two people who have a real connection, who got married to save each other's reputations and families, and two people for whom I vouch. If you could see how truly wonderful and in love they really are together despite the odds stacked against them, and despite the few days they have actually been dating, you would not speak with such cynicism."

"So you really do approve of this match?" The woman in the blue dress calls out, sounding as though she's amazed.

"Yes." Mrs. Felix nods. "If I had to go out in the world and choose a girl that I think would be perfect for my grandson to marry it would be exactly this girl, our own, *darling*, Robin Love. She's kind, she's considerate, generous and her heart is genuine. She's been raised by her wonderful ARMY father with so much honor and love and my Royce adores her, so yes. Of course I approve."

"Robin. Robin! What would your father think of Royce? If he's found, what will he do when he meets your husband?"

The entire room grows completely quiet and when I catch Royce's expression as he presses his thumb into my palm for me to answer, I realize he might be as curious as the reporters. "My father?" I laugh a little. "Well, he's Special Forces and I'm his only daughter, after all, so…" I dart a wink at Royce. "I would assume he will try to kill Royce for marrying me without permission."

Everyone erupts into laughter including me.

"But then what?" Royce asks.

"But then, my father will hear the story, and he will love Royce how I do. He'll also be so thankful that we're safe and okay, because that's what any deployed parent wants for their children, right? Just how Sage and I hope our father is somewhere…" I swallow, going on, only because I know everyone is listening only to me. "That he's alive and that he will be found…soon."

The room grows so quiet it's unsettling, and I pull in a shaking breath before saying more. "I'd like to ask anyone who's filming this, to please run this footage and maybe can you ask the public to give my dad and his best friend, who is also missing in action, one quick prayer, because they really need it." My voice cracks. "Their families need it, too." I swallow the massive lump that has taken over the back of my throat and croak out, "We're all so worried about them."

Mrs. Felix, sensing I'm about to break down and cry, zooms her wheelchair in front of me. "Do you hear how sweet she is? Your stories from yesterday marking her a prostitute would have stuck to her reputation and ruined her life. People would have whispered and torn this nice girl down even more than what you had already done to her, all because you assumed the worst about her when it wasn't true. Today she's safe, and she's married, and we've invited you into the *real* story that's unfolding here. I ask you, this time, to report and do good. Try to help this girl find her father, try to make up for the lives you almost accidentally destroyed."

The press mutters more, but seems to be fresh out of questions for me and Royce. Suddenly a bunch of them surge towards Sage who's standing at the back of the room with Hunter and Vere, eating chips out of a large bowl.

As a few crowd close to ask him a few questions, I can see my brother is nervous, and though I can't hear the questions they're asking or his answers, I can see the expressions on the faces of the people interviewing him. It's obvious Sage is working his charm on them because they're laughing and nodding and taking some of the chips he's offering them.

I try not to look panicked, seeking solace in how we told Sage he didn't have to lie about our dad or how we ran away anymore, so I can only hope whatever he's saying helps solidify our story.

"What about a honeymoon?" One man calls out. "Where will you go?"

I feel my cheeks go completely hot at that question. My heart starts beating so fast that suddenly it feels really hard to breathe. I turn my face to hide it into Royce's bicep and lower my lashes unable to meet anyone's eyes, because the word honeymoon is slamming around my head so hard I can now hardly see.

I risk a quick glance through my lashes up at Royce, hoping his poker face is turning out way better than mine, and thankfully up on his chiseled-calm-face things seem stabilized and not at all ruffled.

He's flashing a smile and nodding while he does this heart-stopping eye-twinkle thing I've never seen before as he says, "Oh hell yes there's going to be a honeymoon and, not that this is *anyone's* business, but this is not rocket science here. We just told you we're in love, and we just got married, so what do you think is going to happen here? It *is* our wedding night."

He laughs, shooting everyone a second wicked grin before pulling me gently closer to his side. "But that's the last time Robin or I will let anyone talk about that side of our relationship, because—*damn—come on people.* Did you not just hear my grandmother's speech? A little privacy and respect is needed where my *wife* is concerned. She's not used to all of this yet. I'm not stupid enough to reveal where we're having our honeymoon, but I can tell you that she and I are not allowed to leave the state. We need to be back here Monday morning to talk with the authorities that are coming in from North Carolina to help us address the situation surrounding the custody of Robin's little brother." He shrugs casually like what he's saying is normal and not at all a big deal, before he adds, "Luckily this is the awesome state of Florida, so there will probably be beaches at this honeymoon, waves, sun and some sand to play in. If..." He winks. "*If* we get outside at all. And on that note, I hope you understand the clock is ticking. We have some travel plans waiting, and so we're out of here."

As the press tries to swarm forward while they shout out more questions for me and Sage, Royce ignores all of them, simply looks down at me and says, "Can I carry you out of here."

I look up at him, trying to match my expressions to his all over again but it's really hard to hold my smile, because my darn corset has been pinching me this whole time. I suddenly find that I can only whisper, "It's actually the only way I'll be able to move. Please carry me." I blink. "I'm wearing a strait jacket thing under this dress and it's made me immobile."

"Christ." Royce laughs, pausing to brush another small kiss on my lips and adds, "But you do look really pretty."

Because the kiss took my breath away and the dress feels like it's gone from one hundred pounds to one thousand in the last few minutes I answer, "Shut up and get me out of here, would you?" I hold my arms up and try to leap into his arms but all of that effort only pushes more air out of my lungs. Frowning up at him, I mutter, "Pretty sure wedding dresses were invented to make it so brides can't run away how they want to."

He bends down laughing some and once again, effortlessly scoops me up into his arms while whispering against my ear, "No more running away, Robin. That's what started this trouble, remember? No more running away." He brushes yet another one of those sweet kisses on my lips, and then puts one on each of my cheeks.

"And what finished it, was you, kissing me, *remember*?" I feel my cheeks firing extra hot with the awareness that every camera in the room is recording how Royce Devlin is planting his lips all over my face!

"I'm only doing it for the sake of the press," he says, voice light—but suddenly he's sounding wounded. "I'm going to need to pull of just one more. Is that okay? One more…kiss?"

I realize he's worried I may say *no*, or that he's gone too far, somehow already. And then I realize that he's staring at my lips in this way that makes my heart flip—makes me want to lick my lips—or heck, melt or, I don't know what… because the look in his eyes and the way the corset is smashing my diaphragm is quickly gobbling up the remainder of of my sanity.

"For the sake of the press. Okay. One more," I agree, turning my face up to his, thinking that if I suddenly die because of this dress, it will at least be in Royce Devlin's arms with his amazingly soft and sexy, smiling lips pressed against mine.

6

ROYCE

ROBIN and I didn't talk much in the crowded limo on the way to the nearby Orlando regional airport. Nor did she seem to have anything to say as the band, my grandmother, uncle, her little brother Sage, our whole entourage, plus whole legal team, were bundled onto the five private sea-planes that were waiting for us all at the airport.

Because, guess, *the-fuck-what*?

We're heading to our honeymoon on these sea planes. A real-fake honeymoon. One that was pretty-much planned and solidified, during the last six minutes of the press conference, because we forgot that we needed to have a honeymoon.

A sixth sea-plane was reserved only for Robin and I.

All for show of course, so we *newlyweds* could be alone. Alone with the pilot and the co-pilot and one flight attendant who has been buckled in and staring at us the whole time, that is because this plane is no bigger than a closet. So who cares? We can't talk about anything anyhow on this twenty-minute trip down to this private island place we're going that's located below the tip of Florida.

At least that is where I think they said we were all going, because right about now I've got a splitting headache and my head is humming and threatening to blow like those nuclear reactors after they've been in a hurricane.

My uncle Gregory mentioned a place called Little Palm Island, and said that it's nice, but that's all I can remember on the details he spewed out to me, aside from the part where there is no real airport on this island, all while I was carrying Robin from the arena to the limo, then onto the plane because of her damn, stupid debilitating wedding dress.

With the press watching us so closely, and because I know Robin would have been sad otherwise, we felt that Sage should be near his sister tonight. So, yeah—another layer of complications has been piled on to us. Which is why we have so many airplanes.

We're *all* going to have a quick honeymoon. Together.

Why the hell not bring as many people as possible with you after you get married last-minute? Bring your grandmother, and her wheelchair, too. It's a fake honeymoon anyhow, right? Bring everyone!

For the first time in my life, I've been grateful, beyond grateful for the money we have. I've been even more grateful for the influence our current fame brings. I've never had to use my wealth like this before, but apparently, when you're famous and willing to pay triple, guys with private sea planes will delay their evening tourist trips to rush into place to transport you wherever you need to go.

It also allows for an entire five-star honeymoon bungalow to be secured for a last minute booking with nearby quarters for the bodyguards as well as for everyone else.

My grandmother, who owns the Orb Hotel Chains, knows every string that can be pulled in the entire hospitality business as well as she has way more money than I have. From the way our trip to this private island is going off without a hitch, and the way every plan about the honeymoon is coming together like we're all part of some well-oiled machine, my grandmother must have really pulled each and every string twice and added on some serious bonus cash.

Honeymoon. I'm heading to my honeymoon.

I slap my hand too hard against my forehead, drawing a look from Robin.

Our honeymoon. We are on our honeymoon. Ha.

I still don't know what's going to happen on this honeymoon. I mean, don't get me wrong, I know what's *not* going to happen, that's for damn sure. Obviously Robin and I aren't going to make sweet love nestled on a bed of freshly scattered rose-petals or whatever the hell newly married people really do when they get to private island resorts after their weddings.

But...we're going to have to do *something*, and shit...what the hell are we going to do? My stomach grows tight...or maybe it's my throat going dry, and I can't figure out what this feeling is at all. But then I get it. This, is simple, white-hot fear. Fear that I'm going to say, or do, or *be* the wrong thing just enough to mess this girl up more somehow.

Looking at her now, sitting so still and quiet with her forehead pressed against the oval glass of the window seat that I can only assume she's as exhausted as I am. She's probably working extra-hard to follow all of the directions we spewed out to her. It seems she's now pretending that she's admiring the view, but from where I'm sitting, I can see that she's not looking at anything but the condensation of her breath against the window.

She's also breathing funny, breathing like…*what?* Like she might cry?

I watch her more closely through my lashes.

Crap. Is she actually already crying right now and doesn't want me to notice? Maybe she's so overwrought by all of this she's already cracked?

I figure if she wanted to talk, she would, and that she just wants me to give her some much needed space. So, I follow her lead, block the view of the flight attendant's stare and turn to look out the same window, pulling in a few slow breaths myself.

I silently applaud Robin for her genius, and when the plane begins its descent for the water landing, I push up the armrest so I can lean closer and whisper against her ear, "You're doing awesome. We're almost there, beautiful one. Are you afraid of landing on water?"

She shakes her head, *no.*

"Soon it will be just us and we won't have to…I mean…" I glance back, changing what I'm going to say to, "We finally will be alone."

"Good," she whispers back as the plane drops onto the water, landing much faster than I'd expected. The way the plane bobs as they taxi us into the floating dock area makes me feel like we're on big, extra tippy boat.

Robin grimaces and stumbles some as we pile out onto a big floating dock and I feel like a jerk for forgetting to help her. I switch my focus off her face and down to the length of her dress, muttering, "The fluffy crap under this thing and the veil has tangled. Hold up." I rush ahead of her out of the plane, so I can lift her up and then set her down. When I do she's oddly motionless next to me. "You okay?" I whisper, watching her trying to pull in a few breaths while tracking the sides of her eyes for any telltale signs of tears.

She shakes her head, *no* but gives me this look that we both share, because we know there's not much she can do but survive being on this damn dock.

"Not long now," I encourage, reaching down to give her hand a squeeze, and smile when she squeezes back.

Thankfully each group, from each plane is hustled onto golf carts and when they get to us, Uncle Gregory steps forward like he's going to shake my hand.

It's an odd gesture, but since we're all acting here, I take it, shake it and pat his back with my other hand in a half hug. His eyes are boring into mine like he wants me to play along as he loudly calls out, "Congratulations, Royce," like he wants everyone to hear. Then, he adds, "Just want you two to know that everyone besides you two will be in a six-bedroom family-bungalow on the other side of the island."

"How was that plane ride?" Sage rushes up grinning both of us.

"Amazing. You happy?" Robin has pasted on a huge smile, but her voice sounds odd.

"Heck yes." Sage doesn't seem to notice as he rushes on talking, "Do not pinch me, Robin. I'm at a private beach resort with my favorite band. My sister has married the lead singer of *Guarderobe*, and I do not want to wake up until after the I've seen the whole island and we go on that chartered snorkeling trip Adam was promising. Got me?"

"Got you." Robin's smile appears to relax some. "But be good, polite and don't let them…spoil you too much?"

My grandmother, who was driven over to collect Sage in one of the resort golf carts, adds, "But of course we will spoil him, Robin. All while feeding him well balanced meals." She winks at me. "Should you need to communicate with him, text anytime we've given him a cell phone and I just texted you both his contact info. My legal team has informed me that as long as we stay within the state of Florida, which does include this island property, we will have a small reprise until the holiday weekend is over Monday afternoon. We all need this extra time to work on your case. Don't you two newlyweds think one minute about it. We have it all handled."

"Thanks Gran," I answer for both me and Robin.

As though she's already dismissed us, she claps her hands in her bossy way, and then taps the arm of the golf cart driver. "Chop-chop, people. The pool and the gift shop are being kept open late. We will be able to purchase whatever we may have forgotten during this fabulous-fast-elopement. I know we all need swimsuits and toothbrushes at the very least."

"Oh yes, I do." Sage, grinning, climbs in between Vere and Hunter who are seated on the back of Mrs. Felix's golf cart. It zooms away while Vere calls out, "I won't let Sage out of my sight. Hunter and I are on waterslide-baby-sit duty. He's going to be better than fine."

I note Robin's answering smile. Her body still looks like she's so tense that she's in some sort of pain because of the dress, and I could swear she's still breathing all funny—again probably because of the dress, but it's first genuine smile I've seen off her face in the last few hours.

If it's not genuine happiness, then at least I know she's happy that her brother is safe. That knowledge makes *me* happy, and somehow it's enough for both of us—for now.

My other bandmate, Adam as well as Evie and the baby, are being piled onto a second golf cart. Baby Apple is the only one that has erased her fake-wedding poker face. Like she can read everyone's mind because we all aren't sure how to properly proceed right now, she's whimpering uncomfortably. I only wave once and smile at Adam my friend shoots me one last apologetic glance as his golf cart zooms away.

When they're gone, my uncle is the only one who's left on the dock with us. Because the pilots and the hotel staff are all watching, all while pretending *not to,* something everyone we don't know or who works at places like these are paid to do, my uncle pulls me away from Robin's side and mutters under his breath, "You and Robin are going to begin a period of... appropriate and notable *private time*. Food will be delivered in to the honeymoon bungalow, and your bodyguards will be on the far perimeters to preserve privacy should any idiot reporter or island tourist try to take opportunistic photographs of you. The rest of us will be out enjoying the island and the beaches. Make sure *if* you're out in public it looks right—perfect even. But, because none of this is very easy, I recommend you simply hang inside the bungalow property together and...shit just let people assume what's going on between you. This is so hard. Do you get my meaning?"

I nearly roll my eyes, but instead I grit out, "You mean make sure we look perfectly in love, and make it look like we just had sex twenty or so times, and that it was the best sex we'd ever had now that we're married?"

"Christ. *Yes.*" He glances worriedly back at Robin. "But...can I trust…I mean. I can *trust*, that you won't…overstep…or take advantage? You know Robin is the kind of girl who will get attached… too attached…and, well…"

"Dude. Remember? I'm the guy who's vowed to never have those kinds of attachments again. You don't have to worry."

"I'm more worried about you saying shit like that."

Confused, I also turn flick a glance at back at Robin before asking, "What? Why?"

"You should form attachments." My uncle frowns, also glancing at Robin. "I was just bringing it up because Robin, she's special and I think you should go very slowly with her, because… I think she could really…"

"I get it. She could really get hurt by me."

"No." He's shaking his head. "That is not what I'm saying. I'm saying she could be something special in your life and that you should consider trying to woo her."

"Woo? Where do you get these old fashioned terms?"

"I'm old."

"You mean…woo Robin like, you 'wooed' Mrs. Perino?"

He nods and my eyes grow wide. "You mean, me…try to date her?"

"Yes. Slowly though. This girl Robin, she's special and she could fall for you."

"You want me to like seriously try to…date her. Hell no." I blink at him, confused as he nods some more. "She is special. I'll agree to that. Why else would I have married her? She's also one of the most awesome people I think I've ever met but as for her falling for me in *that* way?" I suck in a breath. "I won't let that happen."

Uncle Gregory shakes his head again, as though he'd like to argue, but I don't let him butt in again adding, "Look. Please understand my intentions here." I sigh out. "We all love this girl. Myself included. But she's innocent, and we all mean for her to stay that way, including me. *Especially me.* My number one goal is to not hurt her and to get her back to her normal life. Away from mine. And fine, I will form an attachment to her, hell I already have. And…I hope deep down that she forms one for me up to a point." I blink at my uncle. "She I are going to be *friends* by the end of all of this. Once she knows me well, and realizes this life I lead is not for her, she will understand that's all I can ever be to her. A friend. Good friends, I hope, because I need one of those.

Because I've never had a friend like her, and because I think she's already almost there for me on that level." I shake my head, trying to sort out my thoughts. "Hell, so am I, for that matter, and that's awesome. I also think it's okay if *good friends* eventually do love each other, but that's as far as this will ever go. I will not mess any of that up and sleep with her, if that's what you're worried about. I want to keep this girl in my life and sleeping with her—we all know—will send her running away from me sooner than later, because that's what always happens. So with Robin…I'm shooting for something that lasts forever. See?"

"Well, that's messed up logic, but as long as you're working to protect her and that you won't cross the line then I feel much better." He shrugs. "I guess I just needed to hear you say it. Sorry to press the issue."

"I'm kind of glad you did," I chuckle a little. "I needed to hear myself say it, too."

My uncle breathes out a long breath like he'd been holding it. And though his eyes tell me he wants to say so much more, he's holding back which is fine with me.

"Okay. Well. Good luck, son." He pats my shoulder once leap-hops onto the cart as I, head spinning, walk back over to stand next to Robin while he shouts out for the people that can hear him, "Congratulations, again, you two love birds! Happy honeymoon!"

"Royce. Is that cart for us?" Robin points, her voice sounds suddenly strained. My heart drops as I wonder if she'd accidentally overheard what I'd said to Gregory and somehow it's hurt her feelings, because I could swear the way her voice pinched and tight something is up and shit…now I'm worried all over again.

Very aware that the remaining driver, and the few pilots milling around as they wait to return to the mainland are still watching us intently, quickly I answer, "Yes. My lady. Our honeymoon chariot awaits."

Her eyes have gone wide—wild even, as she reaches up trying to get her arms around me, but for some reason that seems to be a fail and her arms fall back down to her sides.

"Royce. Please. Pick me up. I need to…we have to…hurry to the bungalow," she whispers, her voice coming out hoarse.

"What's wrong? *Shit.*" I scoop her close which seems to agitate her versus helping like I thought it would and hop into the cart. As the driver takes us off the dock she twists in my arms, pulling at the sides of her dress and, I think she's trying to straighten her back.

"The dress. It's too tight. Wanted to tell you but, I can't—I can't breathe at all anymore."

"Dude. Can't you drive this thing faster?" I call out to the driver as he's passing a sign marked, Honeymoon Bungalow, private.

The driver chuckles, "You honeymooners. Always in the same hurry." He chuckles again, motioning to a pretty, flat roofed house. "Lucky for you two, we're here. The front door is wide open. Key cards are on your desk, food is here, the door auto locks so kick it closed, but note I was to inform you that there is to be *no* champagne in consideration of the age of your young wife. We have your privacy in mind and therefore—"

"Okay. Yes," I interrupt him already leaping off the cart with Robin, growing limp my arms. "Thank you. Sorry to rush, but you said you understand."

I'M RUNNING into the bungalow listening to her quiet gasps and staring at her ever-whitening face, only pausing to kick the door shut with my foot and quickly making sure it's locked before finding my way to the huge bedroom located at the back of the unit.

Robin's gone so pale she looks nearly grey in color. When her gasps go silent, and her weight goes so limp in my arms, I freak! I want to call 911, I want to shout for help, but I know those would be stupid time-wasters when all she needs is to be able to get air into her lungs.

Working quickly, I search for zippers or something at her waist to release her from the dress, but I can't find shit, so I turn her onto her side and curse when I see a row of what looks like 100 or so pea-sized buttons going down her back—hell maybe there's two hundred. "Fuck, no. What the hell?"

I try to undo one button, but it won't budge under my huge clumsy fingers. "Sorry, Grandmother," I mutter, as I take both hands and *rip-pop-pop-pop* the buttons off the gown so fast they pelt my face like pearl bullets. I yank the dress completely off her and fling it to the side saying, "What is this?"

Her eyes seem to be rolling back into her head as I stare at the under-thing-pop out cage looking thing and unable to find any sort of buttons, I rip it off of her using all of my strength.

"Robin. *Robin? How's that?"* My voice starts to shake when I realize all this effort hasn't changed her breathing one bit, and this time she's gone so limp I think she's fainted!

I turn her back over realizing the next layer, probably the layer responsible for her lack of oxygen is this very sexy corset.

"Holy…mother of…*shit*," Panicking now, I reach for the slippery silk ribbons lacing her up the front and on both sides of the corset. Staying away from the laces going up the middle, I get both sides undone, wincing as I note how her soft skin has been marred into angry red crisscross welts where the corset had bound her, but in seconds and the thing pops free. I leave what's left of it to cover her chest while trying really hard not to look at the tiny lacy curious panties she's wearing below the corset.

She gasps, seems to comes to, and pulls in a bunch of coughing breaths. With a huge sigh of relief I let my own lungs take in a few full breaths and push the veil away from her face. "There you go. There you go. Breathe in deeply. There you go. You're okay. You're okay…"

Realizing she's going to be really embarrassed, I yank at the sheet under her, scattering rose-petals and pillows all over the place as I position part of it over her nakedness before pulling the entire corset off and tossing it on the floor near to where the wedding dress landed. When I'm sure there's nothing else binding her breathing and that she's going to be okay, I leave her and run to the bathroom to get a cup of water and make a wet washcloth so I have options to wake her up more if she doesn't come around how I want her to.

Luckily when I get back into the room, she's sitting up, clutching the sheet to her chest and the pale cheeks have returned to their usual bright, slightly flushed color that I love.

"You okay? Please talk to me."

She's got one hand over her chest like she wants to feel the air going in and out, and she smiles. "I think—I think you saved my life. Literally."

"I think you almost killed me by heart attack."

Relieved, I let myself breathe in as deeply as she's breathing in, but I'm still too freaked out to smile like she is. "Damn, girl. Next time you can't breathe can you please mention it long before you're about to actually *die*? You scared the shit out of me."

"I didn't know. I thought it was me…being nervous, and then I thought it was being near you that was taking my breath away because I always feel kind of woozy when I'm around you, and every time you smiled at me after the wedding I felt like I was choking. I didn't get that it was the dress until just after the plane ride."

"Woozy? Who says that word?" I laugh handing her the glass of water while trying not to let all that she just accidentally said to me go to my head. "Here. Drink water."

When she takes a few sips the sheet slips some, revealing the creamy curves that I've just seen far too much of—that I wish I could see more of, and that I've got *no right* to look at anymore.

Quickly, I turn away, acting like I didn't see all that I just saw, and acting like she isn't the most beautiful and awesome girl I've ever been alone with, ever.

She quickly recovers the sheet, pulling it all the way to her neck which serves to reveal more of her curving long legs, as well as scatters more of the honeymoon rose petals between us. "There's a lot of petals, huh?" she whispers. "Pretty but maybe, a bit over-done?"

"Oh…uh, yeah," I utter, taking in the entire scene. Her rumpled wedding dress, the crazy, now ruined corset and slip things, the pearl buttons all over the floor, and how she's sitting on a bed that I didn't hardly register until now, that is layered, one inch think with fresh, 'welcome-to-your-honeymoon' pink and white rose petals, and *damn-me*, but if you add in her flushed face and the part where she's nearly naked now, it looks like she and I just…

A slam of desire wells up in my soul and everywhere else.

"Okay." I start backing up. "I'll step out and we can—you can —regroup."

She nods, and I feel bad because she's looking all too serious and suddenly guilty as though she's going to apologize for something when there's nothing to apologize for except for the part where I'm about to have one hell of a painful cold shower.

"Wait." I turn back, hoping to change the look on her face from freaked out and apologetic to…*anything else*.

I point at the pile of crumpled wedding wear and bits littered all over the floor. "Please don't touch the dress, corset the buttons, any of that has to stay where it landed." I wiggle my brows. "It looks like we've had one wild time in here already, and we want the staff of this place to make note of that so add any shoes and stockings and whatever you've got left to the pile. When you're done, I'll make sure my outfit is properly scattered around, too."

I kick off one of my fancy shiny shoes to land onto her dress, the other I leave by the door so it looks like I was running out of them, but her worried expression only gets worse, not better.

"But what will we…wear? We don't have any luggage."

I open the closet by the door hoping for some of those fancy hotel bathrobes, but don't find any. Instead, I pull out the set of extra sheets someone had stored in there and hold up one flat sheet. "Are you down for eating a very late dinner with your husband in a toga by our private pool while we listen to ocean waves? I'm starving," I lie, because right now, God strike me down with a lightning bolt, I'm only hungry for her.

Luckily she can't read my mind, and she relaxes under what I hope is a steady gaze. I see her fingers going over the sheet she's hiding behind. "Yes. Okay. I love making togas. Could be…hilarious." Her frown changes into a little smile.

"That's the spirit."

"Give me a minute," she says.

Acting all casual, I turn and head out, I'm holding my sheet in front of my lower half, hoping she can't see how I've lost all physical control. "Take as long as you need—come outside when ready?" I manage, proud as hell that I've said that without choking.

When I'm alone in the living room, I stalk to the bungalow's kitchen and shove my entire head into the Sub Zero freezer to breathe in as much ice-cold air as possible. I start praying there's a spare bathroom or at least a shower by the pool nearby. One that offers cold-cold water.

If Robin looks as beautiful walking around in a sheet as she looked rumpled-up in a sheet while lying on a bed—and if *sheets* are the only clothes she and I have to wear for the next twenty-four hours—then ice cold showers and this freezer are about to be my new best friends.

7

ROBIN

AFTER A QUICK TEXT to Sage to make sure he was settled and happy—which he was, because Adam and Hunter were going to take him on the high speed waterslide soon and he couldn't hang-up on me fast enough—I walk out of the master bedroom with my toga in place.

As I cross into the living room of our honeymoon bungalow, I'm trying really hard not to feel stressed out about the sheer opulence of this place. The hand carved furniture looks like whole trees were murdered to create each piece, and the feel of the crystalized and veined marble floors under my feet feel so ice cold from the air conditioner blasting non-stop, that I swear they make my heels hurt and my teeth chatter with each step. Why do the super-rich like to live and hang out in places that resemble freaky bank lobbies?

I head toward the warm ocean breeze coming in from the opened, floor to ceiling sliding doors off the living room.

I'm trying to poker-face that I'm cool with wearing only a twisted up bed sheet. One that's held up mostly by my upper arms and armpits. And one that's covering the last remaining bit of underwear, those lacy flower petal, n*ot-really-underwear-things*, that Royce didn't rip off of me in order to save my life.

I'm afraid if I sit wrong, they're going to pop off of me, too!

Locking my arms tighter on the endlessly slipping sheet (because, add this to the unnecessary-opulence-list, they're 100 percent satin-silk. And, slippery as heck.)

I step out onto the patio and spot Royce, wearing a toga that looks like it's tied much better than mine. He also looks more relaxed than I do, but of course he does. His job of covering up body parts is easier. If his slips, he only has to wear his toga tied around his waist.

He's hovering around a table that's been set out on the patio with some food laid out on it. After a few steps, I realize it's raised patio that overlooks our own private pool. A pool shaped and colored like a blue opal teardrop, thanks to the amazing ceramic, stamp-sized tiles that make up the whole thing. It was built to 'trick the eye' into thinking that it's connected to the ocean view in the background. It's too dark to tell if it actually works, but with the stars shining down on us, and how someone's lit the whole garden and even created lights that are stuck into the sand all the way to the ocean, stopping probably where the waves are breaking onto the shore, makes me feel like I'm a real bride standing in a travel magazine.

Wow. Wow. Wow. I want to paint this. I want to live in this garden. I want to run to the ocean right now and put my feet in the water!

Resisting the urge to bolt, I force my steps forward, but when I reach Royce's side, I'm unsure what to say. By the look on his face, and the way his eyes seem to be darting around everything on the patio besides me, I think he also doesn't know what to say.

Finally, I start with the obvious. "Uh…could this be any more beautiful and…any more…awkward?"

"Nope."

I shrug. "Any ideas about what should we…say. To…each other to fix that some?"

Eyes, finally meeting mine with what looks like half-relief and half approval of my toga-tying, he finally cracks the smile. "I could apologize for ripping up all of your wedding—er—stuff? And then I could start us off with some sort of honeymoon speak? Like: Hello, beautiful *wife*. Or, ready for dinner, sweetie-pie-wifey?"

I'm biting my upper lip to hold back a nervous laugh, before uttering, "I think that this is now even *more* awkward, my *darling*… uhhh…*hubster*? Husband-dude? Ball-and-chain? Way to make it better."

"Hey." His grin is so big it's crinkling his whole face. "Traditionally the old-ball-and-chain remark is reserved for the wife."

"As you know, this is not a traditional wedding…so…" I frown, not sure what else to say.

He laughs, saving me from going on, and I laugh, too, as he paces a bit in front of the table. "This is harder than the actual wedding, isn't it? What *are* we supposed to call each other? All joking aside, we will need to be able to dialogue with people and ourselves, using the words husband and wife, as well as pepper in all of that lovey-sappy-shit couples spew out when speaking to, and about, each other. Only, we will have do it without any of this awkward happening between us."

His toga slips, and he curses under his breath. "These shiny sheets suck, right? I can't make this side portion stay up." He takes the part of the toga he had going over his shoulder and wraps it once around his waist, tying it there instead. "There." He blinks over at me. "What do you think. Should we try again?"

"What-think-try?" I squeak out nonsense, trying hard to return his smile while feeling the back of my neck heat as I try to stare *only at his face.*

Only at his face. Face. Only.

*Because…*I swallow. *Because.*

Sheet tied low. Sheet tied low. Only at his face.

Suddenly I'm wondering insane stuff like…*was he outfitted with special wedding underwear, too or…*

I realized I've just looked down his whole form. Then back up. Then back down.

Oh no. Just did it again. I've elevator-eyed him. Should I start blinking fast and pretend I just got dirt in my eye? OMG. I think this guy has no tattoos. Isn't that illegal in a rockstar? Maybe he does have some. Down. Lower.

I grit my teeth behind a small smile.

Don't.

Look.

Down.

Lower.

Just don't.

Don't.

Only. At. His. Face.

So what if he looks like Michelangelo's David, only a better version? That's okay to notice, you're an artist. So what?

I realize if I breathe in too much, I'm going to smell the amazing musky smell of him, and if I move my eyes again, I will start to overanalyze the expanse of Royce's tawny smooth skin stretching between his collarbones, and down his whole, now bared torso because…because.

Because…torso…torso! Wow.

Torso.

It's got the real-live, rippling 'V' lines.

Oh crap.

I'm looking down again.

Finally, because he's just staring and shaking his head while I'm certain it appears as though I'm having a seizure or something in front of him, I manage to recover some and ask, "You were saying? Try what?" I breathe in a tiny bit, then back out, shaking my head to clear it while dragging my gaze back to his beautiful looking face while adding lamely, "I'm so sorry. You lost me there. I'm not thinking straight. Not used to being up so late," I continue shaking my head again. "Guess I'm tired and hungry and everything is suddenly hitting me, you know? What are going to try?"

His brow furrows and I'm sure he's now wondering if I'm simple-minded. I could be, after all. He's only known me for a week. I could be exactly the wife Mr. Rochester was tricked into marrying? The one he hid from Jane Eyre!

"Sorry." I say again, wishing I could pour water on my face.

"Shit. I thought I already begged you not to tell me that you're *sorry* for anything that happens between us. This is not easy, and hell yes we are tired, huh? I was just suggesting we try saying husband and wife stuff to each other. Maybe we could do it while pretending we're talking to someone? A reporter maybe? Considering that's who will bust us if we get this wrong," he grits out like that thought pisses him off. "I'll go first." He clears his throat and makes a very serious face before starting in with, "Oh. Yes." He blinks at me and pulls a face. "Robin? She's my wife. And my wife is so nice." He laughs a little at himself, then goes on. "What? My wife, well…she and I, on our wedding night, we had dinner in togas by a pool. My wife and I love eating out on patios where we can hear ocean waves, yeah. It's my favorite, so that's what we did, me and the wife."

He clears his throat when, again I find that I can't respond beyond only blinking stupidly at him. "Hey there, wife. How are you feeling about all of this, *wife*?" He blinks, and adds softly, "Hello? Earth to *wife?* Want to have a try?"

Realizing I've been holding my breath or maybe I've just stopped breathing all together I pull in one burning breath. Then, like it's got a mind of its own, my arm raises and I point— literally point at his 'V'! I'm screaming inside my head but, from somewhere, I quickly blurt out a single, whispered: "*Husband.*"

This makes him crack up, but he nods at me like he's a proud parent who has finally broken through and just taught his kid how to read. "Okay. Go on." Still nodding, he points back at me, copying my move and acting like what I just did was fine when it wasn't. "*Wife.*"

I shake my head, and cross my arms over my stomach, uttering louder this time: "Husband."

Try more. He's still nodding, face all earnest and encouraging. "Wife. My wife."

"Husband. My husband."

Suddenly his face scrunches and the edges of his eyes crinkle deeper than I've ever seen them crinkle and between his ever-increasing grin, he thumps his chest once with a fist and says out, "Me. Tarzan-Husband." He arches one brow, cracking up fully. "You? Jane-Wife?"

"Oh—ha! That was so spot on," I answer, giving into my own belly laugh as I sit collapse into one of the chairs around the table, holding tight to the toga. "I suck at this. How will any of this ever feel comfortable between us?"

"Shit. I don't know. We just have to push through, huh, *wife*?" Laughing more he flops into his own chair, and as we tug at our togas a bit, we both start laughing uncontrollably all over again.

And just like that, the tension in the air between us disappears.

"My husband, *Royce*, he's patient, kind *and* hilarious," I say, not even blushing. "My husband, he doesn't even judge me when I blip-out on him and blink at him like a fool. My husband and I, we totally spent our wedding night laughing, while wearing silk togas on our wedding night. And once we got over some initial jitters, it was pretty awesome. Romantic, even. Because that's my husband—he's so romantic. And you should see how *my husband* looks in a toga. Amazing." I grin over at him. "How's that?"

"Great actually." He raises his brows as if he didn't think I had it in me. "My wife," he says, shaking his head as a last rumble of low laughter leaves his lips. "Well, she's got this way about her that makes me smile from the inside out. I've never known a girl like her."

"Aww. That's a nice one."

"Well, it's true," he adds, meeting my gaze. "I think if we just stick with what's real we will muddle through, right?"

"I hope so."

Still grinning, he motions to one of the platters in front of us, covered up by a large silver dome. "Little, wife," he sweeps his arm wide at the table. "Are you hungry? I took the liberty of ordering us a meal. There were many fancy choices available, but after the day you and I've had, I went for more…comfort food."

He pulls the food covers up high with a flourish and reveals two steaming plates of baked macaroni and cheese, two chocolate milkshakes and two vanilla milkshakes. "It's all off the kids menu."

I gasp. "My husband is an amazing mind reader."

He cracks up again. "Just in case my wife is not into junk-food, I've also ordered two spinach salads loaded with almonds and raspberries, dressings. On the side."

"My husband is also thoughtful," I joke, looking over the plates at him. "This is perfect. A perfect honeymoon meal. I'm sure half of why I just went into a coma in front of you is because I didn't know I was starving."

"In case you haven't noticed, I've been all stop-start-and-stutter, too." He shoves about four fries into his mouth.

I glance up at him. "I haven't noticed."

"Well, that's good." He swallows, expression flipping to what looks like relief as he points at the milkshakes. "I choked on choosing which flavor, but this way we get to have two. It is, after all, a special night for a bride and groom, so I thought we could get a little whacked-out on sugar."

Before I can say anything, or maybe because for some reason he gets that I'm choked up, or suddenly feeling extra low blood sugar, or about to say 'thank-you' when he has ordered me not to do that anymore, he hands me one of the silverware sets and a very fancy linen napkin and says, "Let's eat, okay?"

In less than five minutes the plates are empty, and one milkshake for each of us has been nearly demolished. We both went for the chocolate ones first, prompting Royce to joke, "My wife and I both *love* chocolate milkshakes."

"My husband," I pause mid slurp, keeping the straw half in my mouth. "I have to keep an eye on him all the time. When we're at fancy hotels, he sometimes over-orders room service. Guy is also an ice-cream addict."

Grinning, he stands with his second milkshake in one hand. "There's this awesome double wide hammock under those trees. It's overlooking the ocean. We can't see much, but the waves will sound nice. Are you interested in watching the stars for a little bit with me? I know it's late…" He glances at the time on his cell phone. "Shit, it's really late, like 3AM, late. My whole body feels like it's been hit by a bus, but I…um," his gaze flicks over me, and then to my toga, then back to my face. "I uh…don't think I can sleep just yet. If you're tired, and from the way your eyes look, I'm guessing you are, the bedroom is yours if you would rather go to sleep instead?"

"Oh. Um. Uh." I shrug, annoyed that I'm back to one syllable meaningless words. I eye the pathway leading to the hammock and then, because I'm afraid I'm going to ogle him again now that he's standing, I let my fingers trace space between the lines that make up the pretty teak wood grained table.

"Robin. It's fine." When I glance up finally, those silver eyes of his are hooded. His voice is heavy. Worried again. "Later…it's important that we—for the sake of the maids who might show up early—that we wake up *together*. With your permission, of course."

"What?" I blink at him.

"I'm going to have to sneak in to the edge of the bed after you're asleep. Maybe could stuff a bunch of pillows down a center line before I get there? If that helps make any of this feel less odd?"

I shake my head, again at a loss for words, and he laughs a little to himself and runs a hand through the thick mop of black hair that always flops over his forehead before adding, "Okay, well, maybe it's always going to feel odd, but know that I'm a quiet sleeper, and I realize that it might feel all wrong to have me in your personal space like that, but I'm sorry."

"Hey. I thought we weren't apologizing to each other?"

"Okay. I only want you to know that I promise I won't cross any lines—or try anything with you. Not ever. You have my absolute-word about that. I want you to be able to sleep soundly. Mostly I want you to…feel safe."

He pauses, finishing off the second milkshake, while looking at me as though he's wondering if I've understood.

"I—do feel safe. Royce. I do. And I want you to feel the same. I don't snore and for the record, I won't…you know be…weird." I pause at that, recanting. "Fine, I will probably definitely be weird but I won't bother you and…yeah, no line crossing. It's appreciated that you brought all of that up, but you didn't have to. I know you're honorable." He nods, looking half-strangled as I finish, "But now that you've said all of that, I'm pretty sure I can't sleep either. So. I'm saying yes to your hammock idea?"

I leave off the part where I don't think I can face going back into the bedroom and crawl into the rumpled rose petal bed.

He reaches down for my hand and I place my left hand into his. Gingerly, he pulls me up while I use my stronger, right hand to keep the sheet in place. When I'm in front of him, instead of releasing my hand he pauses to run a thumb over the rings on my finger.

"It was my mom's ring," he says. "I like how it looks on your hand. She'd like you, Robin. I wish you could, hell, I don't know. I wish she could have met you."

I feel my shoulders slump as the weight of what he's said and what we've done tonight—really done reels around my brain: *I'm married, legally bound to this man, and my father doesn't know him—didn't walk me down the aisle, and I'll never be able to meet Royce's mom*!

It all makes the ring feel so heavy that if he were to let go of my hand right now, it—or I—might sink through this deck and be swallowed up into the center of the earth, because I know I don't belong here and…*What have we done? Is any of this really okay?*

Thankfully, Royce doesn't let go, he only wraps his hand into mine, and it's warm, soft, solid, and very much, holding up the weight of the wedding ring.

"I'm sorry about your mom," I whisper, because I am.

"I'm sorry about your dad," he answers, and I believe that he is.

He makes our fingers intertwine, saying, "I have to think they would both approve of this. Of what we're doing."

And when I risk looking up into his eyes—searching deep, he lets me in all the way and I don't see any resentment or dark glimmers of what might be his hidden regrets about this fake relationship hiding anywhere.

He nudges me toward the path leading down to the secluded hammock. I push away my doubts, squeezing his hand tight while trying to make myself believe my own words as I answer, "They would. I know they would."

8

ROYCE

When I first come to consciousness I think I might be still asleep, because I hear the ocean waves I often snooze with in the background, coming off the sleep-machine my grandmother gave to me. I also realize I have no idea where I am.

This is a waking state which is not unusual for me, because I'm forever on auto-exhaustion mode. More often than not we hit the tour bus or the limo after a show, and are led half-asleep into hotels where we don't remember which city we've pulled into next.

But this morning, even half-conscious I'm wishing I could go right back to sleep. Because I'm comfortable. Really comfortable, more so than I've been in a long time.

I register that I'm holding someone—someone who is soft and abundantly curvy in all of the right places and who is sprawled flat on top of me, breasts pressed into my chest. She's got her head nestled on my shoulder and she's breathing extra deep, like she's sound asleep and as comfortable as I am right now.

This, I note, is also rare, because I don't get comfortable with girls after we have sex, nor do I ever let them fall asleep in my bed.

From the amounts of soft, bare skin that's touching my bare skin, I also get that we must have had quite a night. The thought of that and the feel of her is setting up some serious morning wood activity, but who could blame me? She's so warm and the way her hair is tangled softly under my chin feels sexy as hell.

Maybe I'll just roll over and ask if we can wake up and...

A new set of waves crash in, but they're not just coming from my machine, and as I come to more awareness, I also note that I'm rocking back and forth and sort of floating. Do I hear...*birds?*

Birds.

Wind.

Waves.

Robin.

I'm in a hammock.

In a hammock with my new-fake wife.

We must have slept out here.

My eyes slam open.

I take in the very real palm trees above me and the very real sleeping nearly naked girl in my arms, unable not to let my eyes and thoughts linger on how I love the way her lashes look extra-long and curling when her eyes are closed. I find that I've got one hand nestled into her lavender scented hair, and the other is around her whole waist. Somehow in my sleep, I've been also cupping her nearly bare ass. And that ass is still hardly covered by the world's sexiest wedding-night thong, I think that was ever created.

Worse, my pinkie's tangled into the side of it!

Carefully, I look down so I can figure out how to best disengage the pinkie without waking her or tearing the thong. But that move has me in even more trouble, because—*holy shit!*

I can't help but stare long and hard at all that I've just felt and imagined. Her curves and her skin are luminous wherever the sunrise is lighting it.

And hell—two of her curves—as in two of her best curves, meaning her entire chest is flat-pressed into mine and even though I'm trying not to look...I'm looking. And damn, me but I'm feeling all that is her, and for such a small person, I can't understand how she can have all of this soft skin. She is beyond beautiful right now.

Sighing, hell yes, with shock and of course total-body-frustration, I breathe in one quarter of a breath, searching for some control. But when she shifts and moans a little next to my neck—I freeze and stop my lungs from taking in air, because that one little sound causes all of the blood from my entire body to surge so hard below my waist now that my sleepy morning wood has become some sort of awkward-raging-redwood tree!

The impact of it coming on like too fast like a surprise, *Jack-in-the-box* exploding has nearly jerked me off the damn hammock, and could have sent Robin flying.

It takes every ounce of my strength, inner and outer, not to groan out loud as excruciating pain and throbbing-hell-heartbeats pound into me from top to bottom. I keep holding my breath so I can't smell her anymore, then I use every brain cell that might be left (and trust me, there's not many, because my damn pinkie is still stuck in her *thong* right now!) I order each and every muscle (and organs) to remain absolutely still.

The only thing I allow to move is the damn pinkie.

One twist, two twists, soft-soft-skin, and back that finger out of there! Fuck my life!

If she wakes up right now while I'm in this electrified and panicked state, and she finds herself pressed accidentally into all the spots my uncontrollable erection is dying to explore, she's going to know—feel—be freaked out by exactly how I can't control myself around her.

Obviously. Obviously multiplied by ten to the 300th power.

Which is why I'm now going to think only about golf. Old people playing golf. Every video ever shown on Ridiculousness where a guy's nuts are slammed into hard-cold-metal.

Shit, it's not working.

The last thing I ever want to do is scare her—nor do I want Robin to have a permanent, crappy memory about me that she won't ever be able to forget. I want her to wake up with someone she can trust. Selfishly, I want that person to be me, and even more selfishly, I want the chance to hold her like this again. (Minus the stroke I'm having below my belly button, hopefully).

I wrack my mind for images that will kill this thing:

Cooking shows.

Yes. I'll think about every boring-AF, cooking show I've ever seen. How about that insane family from Alaska? Oh. And those gold miner dudes. And every person who's ever been all afraid and naked on that one show.

Yes. Yes. It's working!

Finally, I regain some control. I risk a glance down at her face again to I test how I'm doing while I prepare myself for how I'm going to keep control when she opens those baby-blues. My gaze calmly follows the curve of cheeks, then I look at her upper lip. Then, when I feel ready, I analyze the sleepy pout of the lower lip.

Damn. Damn that lower lip.

Cooking shows and Alaska aside, I'm wondering if I could get away with stealing just one sleepy kiss off of her? What would just one kiss taste like now that we're married. And could I do it without waking her?

No!

One stolen kiss is what got you into this mess in the first place. You swore to this girl you would not cross any lines only a few hours ago. That is crossing the line!

Like she can hear the war going on in my head between my mind and my body, she thankfully, turns her head back down away from me and utters some intelligible words against my neck.

I realize she's dreaming, because she calls out, *"Dad?"*

My mind feels like it's been hit with a lightning bolt as I think —*Did she just call out, Dad?*

All of anything and *everything* I had going on with my misplaced blood flow disappears like someone's poured a bucket of cold ice-water on my crotch.

"Dad? Please. Tell me," Robin cries out louder. She sounds lost, afraid, desolate. "Where? Where are you?"

My heart drops to my stomach, and I feel so damn guilty because this whole time I've been memorizing the softness of her skin and staring at her lips, she's been having a bad dream. A nightmare.

A couple of tears escape her scrunched up eyes. "Dad? They can't find you. Tell me where you are?"

"Shh. Robin," I say, already running the back of my hand against the tracks of her tears. I've matched her whisper with a whispered promise of my own. The same promise I made to her when she'd first agreed to this fake-wedding farce: "We are going to look for him. I promise. Robin, can you hear me? We are going to look for him."

More tears escape her eyes, and because I can't stand to watch her face look like it's in this kind of pain, I shake her a little. "Wake up. Please wake up. It's a dream, Robin. You're only having a bad dream."

When she opens her eyes, we're only inches away from each other's faces. As her expression clears, I register that she knows where she is and who I am all at the same time. "You're having a dream," I whisper again, keeping my face impassive while I act like I *don't notice* exactly when she goes completely tense as she realizes how she's lying against me. I also turn my eyes away while she quickly pulls her sheet up over the parts of us that should not be touching.

All I have to do to stay in total control while she wiggles against me is to think the word, 'dad' and imagine a US Army Special Forces dude who is holding a gun to my head.

Dad. Dad. And, dad. Brilliant.

When her sheet is set, she glances sideways up at me through her lashes, and asks, "Did I wake you?" Adding in a small self-deprecating laugh, she appears to relax a little.

I sense she comfortable and completely safe with me just how I wanted her to feel, so when she nestles her head back onto my shoulder again and sighs deeply, I can't explain how or why I feel so happy, but I do.

"You were talking in your sleep," I answer, not mentioning that I was already awake. I also don't bring up exactly what she was talking about in her sleep, because I'm wishing for her sake, that she can't remember why or who was in her dream.

She rolls off me then and settles herself so she and I are lying both flat-backed against the hammock, looking up at the palm trees. She's pulling more of her sheet up under her arms as she whispers only, "I… uh…do that sleep talking thing. A lot. I hope it's not going to be a problem. Sage does it, too."

I try to joke a little, reminding her of yesterday's conversation and all that we're facing today, "My wife, she always talks in her sleep. I find it very adorable."

Instead of smiling like I'd hoped she would, she lets out a long and shuddery sigh and whispers again, "My husband? He's really nice. He also has no idea how messed up his wife might become if her father never returns home from deployment."

"Well." Those words have made my heart sink. "Here's something I know about my wife." I reach down to find her hand and get it into mine. "She's really strong. And together, she and I are very good at staying positive, despite really crap situations we can't control."

She looks over at me and nods, and I reach over with one finger to stop another tear from escaping her left eye. "She's also got no clue the shit-show she's facing being married to a guy like me." We both study her teardrop drying on the tip of my finger. "I haven't even cried *once* since my mom died."

She pulls in a fast breath and flips her head back to look at me. Her brow crinkles deeply as she asks, "You've never cried? Not once?"

I trap her wide eyes with mine and shake my head, 'no' while I go on with my fake-press interview. "Robin and I? We were both grieving. And we were in the middle of some huge life changes when we met. I never saw her as a nanny and she never saw me as a rockstar. We were both really messed up people, stressed and scared to death, and lying through our teeth when we met each other. Yet, somehow we both had this way of seeing past each other's masks. I think it's part of why our friendship grew so quickly. Why we are so comfortable around each other. Why I'm so happy she married me because…we don't have to face the messed up shit alone."

She shakes her head at me, her clear blue eyes reflecting amazement, understanding, and what I hope is the reflection of that true friendship I'd mentioned to Gregory last night, as one side of her mouth turns up a little in a smile.

"My husband and I? We're messed up people to be sure, and very fast friends—yes. We are that, aren't we?" She whispers, turning to place her other hand over the side of my cheek, then moving it up to the edge of my eye, as though she wants to check to see if I'm lying about how I don't cry. "It's why we're a good match. My husband and I, we've bonded because we are both missing a parent so bad it hurts, right?"

"Exactly. But we don't like to talk about it much. If at all…ever," I say, gently warning her that I'm not good at this shit.

"Only on the day after we get married. The day when we're hanging out in a hammock by the sea."

"Yes. Only on that day." I laugh. "Because we don't like to ponder shit we can't control—shit that hurts like hell."

"No. We don't like that."

Her eyes meet mine and this time she's not searching for the deeper parts of me. She's just raw and open and for once, she's showing me herself. I love how I see all the way into her sweet, brave, sadness. Better, I can feel her absolute trust.

Then and there I vow to somehow to be this girl's real hero one day. My mom is dead, but her father…well there's still hope, right? I will figure out a way to search for him. To find him.

I reach over and tug one of her blowing blonde wisps. "Did you notice, now we don't even have to prep for our press conference this morning. We know exactly what to say."

"Which means we get to order breakfast now?" she says, waggling her brows comically, but she stops because what looks like a hotel pool-cleaning crew has come around the corner.

When they spot us lying all snuggled up in our hammock, they turn away very quickly while pretending not to see us. But that's when two paparazzi come busting through from behind them, each with cameras filming us non-stop and they, unlike the pool crew are making a beeline for us.

One of the pool guys, who was actually doing his job by trying to block the paparazzi, starts shouting, "Security. Security!"

The other guy drops his equipment and starts tugging at one of the photographers back, but the guy is too small to stop the photographer. "Mr. and Mrs. Devlin, we're so sorry. Security! Security!"

This commotion makes Robin try to start out of the hammock, but I plant my feet on the ground first, whispering, "Wait. Wait. Robin. Move slowly. We need some quality 'morning after the wedding night' photos to happen, so this is not a big deal, but please remember, we're in sheets. One naked picture will last forever, okay? No need to run, just keep yourself covered."

I stand first, then manage to stabilize the hammock for her so she doesn't flip backwards, but as she starts to clamber out, all becomes sheet-slipping chaos. In order to make sure her sheet stays up where it needs to stay while ensuring the last photos taken of us look sexy-newly-wed-romantic, I shout out dramatically, "Jesus—you bastards. Give us some damn privacy, would you?" Then, I scoop her up into my arms pull her front against my chest, then stalk away with her in my arms, as she wraps her arms around my neck and buries her head into my chest all the way to the bungalow.

"Thanks," she whispers as I set her down inside, turning away quickly while she gets herself together.

As I slide the large glass doors closed, she points through the window to the pool guys, along with security, who are now chasing the paparazzi out to where they've anchored two Jet Skis just past the surf break we couldn't see last night. It's much closer than I thought it was, and apparently, that's how the paparazzi got in, and now how they're making a fast escape.

"So much for what was supposed to be our private and *guarded* beach. First I thought my grandmother had sent those guys, but now I'm not so sure." I shrug clicking the slider lock, then checking it twice.

"Either way, those particular photos will be great to keep our story going today. They pretty much had to be taken, and, I'm going to call it a bonus that we were caught undressed."

"Why?"

"Now the world will see with their own eyes—that we…uh, *did it*." I pull an impish face, trying to joke my way past this conversation. "Possibly, we did it a lot." I waggle my brows more. "It's not a big deal. We only have to shrug and blush, then talk about how we *don't* discuss *these personal things* when people ask us about our wedding night."

"People will not ask us about *that*, will they?" She's laughing, but I can tell she's once again, uncomfortable.

"Hell yes, they will. That and more. You'll learn. People ask about everything. Nothing is sacred, so practice your poker faces in the mirror." I stop myself from reaching over to run one finger along her adorable, now fire-red cheeks.

Suddenly, we feel too close together again, and her eyes seem to be ping-ponging between my bare chest and then to my eyes, then back to my lips, then to my abs how they did last night. It's like she's never seen a guy wearing a bed-sheet before and…and…she's just so darn cute…

"I need to shower," I nearly shout out, then add, "I mean first. I want to go first. If it's okay?"

"Sure." She shrugs once as I feel my temples pounding again as I fight for control.

Before I can run away, she calls out, "Hey, uh…Royce?"

"Yeah?" I pause, but don't turn back, because the familiar, almost happy and calm way she's said my name has nearly brought me to my knees.

Softly she adds, "I—I just want you to know that, considering… everything. It was a really great wedding night. You know, lying there and looking up at the stars with you. I've never fallen asleep listening to waves. And waking up together like that and…how you stopped me from having that nightmare was really cool. And, even though we didn't, uh, do real wedding night things together." She laughs then, sounding extra-awkward-adorable. "It was still so memorable. Really nice. I'll never forget it. That's all."

I grip the sides of the doorway leading into the bathroom, thinking: *I'll never forget how you just said the words 'do real wedding night things together' or the feel of your damn skin next to mine.*

Fuck. Think about her father. Dad. Dad! And Dad!

"Totally memorable. Happy you're happy," is all I can manage to choke out.

"Good, because I feel like we've got this down already," she rushes on. "And I think, tonight, when we have to do that all again? Like even if we end up in the bed with a whole bunch of pillows stacked between us how you suggested we try last night? Or, even if there's twice as many photographers and people asking too many questions? Figuring it out together, is what's going to make it okay. What I'm trying to say is that you were right. I think it's fun already—just how you said it might be. Are you feeling that? Feeling the…*fun*?"

I dart a tentative glance back at her, and lie my ass off with a quick, "Hell yes. Definitely. Feeling the fun."

Her nod and responding smile all but have me bolting into the bathroom.

In case she wants to follow me to keep *chatting*, I lock the door and I don't pause to even pull off the toga.

I run for the damn shower and blast on the cold water so I can stand under the freezing spray while vowing to never use the word 'fun' to describe this situation again.

9

ROBIN

WHILE ROYCE IS SHOWERING, and despite the part where I just lied to him by saying all of this 'could feel fun' I pace around the room, feeling truly freaked out. Feeling like I'm no longer on Earth, and now I'm living on Mars! Feeling even more like I've been elected the *Queen of Mars*, or something—the Queen of Mars who has no clue how to handle this new title.

I also can't stop this paranoid nervous thing that's coursing through my body.

I've closed each and every blind in the room. But now, the ones that still have little cracks of light seeping through are giving me anxiety, so I return to each one and turn the little poles as tightly I can without breaking them to make them all tighter. I'm trying hard to forget how exposed I felt being photographed in the hammock while I was half naked and wearing *only a sheet*, all while I'm *also* trying to forget what Royce Devlin looked like just now with his sheet slipping off around his waist.

"Because…in Mars, we only wear sheets." I mutter. "And, because the Queen of Mars would like to acknowledge that the King of Mars is so damn hot," I finish, laughing a little about how I nearly became possessed and how I almost stepped up and tried to trace his ab muscles before he ran into the shower. As if that wasn't awkward enough, I was also seriously going to put my hands on that 'V' and figure out what was muscle and what was hip bones. I'm now so obsessed with the two lines below and to the sides of his waist, that I'm actually considering taking the fancy linen hotel correspondence paper off of the fancy ornate desk, and sketching what I remember of Royce's amazing bare torso right now. But I can't. What if he saw me doing that? What would I do with it once I was done? It's not like I have a suitcase or even a purse to hide that drawing in…so I won't. I will just sit here and imagine how my sketch would turn out.

Try to…memorize…every line of his abs. Because why not? I've already memorized Royce's face. I think maybe I did that the I first day I met him. I say it's because I'm an artist and studying faces is what I do, and I also say I can't get enough of Royce's face because his is angular and unusual that staring at the planes of his face have become my bliss. But it's more than that—okay, it's because he's beautiful and handsome and I'm unable not to memorize how he looks. He's So paintable…*draw-able, sculpt-able*…fine, after yesterday I know he's… even very kissable.

How can I not think about that—when he kissed me so many times and I kissed him back?

I've sketched, and recently painted every line of his face, too. I've pondered the exact tones of his skin, figured out the lines of his cheekbones and before we were married, I embarrassed myself by mentioning to him out loud just how I love the straight lines that make up his chin.

I've also analyzed the way his silver eyes tilt up near his nose, and even today, I was counting the sexy-faint crinkles that exist at the outside edges of those same eyes. I've memorized the way his full lips bow and curve along the top lip, the way the bottom lip can pout when he's thinking. So much so, that I've become almost addicted to watching the various degrees of his sardonic-twisty smiles and frowns. I also love when he's in full laughter, how the smile goes up higher on the right side than the left.

But…seeing him in a towel? Being pressed up next to his bare skin —eye to eye with collarbones and shoulder muscles that must have been molded after Gods? Well…I either need to tell him straight up when he comes out of that bathroom that he's actually married a real-live- stalker, or I need to learn or figure out how to fake that I've got some control when he's around.

"That's all," I mutter out again. "That should be easy."

I shake my head, wondering what would he have done if I had just run at him and started smearing my hands all over his stomach while uttering stuff like, *can I please just look at and measure the way your abs line up, have a closer look at your hips—can we talk about your 'V' a little bit?*

I fling myself on the bed, laughing out loud now. "What the hell is wrong with me? Do guys even know we call those sexy lines, 'the V' in the first place? Should I Google if 'the V' is even a thing? It is, isn't it? It is to me…and it's—oh stop thinking about it." I slap my hand against my forehead, wishing my mind would shut up. "It's okay. You're an artist, not a stalker. Now you're an artist and wife. Not a stalker. I'm sure all of this behavior is perfectly normal in the world of fake wives and fake husbands…right?"

I breathe out, feeling better and stand up to pace the room again, telling myself, "Somehow I need to figure out how to be conscious of the fact that yes, he is beautiful, and that he and I will probably see each other half dressed *a lo*t starting now, considering we are sharing hotel rooms."

"And…hammocks," I add, feeling my cheeks fire with the memory of my chest pressed up against him when he woke me up."Which is *why* I need to get over the fact that he's probably beautiful in all of the usual places, as well as also shockingly beautiful in places other mere mortals are not beautiful. Like…I bet that even his elbows and armpits are probably *stunning*, and that even mundane things like his kneecaps are all angled and balanced and very… very…*paintable?*"

My thoughts spin…*Is that the word I'm searching for? Paintable? Whatever. I want to paint him. Every single inch of him, and one day I'm going to ask. One day, when things aren't awkward between us, I will. I'll bet one day, I will be able to ask him anything I want…*

One day…

I'M STARTLED out of my thoughts when the sound of soft knocking comes from the bungalow's front door.

Fearing this might be a trick or more paparazzi, I hardly let my feet touch the marble as I walk to the door so I can peer through the little security-peek-hole. I'm holding my breath and listening at the same time, wondering if I should go alert Royce when I see that girl Clara, the daughter of the lead stylist I met yesterday, frowning and trying to peek *into* the peek-hole as I'm peeking *out*!

"They're not answering." She huffs out a puff of air, making her straight cut bangs flip to the side while she tries to peer in again. "Probably they're still doing it in there—can't—see—anything," she's grumbling. "Let's see if I can hear…something going on."

I jump back a little when I realize she's moved to pressing her ear against the door! So rude. Who *listens* for people *doing it, if that's what she thinks we're doing?*

I back away, thinking I'm not ready to face anyone from Royce's entourage, especially not the one girl who I think might be a possible *mean-girl.*

But when I hear a second person talking, I return to the door and peek out in time to see Mrs. Felix, wheel up to the door next to Clara.

She's frowning at Clara while commanding: "Knock *louder*, dear. I'm sure if they're occupied on the morning after their *most romantic wedding*, well it's to be expected, and who could blame them. Not I. We will call what they are *doing* something proper, well past the words 'doing-it'. Young lady. *Tsk. Tsk.* Did you think I did not hear your crass comments?"

"Mother, do not ramp into one of your speeches," Gregory says, crossing into my narrow view point.

"It's not a speech, it's a teaching moment we're all about to have," Mrs. Felix sounds highly offended.

"Mother. Please. Don't go there." Gregory is backing away, shaking his head at Clara like he feels sorry for you. "I'm going to go help the stylists move the racks up the walkway."

The guy is almost running down the walkway as Mrs. Felix turns to Clara saying, "Royce and Robin are most probably *making love* right now. *Love*, young lady. Your generation, with your *meet-ups* and *hook-ups* and *doing-it* verbiage simply horrifies me. *Tsk. Tsk.* Don't *think* I haven't heard about how you young people do this 'hang and watch Netflix' *ridiculousness.*"

I almost burst out laughing as Clara's face turns from red to panicked while Mrs. Felix zooms closer, cornering Clara against the door with her wheelchair while, ranting on, "Watching a movie is watching a movie. Making love is making love. Never should the two just mix on some young man's dingy couch or unmade, *most-probably* unwashed bed. And at least use *Amazon Prime* to watch your videos. Save some money and get some self-respect?"

She mock-shudders but then my view is blocked as Clara's dark hair is pressed up against the peep hole while Mrs. Felix finishes with, "Self-respect is something you must try to hold on to. I've heard this is a millennial epidemic, dear. Royce and Robin never watched one movie together before Royce proposed, and I think more young people should simply get married and commit instead of all of this…swiping right and swiping left, and-and movie watching-meeting up business that you all do. Do you understand my meaning, Clara? I hope you will let my Royce and Robin be a quality example for the direction your own life should go."

"Yes Ma'am," Clara sounds like she's choking while I step back again, so I can cover my mouth and swallow back some laughter, fully understanding now why Gregory bolted. Mrs. Felix on a rampage is one force to be reckoned with. *Ha!*

"Good," Mrs. Felix adds pertly. "Because the *morning after a wedding,* the bride and groom are *making love*. Do you understand me? Love and making love are two things we should not be ashamed of or joke about, nor should we minimize these acts of beauty with the words 'doing it'. Never again, young lady. Do you hear me? Now please apologize for your slight."

"Yes, Ma'am. I—I'm sorry," Clara adds, and turns back to the door so Mrs. Felix can't see her rolling her eyes. For a moment she looks so humiliated, annoyed and possibly still jealous of what she's imagining we are doing behind this door, that I almost crack up again, straight into the door peek-hole as she knocks softly again.

When I still don't open the door, Clara says, "Maybe I should text my mom to halt the stylists? I could ask them to stop unloading the trucks? We can come back in another hour with the clothing rack choices and makeup crew?"

"Let me try knocking with this." Mrs. Felix zooms closer and whacks the door with the retractable cane she keeps in her basket a few times.

Clara again rolls her eyes and makes yet another face, this time she finds the doorbell and dings it about fifteen times. So much so, that if Royce and I had been *making love*, we would have fallen off the bed and thought there was a fire.

I wait a good five seconds so they think I walked here from far away, then try to act all fluttery and making-love breathless as I call out, "Who…who is it? We—were um…watching a movie," I call out, unable not to say it, while choking down another laugh at Clara's responding glare.

"Robin, dear. There you are," Mrs. Felix answers first. "Let us in. We've brought news. We also have press waiting to interview you and we need to talk about the developments with the attorneys. It looks like we will get early approval on our custody attempts to be co-guardians with Sage. Isn't that exciting? Open up, darling. Please, do?"

I SECURE the sheet and clamp down my arms tight against the sides of my rib-cage before I pull open the door. Mrs. Felix zooms past me in her wheelchair. Clara's eyes are going all around the room and over me as she's squeezing in close behind.

"Do you mean it about the custody? That's wonderful news," I call out, following Mrs. Felix as she wheels past me.

"My dear, Robin. I mean it. I knew it would not be difficult. Everyone *loves* a great love story and that's exactly what you and Royce are, my darling girl. The press has run with what's happened and the courts are all alerted and playing nice. The PR people have told me that you and your little brother have been already branded as America's sad little orphans."

Using the automatic spin control on her chair, she twirls once and then goes on, "Even better, the entire world is in support of our quest to help you and Sage. They have backed your marriage, they adore what the band did last night by including the fans in the wedding, and most especially, people are obsessed with your rags-to-riches tale, as well as over how Royce stepped up to help his girlfriend the best way he could, by marrying the girl he loves right away to help you. It's all a glorious success, darling, and of course I'm so happy to call you and Sage part of the family because from the moment Royce told me you were 'the one' on the very day you two met, I'd been hoping." She glances over at Clara then back at me, and I can tell she's a little worried she may have slipped up and said too much.

Although my chest twisted at the word 'orphans' and then twisted again at the words *true-love*, she's used the absolute scorn that was just flashed to me by Clara's expression has me bending to give Mrs. Felix a swift hug. "Oh, thank you, Mrs. Felix. You're so nice to me. Thanks for welcoming me so easily." Can I ask, how is Sage holding up this morning? Any reports?"

"Sage is sleeping in. The resort left the water slide running for extra hours last night and Hunter and Vere had a blast tiring him out. He had big plans to go on it again with them this morning, but we must see if we need to dress him up to be in the press conference we are planning."

"Where's Royce," she asks, as her eyes skim back to me, going up to my messy hair and then back to how's she's noticed that I'm totally naked under my sheet. If Clara weren't here I'd explain that Royce and I didn't have anything else to wear besides our sheets, but instead I stick to the plan and answer what I can.

"Oh. Royce…he had to…he's…"

For some reason the way she's looking at me so intently as though she's trying to read my mind—or maybe trying to analyze if Royce and I really *did* make love last night or not, that her scrutiny has my cheeks going hot. I'm wishing I'd taken the time to glance in the mirror before answering the door. "He's in the shower." I shrug. "And uh. I go next," I add lamely.

Mrs. Felix presses the controller on her wheelchair again, and it zooms ahead making a beeline past the living room area and goes directly into the wide double doors leading to our bedroom area, with Clara following close behind.

"Oh my lord. The dress. *My dress.*" She gasps and I can't tell if she's being dramatic or serious. "I see you two didn't pause to hang it up? Good gracious." She gasps again. "You two didn't even pause to take it off…properly. I will have words with Royce about *this.*" She waves her hand at the mess.

"Oh. I…um. No. It wasn't like that." I follow her, taking in the rumpled dress, the little pearl buttons all over the floor and the corset with the cut ribbons flung to the side of the bed. Again I want to explain, but I hold back because of Clara again.

"I'm sorry. We uh…I couldn't breathe after we arrived and he was helping me but then…" I glance at Clara's over interested face. "Well. I hope the dress can be fixed."

Mrs. Felix recovers first and says, "I also couldn't breathe on my wedding night dear. My dear husband ruined a lot of my outfits, too. I'm sure with Royce looking so handsome in his tux he and you two were swept away with reckless…wild…" She frowns at the buttons again. "Abandon. I'm sure all can be repaired."

I scour my brain for other things I can talk about and come up only with, "Yes. Well. We went out to the hammock, and…it's by the beach, past the pool, which is gorgeous by the way," I point at the sliding glass doors, "And we were only *now* getting back to the bedroom." I swallow, flushing, because I realize that sounded like Royce and I had been really…very…*active.* I rush on, "We weren't expecting company just yet and…we would have cleaned up some but we—were—uh…you know." I bite my lips and look down at the floor, wishing it could quickly swallow me up.

"Spare us the details, *please.* We get it." Clara crosses her arms. "I have *got* to open a window because now…" She wrinkles her nose before finishing, "Now I can't work in here unless we air things out." Clara gingerly kicks my torn, lacy corset aside with her foot as she passes by. Then, she struggles to open all of the blinds I'd just worked so hard to close, getting each window open a crack. "There. Much better. Fresh air." She wrinkles her nose, acting even more disgusted.

Mrs. Felix and I exchange an annoyed glance as Mrs. Felix asks, "Didn't Royce tell you we were coming?" I asked Vere to text him, she's coming in a minute."

"I don't think either of us know where our cell phones wound up and we haven't—didn't think about even finding them because…um." I glance helplessly at her.

Mrs. Felix chuckles knowingly again. "You two newlyweds are so adorable. Of course you didn't have your phones. We can all help you search for them. Go alert Royce he's been invaded, would you?"

I nod and pad to the bathroom door and give it two raps. "Royce. Your grandmother's arrived and Clara. Everyone else is coming in here right now. *Everyone.*" Hoping he can hear that I might need some backup out here, I add. "Is it my turn yet?"

I hear things dropping on tile and the heavy glass shower door sounds like it's just banged into something. "They are? Okay. Coming now."

Mrs. Felix has followed me and calls through the door. "I'm sorry for the intrusion, dear."

Royce answers, "I know it can't be helped, Gran. How's Sage," he calls out through the door and even though I swore to ignore stuff like that, my heart flips because he's so nice.

"The boy is better than fine. We've worked out a way for him to have adjoining suites near us for the remainder of the honeymoon and also, Robin, we spoke of this briefly before the engagement, but I wanted to confirm that it is okay with you if Gregory and I place ourselves as secondary guardians until your father is found? It will streamline the legal proceedings if we offer him our full financial backing, but we are well aware you are full guardian and the person acting as parent. Is this amenable to you?"

"Yes. Of course, and again. I can only thank you and vow somehow to pay you back for that," I answer, backing up next to the bathroom door as the room fills up with stylists, clothing racks and a whole bunch of people.

"Not necessary, darling." And then, she shouts out, "Royce Devlin, what are you doing in there?"

Because the stylists are circling us now as well as Clara, and suddenly there's too many bodies crowding into the bedroom and whispering about the torn up wedding dress while pointing at the pearl buttons scattered all over the floor, I work to come up with some sort of acceptable chatter, "We've already noticed, Royce spends way more time in front of the mirror than I do."

"That's obvious. Something that needs to probably change on your part," Clara says, with a fake sunny voice while her scathing glare surveys me, ever finding below her standards. "But that's where we stylists come in, isn't it? I hope we can get you up to his level but like…" her voice drops. "We're not miracle workers, are we?" She's said that last part too quietly, so Mrs. Felix couldn't hear it, and she ends it with a look that says she doesn't think I'm going to make it to what an acceptable *rock-star-wife should look like.*

"What did you say, Clara?" Mrs. Felix calls out.

"She's wondering how to make me up, and so am I, because I don't have much experience with all of that stuff, " I say, saving Clara's ass, even though I shouldn't.

"Clara, can you see how Robin is like no other girl Royce has ever met? So genuine and generous—very *au-natural.* We should all strive to be more like her, shouldn't we? And we don't need to make-her up much. Her natural beauty is why Royce fell for her in the first place."

"Yes, I will see what I can do," Clara says that fake-sunny voice back in place, but as she turns she's rolling her eyes so far to the ceiling I'm surprised the girl doesn't spike her own blood clot up there.

The other stylist assistants and people I have not yet met (or maybe I have met them but I don't recognize from yesterday's chaos, have moved the mess of my torn dress off the bed, unzipped the clothing rack covers, all while others are carrying in two folding, canvas director's type make-up chairs with what looks like cool portable, wheeled make up stations.

I can see the living room has been flooded with hotel staff pushing in covered, wheeled room service carts that appear to be loaded with food. As the crush of people coming into the room increases I grow more and more mortified, but all I can do is cower further against the wall and clutch my stupid sheet.

Everyone—has figured out where the sheet has come from, and they've commented on the torn and rumpled wedding dress. And once they get to me they've also walked past and analyzed Royce's scattered tuxedo that's lying all over the couch in the living room.

By their *looking-not-looking* glances at me, it's obvious they're making the wrong assumptions (or as Royce would call them the *right assumptions. The ones we want*) about what happened between us last night.

I suppose if I could trade places with them, I would think that it looks like the groom had undressed in the living room, or that maybe I *helped him* undress, and then *he* obviously got impatient when he undressed me, right here in the bedroom!

While everyone starts gathering up the buttons, I lean over and whisper, "Don't worry Mrs. Felix. Royce was a gentleman and we promise, no matter how things look, this is all Royce's calculated set up."

She leans close and whispers to me, "Of course it is, darling, I'm sorry if I may have doubted you. I just…well…you look so flushed and rumpled, but I know my grandson, he is very good at all of this make-believe."

I whisper back. "He's only been sweet. Protective. And we've been practicing what to say all night. So maybe I'm finally coming across naturally, that's all."

Royce slams out of the bathroom, startling everyone into freezing. Like he doesn't even see them, his eyes go only to mine. "You okay, Robin?"

"Yes. Great. Took you long enough, though," I grumble out, but force on what I hope looks like a warm smile while my eyes and the rest of me goes insane, because…*stop-my-heart-again.* Forget how Royce looked in the wrapped-up toga *before* his shower. Wrapped in a towel with water droplets all over him, with his wavy hair wet and slicked back from his face, and that glistening chest and six pack of his—*oh, help me.*

Please God. Help me on this. Do. Not. Look. Do not stare at the water-wet-V.

I force my eyes away from him and decide to start inching towards the bathroom door for something to do besides look at *him.*

While I do that, Royce address everyone else in the room. "Hello people. I'm supposing your presence here means it's go-time already? Can't even give a guy a proper amount of time to have a honeymoon?" He grabs the crumpled wedding dress off the chair and holds it up like he's proud of it. "And before you make up stuff, let's be clear. It was all me—losing my head and my patience and tearing this dress. Sorry grandmother. I wasn't thinking clearly." He points at me. "And can you blame me?"

I flush so hard as everyone glances at me with knowing and nodding looks, that I get they're all bought in to this. No one is even questioning us. Which means that if Royce's closest circle of friends and employees are bought in, then maybe the judge and the social workers in charge of mine and Sage's case will believe all of it, too.

Believe in Mrs. Felix and Gregory and all of the financial support they're offering to us—is all because Royce and I are so in love that we had to get married to save Sage. I can't even be angry at Clara for being so snide because her surprise and subsequent jealousy is a little part of why this is working.

He stalks over to me and says, "Hold on there, beautiful wife, before you escape. Just one more kiss while you're wearing that sheet, if you don't mind. For the memories…" His thumbs go over my bare shoulders in this way that gives me goosebumps, and when I look up at him with a small head-shake which I hope says:

Don't freak me out in front of all of these people—

He brushes a soft kiss lightly across my lips and escorts me the rest of the way to the bathroom door, whispering, "Make sure it's locked or my grandmother and half of these people will have no problem coming in and bothering you while you shower. It happens to me all the time."

"It does?" I blink back at Mrs. Felix.

"Yes." He nods, and adds, "I'm sorry, Robin. This is the beginning of the end. You must know that?"

His eyes are so deeply bored into mine I'm thinking: *the beginning of the end of my heart, of my soul and all control I have of my body?* I'm so weak in the knees from his short kiss that I ask him out loud, "The beginning of the end, of *what*?"

"The end of your privacy. The end of who you used to be." He shakes his head and then corrects himself. "I hope it's not going to be too stressful for you to live like this." He waves his arm around the crowded room.

"Wait. All of these people barging in here isn't just because we got married yesterday and because we have a press conference? Is it going to be like this every day?" I blink up at him, analyzing his anguished face.

"For the foreseeable future, yes."

I look around, letting that sink in, and when my eyes travel back to his I cling to him for a second answering, "As long as you're here with me. It's going to be fine."

"And when I *can't* be with you?" His eyes flash with panic. "What happens then? *Shit.* We have so much to talk about still."

I shrug, saying only what I always say when I'm scared and unsure: "It's going to be fine. Whatever happens we will work it out together, right?"

He plants another fast kiss on my forehead and pushes me gently into the bathroom. "Right. Together."

I close the door, but as it shuts he starts knocking and knocking, so I quickly re-open it a crack. His face is pressed close to the crack and those eyes have grown worried again.

"Here's the outfit Clara's picked for you. I hope it's okay. I'm assuming you want to put it on by yourself?" He shoves some hangers through the crack at me.

"Yes. I do." I take what looks like dressy shorts and a cool shirt and hang it on the back of the door, as I close it.

"Remember. Lock it. Okay?" he says again, not moving out of the way. "And…could you hurry?" He makes this funny face. "I'm sort of getting addicted to having my new wife by my side."

"Okay. Sure. Worrier." I laugh, pushing the door closed against his weight.

I know he's only being extra nice, but I'm not going to lie, I like how I don't see his shadow move away from the line of light that's showing below the door until I click the lock.

10

ROYCE

"OKAY NOW THAT we have most of the info on Robin, Sage, her father and the background to the wedding we were all curious about. Let's open this up to questions from the other reporters."

Mike, the reporter, and my long-time friend, whom we've invited for our exclusive post wedding interview, happens to be the same guy my grandmother had invited for our set-up 'engagement kissing photos'.

He's now acting as our honeymoon press facilitator. All of the other reporters are gathered in behind him and have been allowed to film, but to keep chaos down, they are not allowed to ask questions until these last five minutes of the interview.

Mike was very well paid for his engagement photo-leaks, and now he's thrilled I've asked him to in charge of this first interview, because it means he will be able take some time off after this once he sells his exclusive photos. He's also just gained huge street credibility with the other paparazzi. I'm happy to help him out, but I've had to be very careful with what I say to him, because Mike, like everyone else, thinks my wedding to Robin is real.

Unfortunately the guy knows me so well, that I'm worried I'm not coming off clear and relaxed with him how I usually interview. I decide to call my nervousness out, just in case he and everyone else are wondering what's up with me.

"Dude. Everyone," I hold up my hands to get everyone to quiet a little. "I'm sorry if Robin and I seem off, but you are aware that my wife and I only got two hours of sleep last night and…" I flush a little, "And well, it was our wedding night, so…yeah, understand if we are distracted and glassy-eyed," I add. "I just have this feeling that I sound and look delirious right now," I force out a laugh.

"Delirious and happy!" One male reporter has called out, trying to charm me, or most probably charm Robin, while Mike clears his throat, signaling his own camera man to start filming.

"Can I go first?" that same man boldly asks.

I nod, shoving on a smile, because I hate pushy people like this, but I think, fine—today maybe *pushy* will serve a purpose. "Shoot."

"We all know about Robin's father." The reporter squeezes forward, now he's leering at Robin. "And we know all that you and your brother went through, but we want to know more of the Robin Love that Royce Devlin fell in love with. The whole world is asking, why would a guy like Royce just lose his mind and get married to a girl-next-door type like you out of nowhere?"

"Let me answer that," I'd interjected, watching Robin's eyes flare with panic before she'd colored slightly and stared at her shoes. "Because, dude, are you mental to try to hurt my wife's feelings in here on her *wedding day*?" I shoot the guy a long look that says he's about to get ejected from this room. "I don't feel like I should even explain this, because we're obviously in love, and that's why people get married, you idiot, but to me—Robin's special. She's everything and she's amazing."

As half of the room sighs, out, "Aww," I look at Robin, saddened that she still hasn't raised her eyes. "Have you all not noticed she's the most beautiful girl in the world—and, when she smiles I go weak in the knees, and that's never happened to me with any girl, not ever before and, hell." I shake my head, "How can anyone answer this kind of question?" I stall for time, dragging up the thoughts I'd come up with back in the limo just before the wedding. "Because when her laughter goes around the room, it feels like I'm standing in warm sunshine. That's why." I shake my head, hitting everyone in the room with my best back-off expression, before adding, "Does anyone have any *real* questions for my wife?"

The reporters start moving in closer, and some have even sighed and are grinning like they love what I've just said and they hope I'll say more. The jerk-reporter makes a hasty retreat to the back of the crowd, but not before adding, "You sound whipped, Royce Devlin. Sorry if I was skeptical, but we all know your past track record with women. What will the world think of this nearly *sappy* change in you?" He laughs.

"They will think I have finally found the one." I fake-grin back at him, making sure everyone sees I'm unashamed that I've just been called sappy by an *asshole*. "Not whipped, dude. This girl is my muse. I'll shout it from rooftops, Dude. Do you want me to? In case you didn't notice, I just married her in a crowded arena, and I'm all about feeling this awesome. Do you want me to shout it out now how much I love her?"

"Uh. Yes?" A younger male reporter asks, hopefully, all while holding his cell phone up high and filming just in case.

Smiling, I pull in a big breath like I'm about to shout something out when Robin, shoves a hand over my mouth. Though I can tell she's trying not to do it, she laughs. "Please stop. Royce. So embarrassing."

I pull her hand away and kiss the back of it, then her palm, before tucking it into the crook of my arm. "In addition to being all that I just said, she's also humble, and a little shy."

"A lot shy," Robin corrects, looking away from the staring people again.

Another reporter, totally taken in says, "I'm going to use the tagline, *Shy and humble: the new sexy*."

Mike takes the lead again on the interview. "Hey, that's pretty good. We *should* use that. Maybe start a trend after all the annoying, loud and obnoxious, entitled, bad-girls we've been forced to interview lately. It's like classy has been forgotten over screaming, hair pulling, high profile bar-fights." He turns back to us. "Royce and Robin, holding hands and acting all sweet how you two are, it's very classy. I swear this reminds me of Princess Dianna's first press interview after her wedding. Doesn't it?"

The reporters and mutter as though in agreement when Robin surprises me by speaking up.

"Okay. Subject change," Robin calls out. "Please do not compare me to Princess Di." She shakes her head. "She's been my idol my whole life, and I'm not at all any sort of well-bred young lady like she was, and I'm as far away from *classy* that any of you could find."

"So you're saying you're the opposite?" Jerk reporter guy calls out again.

I'm impressed how Robin holds her ground. She looks up and makes eye contact with the guy who keeps trying to insult her and says,

"No. Not the opposite. I'm just a normal girl. One who grew up on Army bases doing normal things like…" She laughs, "Dollar store shopping, and running around bookstores and malls for fun. I went to normal schools, speak no foreign languages, have never been to the symphony or the ballet. That kind of stuff." She blinks. "The last three things, I think, are direct requirements for *classy*, right?" The reporters laugh as Robin goes on, "I have no clue how to navigate social situations, and there was no debutante ball on my military base in case you were wondering." She grins then as the reporters laugh again.

"So then, why should Royce have married someone like you? Can you answer that?" The jerk asks again.

"Yes," Robin says, while I lock eyes with one of my bodyguards because after Robin answers him, this dude is out of here. Robin continues, "Because Royce—he is just like me. A normal guy." She looks over at me, her expression begging for me to step in and save her from talking more. "Right, Royce?" she adds.

I can tell she's shocked the reporters by calling me a 'normal guy' so I answer quickly, thinking I need to do a little damage control here. "Well," I start, rubbing a hand over my chin like I'm thinking extra hard about this. "It's true. I've never been to a symphony or seen a ballet. But, Robin, I can't agree that I'm just a *normal guy*. Hell no." Her brow crinkles into a small frown and now I'm worrying I've hurt her feelings, so I decide to run my comments another direction. "I'm not at all normal, because," I tap the side of my head with one finger. "Up here, I'm a total disaster. Despite the part where I do speak French and Italian, and did learn from my grandmother which fork to use for shellfish, and know how and when to touch the dessert *spoon, you know,* over the using dessert *fork*, this—very normal—very cool girl loves me anyhow." I smile brightly then, wondering what the hell I just said, and hoping whatever it was, that it was enough to charm them into leaving Robin alone.

The press seems to have eaten up my answer like I was flinging out gold coins. When I look up, they're all wearing this smitten—soft look, and it's not for me, or for Robin, it's for *'us'*. The new 'it couple', and my heart soars as I think: *holy shit, this is working. This is actually working.*

Another reporter calls out, "You speak French and Italian? How did you learn those?"

"You'll have to ask my grandmother," I answer dryly. "I might be a rockstar, but my mother and I were raised by her rigorous educational standards. We spent all vacations in France or half in Italy, and always with the best tutors. Hunter and Adam were also included in the language tutoring." I squeeze Robin's hand, trying to check in with her if she is okay.

She squeezes back, asking me directly, "Is there really such a thing as a desert spoon and fork?"

"Yes." I make my mouth go all tight trying to sound like my grandmother. "In general, you should eat custards, or other soft deserts —chocolate mousse for example—with the spoon. The fork, surprisingly, is for berries or any other garnishes. Cakes and crepes may be eaten with either of the utensils."

Robin as well as the reporters have grown quiet.

"Wow," Robin says finally, shaking her head, and I catch a flicker that's half doubt, half amazement at what I've just said, crossing her face. "Good to know. I guess."

"Too much?" I ask, laughing, while ever-grinning at the crowd. "I don't just play guitar and sing, you know? I can go to fancy state dinners with the best of them."

"You can?" Three cute little lines have now formed in Robin's forehead. "I mean, Do you? Will we *do* stuff like that?"

I shrug, glancing at the too-attentive reporters. "Hey, if presidents ask, we go. Once, on our last world tour, we wound up having dinner with the President of Indonesia. Loved Indonesia. Everyone has to go there. Amazing place."

"Holy cow. Really?" Her big blue eyes widen as she responds to that. "Again, good to know the people I'm probably going to make a fool of myself in front of while dining. Presidents. Great." She turns back to the reporters. "I guess on record, I can tell you all that I will officially memorize all the things you can do with a desert spoon *and* start studying French to catch up to my husband, starting tomorrow. Aside, what is chocolate mousse? Maybe we should get some in here now?" Robin's brow furrows more, but she covers it with a huge wink because it's obvious she knows what chocolate mousse is, and she's just hamming it up now.

Mike laughs out loud and steps forward, turning to face Robin. "Before coming in here, I'd have even called you two doomed based on how you met, Based on Robin's background compared to yours, I'd also had this idea you two were a no-go. But as we're going on here, I'm starting to see how this marriage could actually work out. You're two people from such *different* backgrounds, yet together you seem so… symbiotic. You balance each other out."

My brows shoot up high as do Robins'. I can tell she's thinking the same as I'm thinking: As in—*Huh? We do?* While I agree fast with, "Hell yes. I'm happy you see it, Mike. I knew you would."

He nods, as do a few other reporters who are also buying in, then says, "So, let me ask Robin a few more questions on behalf of everyone here. Can I?" Mike asks me.

I'd shrugged then, said it was up to Robin, because it really was up to her, and she'd agreed.

She'd laughed at the guy's jokes and colored adorably every time he referred to our 'wedding night' and after all of that, she's now answering candidly to any, and all questions the man has thrown at her about her 'very normal' childhood.

I'd stop her from answering some, because the guy is getting invasive and too many people are going to know personal facts about Robin's past. Facts she might not want anyone to know actually, but her answers have been safe so far. And…*damn me* for exposing her this way, but I want to hear her answers as much as the reporters want to hear them.

As he goes on, I soak Robin up, right along with them. I gain information about what Robin's life was like back when she lived on a military base in North Carolina.

She, without a flinch, told the guy how her mom had left when Sage was just under two years old and she'd been ten. How the woman had been a heroin addict, and how she'd not been back—and, that no one knew if she was dead or alive. She'd told them how she'd all but helped raise Sage. That she'd been his stand-in-parent, all along. Which is why she thinks she and Sage and have a closer sibling relationship than most. It's also why, when she ran away with him to try to keep him from foster care, that choice had seemed so easy.

To her, running had been the correct—*the only* action to take; and it seemed as though the reporters agreed with her.

The only time she blushed during this portion of the interview was when she revealed how she'd slept with a stuffed bear until she was in 9th grade. I learned she loves dogs and cats, but is horribly allergic to cat hair. As in, her whole face and lips swell up, kind of allergic. I'd also discovered that once she had quite the ocean fish aquarium set-up in her basement, where she actually did something called coral-fragging.

It's how corals grow and she got into that crazy hobby, because her favorite movies as a kid were The Little Mermaid, Nemo, and of course, Finding Dory.

She also told one reporter she's been obsessed with paint and painting since she'd first smeared finger paints all over her living room couch back in first grade. Not to be naughty, but to mix colors. To make the couch look better. Instead of getting rid of the couch she'd ruined, her father had understood her need to make the plain grey couch more beautiful. He and Sage had helped her 'finish' the project with more permanent, acrylic paints. Her father was so cool, that (after he'd made Robin promise to leave the rest of the furniture in the home as-is) he'd kept that painted couch in his den, telling everyone who asked, that it was his daughter's first major art work. A collector's item.

When Mike asked her to say the two things she couldn't get enough of in her life, she'd glanced at me and answered, "Yesterday, I'd have said, Frosted Flakes and brand new paint brushes, but today?" Her cheeks had gone bright red as she glanced shyly at me before going on, "Today, I've got *two things* and one *person* that I now can't get enough of in my life. How's that?"

That answer had nearly brought me to my knees. I was the one getting red cheeks after that, because, *hell yes*. Even though it's not true, that was the sweetest damn thing anyone could ever say after getting married, right?

When the guy asked me the same question next, I told him the damn truth. I said, "I can't get enough of my sweet wife's smile, and keeping that smile on her face was all I wanted to do…from now on—hell forever."

Better, as I'd said my answer, I heard Robin gasp, and I got to snuggle her in next to me, pick up her hand again so I could land another kiss on it, then hold it for the rest of this interview.

Because…we did just say we couldn't get enough of each other, after all, so holding her close right now is very much allowed.

As we stand people make comments about my board shorts and shirt, and I answer, "Thanks for reminding me. I'm wearing this outfit because we're supposed to go snorkeling or something after this interview. Can we please end this and move to the still photos we promised? I want to enjoy time with my wife."

Robin makes everyone wait as she pauses to tighten the fabric belt of her high-necked, black, sleeveless shirt. It's a shirt that, though high in the front, is nearly backless. It was something I noticed the second she walked out of the bathroom, because it was the most extreme shirt I'd ever seen her wear. It had been paired with some very cute beach shorts, so even though the shirt alone was really not beach wear, how she'd managed to dress it down was perfect.

Her damp curls had been piled up onto her head by the stylists in this very loose, very sexy bun, which as Robin moves around to get into position to take photos next to me, I realize also brings all eyes to the expanse of skin she's revealing when she walks.

I know for a fact that if a girl's shirt is backless like this…it means they're also *braless,* which on most girls—and on Robin—is as hot as hell. But I don't think Robin's one bit comfortable with that part of this outfit at all—and I suddenly don't like sharing her look—or her skin—with the whole planet, so I work to constantly block her back from view, hoping that it helps somehow. But it doesn't help because it's possible the nearly sheer front of the shirt might be more subtly revealing than the back!

Suddenly, I sort of want to punch anyone who's noticed what I've just noticed—which is, in fact, *everyone.* Worse, now that she's standing versus sitting next to me, and I've got my arm around her waist like this…*damn, but my thumb can't stop creeping in to feel the softness of her skin along her waist. All for, show,* I'm thinking while I swallow down a hard lump in my throat…*all for show, but…damn…this girl is undoing me.*

A woman call out, "Oh, Robin. I wanted to ask about your clothes. Do you know the designer of the shirt you're wearing? It's really different, and we always report what fashionable people are wearing especially if it's something we've never seen before."

"Oh, well then you're going to be so disappointed in me. I think, with this top, I've failed because I can't keep it tight." She looks down, again worrying over the belt. "I'd hoped you wouldn't comment on it. The stylists gave it to me last minute. It's not one I picked out for myself. I wasn't sure how to put it on…and, it was so revealing and strange that when I put it on the correct way, uh…well, look. This is the front." She turns to show her bare back. "I couldn't figure out how to tie the belt, so I flipped it and the best I could do. But wait." She smiles, looking sheepish. "The designer's name is right here…hold on."

Robin turns back, pulling at the high collar under her chin, then flips it down and stretches it out, revealing a tag next to her neck while she reads out loud: "Challa." She shrugs, looking up, and grinning. "I'm wearing Challa, *backwards*."

"How refreshing." One woman steps forward snapping a few more photos. "I'm sure you've started a new trend, and that Challa will be thrilled."

I can see Robin's slightly mortified while more people move in to take a closer look, and to snap a few shots of the ingenious way she's tied this shirt onto her body. I'm mortified because I think they're getting royal-good shots of the see-through parts near her chest.

Again, I get the irrational urge to punch people, but I manage to keep a small smile on my face to let Robin know it's all okay and normal that this is happening. Then, unable not to resist taking a closer look just like everyone else, I run a finger down the lower part of her back, while I pretend that I was only helping her adjust the belt around her waist better. "I think it looks beautiful. Super sexy."

"Very on trend," the woman reporter agrees.

"Last questions," I call out. "Honestly, guys, we are done here."

"Wait. One more. After you go to New York City, when will you two meet up on the tour?" A woman calls out quickly.

"When we get to Europe," I answer her, keeping a straight face while loping my arm around Robin's shoulders as I go on, because I'm not sure if this information has been handed down to Robin yet. "The details are still being finalized, and some of this is a surprise to Robin, but we're *definitely* going to meet up in Europe."

I smile a little as I feel her shoulders tense. I'm dying to look at her face because I want to watch what I'm about to say sink in and flash across her expressive beautiful face, but I hold steady, keeping my eyes on the reporters. "At first we'd thought to spend the summer apart. Possibly, wait until Labor Day to reconnect, because Robin's going to start Ridley's Art School in NYC this fall, and Sage is going to a day prep school nearby. We wanted them to get settled in, get used to living in Manhattan—because there's a lot to be done on that side of the world, without the two of them being distracted by our tour madness."

A few of the reporters are nodding like they understand, and because I can't help myself, I can't resist tugging Robin closer while I add, "As you know the tours can be grueling. It's not any sort of real life. It's hotels and press events and long nights." I sigh. "So yeah, I'd thought to protect her from all of that. I had this idea I would come home on breaks and stay with her in our NYC penthouse when I can, but we can't stand the idea of being apart so much so soon. Not now that we're married. We'd miss each other, wouldn't we, Robin? Which is why I'm hoping they'll come to the European part of the tour with us."

"Yes. We would miss each other, but are you serious? Europe?" Robin's voice is surprisingly solid, but I can feel her trembling some in her shoulders.

"Surprise." I grin. "There's still two months of summer left, and so do you... *want* to go? I feel terrible for putting you on the spot like this," I say, leaving off my worst fears of: *What if she doesn't want to go and now she feels obligated to agree with me. Damn, why didn't I think this through.* "You'll see London, Paris, Berlin. Spain is the fourth stop, and I'm not sure when school starts for you, but we will be sure to get you and Sage back in time. What do you think?"

"Sage will love this idea, of course. And...I've always wanted to go see Europe. The museums. Go up the Eiffel Tower, of course *that* is a dream everyone has, right?" I'm analyzing her breathing and when she pauses, shaking her head a little. I tilt her chin up so I can see her eyes. "But...go to Europe as your *wife*?"

She's whispering, but the entire room has grown so quiet everyone is hearing her loud and clear. "What if I keep messing up and wearing the clothes your stylist gives me backwards? What about the desert forks and spoons and the dinners with presidents I will most probably mess up for you?"

"Then the entire world will start wearing their clothes backwards," one laughing reporter interjects, totally taken in with Robin's reaction. "And no one eats desert these days. Not in Europe, that's how everyone stays so slim. You'll be fine."

"He's right." Mike is beaming at Robin, also charmed.

"We'll keep it casual," I say, searching my brain for words that will resonate with her. "Come on, Robin. Like you said this morning, it will be Fun. So much fun."

11

ROBIN

"Holy cow. You and Royce made the cover of over *ten* magazines." Vere's eyes are bright as she's going through various Instagram feeds. "Ten covers in the same *month*. All the big fashion ones, of course, and then, Rock&Roll, *yes*! That's a score. But this one—this one, PopLifeGo? That is usually all about movie stars not musicians, at-all-*ever* and—*look*!" She flashes her phone in front of my face again. "Cover and feature story."

"Okay. Cool," I answer, turning to admire the marshmallow-castle-clouds floating below our plane, working hard to ignore the fact that under the clouds is all ocean. Only ocean. Deep, cold, water that would sink a plane like a stone should we end up down there. Am I the only one who hasn't flown 'the pond' before? Am I the only one who wanted to cry 'bull-shit' when they told us our seats would float?

"Cool? Robin. Hello. Are you even listening?" Sighing like she's annoyed, Vere shoves the wide arm rest separating us up until it disappears, making our two seats into one cozy couch. Then she reaches the phone up to my face, bumping it against the window so I will finally look at what she's talking about.

The picture she wants me to see is a magazine cover made up of me and Royce with our arms around each other. It's one that was taken during our honeymoon stills. "If only I could stop seeing myself nearly naked in that backwards Challa shirt," I sigh, turning to analyze the design of how, what I thought was a solid wood arm rest, could have moved at all—yet there it is, now an integrated part of the first-class seat.

Every seat in this section looks like real furniture, not airplane seats at all. And I mean furniture with hydraulic seat cushions, and flat screens on the backs of them, and very deep—fits a crystal wine glass with a whole stem on the bottom of it—kind of seat! Because wine is what fancy ladies on the way to London drink while heading to London, and they need to drink it in stemware, I guess..

I, the fraud, of course am having a Coke. One full of ice cubes, which earned me an eye-roll from the British flight attendant. After she'd passed it to me with a look of disdain, Vere explained that in Europe, they shun ice cubes.

What and why?

"Robin. You have got to look at this. You look so hot."

Sighing again, I take Vere's phone before she accidentally bashes me in the head with her excitement, and zoom in to the photo of the magazine cover, shaking my head when I see myself. "It's like they Photoshopped how my nips were popping out. If that's how I looked that day…then…omg, so awkward."

"Not even. You were the prerequisite rockstar wife, naked and sexy…" Vere takes her phone back and zooms in even more. "And wow, I think you're right. They did make you extra perky. Whatever sells, right?" Vere laughs as I shove at her shoulder laughing as she adds, "You know that was such a hot look that Clara picked. Girl did you a favor to be sure. I still can't believe you went for no bra, knowing you. And you haven't done that since but maybe it's time to bring those now famous boobs back to the public."

"No. Never." I snort. "I wasn't given the choice to have a bra that day. Royce had torn my corset in half, there was not any appropriate underwear in sight, and I was literally a zombie that day from lack of food and sleep, so I hardly remember us taking those photos."

"Well the world remembers. Look at this one." Vere scoots over even more, nearly lying on me this time so I'll look at her phone again. "Holy wow you got the feature," she squeaks out, eyes twinkling. "*This* story is three pages longer than the article they wrote about Madonna's awesomeness when she was at the Women's March. Remember? When she was dropping the F-bombs like crazy on live-TV right after Trump was elected."

I nod. "And the extra pages mean something important because...*why*?"

"Because no one ever gets more than two pages max in this magazine." Vere's turning more and more pages. "This article is longer than the *after Oscars* party feature. Longer than the best and worst dressed from any awards show. No wonder we were mobbed at the airport by people recognizing you. You're famous now Robin!"

"People were recognizing Royce. Not me." I protest, dropping my voice and pointing at Clara and motioning one finger over my lips to remind Vere to keep it quiet. Clara and her mother, Jennie, are in the two first class fancy seats facing across from us. They've been reclining and I think, sleeping like that for at least an hour.

Vere opens the Notes App on her phone and types: *They're only pretending to sleep, you know that right? It's how Clara eavesdrops.*

I shake my head again, almost laughing out loud as I take the phone from her to type my own answer: *I thought they were such seasoned travelers. Are you sure?* I nod in their direction again, and Vere and I take in how they're both wearing those silky black eye covers with cold-gel packs inside of them.

I add: *I saw Jennie take a sleeping pill. I'm sure she went right to sleep.*

Vere takes the phone back, answering: *By the way Jennie's got her mouth hanging open maybe she is out, but Clara's frowning every time I gush about how famous and awesome your boobs are. Ha. She's not sleeping one bit. I swear that girl has so many jealousy issues these days. For no reason.*

I type: *Right? Considering she's so beautiful, has the best summer job in the world, she always looks so put together and sophisticated. I know she could get any guy she wanted. I've never known anyone who could be an actual real model before, and I think she could, right?*

Vere frowns at what I've typed adding: *Totally. But the problem with Clara is that she can any guy EXCEPT for Royce Devlin. Which, I guess, is who she was really hoping for? Talk about unrealistic goals, huh?"*

I bite back and laugh under my breath, stopping it by biting my bottom lip. *"Well...why shouldn't she have those. Royce married me, didn't he and that's the must unrealistic and incredible thing ever."*

Vere shakes her head making this bug-out incredulous expression while typing more: *Yeah. Maybe. But you weren't trying to hunt him down. It just...happened. I swear before all of this she used to be normal. Kind of nice even. I'm sure soon she will get over your marriage to her dream man. She has to.* She types a winky-face, then: *For the rest of the flight, though…watch what you say just in case.*

I type back: *How about for the rest of…always.*

Vere rolls her eyes and agrees with an exaggerated nod.

NEITHER OF US want to slip up and talk about the fake parts of my wedding, my relationship, or any of the very successful interviews we'd had after the courts had granted me full custody of Sage.

In the days after our wedding and we had permission to leave Florida, the press seemed to get attached to following the story about me and Sage. We became part of the American nightly news. People loved the story of our wedding, but the media attention reached a peak when we'd had to return to North Carolina and go to court in order to gain legal custody as well as clear me because of how I ran away.

The judge who saw to my case was x-military, and he, thankfully took my side in the story. Understood my motivations were sincere, and told me I was lucky as hell Royce, Mrs. Felix and Gregory had stepped up to offer their combined support. We only have to check in with our case worker once a month and file an annual report including Sage's grades and a psychological evaluation until he's eighteen like me. Or, until my father comes home.

After all of that news exposure, it was like people were sort of addicted to checking in with what was happening with Sage and I. To keep the story alive, because we were told this exposure would speed up the search for our father, we took full advantage of that attention and did any and every interview people asked us to do.

When Royce and I had gone directly with Gregory and Mrs. Felix to New York City, those interviews were even easier to access because all of the big morning news shows and talk shows are based out of NYC.

I even had to bring a film crew into our apartment after Royce had left on the Asian part of his world tour so they could check out our four bedroom, *newlywed's apartment.* One that was being refurbished to add in Royce's, amazingly kind, too-thoughtful, wedding present to me.

An art studio—built along the windows of his living room.

Although, I'm supposed to be calling it *our* living room now, but it's been sort of difficult to remember that, considering it is just not my living room. Not my penthouse apartment. Because people like me don't really live on the second highest floor of the Manhattan Orb Hotel in a sky rise home that feels bigger than half of my high school, that is also located just below Mrs. Felix's amazing penthouse apartment. Royce Devlin rockstar lives there. Mrs. Felix, hotel maven, she lives there, but Sage and I? It's not ours.

I swallow again, trying to make the stomach churning stop. We're just...visiting. Just how we're about to visit Europe.

As for the art studio Royce had ordered built for me?

For me, the visitor? It was over the top.

The first time I'd been able to see it not taped off, was during this big, staged reveal. I had to go in with Mrs. Felix and an architect along with the morning show crew to see it in person. I was so choked up I'd teared up. It had work tables, and beautiful distressed wood storage shelves built all on the back of these cool, moveable dividers that would allow us to keep the art and work space open. Or, I'd told them, after I'd pulled myself together, that *Royce and I also wanted the option to close it off completely. You know...should we have a dinner party or something after Royce's world tour.*

My stomach pinches even more at the memory of me uttering those words with a straight face right on live TV.

Royce had seen the footage and had called to tell me it was my best performance to date. And when he'd asked me how I liked the studio, really liked it? I told him the truth. That it was too much, that it was simply the most perfect art studio anyone could dream up. Then, I told him how I was really happy that he'd designed it so it would be easy to disassemble the sliding dividers and return everything back to normal after all of this was...over.

He hadn't been able to call me after that. And I didn't try much to call him because as I got wrapped up into more interviews and the hundreds of photo that were taken of me and Sage non-stop every time we left the apartment. Then I got sort of too tired, or so much time had passed that it felt awkward to call him which is about when I practically became a recluse in our apartment or hiding upstairs with Mrs. Felix in her penthouse.

I started telling Mrs. Felix that I didn't want to go out. Vowing that I only had two weeks to get settled in with Sage before leaving with him to go to Europe.

I'd assured her that I was tired. That I and wanted to sit around and just read, watch TV, and paint. It was partly true. With the amazing art studio they'd made for me…well…why would I want to spend one moment outside of that beautiful space? I'd become addicted to the floor to ceiling windows and my million dollar view of New York City. It even included a small glimpse of the Hudson river in the background.

I think she knew that I wasn't tired, but that I was simply afraid to have public appearances without Royce. Because…heck yeah, it's scary when people recognize you, then rush you and take photos, ask to have a selfie, or call out random comments to you while you're just walking down the street.

I also tried not to miss the guy, but I did.

While alone in the studio, I wound up having endless conversations with myself about *why?* Royce and I still hardly knew each other. After all, our total time spent together was one week before the wedding and about two weeks after.

Three weeks and a few days, that's it. No reason to miss him.

Only…during that time we'd been inseparable.

He'd been holding my hand every day, laughing with me, sitting by me, and hardly ever once leaving my side which had made all of this fake marriage stuff seem easy. We'd goofed off and spent countless hours on coming up with daily strategies on how to do our relationship better. How to make it easier. More real.

Like the sleeping-plan. We'd agreed that outside of our Orb apartment residence, like when we had to stay in hotels, where there was a bunch of staff that would gossip, for example, we would sleep in the same bed, fully clothed with the pillow towers in place, of course.

While at his apartment in NYC, we could lock ourselves in the master bedroom. It has this massive living-room area inside the bedroom. One with a huge leather couch placed facing the windows. While he was at home, we'd slept together with Royce on that couch and me in the bed, but after he left to go on tour, the room and the massive apartment had seemed so empty so I'd started sleeping upstairs with Mrs. Felix in a guest room next to Sage's.

Once I'd stopped leaving the apartment, Mrs. Felix took it upon herself to help me figure out how to navigate some of the things that will come with my future jet-set life in Europe. Daily, she'd give me funny lessons like, how to eat crab legs with odd shaped metal crab crackers. We'd watch YouTube videos about the UK Royals so I would know who is who, who lived where and how many babies people were having, in case any of us crossed paths—something that was apparently a huge possibility.

When I worried over the foods of France, she showed what this grey-paste looking stuff called foie-gras (pronounced fwaa graaa) which is essentially sliceable meat-goo. Think fancy SPAM that is often served in fancy restaurants in France. It is to be spread on crackers or old bits of baguette. Often, it's served at the same time the French would bring out caviar. Which, by the way is full-on, tiny jars or cans stuffed full of creepy, tiny, salt-popping-watery, tastes like saltwater-air-poo, supposedly edible (but not to me) real fish eggs!

After my initial reaction, the poor lady tried to show me how to eat both of those things without endless dry-heaving, which is what happened every time I tried to lift my fork toward my face and caught the scent of either of these two *rare delicacies.*

Then, because I could not stop the dry-heaves (which is a good-manners-no-no) Mrs. Felix considered making me a pretend vegetarian, but that's where I put my foot down.

I had this horrible, embarrassing tantrum.

Over meat.

Maybe because I was exhausted, or frustrated or disappointed in myself for not having the strength to swallow down the fancy food even though I really wanted to be able to do it, I'd nearly shouted at the sweet old lady.

It went something like: "After Paris, we go to Berlin, then Venice and I'm not giving up salami, prosciutto or any other of my Euro-meat-dreams. And believe me, I have a ton. I'm going to need some sausage with a side of bratwurst and extra Kassler on the side, the minute we hit Germany. And—and—just because the French have stinky, grey-paste, snails, fish eggs and frog legs for *meat? Meat* that makes me want to barf, that should not force me into becoming a vegetarian for the summer!"

It was a low moment. For me and for Mrs. Felix.

I did apologize, and Mrs. Felix recovered from my outburst by, as usual, remaining calm and classy and not holding it against me.

She'd said I was 'hilarious and so 'refreshing' even though, this time it wasn't true. In the end, she let me remain a carnivore and told me to pretend I had a food allergy should I be presented with a plate that I could not eat.

I was also ordered while in France, I should carry a perfume laced or linen handkerchief in my purse or hidden into my dress sleeve. Apparently, this is how the true-proper-ladies of the past handled smells. But it only works only should I have a dress with accommodating sleeves, which I do not. I didn't tell her that I don't even carry a purse, nor did I bring up how girls from my generation do not own handkerchiefs of any sort, because that information might freak her out even more than my dry heaves.

On that topic, I was also directed to act carefully. If my stomach started swirling and I felt even one little burp coming up my throat, I'm to exit the table quickly, and under no circumstances should I let myself dry-heave in front of anyone how I'd been doing.

According to her, I sounded like an elephant who'd swallowed a vacuum cleaner and, "In a girl as tiny as yourself, Robin. The effect is both shocking and rather disturbing. While in Europe, or with cameras rolling, we do not want you to be *that*, darling. No. No. Not ever. Am I right?"

No. No I do not want that. Ever.

12

ROBIN

I WAKE up when there's turbulence and I hear the captain ordering the flight attendants to take their seats for safety.

Suddenly, I'm in a full sweat, eyes going directly to the flat screen TV / computer / tablet thing in front of me as though it's going to have some answers about why the plane is bouncing all around. Sadly the thing only makes me more stressed by blipping out to a black screen then back on while hi-lighting how we're over water with no land in sight.

I make eye contact with this random lady who's walking briskly past me holding her iPhone while pointed at me, all while the stewardess says to her, "Ma'am. Ma'am. Please take your seat. Now." After she escorts the woman past the curtain, she apologizes to me. "So sorry. It keeps happening."

WTF. Were people walking up the aisle and taking photos of us this whole time? So. Weird.

I glance at my watch and realize that I must have fallen asleep for an hour or so, but according to the darn map, it appears we've hardly made progress toward the final destination goal of London's Heathrow Airport.

When there's more turbulence I start breathing all funny, and I think I'm having a panic attack, because suddenly I want to ask Vere, who's reading a book on her Kindle, if she's ever afraid of flying over oceans. I also want to whisper how I hate that we are forced to stare at this fancy flat screen map showing our tiny plane above the planet because it makes me realize how I'm inside that plane. If the plane looks small above the earth, then the part that makes up *me* inside of that plane is smaller than half of a half of a corner of dust!

I start sweating a little more. The clouds outside no longer fascinate me because they look dark and freaky and—*is that lightning?* I'm about to beg her to trade seats, because obviously asking for the window seat was a *bad-bad idea.* I want to shake Jennie awake and beg her for one of her sleeping pills. Maybe get myself one of those black-out eye masks, too. Because… *because what if the worst happens right now, and we start crashing, and I've got a perfect view of the ocean below, and I die and I'm not with Sage? What will he do without me?*

I swallow, dragging my gaze away from the window. I work hard to shove this irrational panic away, then manage to tamp it all down only because Clara and Jennie are moving around like the turbulence has made them wake up, too.

Maybe, eventually I'm going to have a nervous breakdown because of all of these life changes happening so fast, but I'm sure not going to have it in front of Clara and a whole bunch of strangers wielding cell phones. Not so they can film the whole thing and somehow share it on social media as well as the news and hold it against me forever.

I conjure up an image of Royce and his kind, 'you've-got-this-Robin' expression, while I force myself to contemplate things that are less scary than this plane falling out of the sky right now.

Will it be strange to see him? Will all of our walls be built up again? Will he and I be able to be genuine and easy with each other? Will there be mobs of press waiting at the London airport? Will he joke with me and call me 'wife' and hold my hand, or will the two weeks apart have made him realize this is madness and that he wants to cry off and start the divorce? What if someone finds out this is fake, and the courts realize they've been set up and change their mind about giving me, Mrs. Felix and Gregory legal custody of Sage?

As the turbulence settles, I'm able to calm down and make myself believe that everything, and every situation and even the plane is all *fine.*

Trying not to distract myself more, I pull out this fancy, lace edged pillow and a nice beige blanket all packaged up in a cute triangle that has been stowed in a little mesh basket under the window this whole time. I stuff the pillow behind my head trying not to feel guilty that I know the entire economy class behind the blue curtain, only has little square sized pillows and thin blue blankets, and that neither one of them came in pretty packages like mine did.

Vere curls onto her side and leans on her elbow and sits up eyeing my face. "You still awake? All okay?"

"Sort of, and sort of," I whisper. "I guess I'm nervous. About…everything."

"Don't be. I know it's strange for you. I've been in your shoes. You're in for a wild ride, but it's going to be so great." She reaches over and places her pillow against my shoulder. "I'm so happy I get to be part of your London debut. We will shop, and see all the museums, maybe there will be time for a show. London is amazing."

I toss her a grateful smile, snuggling closer to her. "Vere. I'm so happy you're here with me right now. That we're friends."

Vere quickly puts her hand over my mouth, and shakes her head. "Aww. Back at you."

Clara grumbles, "Can you two *please* be quiet? I had to pack all of Robin's junk late into the night, so you should feel sorry for me and let me sleep through this flight before I'm forced to unpack it all. This is the only first class moment your *servant* will be allowed on this entire tour."

Vere rolls her eyes. "I thought it was a paid internship? You also didn't pack her stuff, you packed the stylists supplies, which is what you hope to do as a career?" She throws a crumpled up napkin over at Clara as Clara pulls off her sleeping mask. "I heard you're getting something insane, like twenty-five dollars an hour? And doesn't this internship include a free summer in Europe with the world's coolest rock band? Clara. Please. You have to stop the pouting bit. It's getting so annoying."

"Fine. All that you said is true." She puts her own fancy-pillow over her head, speaking through it. "But it still sucks that I'm a lower tier staff member when I should have been dating Royce or Adam by now. From where I sit, with Adam and Royce married, and Hunter permanently taken by you, I feel like I'm Cinderella and there's no princes left. I won't even get to go to the ball."

"Yes you do. You get to sit at the music awards table with all of us." Vere giggles. "You're also in first class and you get to see every concert side-stage. Your VIP pass looks exactly like mine does which proves we're the same status level. Clara, are you *really* asking us to feel sorry for you, really? Because I think you also get school credits for this summer."

"I don't care." She whines out. "Please. Feel sorry for me, this all hurts where Band-Aids can't touch." Clara huffs again from under the pillow. "Robin stole my almost boyfriend and Adam had a baby with a girl called Eve and they named her *Apple*, which is so ridiculously adorable that you couldn't even *make it up* if you tried. And I will never get over either scenario. Never. I am seriously traumatized and still endlessly single, because no guys will measure up to the guys in Guarderobe and you both know it. Feel. Sorry. For. Me."

Vere shakes her head and we both laugh. "Clara you're killing us. I'm going to sleep." She pushes the reclining button in her seat, and because I didn't know where the button was until I saw Vere doing hers, I find mine and recline along with her, watching with amazement as the mahogany arm rest miraculously comes back into place between us.

"Don't mind her overmuch—she's just slow at accepting change," Vere says loud enough for Clara to hear. "Did you know she also goes to my college?"

"I think you mentioned it."

"She will fall in love with a new boy, probably the day we arrive in London, and she will calm down and stop acting *psycho*."

"Vere." Clara's voice comes out clipped and prissy. "You do not need to tell *her* my whole life story."

"Yes I do. I want Robin to know that as you travel on to Paris, where I won't be able to come along, that you are always more bark than bite. You know it's true."

"Wrong." Clara snorts. "In this horrible situation, I'm *all* bite."

Vere rolls her eyes. "She'll take great care of you in my absence."

"Not. I'm going to throw her into the Seine as soon as you leave for the airport."

I raise my brows and make the crazy sign with my finger next to my temple, mouthing the word: *wow*.

"You'll get used to her. I swear," Vere giggle-whispers, then laughs at the doubting face I'm making, adding, "She's funny after a while. Maybe she will even go shopping with us."

"Nope again." Clara grumbles. "Not funny. Not shopping. No. Count me out. I'm here to work not to make any new friends."

I shake my head, praying that Clara doesn't go shopping with us while biting back how I don't want to be friends with her anyhow, because I don't hang out with *mean girls*. But, instead, I hold my tongue and snuggle in again, closing my eyes to think, because Vere looks really tired. I think if it looks like I've nodded off, she will relax and stop mothering me how she does and get some rest too.

WHILE LISTENING to Vere's steady sleep-breathing, I keep my eyes closed and ponder the shopping idea, because I've been encouraged more than once, to go shopping since I've married Royce, but I just haven't had the heart to do it.

Mrs. Felix, Gregory and Royce even gave me my own bank account along with some credit and debit cards to go with it. It's an account that they set up using the thousand dollars they'd owed me in nanny fees, so it's not like I'm broke or anything because that 10k is money that I'd made while working for them. When the paperwork settles I will also be getting my dad's ARMY support paycheck auto deposited into that same account. That will come in once a month, but that hasn't started up yet as it needs to be changed from our past guardian's account back in North Carolina.

Only, my account has way more than my earned ten thousand dollars in it. It's now holding *forty* thousand dollars.

Forty. Thousand.

Mrs. Felix put it there last week, explaining that the extra amount was *normal rock-star-wife expenditures* that will crop up for me.

Whatever-the-heck those might be, I'm not bold enough to ask. I've also realized that I've had no need for *anything* since our wedding day. That's because everything, down to the soft travel-slippers on my feet, has been hand delivered to me before I even know I might need it.

Before I left on this trip, Mrs. Felix had noticed I hadn't been spending my money, and she encouraged me to go ahead and use it how I saw fit. She also said that I could shop as much as I wanted to when I was out with Royce while on my travels around the world. That it was expected, and not to worry that there would be 'more to come', I was only to ask if I wanted more.

Only when she'd said that, I didn't feel excited. I felt nervous. Guilty. Overwhelmed.

Maybe I felt—still feel—like a fraud. But who, in my situation wouldn't feel that?

Touching that money would mean touching the credit cards that are typed up with a name that doesn't belong to me, but that people call me now.

I'm Mrs. Devlin. Robin Devlin. Mostly, people just call me Royce Devlin's *wife*.

Gregory even took me out to get a NYC driver's license with my new name printed on it. My Passport has been changed, too. It's been hard enough to flash the license and the passport to airport security today, because each time I see that fake name, I think to myself…I'm Robin. Robin Love, and I keep waiting for everyone to point a finger at me and call me out about this whole farce.

As for spending that money? Heck no. That is not ever going to happen. I feel like I should be paying them back for all that they've done for me, not spending more.

I know the legal costs of just one, *so-so* lawyer is about $150.00 per hour. Mrs. Felix's team of attorneys is top notch, and they've spent hours—days even—drafting up paperwork and appearing in court again and again with me or on my behalf. They explained what was going on, using smaller vocabulary words so even Sage could understand which took forever for them. The part where we finally did win custody of Sage was awesome. Mrs. Felix and Gregory are staying behind this week, to sign on as legal family guardians for Sage. They're drawing up special documents stating they will step in and support Sage until he's a full adult, including his university fees, should I accidentally pass away somehow. They even made me something called a *living will* where I stated all of my wishes for Sage, should that happen. Which took even more legal papers and time.

I know, by this point, Sage and I have cost them thousands of dollars. They've also hired a special private investigation company that is currently working on locating information about whether my father is dead or alive. It's a company that has brought back hostages and found 'missing people' who weren't really missing rather taken, and they've had successful extractions (that's what they call it) all over the world.

Attorney fees I can guess at, but there's no way I can guess at how much this private mercenary company costs to hire. I creeped on their website and it was slick, and swanky. All silver with grey and serious sans-serif fonts. The site listed what the company does, but said only that fee structures were to be *individualized per case requirements*.

So…yeah. More and more thousands must be flying around to that company, all because of me again. Mrs. Felix and Gregory have assured me that none of this, or the fees, are any sort of *hardship* for them. That they're happy to help us. That it makes them happy.

Mrs. Felix even tried to flip my worries by telling me that Guarderobe has sold more albums and individual song tracks on iTunes than they've ever sold before. She, like Royce, has also hinted that it started the day Royce and I got married. She assured me that the band is making tons of money off of the publicity our situation is creating. She even told me the Orb Hotel NYC, as well as the world-wide bookings of her chain are way up because people have this idea they might see me and Royce staying in one of them. Now that the world now knows it's the preferred and obvious residences for the band, they're nearly sold out all of the time.

I think she just told me all of that to be nice, to make me feel better after I'd asked her to keep track of the spending on my behalf so later she could present me with a smaller bill that I would work hard to pay back. But…I'm keeping track, with or without her.

I also told her I wasn't going to buy any of her invented stories about how Sage and I are creating money out of thin air. I know that after living in two ORB hotels, I argued that bookings are up because the Orb chain offers the best luxury hotels in the world.

I also asserted that if Guarderobe is selling more and more albums and tracks, it's because Guarderobe is talented and awesome and has worked long and hard for their fame and that their successes have nothing to do with Royce marrying *me*.

Vere jostles me out my thoughts by accidentally whacking me with her backpack while stuffing all of her clutter back inside. I take it from her and do up the top zipper while she makes this hilarious show of making her cheeks go red and her eyes bug out while forcing air into this giant, bright red, soft coated, plastic neck pillow. She throws it around her neck and flutters her eyelashes. "Sexy, isn't it? But I can't sleep on a plane without this baby."

I laugh, raising my brows at her. "If you say so." We stow her backpack again and nestle back down facing each other. "I'm so excited about London," I whisper. "But I'm also really scared. London is so sophisticated. What if I mess up and wear my clothes backwards again."

I grab the Entertainment News magazine and point to the photo of me and Royce laughing at a Hot Dog stand. "What if all the things I'm expecting to eat taste like the hot dog I spit out here? Thankfully, no one took a photo of me dumping it in the trash."

Vere blinks. "All of New York City knows some of the stands don't have good dogs, and some do. You got a bad dog and threw it away. So what? People overreacted."

"Clara told me that the whole world is *watching*. That a whole city would have had its feelings hurt if I'd have been caught making a bad face or spitting that hot dog out, or trashing it. She says there's always big organizations watching us, like…she said I could get the band in serious trouble for dumping that hot dog in the trash."

Vere's brows shoot up. "What? With who? Like…*who* is she talking about?"

I shrug. "Maybe something like… the Hot-Dog-Collation-Union of America would post on their website that all hot dog lovers are never to buy Royce's albums again. All because my actions were a direct rejection of the entire hot dog industry? Or…hog farmers could be angry? Or people who track food waste? I don't know. It's a lot of stress to think about this extra stuff. Clara just told me that I need to be really conscious about every move I make from now on."

Vere laughs, then whispers, "It's possibly true, but Clara shouldn't have you worrying about this kind of stuff."

I press on, "It's such pressure being in the public eye, isn't it? I'm serious Vere. What will happen if I mess up again and accidentally insult entire countries because I have a weak stomach and a strong sense of smell? I'm terrified."

She laughs again. "You're bound to mess up. You're only human. But look, right now the world seems to like how you goof up. You're so real about all that you do." Vere pulls out her phone again, then searches something. "Look." She puts the phone between us so we can both see, pausing on photo after photo of girls dressed in too-short shorts wearing the same Challa shirt I wore to that first honeymoon interview. And the shirt is being worn backwards and tied at the waist, exactly how I did it. "When you mess up, you set trends. You're the new 'it' girl. You and Royce are America's real live fairytale couple. Just be *you*, because I've learned in this life, that's the only thing you can be."

"I guess that makes sense." I drop my voice to the quietest whisper so I'm sure only she can hear my deepest fear. "But what if me being all real and awkward isn't ever good enough to be standing next to a guy like Royce? I really could mess up the career he's worked so long to grow."

"Please. Robin. Listen to this." She rolls her eyes. "When I first started dating Hunter and these photos broke of him kissing me. It was the day he asked me to officially go out with him. It happened in front of a whole suburban neighborhood while the local news stations had cameras pointed at me. I'd just been crying, and I was all blotchy, and everyone on the planet was literally, overnight, asking: *What the heck! Hunter Kennedy is dating some hot mess from Colorado.*"

She widens her eyes and points to her chopstick-crazy-bun. "In addition to this untamable mess of hair, I had zero fashion sense. I wore baggy hoodies I'd stolen from my brother, as well as my dad's old jeans that I'd hacked off and made them into tattered shorts. I wore them nearly *every day.* Like a bad uniform made out of *WTF.*"

Her scrunched up face makes me crack up.

She goes on, "I would belt them to be all tight around my waist and they were beyond monster huge on me with the cut-off strings going all around my legs. It was the worst look possible for anyone to copy and suddenly half of the planet stole their father's jeans, chopped them up and started walking around in them. Stores started selling shorts that looked like they were made from my father's old jeans!"

"Wait. You're taking credit for that entire trend. Come on. You sound insane."

"Yes. It's true. It's because those shorts landed in in every magazine just how you have landed in every magazine. I was always listed under *new trends.*" She blinks her eyes wide, twice. "And this messy clump of hair kind of bun also went from everyone's couch onto runways! There were whole magazine articles and YouTube videos on how to perfect it."

I shake my head, thinking about what she'd said, as Vere presses on, "It wasn't me that started this hairstyle or cut of shorts, but it was the photos of me kissing Hunter while sporting these looks that made it go viral. All of the girls thought messy buns and bad shorts were what rockstars and cool guys were looking for in a girl. And so, I was like their tipping point. I accidentally led innocent girls into my bad fashion choices."

We both crack up again. "I've copied stars, too. Or wanted to, anyhow," she says. "Remember when Fault in Our Stars and then, Divergent came out? The movies?" She blinks her eyes wider. "I wanted to cut all my hair off super short. I was obsessed with the word *dauntless* and I was sure short hair would make me look, strong and get me to that moon and back feeling. Admit it. You know you wanted to chop your hair, too."

I snuggle down closer to her, nodding. "I did. Okay. I did. To act all 'Dauntless' was my life goal because obviously I seem to lack that capacity. I also dreamed about cutting my hair like that non-stop. I almost went for it, too, after I found out Veronica Roth, the author who wrote the Divergent series? She also had awesome short hair at the time."

Vere sighs. "Yes. I knew that. I love those books so much. And *this* is why we were such fast friends. You and I have similar hearts and minds." Vere lies back adjusting her crazy neck pillow. "Clara is right, people are watching us, and maybe it's millions of people. But for the most part, I think they're simply watching because they're looking for inspiration."

"That's for sure. But what if I influence someone badly? How do you deal with the pressure of it all?" I fix my own pillow under my neck.

"I just try to think that everyone who's watching wants a catalyst. Something that helps them dream big. That little push to be courageous enough to try something different so they can tear off the mask and show the world who they really are without being afraid."

She turns over on her side, the expression in her eyes going all dreamy. "I think we all carry this hope that these little changes, like hair…or new shorts, or wearing clothes backwards, will give us an added layer of armor against the world. They're not really looking at us. It's not personal. You know? Like, you and I weren't really looking at the actress from the Divergent movies or trying to be her *exactly* by wanting to cut our hair. It was more about emulating the 'cool-dauntless' she invoked in both of those movies. We were hoping to feel a little bit braver in a world that seems so scary and out of control. That's what I think, anyhow." She shrugs. "I like to think that maybe somewhere if I just stay real—do me as hard as I can without doubting myself, then I'm helping someone out there feel brave and stronger, too. As much as it's scary, if you can think of it like that then you don't have to worry so much?"

"Maybe, but it's really hard to squelch the feeling that I'm lacking something," I sigh out, as new doubts crowd in. "For example… I never cut my hair off, because I wasn't brave enough to actually do it. I'm also the last person anyone should be looking at for inspiration, because despite the part where I say everything is going to be fine all the time, I'm sort of endlessly feeling like all is crumbling around me."

Vere smiles. "Don't you get it, Robin? We're all walking around with scotch-tape holding our lives together. We're wondering what the hell we are going to do to keep it together tomorrow and I don't think anyone our age ever feels like they're standing on solid ground. All of us. And in this rockstar world it's so much worse. None of us know what we're doing, all while we have this anvil over our heads, because we're waiting for the ride to end like everyone says it will."

When I answer, "Okay. Well that's sad."

She smiles at me like she's a teacher who's breaking through to a new student. "Whatever happens, Royce is going to be there for you how Hunter was for me when I was new to all of it. He's such a solid friend. He won't let you slip up. No way. That guy is so into protecting you that when you're in the room his eyes hardly leave off tracking you. Together you and he have got this."

"Yeah. That's the exact line he and I keep saying to each other, actually." I answer, mostly for show because the stewardess was passing by, and because Vere and I both know Royce is sweet to me, yes. But her words *so-into me* are not sitting quite right.

I'm unable to meet her gaze any longer. I can tell from the look on her face she's just caught up to my line of thinking. The crease going across her brow deepens and it now tells me she's reached the same conclusion, and that she might feel sorry for me. She drops her voice to a super quiet whisper how I did. "Well…you're friends. Good friends, right?"

"It's fine." I answer with a small shrug. "Better than fine. And I've got you, too now, right?" I wink at her answering nod, then I fake a yawn and roll over to my other side, busying myself opening the sealed packaging on my blanket while reading the words: *100% Real Cashmere, with our compliments,* that's printed on the bag.

When I shake it out and pull it up to my chin, I almost sigh out loud, because I've heard about cashmere sweaters before, but I've never actually touched one. This blanket is like getting a hug from about two thousand baby rabbits.

My throat tightens as another random panic attack surfaces, this time about the blanket, because… *maybe it's not made from rabbits.*

Maybe it's from baby lambs? Baby camels? Maybe Cashmere is the name for some cool synthetic fabric?

A lump forms in my throat, because despite what I've said to Vere, even here with no cameras pointed at me, I've failed. If I don't know what this blanket is made out of here in my fancy first class seat. I'm not going to know 95% of what's thrown at me in London, despite all of the table-manners training that Mrs. Felix gave me. And when I get to Paris, a country where I don't even speak the language? I'm dead.

Thankfully, this fancy seat comes with free internet on the touch screens so, I sit up a little so I can Google the word *cashmere.*

Before I can type anything though, Clara sits up and rips off her mask. "What are you doing? Stop fidgeting around. Between you and Vere I'm getting no sleep on this flight." And then, as though she just read my mind and wants to rub salt into my wounds, she starts cursing me out in French! And it sounds legit and perfectly fluent. She's also got that model-perfect, sophisticated glare-pout on her face while she's talking, and suddenly I'm imagining her saying: *Robin, when I was born I was wrapped in a cashmere blanket. My first word was Cashmere. My Christmas stocking is Cashmere. My cat's name is Cashmere. But you're 100% cotton all the time.*

Quickly, I work to force any doubts and my insane worries out of my expression and pout-glare back at her like she and cashmere-*whatever-it-might-be* hasn't just shaken me down. "I was going to watch a movie. I'll use my headphones," I bluff.

"You better." She rolls her eyes and flops back down, still watching me like I'm some sort of bug in a jar she can't figure out.

Maybe she's all-bark-no-bite. And maybe like Vere says, I'll get used to her *funny* sense of humor; but after one month of trying hard to make this girl like me every time we interact, I suddenly decide I don't care if she does anymore.

So, for the first time since meeting Clara, I decide to do a little barking-back for myself. I pull the blanket up around my chin saying, "Don't you just *love* these cashmere blankets, Clara? Royce has these adorable pajama pants made of this stuff. I love them." I add in another lie, then sigh while I fake-smile dreamily at the ceiling. "It's so great for cuddling up to, right? I cannot wait to see him." When she doesn't answer, and rolls back over, shoving her mask back onto her face I add, "Oh…sorry. Right. You wanted to sleep. Sorry."

Clara doesn't answer again, just rolls over further, covering her face up with her blanket. It feels like a small victory, because now, I don't have to see her sneering under that mask anymore. Thankfully, she doesn't move again until we begin our descent into London.

By then, I haven't slept a wink. But I've done my research and then some.

Cashmere is a wool. Made from fancy goats—but only the neck fur of fancy goats. And even though it's a goat, people still call it a lamb, so we can also call cashmere *lambs-wool.* Yep.

I've totally got this.

13

ROYCE

We don't get back to the London Orb hotel suites until 4AM. That's because in big cities all over Europe our stage time never starts before midnight. It's the way it is here.

Dinner restaurants serve starting around nine, night clubs only really get hopping at midnight, because no one would dare go outside before 10PM. And, as my PR people assure us, a band like Guarderobe would never insult the culture and play one riff before 12:30 AM.

I've been told Robin arrived during the concert, but as I make my way into our suite and kick my shoes off, the only sign of her I can find is a pair of leather sandals with long thin straps that Robin must have left by the door.

Without thinking I pick one up and turn it over, pondering just how much smaller her foot is than mine. Pondering more how I can tell that these sandals look new, yet they're also slightly worn in this way that says she's had a whole bunch of adventures in these sandals.

Adventures that I've missed.

I smile when I pull open the entryway closet to hang up my leather jacket next to this very cute, very feminine light-blue rain coat with a long belt that also has to be hers.

Desperate to see her now, I almost sprint across the suite toward the bedroom, hoping she's still awake. As I get closer I swear I can smell a whiff of her lavender scent in the air.

I quietly open the bedroom door, and yes! She's there, but she's sound asleep.

My own breathing goes deeper, gets calmer maybe, as I tip toe to the bed, taking in her moon shaped face snuggled into one of the pillows that's so big it makes her look even punier than usual.

She's so beautiful when she sleeps, and I've honestly missed her so much—as much as I missed my mom after she died—that I almost touch her to see if she's real.

I want to hear her say that she's safe, that her brother is happy and that despite me being stuck in the middle of her life, that things have turned out exactly how she wanted.

Has she been able to relax some now that all of the paperwork has come through? And even though it's not real and our marriage is in name only, most of all I want her to wake up and ask questions about what we're going to do in London tomorrow. Because if she does, then that means she wants to hang out and that somehow she's still a little bit…mine.

Mine for a little while longer.

My wife, Robin.

I open the curtain a crack so I can see her better and have to smile because she's worn her giant hoodie to bed. She started doing that around the second time she woke up wrapped up in my arms. The first time that happened was in the hammock at our honeymoon.

The second time, was in the extra-large king sized bed *inside* of our honeymoon suite despite the pillow tower we'd made to separate us from each other.

The third time, it was also in our honeymoon suite, but that third time was when she showed up with the hoodie she's wearing now.

I'd laughed, telling her she'd be too hot, and that I didn't mind that she was a chronic cuddle-addict. She was adamant that the hoodie would act as a wall or some sort of physical boundary between us if the pillows failed. We also agreed to tell anyone who might question her odd pajama choice, that Robin was simply freezing cold all of the time, so she loved to wear hoodies to bed.

To help her out and to be fair (and in case I can't contain myself) I started wearing the provided hotel bathrobes to bed as well.

We've had no problems convincing people that our wedding was consummated, and then some. The press, of course, instantly made up lies about us that we have never refuted thanks to the nearly naked toga photos that were taken of us. In one of our 'honeymoon expose' articles, some reporter had written that I sleep in the nude and that Robin does as well!

As far as I know, underneath that hoodie, Robin could be dressed in something like chain mail. Hell, I actually hope it's true because I need all of the help I can get here. I've promised her, myself, my family, and God himself that I won't take advantage of this situation, or of her. And every time I see the hoodie, I fight a war with myself to try to forget every silken curve I know exists under that thing.

Keyword, *try*.

Second keyword, *fail*.

Despite the utter physical pain and mental torment those things I *can't* forget about Robin have caused me, tonight just like all of the others, I don't care. I'm just excited that she and I are back to sharing a room and a bed. All I want to do is hold this sweet girl in my arms, match my breathing to hers, and watch her sleep. When I left NYC and had to go to Taiwan I'd grown so used to her being there, breathing in and out near me, that I've had to resort to taking sleeping pills for the past weeks.

Back in New York there was a couch in our bedroom, so I (against my will) took the damn couch. All of that worked, because she was right there across the room, breathing away feeding my new-found addiction to her. But I'm not going to lie, I've been really looking forward the hotels we're going to have to share over these next few weeks. European spaces and hotels are different than those in the United States. They're much smaller, even in full luxury suites like this one, there's only room for one small sitting area.

In France, *the city of love, as people call* it, the bedroom is only for a bed. No one would think to place a sofa the size someone could sleep on in a bedroom in France. They have 'salons' for that. They did invent the chaise lounge, a half couch half chair thing that's often put into the hotel rooms, but that piece of furniture is way too small for sleeping.

I know this was Robin's first flight over the ocean, and all day I've been regretting what I missed not being with her on that exact plane. What did her face look like as she peered out of the window? Was she nervous? What did she eat on the plane? Drink? In the airspace on the way to Paris there is no drinking age, because it's not the USA anymore. Did she taste the Champagne they always pass out with dinner?

It's also her first trip to the UK. How wide did her eyes get as she drove in the limousine on the way to this hotel? Has she glimpsed Big Ben yet, or did they save that for me? What else has she seen, and will I have time to show her around London how I want? Based on what she's told me about how little she's traveled, I bet she's never even been on a subway before. But can I even taker on a subway without creating mayhem and chaos on the London Underground?

At least I will get to sit next to her on our flight to Paris. I also know that even more than London, *Paris* is the city Robin craves to see. It's the one with the art galleries and museums she has dreamed about for her entire life, and I seek solace in all that I've missed in her life because I know I will be the one who gets to show her the Eiffel Tower for the first time.

Smiling now, and noting how my heart has grown so light I hardly feel tired at all anymore because I'm so happy to see her, I tip-toe into the slick, hipster-minimalist bathroom that matches the rest of my suite to brush my teeth. Cool, modern and sleek is the trademark decor of the entire Orb Hotel, London. It's all grey and white marble, black furniture and shocking pink Orchids with window seats and empty book shelves. It's a pretty style, but not at all my favorite, because if you leave just one thing lying around, the entire place feels messy.

I grab my toothbrush out of the slick black marble toothbrush holder, brush my teeth, wash my face, and head into the back closet to slip on the hotel-issue silk pajama pants. Then, even though it's hot, I add the light weight cotton hotel robe we'd agreed I would wear while she's wearing the hoodie.

When I get back into the main bedroom and stare down at her again, my stomach clenches with guilt. I realize I can't just crawl into bed with her and pull her into my arms how I want.

That's because we aren't really married, heck she's not even my girlfriend officially. It's quite possible that she's like…forgotten me or heck, I don't know, that she will be scared to wake up with me clambering back in her bed with no warning. So, despite how knocked out she looks and how comfortable she looks, I need to wake her up to ask permission to do this.

"Hey," I whisper, while I crouch down next to her side of the bed and pick up a strand of her hair, leaning in so I can survey her face a little closer. I bite my lower lip and grin at how she's totally slack-mouthed and out, while I let one of the curls I've grabbed coil around my finger. Her beautiful hair has a mind of its own, and I love it so much. "Hey, Robin?" I try speaking louder. "It's me. Sorry to ask you this but…can you wake up? Can you?"

"Mfrmn." She rolls toward me and makes this funny little smile like she's dreaming. "No…the *goat's neck.* Only the neck. Wool, okay? Wool," she murmurs. "Cashmere. Mhm. That's why it's extra soft."

Smiling more now, I call out again, "Robin?" This time lightly running my hand along the edges of where her hair meets her forehead, and then I caress down the round line of her cheek until I have my forefinger twisting again into one of those longer soft blonde curls that are coming off of her ponytail.

My heart thrums with anticipation because I realize how terribly I've missed the sound of her voice but I'm completely unprepared for how my spine melts when she turns toward me. Half opens her soft, sleep heavy eyes, licks her lips and smile-mummers my own name up at me, "Royce." Then. "So good to see you. You don't have a beard anymore."

When I don't—can't—answer, she blinks herself more awake, eyes finally focusing on my face she adds, "*Hi.*"

"Hi," I echo, loving how her voice had come out all scratchy—how she's staring at my chin with a little question in her eyes. "The beard grows back in a day or less," I tell her. "We're still experimenting with my look."

"Looks nice." She reaches out and touches the edge of my chin, then pulls her finger away. "Like you're closer to my age today, instead of some jaded old man. You know?" She smiles directly up at me, while rubbing her eyes.

"I am close to your age, but still very jaded," I answer, trying to joke and I want to say more, but my reaction to her sleepy-smile has made my body betray me. I've just spiked an erection that is so painful and jarring that I have to stand quickly to gain some distance between us before the weight of it sinks me to the ground! Because if I don't, I'm going to kiss that smile off her lips and I'm not going to want to stop.

Unaware of my torment, she sits up on her elbow and my eyes involuntarily track the blonde waterfall of curls slipping out of her ponytail while she meets my eyes with more of her wide-open-blue happiness. Then she says all the wrong things, like: "Hey. Come back. Are you coming to bed? If so, *yay*. If not, what are you doing?"

At that point, I'm running from her back to the bathroom.

"Thirsty. Forgot to—brush my teeth," I lie. Then I lie some more. "And I forgot my glass of water. You want one? After you fly you should drink a lot of water," I leave the door cracked like it's not big thing me being in here holding up my shaking legs by leaning on the marble bathroom countertop.

Thankfully, she can't see me or my face from where she's lying, because when I look at my reflection and stare into my own eyes, I realize I've melted.

Heart. Body. Soul. Now, unrecognizable.

"Sure. Yes. Thanks. Water sounds great." She yawns loudly while I crank on the faucet then all but shove my head under the stream of ice cold water, working so hard to erase the sound of her voice asking: *Are you coming to bed…are you coming to bed? Yay. Yay. Yay.*

I stand at the sink, looking at myself in the mirror, wondering what she'd think if she could see my face right now. Could she read the red-hot desire behind my eyes? Will she notice how I'm having a difficult time controlling myself under this bathrobe?

Damn, me. Think about something to take your mind off of her sleepy-sexy. Think about her damn dad.

Dad. Dad. Dad.

Tightening the belt on the robe, I run the faucet and soak a washcloth into the sink then place it along the back of my neck, squeezing it some so droplets of cold water attack my spine while I call out, "I had to wake you because I didn't want to scare you by just climbing in bed with you, and, yes, I'm tired so…sorry if I seem all distracted and scattered." I'm amazed my voice came out steady, because listening to the cute sound of her yawning again has wrecked me a second time.

I can tell by the sounds she's making she's moving the bed covers around. After the honeymoon, and having had to share a few hotel room beds with her already, I'm certain she's setting up the prerequisite wall of pillows.

"I'm glad you woke me because I—um. I mean." She pauses for a long time. "Can I say that I missed you? Is that okay?" She says the last question all quiet, breathlessly—as though maybe she regrets uttering them, and my chest swells because—*did she just say she missed me?*

I want to kiss her. *If only I could…*

Unable to respond because the only thing that wants to come out of my mouth is a painful groan, I re-cool the washcloth and slap it over my whole face, wondering if she would think it strange if I brought this to bed with me.

Maybe I could fake a headache. Sleep with this thing over my whole face so I don't have to look at her or better, maybe I can figure out a way to ice it double and tie it below my waist.

"Anyhow…uh…how was the concert?" she adds, but now she's the one with the wavering voice like she feels awkward that I didn't say anything after she said she missed me.

Yep. She's regretting her words.

Quickly I clank down a glass and make sure it's really loud against the marble countertop while finally turn the faucet off. "I missed you, too, Robin. So much." I call out extra clearly, noting that it feels amazing to say it. "Sorry for the delayed response. Was flossing. Show was great. London is one of our favorites."

She's muttering something but I can't hear it while I splash cold water down my front, trying to get control of my body while lecturing myself that it's my job to pull the awkward out of this endlessly awkward situation.

I have to regroup and make her feel like this extraordinary situation, of her flying into my hotel rooms, is simply ordinary because this is going to be our new normal.

She and I got used to each other and how this marriage was supposed to work back in New York City, but how this tour portion is going to go is all uncharted territory, and aside from her being inside of it, it's not new to me, but all is foreign to her, so I'm the one who needs to step-the-hell-up.

I ditch the washcloth and fill two glasses of water, but as I turn I catch my look in the mirror, I almost laugh at myself, because my expression, arms and my back are so stiff it's like I'm the fucking Tin Man from The Wizard of Oz. One who's holding water glasses like they're a body shield.

I breathe in and drop my shoulders and arms so they look normal and seek solace in the idea that if something goes wrong I can dump both of these water glasses on myself if needed. Bending each leg a couple of times, so I stop walking like my knees don't bend, I step back out into the room, determined to make her feel comfortable.

Walking gingerly around the room I busy myself with setting each of our water glasses on our bedside tables, then I pace the room, pausing as though I want to look at the view. Then, like I'm trying to help her, I yank a couple of the square decorator pillows off the chaise by the window and walk to the bed.

When she's turned away to sip some of her water, I quickly dive under the comforter and get myself to the furthest part of *my* side of the bed. My motion has made her startle, and I feel bad watching her quickly scoot to the furthest edge away from me on *her* side.

Like it's no big deal I add my pillows to the top of her fortress and work to not stare at her sleepy-cute face, or notice her form under the sheets as I peek over the pillow-mountain.

"Like the Great Wall of China, tonight," I say, trying to joke a little, noting how her hair seems twice as bright as I remember it. That, or she's been in the sun since we've been apart from each other and it's lightened up because, yes…her cute face is completely tanned now. Which has me wondering if her body is also…

I pull back, screaming at myself inside my head: *No. No. Don't think about her body.*

"I heard you got to see the Great Wall." She pats a pillow proudly on her side, popping up so she can see my face this time, adding, "Was it cool?"

Boom. And it's back. Full throttle. Someone help me.

"Big." Is all I can say and damn-me, but I am talking about my own boner not the Great Wall of China.

I can't stop my eyes going to her sweet face. I'd forgotten how fresh she always looks—how the roses in her cheeks never fade—how the bow-shaped curve of her upper lip drives me wild. How, when she bites that lower lip my entire body-and-soul overreact.

"So tell me, why?"

"Why what?" I croak out, panicking. *Can she read my mind? Does she want me to answer why my lower body is cracking off, or why her upper lip drives me wild, or why that freshly chewed lower lip will make it so I can't walk or move for the next hour at least?*

"When you were in the bathroom I asked, *why* is London a favorite of yours?" She moves a couple of pillows away so we can see each other's faces better, then leans back against her pillows that are backed by the headboard, stretches her arms up high, nestles one forearm under the back of her head, regarding me calmly like she's not even nervous around me, like she can't tell I'm about to jump out of my skin.

"Oh." I blink. Forcing myself to settle back into my own pillow. "We love London because everyone speaks English and so when they sing the hit songs, they really go for it. Nothing feels better or fills my soul than when words we wrote come back to me on thousands of voices. Besides, people in the UK make everything sound better when they talk and sing with that accent. Makes us feel like our songs are twenty percent more classy or something." Quickly, before she can ask me more questions, I fake-yawn as big as she's real-yawning. Then I do it again.

I know that despite how tired I might be, until my heart and every drop of blood in my body calms down, and until she stops glancing over at me and smiling at me like she's—damn her lips—there's no way in hell I'll be able to sleep. "Do you think *you* can go back to sleep?" I croak out, adding in a bit of a cranky-note to my voice, scooting down so I can't see her very well anymore. "Because I'm so tired."

"Yes. Sorry," she says, words tangled into a yawn, misunderstanding me just how I want her to. "We can talk tomorrow because I probably won't remember any of this anyhow."

"Me either," I lie, pleased that she's not offended, how she really should be by how I'm acting all grumpy. I suddenly want to pull her into my arms and to tell her the truth. Tell her so many things I shouldn't—about how cool and beautiful she is, about how my heart feels different ever since she married me. About how each day, it's constantly full and endlessly beating just a little too hard. And I want to tell her I've never been so happy—and that I'm triple-happy now that she's here with me again.

But…of course I don't say any of that shit. Because who says that kind of shit?

"Night." She mummers. "Or…morning, or whatever time it is…"

"Night," I answer, listening for her to drift off. It doesn't take her long.

Moving slowly, I click out the light and turn a little, examining what I can see of her face in the dark, then I frown at her mostly untouched water glass, worrying that she's going to be dehydrated from traveling.

The London traffic sounds grow quiet as fewer and fewer cars pass along the road far below us. I let myself be lulled to relaxation by matching my breathing to hers. I already know that as she dreams, she rolls towards me and like clockwork, it's already happening.

As she gets closer, and though I know it's wrong, I move three of the highest pillows and place them out of the way, then I bump a couple off with an elbow, while I grab the rest and toss the remainder on the floor.

After thirty more minutes, she's rolled close enough for me to make my move. Knowing from memory just how she's going to fit in next to me, I scoot up slightly and pull her close so that the next time she rolls she'll be facing me. And when she is, I pull her up and in, then settle my arms in around her as her head finds the same spot against my heart that it always finds. One arm goes up by her face, the other nestles around my waist like it belongs there.

I pull in the first deep breath I've taken since I left her, and turn a little more so I can plant a light kiss on top of her head then nestle my chin next to the softness of her curls just how I love.

Her scent envelops me and thankfully, I'm so exhausted that the desire for her fades into something controllable and comfortable. Just before I nod off, I feel one of her arms curl across my chest then her hand twines up to lie against the side of my neck.

I'm not sure if it's a dream, my voice, or Robin's voice that whispers: "I really missed this."

14

ROBIN

WHEN I WAKE UP AGAIN, it's to the sound of an ambulance's siren.

Only, as I register it, I get that it's not the long, wailing-jarring ambulance sounds I'm used to hearing. It's a sound I've only heard on TV. This ambulance is all kinds of UK adorable with its *wee-woo wee-woo* sounds.

Because I'm in London. Heck, yes, London England. Oh, my-yay.

I crack open my eyes, trying not to move one inch, because I'm warm and comfortable and there's a living breathing beautiful guy underneath my body.

My thoughts spin sleepily: *I'm in London, and Royce has me wrapped up in his arms while he's sound asleep just how we slept every night together since we've been married. Things haven't changed. A second, yay!*

As usual, I'm embarrassed that once again, my pillow tower didn't work. That's because I'm the one who tosses and turns too much. I'm also the one that winds up curled up onto Royce's chest, no matter how I try not to do this.

But, fine I'm also going to admit that I love how—how *he* and his *skin* and his *heartbeats* feel amazing when he's relaxed like this.

When he's so close to me.

As I wake up more, I process every breath he takes and try not to be dumbfounded that this exact morning, this kind of morning with a sleeping Royce Devlin pressed into my body while sheltering me in his arms, has become my temporary reality.

More insane is the realization that I am in a sophisticated city that I know very little about. I'm residing on a street I was delivered to by limo, and led inside a building that I wouldn't recognize if I went outside this morning. Honestly. If I walked to the corner and turned myself around three times, this is a place I couldn't find again without asking someone!

I'm all but lost—a total fish out of water. Yet, here in the circle of Royce's carefully placed arms, while I'm breathing his same breaths in and out…in and out…I feel completely found. For the first time in my life I feel like I belong somewhere, and that somewhere, though transient and impermanent, it is the best place I've ever been.

For the first time since my dad went missing and for the first time since I married Royce, I feel completely and utterly safe. And even though I should have wicked-bad jet lag beyond this small headache, I think I just slept more soundly than I have in months. Instead of feeling fear or strange, I just feel this sense of trust, happiness and wonder. And…I'm so thankful that Royce Devlin has turned out to be such a great friend.

Knowing I can't lie here forever, and also knowing it would be really awkward if he woke up right now, because he might wake up and comment on *who rolled toward who?* (Because I'm the one who's all the way on his side of the bed while he hasn't budged very far from his original spot from last night.) I slowly scoot out of his arms, and slide off the bed, making a fast break for the bathroom and my toothbrush, because if this is going to be awkward, I may as well have fresh breath.

As the door clicks behind me, I hear him groan. Then he groans again.

Like I woke him up? Like maybe he wasn't nearly as comfortable as I was, but that he was letting me sleep all while I was paralyzing his neck and back?

"I'm sorry." I call out, through the door. "I didn't know I was hurting you."

"I'm the one who is sorry. Truly because…" I lean on the door, but I can't hear how he's finished that sentence, because it seems as though he's suddenly talking into a pillow.

I glance at my phone, reading a text from Sage that says he's fine and well, and after I send my reply that he's going to love the UK when he gets here, I call out again. "It's way after noon. I wonder why no one woke us up."

He chuckles. "We're newlyweds. Catching up on the *love.* Remember?"

"Oh. Right. That's us. Always. Like rabbits." I laugh through brushing my teeth.

Like he can tell I almost choked on those words, he chuckles. When I turn the water off I can hear that he's now out of bed and moving around the room doing something.

He pauses at the door, saying, "I gave death threats to my staff last night. My uncle is also protecting *our love*. Sadly, our peace is down to a couple more hours. Gregory's just texted to say a crowd has formed outside the hotel. Now that you're here we need to make a quick public photo appearance. Then we've apparently agreed to some sort of small press event. Usually after those, we exit the premises with a huge obvious show that we won't be back for a long time."

I'm splashing water on my face wetting down some of my curls while running my fingers though my hair. "Why?"

"That's so the crowd can dissipate. We have to do it all the time. Usually we can go around the block a few times, swap into different cars, and sneak back in via the basement parking garages or well-placed fire doors. That or…we can look at your London bucket list and actually go do something. Vere told me it's really long."

I click open the door, and walk back out, and sitting on the chaise by the window, curling my legs up into my huge hoodie. "All my stuff is kind of cliché. Maybe you'll think it's lame?"

"Robin." His voice goes all low like I've hurt his feelings. "You know I won't. Tell me your exact list and we will try our best. Are you up for it? We can start with breakfast. Any goals there?"

I blink. "Uh. Okay. I'll start with food. I know scones come from here. Wait. What about that famous beans on toast stuff? I heard about that in the movie Bend it Like Beckham. Do you know it? Soccer? Romance? Best movie ever?"

He shakes his head and I flush, because of course cool-guy, Royce Devlin doesn't know random romance movies that only people with no lives like me, have seen. He, for years, has had an actual life.

"Well," I shrug, recovering while trying to act all cool. "Is there a fresh-scones and beans-on-toast restaurant we could search out?"

He laughs. "I'm not an expert, but I'm pretty sure those are both snacks that happen after lunch, during what the Brits call tea time. Let me Google." He drags out his phone. "It says the most cliché breakfast here in London is poached eggs, sourdough toast and avocado—served up with different cheeses and toppings."

"What has the different toppings? The toast, the eggs or the avocado?"

He scrolls through the phone. "No clue. But people won't judge us if we do it wrong, simply because we'll be eating it in here with room service."

I laugh. "Perfect. As long as I get to try the other stuff later, though." I pull out my own phone, firing off another text to Sage then take a photo that reflects the cool old buildings across the street and send it to him as well, reading what I'm typing out loud so Royce can be included: "Sage. Look at the street below the Orb London. You're going to love it here."

He replies: "Cant' wait. Mrs. Felix says hi. Please say hi to Royce.

"My brother says hi and so does your grandmother." I show him my phone.

"Say, 'hi' back to the kid." He grins, waiting for me to send my reply. "Are you trying to distract me from your actual bucket list? Come on, Robin, aside from food, why are you being shy about what you want to see?"

"I—I don't know what to put on that list Royce. I never thought I'd come to London, and I didn't have much time to research things. I only know I want to see a castle. Any castle. Maybe one with a moat or a maze, and a dungeon maybe? And I want to ride in a black cab, and take a ride on the London Tube and take a photo of how that looks, because I've never been in a subway before."

"I'd already guessed that." He blinks at me, flopping down on the bed and rolling to his side, grinning.

I don't grin back, only raise one brow in question. "Why? because you assumed your wife is a total small-town hick? Ouch."

"Hardly, Robin." His grin is wiped away and his tone turns serious. "Just because you haven't travelled much doesn't make you a hick. And what does that word mean anyhow?" He's Googling it while speaking. "It says here hicks are referred to people born on hog farms. Is that you? No. It is not."

I shrug, calling him out, "I know you well enough to know you're only reading the one part of that definition that doesn't apply to me. The hick. If that's all it says show me your phone."

He colors slightly and turns off his phone fast. "This definition doesn't apply to you. It even says hicks are seen as rude and you've never been that. You're simply…you know, under travelled."

I roll my eyes laughing. "Okay. Whatever. I'm just saying, I might be too… *under-travelled* to make proper bucket lists."

"Well you had a top three list, what is number four?"

"Well. Fourth is a photo in a red phone booth. And, oh…I want to see Trafalgar Square, and that pretty gold Victoria Statue, and it would be cool to see the National Galleries." I blink up at him. "Oh, and cobblestones, I want to run around on some cobblestones, and see some dark narrow streets full of fog and pubs, so I can get my Sherlock, Dr. Who, dark streets of London history shivers going."

He laughs out loud. "Now you're talking."

Encouraged by his bright smile, I go on, "Oh, and we must eat fish and chips of course."

"Of course. With malt vinegar, hopefully from a food stand in a market or a small pub."

"Oh, and I heard there's this soft serve ice cream cone everyone gets called the *ninety-nine.* I always see photographs of it on Instagram. It's one that's got a chocolate Cadbury stick shoved into it—a 'flake' it's called. Honestly, if we have to minimize I'd be fine with only doing cobble stones and the ice cream, and that we can bring into the hotel. Okay? Have you heard of this ice-cream awesomeness?"

"No. Never, but from the look on your face, I now want one very much."

"Well, maybe…like us…maybe it's not real. Like maybe it's all lies someone made up and posted on the Internet for the world to believe?"

He frowns and his face darkens with what looks like hurt surprise, then his gaze grows so shuttered that I wish to my core that I hadn't joked about that. Us. Quickly I add, "I am also good just hanging here at the hotel with you. Or like…you can go do other things, without me. You don't need to entertain me or be by my side because I'm self-sufficient. When Sage gets here in a few days, I'll have one full day to do all of this stuff with him." I shrug. "So…it's whatever you want."

"Robin. Honestly? My goals are to…simply, be with you. To show you London and to make you smile this week, because it's fun for me to see the world through your fresh-seeing eyes. This list is great, I'm only frowning because I'm afraid I can't show you some of these things without causing riots. I need to come up with plans and creative methods of how do it all so you won't get mobbed."

"Which is why I say we *don't* have to do them. The ideas are too touristy. I know. That's why I left off the Tower of London and like… that London Eye and Big Ben which both were really on the top of the list, but I already know they're impossible. Let's just go for the little stuff."

"No. We've got this. It's your first time to London so we are going to do some cool things. Just…give me time to make the plans."

15

ROBIN

While Royce and I are finishing up the room service breakfast he'd ordered in, consisting of the promised poached eggs and ham, the incessant knocking I now associate with the stylists, has begun shaking our door.

"Damn." He stands up, rolling his eyes toward the knocking. "Would you mind if I grabbed all of the shit they're going to want us to wear, and tell them we can do it ourselves today? I don't want to share you just yet."

"Um." I blink, tamping down butterflies because of what he's just said…*because, aww. So sweet.* "We're allowed to do that? Dress ourselves?" I ask.

He pulls in a breath, shaking his head like I've surprised him. "Robin. We are allowed to do whatever we want."

"We are?"

"These people work for us, *you* included. They're not jailers. Watch and learn how it's done." He crooks his finger at me and I pad along behind him in bare feet to hear what he's going to say when he opens to door.

"Well good morning, Clara." He wedges his body into the four inch crack he's made in the opening so she can't see behind him or me at all. "Where's the rest of the crew?"

Her voice pipes in from the other side of the door. "Oh. I told them I could handle this by myself. It's only two outfits, after all. But you,

Royce? You could totally get away with just going down to the lobby in that robe it looks so good with your skin tones and all." Clara suddenly sounds sort of breathless.

I can only imagine she's fluttering her lashes and flipping her hair how she does.

"Well that's nice of you to say, Clara." His voice is polite, friendly, but also clearly distant. "Robin and I also thought we could handle getting dressed by ourselves. The part where she is still *undressed* is why I can relieve you of everything right here. Thanks for bringing it all up, though. Can't wait to see what we've got."

"What. What do you mean?" Clara's voice swaps into panic. "What if you do it wrong and I get in trouble. You should let me come in and help."

"It's only a morning press conference. Not a red carpet event." Royce rolls his eyes again, making me smile.

"Yes. But..." Clara's all but stuttering now. "It's the first time you've been seen together in weeks. This is really important that it goes off well and that Robin doesn't screw it up again or look...like a hot mess..."

I see Royce's back go stiff and whatever expression he's holding on his face makes Clara change her words to, "I mean, I just want you *both* to look your best."

"Well, again that's very nice, but I'm sure you can respect how my *wife* and I want to be alone as much as possible this morning. It's been too long since we've seen each other, and I'm feeling really stingy with every second of her free time. It will all be fine. If we can't figure it out, maybe we can take your suggestion and we'll both head down in our robes because her skin tones are *way* better than mine."

"P-please don't do that," she adds. "I'd get in trouble."

Royce's voice grows taut, slightly harsh and very firm. "See you down there in about a half hour in whatever we choose to wear. And thanks again."

With that, he starts backing up, dragging in a small cart hung with hangers with a few boxes stacked below. Just before he shuts the door I peek around and lock glances with Clara who's standing there with her mouth hanging open.

When she sees me she closes her mouth fast. Her eyes scour over my loosely tied robe just like the one Royce is wearing, and then go over my hair and how it's flowing down all over the place in its usual, curling-damp, post-shower mess. "Hi Clara," I call out, with a small wave, trying not to act too smug, but it's really hard considering she was flirting with my—sort of—husband. "Thanks for bringing the stuff up," I echo, acting like it's totally normal for people to deliver outfits to me like this.

Clara nods, but she's flushing bright red—not with embarrassment but with unmasked jealous-fury. She spins away, calling out in a light voice that did not match her expression, "There's a hair brush and some special make up for you, Robin. Try to use everything correctly."

Thankfully, the heavy door has closed all on its own, so I don't have to answer her.

"Wow." I sigh eyeing the cart. "Does she flirt with you like that every day?"

"Unfortunately, she does. Does she insult you like that, every day?"

I shrug but don't answer that, because I don't want to make waves. Royce, being Royce—mistakes my silence for me being mad that Clara was flirting with him. "Look," he starts, going all serious. "I only tolerate Clara more than others, because I've known her a long time. It's because of how her mom has worked for the band for years. So many girls do that flirty-shit, though. They think, because of my job, they should just openly hit on me, or show me cleavage or do something creepy-random like complimenting my skin tones, how Clara just did, instead of just having a normal conversation. I never just hear the words, 'nice day, huh'?" He laughs. "So messed up. Skin tone. *Please.*"

I laugh a little. "I honestly don't mind what Clara does. She's annoying, that's all. And…not that I want to take Clara's side on this one thing, but…" I eye him up and down. "Speaking as an artist and a friend here, you do have pretty awesome skin tones. Rare even. I can hardly blame her for the comment. She's dead on correct in her observations."

"What? No. Don't even start." His brows shoot up.

"Yes. You're made up of mostly olive skin tones, but with this very clear beige-taupe overlay. That's what really features how it's possible you were born with no pores whatsoever. It is quite the 'wow' effect." I breathe in, holding up a finger as he's opening his mouth to protest again. "*And* when you're suntanned I've seen real hues of salmon glinting through here and there. Also very cool." I shrug. "The white robe does bring it all out."

His brows go up more as he stalks over to stand next to me by the cart and starts peeking in boxes and unzipping the clothing bags while chuckling. "Did you say *Salmon*? Please."

"Yes. One of the many varied colors of pink coming from the primary color red. You also have a whole bunch of coral. Oh, and when you're all flustered you don't go bright red like I do, because I have zero olive tones, in case you didn't notice. You have so much olive that you go sort of crepe colored."

"Crepe?" He sounds twice as doubtful as before.

"Oh yes. Crepe and more." I say. "I won't bore you though, because I could literally talk about the color palette that makes up *you*, Royce Devlin, all day long. Your eyes—straight up silver is hiding in those, and the inky-hair?" I point at his rumpled mop. "That's hiding some major magenta and navy."

He finally cracks up and holds his hands up high, turning to face me. "Okay…well…stop for now, would you? Clara's comments were annoying, but with you saying this? I—I'm feeling all kinds of flattered. Hell, I might even feel touched that you've spent time studying this. I feel like…" He tears his gaze off of me and returns to unzipping the second clothing bag. "I think it's making me stuck up… or…something."

"You're married to a huge color nerd. And textures. You might as well know this about me. I might drive you insane with this stuff," I add, eyeing how his chin, baby smooth last night, now has this soft-scratch stubble covering.

He pauses to survey the rack again. "This one is yours," he says, motioning to what looks like a strange red mini skirt paired with a white blouse, but he's not looking where he's pointed. His eyes are back to going over my face like he's admiring me, or rather, admiring who's inside of me. And I mean he's seeing that nearly OCD artist-girl whom I try hard to hide from everyone.

When my answer to him is only a shrug, he says quietly, "You're a very cool, very smart person, you know that, Robin Love? And way out of my league, if you must know." He falters, laughing a little. "Shit. I meant to call you, Robin Devlin." With a fast head shake and a very flustered expression, he adds, "Damn-me, but that made me realize just how much I really miss your last name."

"So do I," I've whispered, wishing I'd held silent, because my reply has my chest lurching down too fast, because he's made me remember my whole past life.

Only from where he and I both stand, we both know it's a past life that feels completely erased all of a sudden.

I work to joke over how I'm faltering inside by adding, "If we took my last name instead of yours the world would be calling you, "Royce Love."

I shake my head and I mimic one of Mrs. Felix's disapproving faces, as I try to add in her voice as well, "*And that name, young man. With your skin tones plus the extrovert job you already have...would just make you seem very obnoxious.*" I drop the Mrs. Felix voice, laughing along with Royce. "Right?"

"Totally obnoxious." He agrees, picking up his whole outfit and holding it high so we can both eye a pair of dark jeans plus a soft grey, summer weight suit jacket. "This is kind of nice. I'll change in the bathroom. Shout out when you're decent and I'll come back out. No hurry, I'm going to figure out how to get to your bucket list while I'm in there."

16

ROBIN

TWENTY MINUTES later Royce and I are all set.

I'm squeezed into the red skirt that is one size too small and three shades too shiny. If *shiny* can have shades, that is.

I'm wearing the skirt with the waist belt undone, and I've fixed it so no one will see. That's because the white shirt is like four or five sizes too big.

I've solved all of the problems by taking the tight, white, laced trimmed undershirt I wore on the plane yesterday, and made the too-big shirt into what I hope looks like a 'boyfriend' shirt. I've kept it mostly unbuttoned down the front, yet have left the bottom closed in just the right spot to hide the open button. It also hides most of the horrible skirt. Bonus!

I'd added only one necklace instead of the four I was supposed to wear all at once, then picked one bracelet and ignored all but one of these ten-or-so, odd, fabric friendship bracelets Clara was going to have me wear.

I also didn't go for the giant dangling earrings she'd sent along, because they sort of looked like Mercedes Benz hood ornaments. Because of that, I'm going without earrings.

I've managed to find the brush Clare mentioned and use it, as well as, I've applied some of the makeup.

Based on the way Royce stared too long when he came out of the bathroom, then stalked away kind of fast after I asked him, *how I looked*, while muttering, "Absolutely perfect," I *think* I did okay, but it's hard to know for sure if Royce isn't just being nice about how I look, like he always is.

When he comes back out of the bathroom again, saying something about how he'd forgotten to brush his teeth, I've just squeezed into the heels sent up to match the outfit—the three inch hooker stilettos, that I think have already made my toes bleed.

"Ready?" He asks, eyeing the shoes.

"Yep." I answer, lying because I know the clothing cart is the only thing keeping me upright and I'm not ready, or capable of walking in heels like these, but I don't want him to know it. "Totally ready," I add, starting to pray to God for some assistance.

He glances at the door then back at me, but doesn't move an inch in any direction.

"What's wrong?" I ask, deciding that if he doesn't move, I don't move.

"I don't want to go out there. I feel like if we do, this cool time we've had hiding out up here will not be recreated. Which is why I've been thinking…about your bucket list, about tons of things actually."

Happy for the excuse that is keeping me from shaming myself in these shoes, I ask, "Okay…and what have you been thinking?"

"That we should pull an Adam-move."

"An Adam-move?"

"We should run away for a couple of days. Together." His silver-blue eyes have started twinkling.

"What? How? Why?"

He moves to sit on the edge of the bed, facing me. "There's no way I can show you the stuff on that list I want to show you, if you and I don't do it while hiding out. I thought we could get disguises and do it, and then I thought we could try to run away and see some of it fast, waiting for the fans to catch up to us and force us to go back to the hotel, but then I thought let's do all three. Let's go all out and really hide and really see some stuff together. Just for a couple of days, what do you say? Could we? At least could we… try to do what Adam did so many times?"

I shake my head once, and then when I realize he's sincere, I grin and answer, "I'm up for trying it. Sure."

He frowns, cocking his head to the side. "The face you're making tells me you think I'm insane. It's a good idea. We have this whole week off to explore, and I don't want to do it with the whole world staring at us like we're under a microscope. Today made me realize I hardly know the real you at all, but that I like what I'm getting to know."

My heart flutters up to my throat as a flood of embarrassment mixed with pleasure has me answering quietly, "Well…back at you, and…thanks."

He grins, eyes tracking my flushed cheeks. "Today also made me realize I want to get to know you for real—but like not just in stops and starts how we're forced to interact. I want to have a few days *away* with you. With us. Being…us." He pauses, looking over at me with doubt crossing his features. "If you want to, I mean. Do you? Would you want to…know me better, too? Without all of the entourage, and fame, and fans, and running from thing to thing going on? Without all of the… noise that's always around us? We could be just two normal friends, hanging out being regular tourists."

Goosebumps of excitement start trickling down my spine "Yes. I think that would be really cool. I've got such experience at being a nobody. I could show you how to do it well. I'm also good at running away, if you didn't notice how we met," I add in, joking.

I smile when he laughs, his expression happy, elated even. And… this makes me wonder.

Is he relieved that I said, 'yes' to this idea? Does he really want to have days alone with me?

Quickly, before the silence hanging between us stretches to awkward instead of awesome, I add in a smile. "Running away could help the whole fake-relationship. We would have a couple of days to just…be real with each other and solidify our…close…close…uh…" I flick him a glance, but he's looking away from me, as I finish with, "*friendship*." I nod, but still, he won't look up. "Considering I think that's the direction we're both going here, right?"

"Yes. Right." He pulls out his phone. "Going to text Adam to call me so I can ask his advice. That guy hid out with Evie for nearly a year. He will be able to tell me how to hide for a couple of days, right?"

I blink. "Adam's not here in the hotel?"

"Oh. No. He left with Evie and the baby right after the concert last night. They were driven to her parent's place in Wales. It's about a six hour drive from here. They're spending the week off making the baby's grandparents happy, but they'll meet us in Paris."

"Ah." I nod, watching his fingers zoom over his screen as he fires off a string of texts.

When there's no immediate response from Adam, he pockets his phone and grins. "He'll get back to me. In the meantime. Let's quickly pack some stuff."

"Pack?" I frown, nearly toppling off the clothes rack with my surprise. "You mean run away *now*? Today? As in…after the press conference?"

"Yes." He grabs his messenger bag and dumps out a load of books and his computer, shoving that into the safe, pausing to give me an impish smile. "Hell yes. You down? This has to be easier than doing a whole wedding in one night, right?"

His grin is so contagious, I have to grin back. "Why not?" When he's not looking, I save face and manage to teeter over to the spot he'd just vacated on the bed and kick off the stupid stilettos so I can dash around packing my stuff without wearing them. "Hmm." I mutter, glancing around the room. "I don't have a lot of options for alternative outfits, because I haven't sent for my luggage yet, but I have leggings and my grey pajama hoodie." I hold it up.

He snorts, giving the hoodie a look I can't quite read. "Bring that thing for sure. It's necessary, right?" He clears his throat. "Because the UK can be cold."

"Very." I laugh at his odd expression, grabbing up the shirt I'd worn on the airplane yesterday along with my black leggings.

"Let's just take the basics, and then we will try to stop and buy some clothes along the way, okay? Adam will, again, tell me how to do that." Royce dashes to the bathroom then comes back saying, "I've got your toothbrush and little make-up bag thing in here." He slings it onto his shoulder, then checks how it looks in the mirror. "Does this seem too over-stuffed?"

"Looks fine. What about my designer mega-purse? Too obviously over loaded?" I hold up this horrible, giant, rectangular, hell-purse that Clara had sent up. Red to match the outfit. Bad red, plus shiny, times two. I had meant to leave it hanging on the cart with a big 'no thanks' note attached to it, but like Royce has done with his bag, I've now slung it on my shoulder. I'm standing at the mirror with him, squishing down the sides of it.

"That purse is…wild." He gives it a look like he's as afraid of it as I am. "It's a wonder."

"Yes it is. We will need to ditch it as soon as possible," I laugh, cracking open the top, checking to make sure the hoodie is tucked in, and hasn't shifted. That hoodie is hiding Royce's plain canvas VANS *and* my flat sandals, as well as a wrapped up change of underwear for both of us.

His and mine. Shoes and underwear. Blush.

"These bags all for the 'just in case' scenarios. Because honestly, depending on how the crowds act downstairs, and depending on who spots us as we try to make our escape, we could be back here in two hours." He runs a hand through his hair, grinning even wider, "But maybe not, right?"

His phone starts buzzing in his pocket and his eyes go more gleaming bright as he lifts it out and gives it a look. "Adam. He's got tips for us."

He moves in close so I can read along with him: *First. You need to change or hide your hair drastically. And do it within minutes of the press appearance for it to work, because people will post live what you are wearing top to bottom. I've shaved my head, I've dyed my hair, I've put on ski caps, hats. Whatever. Robin's hair is going to be the most difficult to hide.*

"I'll go from hair down like it is now, and swap it up high, into a bun or something. Do you think he means I should change the color?"

"Over my dead body. I love your hair color. Not allowed."

"Okay. Okay. Fine. Maybe that's too extreme."

"We will both get hats, or…something…" he's saying as I nod, heading back into the bathroom to grab some hair ties and the brush.

When I get back, I see that Royce has pulled a beanie out of his closet. "Just in case we can't find anything else?"

We shove it, and the hair ties and brush into my purse just under the hoodie, as well as Royce's phone dings again.

Grinning, Royce reads it out loud. "Second: I'm sure you thought to bring sunglasses. Remember you need any little thing like that as you go from point A to point B. And then at point B, do a full costume change en-route or the final destination—point C. That's how I did it. A. B. C. Run, get to a staging spot, change more as needed, then have extra outfits in case you have to change again. Got me?"

Royce frowns handing me his sunglasses to put in the purse next to the ones I've just fished out of my carry on backpack from yesterday. "Maybe we won't be so good at this." Royce frowns more, swallowing hard. "I forgot the easiest most obvious thing to bring along. Sunglasses are textbook. Level one kind of shit, and I forgot them. Is this a bad idea?" His eyes have lost their silver-sparkle and are now leaden with worry. "It could be dangerous."

"We're fine. It's a great idea. What else does he say?" I ask, smiling at how his face is so very cute when he's worried like this.

Royce comes close again so we can both read the next texts together: *Third: Tell me and only me exactly where you are going should you need someone to create an exit plan. You need one safe person to know. Besides, I'll cover for you. Hell, how about once they realize you've disappeared, we can hatch a story that you came to see me in Wales. That will buy you a day. Then, if someone catches on, I'll tell them you never arrived in Wales. That should spin people all over the place in opposite directions for at least one more day. As long as the fans don't spot you, you'll be golden.*

Quickly Royce texts back: *Thanks dude. Will do. I'm formulating my final destination—C plan as you call it—right now."* I shoot him a questioning glance while he finishes texting Adam with: *Will keep you updated. In the meantime, prepare for my grandmother to call you wondering if you know where we went.*

We read Adam's reply: *Awesome. Be careful. It's not as easy as I made it look when I did it.*

Royce answers, giving me a wink: *Dude. You never make anything look easy.*

Adam's answer to that insult? *Whatever. Good thing you're already married. But…don't you two come home with a baby like we did. Or else.*

Royce laughs. Then he types: *F-you. ;)*

ROYCE's last words to me before we left the room for the publicity appearance were, "Follow my lead and whatever happens, you just play along, okay? I'm trying to surprise you with what I have planned, but I also want you to be safe and to feel comfortable." He'd grabbed my hand and looked into my eyes. "If you find this stressful instead of fun, you can abort the running away at any time, okay?"

He'd surveyed me top to bottom, then as he watched me put the stupid stilettos, he'd added in a low whistle, "Damn. That red skirt is short, isn't it? You look amazing in it, but…holy shit I think this is the first time you actually don't look eighteen anymore."

"Credit to Clara's styling expertise," I say, leaving off the part where I want to tell him how much I hate the skirt as much as the heels.

I also want to condemn this purse as absolute 'garbage' because I saw it came with a $5,000 price tag inside of it, but because it's become our escape bag, I kind of love it now. Because we're in a hurry and because it doesn't really matter what they make me wear, I say what I think needs to be said, "Clara and her mom know what's in fashion. And clearly, I don't because I'd never wear any of this." I shrug. "I only want to look like you and I somehow…match. Like a rockstar wife should look, or whatever. I'm glad you approve of the look though because it really helps to know you like what I have on, because these press things freak me out, you know?"

"I never said I liked the outfit." Royce pulls a face. "I thought you had directed them. Told them what you did like because that's what me and the guys do." I shrug, tugging at the skirt and staring at the tips of the shoes. "Robin. I don't want you wearing what you don't like. You're so beautiful and you have your own kind of 'cool style'. You could stand next to me in a cardboard box and look like you matched me."

I shrug, still looking away. "Well. Beyond jeans, shorts and hoodies I don't know what I like in the world of Haute Couture that you all wear, so…maybe what they give me is not what I would choose but it's cool. Like…I don't mind."

He frowns. "Shit. I guess I take all of this for granted, don't I?"

I nod. "Look. I don't know how to choose the clothes that belong in your world." I motion to the outfit. "This buys me some time while I learn despite how whack-ugly this skirt and purse seem to be, maybe they're straight off the runway, right?"

"Probably." Royce laughs. "But if it's not cool with you I can call Clara and ask for her to send something different?"

"Please don't call her back up here." He laughs as I roll my eyes, tugging at the skirt again, adding, "I won't wear this for very long. You say we're changing straight away, right? So I'm good."

He nods, scanning my face doubtfully, while reaching out to grab a long lock of my hair, running his finger down the length of it until it pauses at the hair's tips and we both watch as it curls around his finger. "If it's okay, I'm going to at least beg a change of shoes for you. Those don't look good for running away. I also noticed you can't walk in them."

"They're really tight," I lie, not admitting that I'm not able to handle myself in heels. "I have the sandals in my bag already, and one pair of black VANS I brought on the flight yesterday. They've got a white stripe and they might match this look just fine."

"Hell yes. Do it. I think you'll need the VANS for what I have planned, anyhow."

"What do you have planned?" I try to distract him but he reaches out to offer a steadying arm while I kick the shoes off, frowning again at how red and pinched my toes were in those shoes.

When the VANS are on, his smile is approving. "Okay. Now I feel like you're half safe—like you could at least run if you needed to. But I'm still worried. You don't know how bad it can be out there." He jerks a thumb at the window. "Stalkers, fans, crowds, cameras pointed at you, dangerous mobs chasing you in the street."

"Come on. It's only *people*, after all. Worst case, if we're spotted, we'll stop, you sign autographs, and we will both make some new friends. Come on now. Try not to worry so much."

He'd laughed and escorted me out into the hallway, saying. "That, little wife, is an impossible request."

———

SOMEHOW, while I was packing and changing shoes, Royce had convinced Hunter and Vere to come down and meet us at the press event. Their job was to add some distractions so the eyes wouldn't all be trained only on me and Royce.

While I was being interviewed, Vere was right there with me, and Royce had stepped away to tell the entourage that the four of us had planned to circle around London on a 'driving tour' after the press event.

Then when it was Royce's turn to be interviewed, Hunter was with him. They'd told everyone in the room *exactly* what we were going to do and see today. As in, Royce told everyone with a smile we were going to *maybe* go see the Tower of London together. That, or possibly catch a musical.

I'd smiled happily and agreed while he'd said that, as did Vere and Hunter. It was easy for me to tell that he was lying, but the press bought into all of it.

As the press conference ended, and the four of us entered the limo, Royce paused to whisper something to Hunter and then to Vere.

Whatever he'd said had made Vere color bright red and throw me a huge smile. She gave me one fast thumbs up while we buckled in, which told me that he'd informed them about how we'd planned to run.

So much for telling only *one* safe person. Royce now had informed *three* safe people, Hunter, Vere and Adam. But I figure that's okay, considering they're all safer than safe.

Hunter, who was frowning and acting more worried than Royce usually did, shook his head then reached into his pocket, quickly pulling out his wallet and passing Royce a huge wad of cash. Then he leaned over to whisper something to Vere who then opened her purse and handed over every bit of cash she was also carrying.

Royce pocketed it with a only a nod, then pulled out his phone, scooting over to me so we could both read Adam's latest text: *Do not use any sort of credit cards. Cash only.*

"Ahh," I say, nodding with understanding. "Very good idea."

Royce snorts. "My second fail after sunglasses." He shakes his head at me. "This is stuff I should know like breathing."

Royce glances up as the driver enters the limo but thankfully the guy has his eyes only on pulling out of the hotel parking area.

Royce tosses me a little excited look as he activates the car-intercom system once we're safely on to a street. "Sir, excuse me, they told you we were touring around, yes?

"Yes, sir. They did. Whot-do-ye-ken viewing first?"

My brows shoot up and I grin ear to ear, squeaking out, "Scottish. A *real* Scottish accent."

This makes Vere crack up and I see the driver smiling at me through the mirror as Royce answers all cool and collected, "Could you drive us past the big flea market place? We'd love to see what that looks like."

"Sir, there's more-than-the-one. For touring, most of ye-Yanks go to Greenwich Market. Tis-a World Heritage spot. Verra-pretty."

My eyes grow wide and I nearly die smiling at how he's drawled out the r's in the word heritage, but then nearly gobbled up the last syllable of that word and the word 'very' into his throat. I shove my hand over my grin so I don't shout out more about how cute I find his accent again.

"Greenwich Market, it is, then." Royce turns off the intercom and leans back, acting all calm. Vere, Hunter and I follow suit, but because I have tourist-issues I shout out and point: "Red phone booth! Holy cow.

Black cab! Anyone see the Prince of Wales, or the Queen, you let me know."

They all laugh at me again, and Royce gives me this look I can't decipher, but it's warm and makes my belly churn because his eyes seem to be alight with laughter or admiration…or something, but I get that he's trying to hold back.

Hunter, after a long moment finally whispers, "Dude, are you sure this is a good idea? I mean, really. The flea market might not be the best launching point. Maybe Vere and I could come along with you? Just in case you need back up?"

'You'd draw too much attention." Royce shakes his head. "I want you to stay in the limo, then return to the hotel and make some sort of second appearance to cover for us, and then spin some story to Gregory and Mrs. Felix as well as any of the entourage or bodyguards who will be flipping out when we don't come back with you? Robin and I have never really been alone together—and I mean *alone-alon*e. Minus the circus that follows us all around. I want a chance to get to know my *wife* how you got to know Vere, and how Adam got to know Evie. Even if it's just for one day or two, I want what you two had."

"One or two days? Where? Wow. How romantic." Vere leans forward, locking her eyes onto mine in this way that makes me feel guilty and blush all at the same time.

"Nothing's *romantic*," Hunter protests. "She's your fake wife. Not even your girlfriend." Hunter grits out, then glowers between us. "So… you already don't have what me and Vere have or what Adam and Evie have. Unless…" He flicks me a worried, rather stressed-out look. "Unless. *Dude. What the hell*, because I thought you promised. Double promised."

"I did!" Royce sighs out, sounding both frustrated and embarrassed. "We're *friends*, Hunter. That's all. We're trying to make this." He makes fake quote marks out of his fingers before continuing, "*relationship* work. We can't do it well if we're not better friends and we think this will fast track that."

"Robin. Do you agree?" Hunter looks at me like I've grown two heads.

Before I can answer, Royce gives him a shove, his shoulders going as taut as his expression. "Dude. You're not my dad. And what the hell? I don't need this shit from you, too. I've already got my grandmother and Gregory living in that space."

Suddenly my cheeks are burning so hot, I don't know what to think or how to answer so I only nod.

"Hunter." Vere pipes in. "What's your problem? Why do you just keep staring at them? I think it's a good idea."

Hunter shakes his head. "I guess I wanted to remember Robin and Royce, and this moment—the very moment the girl next door stole away Royce's—"

Royce punches him in the arm. "Shut up, would you? No one's stolen anything. We're having a tourist-adventure. We're making *friends*. Nothing else."

"Yeah," I finally choke out my response, relieved that Hunter didn't finish that sentence. Because what would he have said? Stolen Royce's *Sanity? Mind?*

"Which reminds me. Vere, do you happen to have some of those make-up remover wipes in your bag? I wanted to take this gunk off my face. Look less…obviously…pretty."

"As if that's possible," Royce laughs out, making my cheeks go hot again while, drawing another odd look and a whole bunch of head shakes from Hunter.

"Of course I do." Vere pulls out a flat package of Aloe loaded wipes. "And Royce is right, I'm not sure if you're more beautiful with makeup, or without. Either way, this pretty *face* of yours…" She's pulled out one wipe and is quickly wiping off my cat's eyes eyeliner. "It does draw attention."

I shake my head at their compliments. "Well, I'm more comfortable without."

Royce has handed me the bag with the change of clothes and on turning back he's punched Hunter hard in the arm while saying, "Turn away, jackass. She's changing into leggings."

With Vere making this face like she's about to crack up laughing, I quickly scoot the leggings up first, then peel the offensive skirt down and off. I decide to keep the white shirt as is, buttoned up and hanging long for under the hoodie.

"You all can turn back now," I say, shoving my head through the top of the giant hoodie.

I hand Royce his VANS so he can change out of his shoes, while Vere hides my rejected skirt into her purse, then shoves Royce's leather shoes into her bag as well.

Royce folded the soft suit jacket, and I tucked it into the spot vacated by the hoodie for 'just in case it gets cold in the evening' as he pulled on his beanie cap and dragged it down low over his forehead.

In silence, everyone watched me part my hair down the back and pull both sides of my curls into two, small, tight buns at the base of my neck.

When I was done, Vere grinned, saying, "Wow. Those are *so* cute. I'm stealing that hairstyle. You look adorable."

"But do I look completely different?" I whisper.

Shaking his head Royce passes my sunglasses saying, "If this is you trying not to stand out, we're in big trouble. I think we're going to need to get you a hat as well."

I point up at his beanie and toss him his own pair of sunglasses. "Well you picked a beanie color that makes your eyes even more beautiful and bright then the black hair peeking out does. No one is going to be looking at me if I'm standing next to you, anyhow. It's possible we both need way better disguises."

"Hell yes you do. And fast." Hunter's still shaking his head at Royce but says to me, "Take care of him, will you, Robin? Guy is not street smart."

"I will. You know I will."

Hunter nods, adding, "That's the only reason I'm letting him leave the limo with what I think is a very *bad* idea. Gregory and Mrs. Felix are going to freak."

"We should be allowed to go and do and see what we want, right? Be free for a little while?" Royce's grin turns into a defiant glare

"Yes. You should. But what about your biggest fear? That Robin might get—"

"My new biggest fear is that Robin might not get to see what she wants to see in and around London. And then I'm even more afraid she won't get to see what she wants to see in Paris. Meaning as a normal person, not like a prisoner or like a goldfish in a bowl, how we all live. I want to try this."

"Wait." Hunter crosses his arms. "You can't be saying that you mean to do this on all of our other European stops."

Royce shrugs. "If this works, why not. One city at a time, right?"

"Uh. Royce. Please no. Once is okay, but like…only once."

Before he could say more, Vere interrupted, "Aww. It's so cute. I know it's going to work."

"Vere, you *would* say that, because you think you are going to win the lottery every time you buy a ticket." Hunter picks up her hand and gives it a squeeze.

"Are you saying I'm *not* going to win the lottery?" Vere pulls a face.

Hunter shakes his head, sighing out, loud and long while Vere claps her hands, her sparkling brown eyes going wide and soft as she adds. "Does this mean we get to make an appearance at the Tower of London, to greet the fans that I'm sure are gathering there to meet all four of us?"

Hunter sighs out. "Oh, hell. Speaking of our hellish life inside of a fishbowl. I must love you dude, because the shit I do to cover your ass. The Tower of London is going to be one long day for me." He pulls out his phone and opens Instagram and shows us the crowds forming there all because Royce announced that we were going to be heading there.

Vere claps her hands again. "Not it's not, it will be amazing. I've always wanted to see it."

"Thank you both," Royce whispers, eyeing the street outside the limo as it starts to slow.

The driver pipes in over the intercom. "Excuse me. Sir? We're nearing the market, but it's rather extensive. Do you have a particular spot you'd like me to stop?"

Royce leans toward the driver and pushed the intercom for the chauffeur. "Is there a portion of this flea market that sells clothing?"

"Yes sir. Many booths inside. The market opens just now, so it won't be crowded. I know where to go."

Royce grins. "Thank you. And if possible, when you park, could you be a ways down the road, and not get out of the car to open our door, okay? We're trying to slip out and inside unnoticed."

"Yes sir," the chauffeur calls out again, pulling into a spot on a narrow side street. "It's just up there." He points ahead of where he's parked. "You'll see a white arch with capital letters spelling Greenwich Market on it."

"Perfect spot." Royce sits back, eyes gleaming with excitement as he looks out.

Hunter ducks to look out the windows, too, but eyes flashing with worry, as Royce continues, "I've got this app that says there's a London tube entrance right near here. Hold on." Royce opens the app. "Let me look up which trains connect to here." After a moment he grins. "Well, heck yes. So many that will connect to larger stations. We're good."

"*The tube?* You can't mean to be going on the London Tube in the middle of the day with no bodyguard and you mean to go to *larger stations*?" Hunter is almost shouting now.

"It's not the middle of the day yet, it's still morning. And, how about you don't shout that out? Yes, we're going on the tube, if all goes well on the tube, we're going to ride a real train and we're going eat fish and chips as well as see a castle today. One with a moat."

I pull my hands up to my chest and half laugh. "Castle? Moat!"

"Oh, hell-no." Hunter's face has turned nearly purple. "Public transportation is not allowed. You know what happens."

"Nothing is going to happen. Dude. Calm down." Royce opens the door and jumps out, before holding up his hand to help me out. "Ready?"

Vere had leaned out and said in a rushed whisper, "Good luck, Robin. Call if you need us to get you an escape route."

17

ROYCE

"WELL, I'm blaming Hunter for this damn panic attack," I say, glancing sideways at Robin. "You okay?" With our heads bent low, we manage to make our way down the street, around the corner and head toward the main entrance of Greenwich Market.

"We're fine. Better than fine. Hunter was unprepared for the surprise we threw at him, that's all."

"Well, that freaked-out fear-mask he threw at me when we hopped out of the limo hit me like a punch. He knows I'm a worrier and now I can't get the look that was on his face out of my mind."

I glance down at her again, trying to invoke some of her inner calm into myself because it's going to be hard to watch over her if I can't see through the fear clouding my eyes. Considering we're entering a funnel of people who are now going inside the market along with us, my attempts at finding this calm doesn't work, and I catch myself gripping her hand too hard.

"Again, we're *fine*." She laughs up at me wiggling her fingers loose and flexing them while making this face that says instead of judging me for being possibly OCD or simply insane because of my chronic worrying, she finds it—me—sort of cute.

As we enter the main doors we both pause at the entrance and look up, amazed at how the whole thing has this glassed in ceiling, industrial greenhouse look to it.

"Wow. *Cool*," Robin calls out releasing my hand and spinning around to take in the space.

I don't take time to look at anything else, but that's because I'm about to vomit because I'm sure people are now taking note of how Robin's face is so enchanting under the light.

Quickly, I start looking for shelter. When I spot a booth that looks like it's got clothing inside of it. It's also one of the few booths that is not just an open table. This one looks rather big, and it's tented off on three sides. I intercept Robin mid-spin and take up her hand again. I know I'm all but dragging Robin towards the booth, but that's because…hell, it's either this or run back out and try to get us into a cab.

WHEN WE GET INSIDE, my heart is galloping so hard I can't speak from the panic attack I'm fighting. I also calm down so, even though the place is empty and I know I'm being irrational, I drag her to the very back of the booth.

"What? Royce? What?" She says, and suddenly her voice seems too loud and shit…did she say my name out loud?"

I've all but shoved the poor girl into one of the circular clothing racks. "Have we been spotted?" she whispers, questioning me again.

"No." I'm finally able to speak as I toss her an apologetic glance. "But should anyone look back here, it looks like I'm all alone. You know, like one person. Not with anyone. And Robin. Please. Don't say my name."

"Okay. But you just said my name, too." She pokes her head out of the rack. "I'm also not the one people are going to notice or swarm. *You* should be standing in this rack." She giggles a little at my glower.

"Humor me. You in there, somehow makes me feel better." I chuckle a little, too, as she giggles up at me again. "Stay in between those clothes and see if you can, you know…shop from the inside out. Maybe find a couple of outfits that might work for you, and I'll do the same. But…let's do this really fast, okay? We need disguises now. Five minutes ago. Yesterday."

"Okay. I'll try." She tucks her head back in, this time full-on laughing, but she stays in there and from the way the hangers are moving, she's already going through the rack.

Hell. It's the first time I don't like the way her laughter sounds because it's as noticeable and as cute as she and her damn-gorgeous face is. There is no way I'm not going to be spotted with this darn girl by my side.

I whisper into the rack, "Put whatever outfit you find *over* your current outfit, and pull off the tags so I can pay for them. Anything else, hand to me I'll get it up to the register or into a bag. *Damn.* That reminds me, we need a backpack or a suitcase or something to hold all of the stuff for this adventure."

"Go work on that and get your own outfit swapped out some. I'll be fine."

A grizzled old bald man who's up at the register keeps looking over at me. It's possible he's seen me stuff my girl into the back of a clothing rack, but like he's seen every kind of person and situation at this market, he does a funny little eye roll at us and stays seated at his stool while he calls out, "I'm not trying to insult you, because you two don't look the type to steal or pull sexy-time shenanigans back there, but I want you to know the back of my place has a video camera recording everything and I'm not sure what your friend is about back there but if you break the rack, you will be responsible for buying it."

Robin cracks up again, but like, I can't even find one bit of humor in any of this now. Because…cameras! "Crap," I utter out, ducking while trying to see where the camera is located. When I spot it, I turn my face away from it, giving Robin a wild glance, saying "Crap, this whole thing has been recorded, probably with sound."

Ignoring my next wave of panic, Robin climbs out of the rack and waves, still laughing as she answers the old man quickly, "Yes, sir. And you're correct. We aren't the type. Please don't worry. It's not broken." Then she smiles up at me, reaching out to take my hand this time. She gives it a hard squeeze, saying, "Hey. *Husband.*" She lowers her voice to an imperceptible whisper, "It's okay, even the camera is okay, as long as he doesn't recognize us." She shrugs. "And even if he does, so what. He's got a good story and we're out of here fast. Royce. It's fine."

"You. Said. My. Name."

She blinks up at me, shaking her head, the laughter in her blue eyes disappears and is replaced with genuine concern. "Come on. Breathe. For real. If you don't want to do this, or if you think you can't…it's okay. We can bolt. I'll totally understand. I didn't know that this would be so extreme for you."

I pull in a huge breath, letting my gaze rove over her flushed face as I almost take her up on her offer to bolt, while at the same time I'm telling myself to carry on.

Because…damn, suddenly…I'm down to get mobbed and mauled because the way she's caring for me right now feels nicer than anything I've felt in a long time.

I go for one more long, deep breath. "This all seems harder than I thought it would be. I guess I take the bodyguards for granted and…" I shrug. "And, I'm in. Okay, with whatever happens, good or bad and…" I swallow. "I'm sorry I'm such a freak."

Dismissing my statement with a small head shake, she reaches up and presses the creases out of my forehead, then nods like she approves of the result. "Good. Now get shopping. I want to see that castle."

"Can I help you *two* find something?" The man calls out as Robin starts pushing hangers aside on a ladies dress rack. "We offer a selection of new and vintage, so if I can direct you from here, shout out your questions, okay?"

Robin pulls two dresses off the rack and brings them to stand in front of a mirror a little away from me as the man goes on, "I'd come assist you, but can't leave my post until my wife returns from the coffee shop.

"No problem." I say, finally able to muster up what I hope is a normal sounding voice. "Hats. I'm looking for all kinds of big…hats."

The man points. "There. In that basket on top of the other round rack."

"Thanks and, also…" I try to modulate my voice to not sound so American. "And…have you any of those *baggage*-valise-type-things?"

Robin snort-whispers, "Most questionable English accent I've ever heard." Then she laughs outright at my responding attempt to not laugh out loud, along with her.

"And what in the world is a valise?" she asks.

"You never watched Downton Abbey? The Royals?" I whisper.

She shakes her head, *no* and I slap on my crap English accent attempt again to answer her, "A valise is a fancy-man-bag. Usually packed and unpacked by a valet."

"I thought valets were guys who parked cars at hotels."

I ramp up my fake accent even more and pull my posture up to stiff and haughty. "Only in this century, my darling, young lady. Back in the day, a valise was a suitcase. A valet was a fancy man-maid-advisor. And all gentlemen who were anyone worth their salt, had one on staff. Both words are very UK."

When a couple pauses at the door of the clothing booth and peeks in, I tense up and whisper, "Would you consider going back behind the racks?"

She shakes her head at my paranoia, but does turn away a little while answering me in her own horrible, fake English accent, "Proof again you've married a *commoner*. The only UK word I know is, "Bloody. Oh, and I know apartments are called *flats* and…I also know *woolly-jumper*. That's a sweater. It is the most adorable thing, wooly-jumper, isn't it?"

I hold my body stiff and poised to run, but thankfully the two women move along and don't come inside the booth.

"Did you say wooly jumpers?" The man up front calls back. "Those are out of season, but you can find some in a box up here by me as well as I do have some vintage suitcases, if those would work for you, sir. I overheard you say *valise*."

"Go pick one. Practice breathing in, then out, and prepare yourself because I'm going to follow you in about two minutes." Robin shoves at my shoulder, then winks at me. It's so surprising the lower part of my belly spins with butterflies and heat and something that feels like pure delight.

"Okay." I stalk ahead of her, pausing to flash her a smile that tells her I really am under control now, and then I wave a couple of floppy beach hat options from the basket I was just plowing through.

Following, as promised, she chooses a wide brimmed straw garden hat for herself while whispering up to me, "You—take that beige one. The one with the string on it and the wide brim."

"I think that's a fly fishing hat, but okay…" I eye the one she's talking about with some skepticism because it looks so ancient I'm afraid it will crumble as I start tugging it on my head. "This is pretty old…but it does fit."

"Oh. It's perfect." She blinks up at the hat. "That can be our inspiration piece. We'll both dress all Grandpa and Grandma chic. Like we're from another time. When you're at the register see if there's any eye-glasses. You know, the cat eye ones with little rhinestones at the edges for me."

"Like granny-readers?" I crack up.

"Yes." She waggles her brows. "Oh, and here, if you like my hat idea, I'll choose all of these dresses, but only if you search out a woolly-jumper-vest to wear. One that might go with the hat?"

I shake my head. "I love this idea, but I draw the line at wearing a vest."

"Okay. Fine. No vest. What do you think of these?" She hands over two hangers with what look like pretty cool, 1950's housewife-looking floral dresses. "They're very *I Love Lucy*—Leave it to Beaver style. I *love* them."

Before I can answer she jumps to a small belt rack. "The vintage stuff seems legit. It's also kind of expensive. Hope it's okay. Each dress is around sixteen pounds. Do we have enough money for me to get one of these brown leather belts, as well? That way, if things don't quite fit, I can improvise?"

"Of course we have enough. I love the dresses, too. And the belt is a good idea, can you grab one for me?" I shake my head, amazed at how she worries about things—*money*—when I always take that for granted. I wait for her to pick the belts and add it to her pile, stepping away. "I'm heading to pay. If it's safe I'll give you a signal. And just in case, track the back of this tent space for some sort of flap so we can run out of here, if needed."

I see her rolling her eyes as I re-adjust my awesome, canvas, old-man hat low on my forehead so I can hide my face when I get up to the register dude.

I pause at a rack of button down men's shirts and grab a few that look like they might oddly 'match' the old dresses Robin chose. Some have formal glossy prints going through the fabric, some are funny, casual stripes. One is so cool I pause, place her pile of things on top of the shirt rack while I shrug it on over the top of my outfit.

The one I've tried has an extra straight collar, vertical grey stripes, and from the crisp feel of the fabric as well as the steep price of nearly 30 pounds, it's possible it has real abalone shell buttons on it.

Like Robin said, it's true vintage. And very cool.

"The cut has to be easily from the 1940's or 30's even, what do you think?" I ask the booth owner.

"Dead on, young man. You've got a nice eye. The one you're wearing is 1929."

I pause at the mirror he's got stuck on top of a jewelry case to check how it looks. I decide to button it all the way up to my neck, tugging the tag off of the arm, as well as tugging the tag off the hat in front of the owner handing them to him as well as Robin's pile as I reach the register.

"Do you mind if I wear these out?" I ask. "And my wife, can she wear some things out, too?" I pull out my wallet.

"Please do, sir. Is that all?"

"Well, you know how it is shopping with a wife. I'm sure there will be more." I glance back at Robin, who's rolling her eyes at me again, but is still waiting at the back of the store for me to wave to her.

Before the booth owner can get a good look at me I find the exact glasses Robin was hoping for on a little rack by the register and wave them in his face. "Can you add on these as well, sir. If you don't mind." They're made of some sort of silver metal and very old-lady as Robin requested. On impulse, I grab a pair of men's black framed glasses for myself off the same rack, thinking, why should Robin have all of the fun? "And these."

As he's ringing those up as well, I pop out the lenses in my glasses because they turned out to be prescription. It's too impossible to see out of them. Once I have them in place on my face, I check how I look in the mirror again, and decide it's safe enough to call Robin forward as I ask, "How much are the suitcases? They seem really old."

As Robin wanders in my direction looking at a few other racks, the man looks me up and down as if assessing how much he thinks I'll be willing to pay before answering my question about the suitcases. "They range from 10 pounds, to thirty, young man."

I pull out the second smallest suitcase. It, like the shirt I'm wearing, looks like it came from the 1930's. It has muted color. Greens and grays, plus wide brown leather strips going across the sort of waxed burlap fabric that makes up the front and sides. The handle has this cool yellowy tortoise shell pattern on it as well. I push on the funny little metal buckles up top until they click open. I'm happy to note it's lined with what has to be original, salmon-colored satin, and that it looks virtually untouched despite its age. It's even got little sewn in, elastic pockets under the lid. For some reason, I get the idea that Robin will love it. "Is there a price on this one?"

"That's the finest of the lot. Again, you've got a good eye." He grins, his eyes going from the bag, to my wallet then to Robin who's paused in front of a mirror to fix her hair. "I'll give you the whole lot, case, clothes, glasses and hats for one hundred fifty."

"One hundred forty, cash," I counter, because I know in a flea market you have to counter or you'll get no respect.

"Done." The guy all but grabs the bills from my hands as soon as they're out of the wallet. I smile at the guy, pulling my hat down lower and trade my fake glasses for my usual, darker sunglasses as a pair of grey-haired ladies enter the booth and head toward the racks in the back, thankfully without glancing once at me or Robin.

Robin joins me at the register and I quickly hand her one of the dresses and pull out the granny-glasses, happy at the pleased look on her face, and suggest, "He says we can wear stuff out. It will be fun."

Robin gets this is more of a command than a statement, and takes the dress, pulls off the hoodie and buttons it over the white shirt, leggings outfit, pulling the leggings up so you can't see them anymore. "Yay." She puts on the glasses. "This is all so perfect." Thanks to the glasses, her eyes have gone fishbowl-huge when she pauses to blink up and me. "Wow. Bifocals. These are making me dizzy. Wait." She laughingly positions them halfway down the bridge of her nose and squints up at me as she twirls in the dress. "What do you think? Granny adorable, right?"

"Perfect," I laugh at her scrunched face and gently place the wide brimmed hat she chose for herself over the halo of blond curls that have started to escape from the two buns she'd made to hold her hair tight, yanking it down a little too roughly, as two more people enter the booth.

I hand Robin the suitcase and she admires how beautiful the old suitcase is, just how I thought she would, as she places our items inside of it. "I love this thing," she's whispering. "I love all of this."

The man at the register asks, "You two going to a costume party or something?"

"Yes. Yes we are, and we're late."

It takes all of my strength to turn my latest anxiety attack into a laugh, as I take the now packed suitcase out of Robin's hand to carry it, while Robin quietly thanks him for helping us, and I nudge her toward the door.

In seconds, we're out of the clothing booth, and have exited the entire flea market. Even though there's no need to run, we're slightly jogging down the street toward the tube entrance. I look behind me, wishing the limo with Hunter and Vere waiting inside of it could miraculously appear, but it's long gone.

My worrying-ways surface again as we purchase our tickets from the machines and go through the turnstile. When we make it on to the correct subway, and we manage to grab two seats in the back facing the wall instead of facing the crush of people inside the care and still *no one* has given us a second glance, I start to let down my guard and breathe and allow myself to be distracted, mesmerized and enchanted by Robin's reaction to everyone and everything she sees.

Like right now she's grinning up at the tube map that's posted inside our car while trying to figure out where we're going. At each stop, she leans near the glass of the subway's window to get a look at the inside of each station, quietly calling out the name tiled into the wall, then pointing it out on the map in front of us like I can't read it for myself or something. "Come on. Throw me a bone. Which station will be our exit?"

I study my app. "The final goal is Victoria Station. We got on at Cutty Sark, we will have to hop off this one and change to get to a place called Waterloo which gets us to Victoria. That's where we will have to get off, get new tickets and swap to a commuter train."

"Wow." She waggles her brows, then studies the map some more. By the ways she's frowning and looking at the intersecting lines, I can tell she's about to say something like, *hope we don't get lost*, but she knows that's what I'm already thinking, so she quickly changes the subject to: "A commuter train? Really? That means we're heading out of London? Just where is this castle. What's it like? Tell me more."

"Nope. Some of this is a surprise. And this is our stop. Canary Wharf. We are looking for signs to the Jubilee line which takes us to Waterloo."

I pick up her hand and twine my fingers into hers as we hop out of the first subway. "Waterloo," she's saying. "Like the Abba Song. Do you know it? From Mamma-Mia? One of my favorites." She tugs me along. "There's an arrow that says Waterloo. Come on."

I don't let the panic take over this time, nor do I analyze or track what anyone else around me is doing for once.

Instead, I keep my eyes only on her. Despite the crowds and how I've got the app on my phone, I let myself be pulled along, and I relax into her confidence.

I love how I feel drunk on the way the edges of her eyes crinkle slightly when she smiles back at me every time I slow down to avoid bumping into someone. I've already grown addicted to how her hand feels warm, tight and so very right nestled into mine as she bossily tugs me along. I've endlessly fallen in love with how this girl never asks or expects more from me than just the moment we're living in—how she loves the here and now.

It's as if she thinks whatever we are doing *together,* no matter what that might be, is enough…is…*the best.*

This morning, she made this same crinkle-eyed smiling face when we were in the hotel room doing nothing but waiting for room service. And she's made this same smiling face to me, during the crap-press conferences we've had since the day we got married. She's even done this while doing shit that is not easy for her—like getting jostled between bodyguards and roped off crowds, after we've been tossed into limos—or hell—into whole clothing racks—like I just did to her back in that flea market.

Right now, I get this feeling that hopping from subway to subway in thrift shop outfits has become everything she's *ever* wanted to do—but it's more than that it's everything she's ever wanted to do…*with me.*

Only, the 'me' I'm referring to right now is someone I hardly let out for the world to see. Because…*shit*…that guy, he's a mess and truly, who am I without my guitar, my bandmates, my fame, the money, the entourage and the bodyguards?

Who?

I swear, this girl seems to have the answer, because her smiles and the way she bores those eyes into mine make the hidden parts of me feel *seen.* Exposed even. But now that she and I have been hanging out, she makes the all that is seen feel *known,* feel welcome and accepted. All with her style of zero judgement and unconditional love, to boot. Something I can't even give to myself.

As awesome as that feels, because don't get me wrong, it's incredible, it's also forcing me to acknowledge that this 'me' this 'real me' is a person who has been so lonely and craving a solid connection to someone so badly, that I didn't know how deep the holes in my heart truly went.

Not until Robin's friendship started filling them back up, that is.

Once again, our time in the train station goes off without a hitch.

We buy tickets and get lost in the crowd along with everyone else going through the turnstiles who were trying to exit or switch trains like us. We'd even paused to listen to an amazing classical violinist who'd set up her violin case for tips between the tunnels. The music is so pure and haunting as it echoes, it's like Robin and I have been struck frozen there, along with everyone else. All eyes on the musician, all ears listening to her magic.

When Robin takes up my hand the next time and gives it a tug, I realize we have to run to make it onto our next train. Once we find the track, and leap on, my chest swells with the success of this day and how happy I am doing this with her, that I start grinning wildly.

"What?" She half laughs, breathless as we take our two seats near the back of the train again, luckily this time, the car is nearly empty, with only two old ladies who are sitting way up front.

"No wonder Adam ran away every weekend for years," I whisper. "If this is how anonymity feels, I could get addicted to it. I suddenly understand *why* he stayed in that small town in Wales called us once in a while, but then never came out." I risk glancing behind me as the doors open and close at the next stop which lets on only one more passenger who chooses to sit up front. I keeping my eyes shaded under my hat, before whispering on, "It's so cool being ignored, isn't it?"

The sides of her lips turn up and she adjusts her own hat. "Is it really that bad, people admiring you?"

"It's not bad if it's one-on-one. And I do like when people enjoy the music or the lyrics we write. Of course I *love* that, but it's the energy people send out when they're in a big group and they spot us out in public. Do you know anything about mob mentalities?"

"Not really." She shakes her head. "But I wouldn't call your fans a mob."

"They're not, but like…any big group of people can *become* a mob. They feed off of each other. I've seen it happen. People will swarm and follow others, and once they realize it's a famous band or a movie star, they think they want to meet or get close to them—things can get crazy. They don't care if you're just trying to eat dinner, or walk down the street. Worse, they don't acknowledge you're a living breathing human. Paparazzi can especially act like that, especially European and UK paparazzi. Over here, they have a different, much closer 'comfort-bubble. In the states, we stand further apart. But here, there is not that much space in general. Plus there's twice as many people, so it seems normal to crowd in. Normal for them, not for someone who has trust issues as well as a who is a chronic worrier, like I am, that is."

"Trust issues with people, huh? That's how you define your worrying?" She's staring up into my face like she'd like to know more. "Why? Like…is it all people or just fans?"

I shrug. "Never really thought about it. When I'm out in public I have this constant feeling that I can't breathe, because I'm never sure which random person is going to invade my space, force a smart phone at me, one that's probably on video record. I get exhausted tracking all of the *motion.* More so, worrying about which person is going to try to grab me or ask for free stuff, tickets, or to sign their stuff…purses, t-shirts, and even sign their *skin,* for crap's sake!" I lean back into my seat, dropping my voice again. "I hate that request the most, because what's the point of making me stop my life and do that, when people are going to just shower it off in a few hours? Or hell…often it's not even the physical contact that gets to me. It can be verbal randomness as well. I'll be walking down a street and have to listen to complete strangers say insane things to me, like how they hated a song, or how they think our music was ripped from another song, or, stuff about how we overall 'suck' which, by the way, is shouted at us a lot in public. Why do people think that is cool, I'll never know?"

She frowns. "Wow. For real?"

I nod. "They even say stuff like: *why did you even write your last album*, or how we're *so boring and so over*. As much as fans grabbing me makes me stressed, comments like that can crush my creativity. I know it's not supposed to, that we all need to have thick skin in this business, but like…damn, It's not like you can go out and order extra layers of thick skin from Amazon.com, right. If only."

She laughs. "Right? I wish. I'd order boxes and boxes of it."

"Crowds can make Hunter shut down completely if we're not careful. You've heard the stories about how, when we were in high school and Guarderobe was part of the Newt TV channel network—how he tried to commit suicide?"

"Yeah. Vere told me. That he was sent to Colorado to hide out and rest."

"They called it *un-making*. Unmaking Hunter Kennedy was the title of the news articles that hit the world circuit. Sold a ton of albums because of the attention, kind of like what's happening now thanks to *this*." Royce laughs and taps the ring on my finger.

"Please." I shake my head and ignore the sales comment, keeping the conversation to things I understand. "Hard to believe Hunter and Vere have been together since high school. I think he's an inspiration to so many because he spoke so openly about his anxiety and his depression."

"Yeah, he did. And he is an inspiration. But one day, you're going to spot the scars on his wrists and you'll flip. They're gruesome. What that kid went through was tragic. He didn't know who he was, and we didn't know where or how to be proper friends to him. We were all so damn young we could hardly process what he did to himself. We were just kids, trying to grow up inside this freak-show. The crowds, the fame, the endless soul-sucking judgment that happens to us is part of why he did that. Adam, he laughs it off mostly; but that guy, after he met Evie? He was seriously thinking about never coming back to us. And I mean…never."

I shake my head leaning forward, my eyes going over hers as she's processing all that I've said. "Talking about this makes me worry."

She grins, and raises one brow. "It is?" She laughs feigning mock surprise.

I don't return her laugh, instead I ask, "But what about you. Robin? Is it—the exposure—getting to you?"

"You mean the magazine articles that have been written about us? So far, so good." She shrugs.

"No. I mean the other stuff. I'm sure you've seen the hate and endless gossip going on about you all over the internet?"

"No?" Her brow furrows. "I heard there was some chatter," she frowns, shaking her head. "But I haven't looked actually. I suck at Instagram and Snapchat. I'm trying to ramp up, but by the time I go to bed, I'm just too tired. Is it really so bad?"

I tug the brim of her hat low so she can't see my eyes anymore and lie to her, "Not so bad. Maybe you should try to never look."

She pushes the hat back up. "It must be bad for you to say that! Tell me."

"There's stories that call you a gold digger and ones that have brought out all school pictures ever published of you in yearbooks."

She gasps and covers her mouth. "Including middle school?"

I have to crack up then, "Hell yes. And I'm not going to lie, you were really cute with those braces."

She leans back groaning. "Oh no. What else…come on. Don't stop."

"Most keep saying you're pregnant with my baby."

"Wow. But we told them at the first press conference that I wasn't."

"Well…now they're waiting to see if your belly swells."

"That rumor will take time to disperse. Maybe in September we can go to Hawaii where we let photographers take photos of you in a swimsuit so they can you are not at all pregnant."

She grins, impishly, patting her stomach. "Maybe in September I will look pregnant with twins from eating all of the food I have on my European bucket list."

"Really?" I raise my brows, curious. "This morning, I thought you said you didn't know what you wanted to see here in Europe."

"Seeing is not *eating*. And I'm starting with the promised fish and chips this afternoon. In France, we're going on non-stop, Tour De Cheese. Germany it's going to be sausages and bratwursts all the time, and in Spain we're going to be all about olives and *tapas*."

I rub my own stomach. One that has started to growl after all of her food descriptions. "As soon as we switch trains one more time we'll hit the first pub we see for the fish and chips." I glance at the app, then at the time on my phone, feeling my own stomach starting to growl with our future lunch-time plan. "Can you wait about one more hour?"

"I can wait," she jokes, patting her belly again and grinning over her scarf. "But the twins…they can't!"

18

ROBIN

We ride the tube to Victoria Station but when the train slows, Royce seems to get quieter and quieter. He's eying the sea of people waiting to get on this tube after our group exits. I can tell he's warring with a new wave of doubt.

We wind up stairs and head through the tube exit turnstiles, heading for the main station. Once there, we stop at one of the rail ticket kiosks where Royce expertly inserts his credit card, then says, "Don't look. I'm still trying to surprise you a little."

I turn away, watching his finger move out of the corner of my eye over a touch screen as he finishes his ticket transaction. The machine spits out a pile of cards and he looks at them reading out, "Platform Three." Then he glances at his phone app, muttering, "That's located at the other side of the building. Damn."

"It can't be far," I say, keeping my voice sunny.

"We have to cross through all of those people." Royce nods toward the crush of commuters swarming like ants in every direction, then swallows in this way that looks like it might have hurt. "Oh, man."

I squeeze his arm. "Remember? This is fun. Whatever happens. Fun."

"Fun." He nods, repeating. "Fun. Okay. But if we survive this, we're both going to have a beer when we get to that Fish and Chips pub, because the legal drinking age over here is eighteen and we will have both earned it."

I laugh. "I'd already planned to taste my first alcohol by trying Champagne in Paris, but if a beer puts a smile on your face after this, then I'll try one of those today."

His brows draw together. "You've *never* tasted alcohol. Not even a beer?"

I shrug. "Not even a beer."

His silver eyes have narrowed and he's shaking his head. "Of course you haven't. Why am I not surprised?" Looking even more distraught, he glances again at the throngs of people, then runs both hands over his eyes like he's suddenly got a headache. He starts muttering so quietly but I catch him saying, "What am I doing. Really. What am I doing *here* with this *never-tasted-beer* girl? Hunter was right. What in the hell am I doing?"

"You're taking me to see a real castle, remember?" I whisper-joke, cutting in, but then get I worried, because he doesn't smile how he should have. Worse, the expressions crossing his face as he glances between me and the crowd are getting steadily darker.

"Royce?" I pick up his hand and search his eyes. "Like I've said all along, it's your call if you want to call this off. Honest. Fish and chips can be handled via room service. If it's causing you this much stress or if you don't think it is safe, then we can stop and just hang out."

I feel like I can hear his heart beating through our connected palms, but finally he utters out, "I *don't* think it's safe. Not at all safe for either of us. But, shit, Robin. Is any of this?" His laugh is short and sounds sarcastic. "If you learn one thing about me today while we get to know each other better, it's that I'm stubborn and I think where you're concerned, I'm horribly selfish."

"What do you mean by that?"

"I mean we *should* get a cab out of this station *immediately* and return to the hotel, but I don't want to stop any of this… *fun,* as we're calling it. I also don't want to stop this feeling I've been having all day… nor do I want to stop this journey or this friendship we're forging together, or—whatever it is we're calling what we're doing or becoming together as this fake married entity."

"Then don't. Don't define it or us. It's probably impossible anyhow." I shrug. "Just…live it. Love it. That's what I'm doing."

He pauses and his curt-cutting laughter sounds very self-depreciating. "I've been doing the same, yet my whole core tells me I should shut this down. Stop it now. Stop… *us* from going forward because I worry you're going to get hurt."

"Isn't that also part of your core? You've been worried about that since the day you met me," I try to joke again, but that line only makes his frown darker.

He sighs and this time he sounds sort of sad as he answers, "Yes, but that's where the selfish part begins. That core—it also tells me to move full speed ahead with whatever happens between us. It urges me to gobble this all up carelessly, like people do with candy Halloween night. Only. I care. I know this is bad for us somehow, bad for you, but…"

His gaze is tormented and confused when it finally meets mine in earnest. "I just want to keep being this normal guy. The one who gets to hang out with this beautiful girl. Mostly because I've never been that normal dude before, and it—this?" He gestures around the train station where no one is looking at us at all. "This feels amazing. To be free and unwatched and unnoticed, is addictive as hell. It's made me truly want to play out what it would feel like to be this real couple on our way to tour a castle for a weekend."

I blink at him. "But…that is exactly what we are doing. Like… if anyone does discover who we are, we're going to tell them that we are a newly married couple, sneaking away on a romantic weekend. Right? Nothing is going to happen. Nothing." I beam at him, trying to jog him out of whatever dark thoughts he's having. "I also get to be the beautiful girl inside of this scenario. And, if you've never felt normal before, I can admit that I've never felt like the beautiful girl before. So…there. See? Added awesomeness for both of us."

He locks gazes with me like I've startled him. "Robin. To me, you've *always* been the beautiful girl. Always."

"Aww." I shake my head, playing off the surge of pleasure and the fluttering-spin his words brought to my stomach with a little shrug as I quip back to him the first thing that comes to my mind: "Well to me, you've always been a very normal guy."

Shaking his head, he reaches forward to run a finger along my cheek and then he takes up my hand to pull me closer like he's going to whisper something to me.

I step into the circle of his arms, cocking my head to the side, waiting to hear what he's got to say next. Which is when this sensation that he's thinking about *kissing me* hits me so hard it makes me turn my head up and stare at his beautiful, smiling mouth as much as I think he's staring at mine.

It...*he*...the pressure of his hand, the way his silver eyes seem to have turned to molten-fire makes me hope...wish...*want things* I've got no right to want, when he's only being nice to me. Involuntarily I lick my lower lip in anticipation I think he's started to dip his head low, but instead he utters. "We're going to miss the train."

He's spun away from me so quickly, I'm nearly reeling from his disconnect and from how the temperature between us dropped about ten degrees instantly.

As I pull in a shuddering breath, wondering if I'd imagined all of that, I make my feet follow him as he calls over his shoulder like nothing at all had just passed between us, "Stay close and don't call out my name. Okay?"

I think I've answered, "Okay," in what I hope was a loud and cheerful voice, but I'm not certain, because the rush of my absolute embarrassment is pounding too loudly in my head to let any other sounds enter.

19

ROBIN

WHEN WE MAKE it to the platform, his expression is hooded when he motions to the train waiting there. "There it is. The one that says Edenbridge. That's actually our final destination. Let's climb on."

"Edenbridge?" I ask, keeping my gaze carefully off of his beautiful face (and of course off of those lips that made me lose my mind a few moments ago) while I take his offered hand.

My poker face might be on strong, but I'm still walking on rubbery, *almost-kissed-Royce-Devlin-in-a-train-station* legs, so I let him literally haul me up the extra high first step, and then up into the train itself.

"Thanks." I whisper out.

"Edenbridge is the name of the town where we're going."

"Is it also the name of the castle?" I guess.

"Nope. Come on."

He starts off down this narrow train corridor lined with windows on one side, pulling out the cards that had come from the machine to read them. "I know we're trying to stay incognito, but I booked us first class fares for this portion of the trip. That was the only place I could guarantee seats. And to be safe, I bought out a whole berth so we can close our door and be alone." He hands me the stack of tickets and I note that there are, in fact, six tickets instead of two. "Our berth is down at the end here. Number 537" He shows me where the numbers are on each door, while I whisper the word 'berth' to myself, because who knew that's what these little rooms inside of trains were called?

Glancing around I realize there is no one else in this car yet—not even in any of the *berths*, so quickly I call out, "I think we should also swap our outfits here. You know…how Adam suggested? And…*oh wow*," I add, losing my train of thought…because…holy cow. I've started to look inside each of the berths. There's eight total in this car, and each of them has six seats inside with windows looking out of the far side over the tracks. They have little drop down tables and on the side of the corridor where we're walking, there's additional frosted windows for light and, a sliding glass door.

"Oh wow, *what*?" He pauses, and glances back at me.

I want to shout out to him that this is my very first, real above ground train ride *ever.* (Not counting Big Thunder Mountain at Disneyland, but that is a roller coaster made to look like a train, not a real train). *And* I also want to shout out that this train, *if he can't notice it for himself, looks exactly like the Hogwarts Express! Exactly!*

But I don't.

Instead I bite my lip and say, "Oh. The train is very cute, that's all." Because after his reaction to my 'never tasted alcohol' comment, and how I licked my lips and nearly randomly planted one on him like a complete psycho a few moments ago, I think I'm done embarrassing myself for the day.

Only, despite my extreme control on the outside, inside…*oh man*! As we pass each adorable berth…I'm thinking of chocolate frogs and Ron and Hermione meeting for the first, time all while internally screaming: *So. Happy right now. Ahh. Ahhh this is going to be so cool. So. Cool!*

"Good idea on the costume change." He pauses to put our suitcase into the last room of six seats. "This one is ours. Let's do that first before other passengers load up." Royce nods, motioning me to the empty, adorable train *bathroom* located at the end of the corridor nearest our berth. He steps in first, I'm assuming to make sure it's empty, before nodding again that I should go in. "Hand me all your stuff except for a change of clothes, and I'll put it in our berth, then guard the door from here. If no one comes I'll swap my shirt out very quickly before you come out."

"Okay." I close the bathroom door, noting that it is also glass and frosted. There's a tiny sink and the entire floor is tiled with these postage stamp sized tiles. Thankfully it's also very clean. "But like…step away from the door a little. Would you? The glass door is making me feel… awkward. Like you're too close or something."

He laughs and so do I, calling out. "How can this be more awkward or I be more close than us sleeping together with a pillow mountain between us while you hide in a hoodie and I wear strange bathrobes to bed over my clothes?"

I don't answer that, because he's right, and when I come out the train has started moving. He's already changed into a cool paisley print shirt and swapped his pants to some soft looking grandpa-grey slacks.

He turns away from the window he'd been staring out of and looks at me in my new-old dress up and down, letting out a low whistle as he pauses to straighten out one side of my rounded, lace collar. Tapping the granny glasses that have slid down my nose again, slightly back up, he says finally, "You look half hipster, half messy-housewife and all amazing. The belt was a great idea."

I smile, spinning a little and adjusting the belt around my waist because he seems to be staring at it a little too hard. I'm thinking, *maybe it's not right*. "It's so cool, isn't it? Can you imagine a time when women had to wear stuff like this every single day? This one has this sewn in, puffy-scratchy-slip thing underneath the skirt that makes it pop."

"A crinoline, maybe?"

"Who knows? I'm shocked that you even try to guess at what it's called."

"Sorry. Years of stylists, time on studio back lots, and stage costumes gives me an odd knowledge base. And…on my last Netflix binge?" He colors a little before going on, "I did binge watch Downton Abbey, Poldark and Sherlock back to back. I'm now a huge donor to BBC programming."

"Wow. No, way." I grin at him, noting that my crush on this guy has just doubled because…he's so cute admitting this to me right now.

"Whatever the slip thing is, it's really fun to wear." I add, wiggling a little in my dress. "See how it poofs out all by itself? It's why I look so fabulously ready to swing-dance or do the twist or something, huh?" I twirl around once, but accidentally crash into the side window. "Ow."

He grabs both of my upper arms and catches me so I don't slam into his chest as I add, "Did I mention I *can't* dance?"

"Looked like okay moves to me." His voice is oddly low as he steps behind me and I lead us back into our berth.

Inside, I'm struck silent. I'm trying so hard to hold my breath as I gaze around, because, because…wow. *Best. Train. Ever. Wizards!*

Because I'm determined to be sophisticated and grown up, and not at all embarrassing, it takes all of my strength to bite my lip and not say one word as we choose seats across from each other.

Only, when Royce leans over and closes the sliding glass door then turns to me, waggling his brows high saying, "Totally Harry Potter awesome, in here, right? I'm Gryffindor. You?" I know I'm lost. I'm totally done for—I'm not going to be able to keep quiet.

"Ravenclaw," I blurt out, flicking him a glance, praying he won't judge me after this. "But once I did the quiz again, and wound up Hufflepuff so…I'm not sure. I guess I just want to be both," I add, because the simile he's giving me is so knowing—so sincere and *approving* that double crush I'd been forming just hit triple-crush.

"Right. Why can't we be two or three?" He nods. "Slytherin is so attractive to me sometimes."

"Dark-sided, rockstar," I accuse.

"Hell yes, I am." Suddenly he's grinning so wide and nodding and laughing with me, all while telling me things like how he and his mom read each book, side by side and cover to cover, each release day. How they needed two copies because they couldn't wait. How he sometimes gets sad from missing her when he comes across the movies playing on TV.

I tell him that I read each book to Sage out loud—because he was too little to really read his own. I shared how my father listened along with us, though he always pretended not to care. Only, Dad was the one who made sure we were at every movie opening night—all of us wearing movie t-shirts he'd purchased from Hot Topic. Which, for a Special Forces guy is not a natural place to shop. But for us… our dad, he did it.

I told Royce how Dad even let us both miss school and how he faked sick for work once, just so I could keep reading the end of last book.

We realized that we never noticed how much those books shaped parts of our whole childhood experiences, but they did. And I agreed with him, noting that I also get sad now when the movies are on TV. When I see them, it makes me wonder how in the heck Sage and I grew up so fast—like how could I be eighteen right now, and Sage… heading into high school? It also makes me think about how the whole family used to drop everything to watch those re-run movies, all over again. Despite having other things to do, Harry Potter is always the best and first choice.

Then, as the train pulled in to the final stop, we talked about how one day, he and I will go together to see the actual *Wizarding World of Harry Potter* inside Universal Studios, Orlando. I told him Sage nearly died of sadness, because we didn't have the money or the time to go inside.

That's when he vowed to go back, and take me there all over again. Together, we visualized how we would choose wands and find the Butterbeer, and go on the rides and eat chocolate frogs until our stomachs hurt, and…yeah, *next time.* We'd do… everything, just…everything.

That last part, probably won't happen, though. Because he's really not allowed to go to theme parks unless he wants 2000 fans following behind him. And frankly, going in would probably ruin what we'd dreamed about together so perfectly on this most perfect train ride.

This past year has taught me that reality can kind of suck. And now that I'm getting older, I wonder if some dreams might be better when they stay inside your head. This dream, above all…is one I think want to keep forever, *as is.* Because right now, it's all floating possibilities, and exciting huge promises, and giving met that chest-expanding anticipation I love.

That's enough, right?

When I'm back in Orlando again, it will mean our marriage will be over. Sage and I, if we don't find my Dad by then? We might even move back to Orlando and be with the Perino family permanently. That's what we had originally planned before I got married.

They're waiting for us to return, and we actually can't wait to go back there. And when we do—whenever that may be, I'll take Sage to the park and do all the things Royce and I talked about together, instead.

Because…that's my real life.

My brother and I had that plan, long before we dropped into Royce's fake life.

I contemplate the dips and planes in his gorgeous profile as the train stops and he stands to take the vintage suitcase down while sending me a silver-eye-twinkling, excited smile while pointing to a faraway castle we can both see out of the train's window.

I can't help but smile back, thinking…by then, Royce will be somewhere far from this place. He'll be touring with Guarderobe again probably, being the amazing rockstar that is *him*. Hopefully, he and I will be friends, but most probably, he will be married to someone else.

Really and truly married. Not fake married and not planning trips with his 'child-bride' as people call me, to an amusement park, that's for sure.

I shake my head, following out of our train berth, looking back once to re-count the six seats back there, and smile. Because… whatever… it was fun to make up the dream…

20

ROBIN

The castle...Hever Castle, is what our castle—*my castle*—the castle Royce Devlin picked for me to see, is actually called!

Ahh!!

It is also above and beyond my expectations of what a first castle should look like that my heart has galloped like ten racehorses fed only energy drinks ever since we arrived here. It's so bad, that it's possible any minute that my heart will simply flat-line.

Which is fine, I suppose, because at least I'll be dying in a castle. Dying in a castle with a beautiful rockstar watching over me.

All good.

This place is so old and so covered in ivy. It's got rock lined pathways and rolling green hills going off in every direction, sparkling clean, tall skinny windows, with secret gardens housing fountains and cool marble statues stuck all over the place. Time after time, I've caught myself of holding my breath, and I practically need to slap my own face to remember how to breathe. I've also become so certain I might be dreaming all of this that I've been afraid to utter one word, because I do not want to jinx this. Or wake up.

Which again, is fine, because...ahhh!

When we arrived, I found out that this castle is attached to a B&B.

Meaning, we're going to stay here. This castle itself is our overnight destination.

Again. Aaah!

We've checked into a room located at the top back of the house, which was, according to the owner, the previous apartments that housed the butler. Back when butlers were sort of the acting bosses over all of `the servants, even though he was a servant himself. Everyone who was anyone (and certainly anyone who owned a castle) had a butler.

His quarters have been made over into a two room suite. It has it's own back staircase, polished wood everything, and the most privacy in the whole place. It's also located over the kitchens and the old stables and is separated from all of the other rooms and hotel areas. Royce also paid double to secure it, and it's welcome privacy, for us by telling her that he and I were newlyweds.

Thankfully, the woman checking us in appeared to be in her sixties, seemed to love newlyweds and young love. She also didn't seem to be the kind of person who would know the band Guarderobe, or who we really were, so she didn't even stare at us past saying hello and calling us a *lovely young couple.*

The whole check-in almost went sour when we told her we didn't have our passports, ID's or credit cards with us. Her acceptance of what she'd said was very 'out of the norm' came only after Royce explained, how this was a last minute honeymoon, *run-away-adventure*. He'd lied, saying we'd been on a family reunion, and that we were the youngest couple without children so we'd been stuck babysitting a lot, and that we loved them but we'd decided to take a couple days and see a castle by ourselves by making a break for it on our way to the supermarket.

She'd laughed and said she did understand how, had we returned, we'd have been sucked back in, because big families can do that. And then she'd laughed again, calling us "poor dears."

What really calmed her down, though, was that Royce had so much cash on him that he was able to pay in advance for the room, as well as leave a room deposit that was large enough to satisfy any of her worries.

"I hope you enjoy your stay here," was all she'd said after Royce also tipped her about fifty British pounds for just *being so nice to us and understanding the impulsiveness of young love.*

When a bellman appeared looking for the luggage we didn't actually have, beyond our tiny suitcase, Royce flipped him some of the cash in his wallet, too.

That's how he secured us our promised Fish and Chips. They've just been delivered, having been motorcycled here from the nearest town pub.

The whole package was wrapped up in brown paper and newsprint. Apparently that's very UK, and to me, it's very cute.

Royce and I decided to hide out in here and eat until 6PM which is when the castle grounds will be closed to the day tourists. It's also exactly when he and I, and the other few guests who are sleeping over in the main part of the B&B, will be allowed private access to the extensive property, mazes, pathways through what the owner called 'the hedgerows' beyond the gardens.

I've personally translated his UK 'hedgerow' word to mean: rows of hedges. But I've learned not to trust my ideas here across the pond because this place is tricky. Even though I pretended to know what these hedgerows are, hedgerow could also be the common word for wild ducks or something.

The castle grounds are so huge, there could easily be a petting zoo hiding somewhere on this property, but either way, we've got private access and that's all we care about. We also found out by way of casual conversation, there are only a few other couples on the property tonight because it's Sunday and off season. So if we're careful, we won't cross paths with anyone until breakfast time tomorrow.

When we first got to the room, Royce was talking about how he was slightly disappointed with the castle's size. In his mind, I guess he'd wanted to take me to some huge, Medieval castle, way up in Scotland that he'd been to before, but told me this was the best he could do on short notice. He's also already promised to take me to that one someday.

Like his promises to take me wand shopping while we stuff our faces with chocolate frogs in the imaginary future that is not going to happen, I've humored him again by telling him how going to see castles in Scotland would be…

Cool, great, amazing…

I'm not sure which word I'd actually muttered at him, because he's now talking more about Scotland while I've unwrapped the steaming hot fish and chips and I'm biting in to the most amazing bite of breaded and fried fish I've ever tasted in my life.

I also lose all rational thought right then, because at the very same time that I have my second bite of this fried-fish-heaven, Royce takes his first bite.

The guy has paused mid-sentence to utter low-rockstar-voice-rumble out stuff like, "Mmm-damn—Robin—this is so good, huh?" All while talking with his mouth half full.

With every bite, he gets this dreamy-food-drugged happy look on his face which is something I've never seen him do before, which has me imagining how Royce Devlin might have acted when he was younger—which is really doing something to my heart because I swear, I suddenly feel like I know him really well.

He also keeps licking his lips and finger tips while explaining how *gorgeous* the coastline looks. I try to engage with what he's saying, like now he's going on about a place called the *Isle of Skye*, but all of his words are running together, because—cute—eating fries—finger-licking-good—wow.

And now, it's all I can do but to keep chewing, keep my mask in place and hide my massive, *I-think-I-love-you-way-too-much* expressions from him. *Because let's talk about how gorgeous the 'Isle of Royce' looks right now. Can we?*

Butterflies twist down low in my belly, and the part where I could already hardly breathe gets worse. That's because instead of getting any sort of control, I've let my mind go. I've started contemplating how, when he's happy and trusting—when he's completely open or…*free* with me—like he's being with me now, Royce's eyes aren't just silver-bright, they're like fast-moving mini-comets. Every time he beams them at me, it actually feels like I'm getting painted with warm starlight.

While I chew through fish piece number three—yum—I've begun staring at how the sun's last rays are cutting into our many-paned thick glass, iron framed window. The light gets split by the beveled edges on each pane, creating a prism effect on the walls and…yes, on to his skin.

Better, it moves through his thick, black curling hair lighting all of the blues and blacks and—yep, there it is. The dark magenta that's hides on the edges of every curl is highlighted now, too.

My fingers itch to find paints or even colored pencils. All I want to do is capture how he's being right now. How this light, the smile on his face, the way his laughter moves the cords in his neck, and even how his always tense and squared off shoulders are truly relaxed for the first time since…since I've met him, actually.

This late sunlight also has me contemplating how truly sexy it is when men can grow a five-o-clock-shadow onto their chins in just one day. Because…wow when the chin and jawline are all chiseled square it's an A+ effect. His chin alone makes me crave the box of willow charcoals I have in the studio back in New York City.

Royce Devlin…swoon…he should be sketched drawn or painted every single day, right? I shake my head, half-checking myself back into his chatter—tracking that he's still on the Scotland topic, which he is.

I manage a smile and nod, hoping I've done it at the right break in the conversation to make some sort of sense, then I almost laugh at myself as he quirks a brow at me—as though he knows I'm full of shit.

I toss him a little shrug and another forced smile which is when he stops talking, giving me one of his unreadable looks. I pretend to ignore that he's caught me red-handed ogling him, by dragging more delicious salt-soaked fries off the newsprint and eat them.

When he doesn't start up his happy chatter again I feel kind of bad because how he's slightly frowning, and I'm wondering if I should try to take a turn and talk about something when he suddenly jumps up and walks to the window to looks out and says, "This moat doesn't even go all the way around. Are you suddenly freaked out by us being here? Do you not like it? Or…what?" He flashes me a such worried look over his shoulder that I feel guilty for keeping silent for so long.

I panic then, because I realize my silence must have hurt his feelings. "Royce." I start, forcing myself to pull in breaths. "How could I be bummed about any of this?"

He gives me this look like he doesn't believe me. "But you've hardly *talked* since we walked in here. What's going on in your head? Is it me? Is this about me—I've bummed you out or done something wrong somehow?"

"No. Um…no." I decide to just tell him most of the truth. "I'm… uh…just overwhelmed. I'm humbled that we're here. Honored you brought me to do this, *and* that it's so amazing. I'm…quiet because I'm trying to memorize every second of it. You know, so I can keep the memory forever?" I grin, motioning around the room. "We're in a castle, a real castle, and I get to sleep there," I point at the ridiculous-velvet-draped-princess-looking hand carved bed. "And everything in here is more than one-hundred-years old, maybe two-hundred. And…"

I force my eyes away from those moon-beam things of his to crumple up the newsprint and the scraps we'd left behind. "I—I'm also trying to remember how the Fish and Chips tasted, and how this Persian rug looks so perfect in here against the old wood floors, and I want to record how we've set this very basic meal on a silver tray that is probably older than the bed." I point at it, not mentioning the part where it's really hard to talk when you're going to share that bed with in a few hours. "And..." I suddenly feel way too hot. "Then there's this part where we've set *this food tray* on top of a hand carved, little lion footed, billion year old, gorgeous coffee table?!!" I pull in a long breath, finally turning back to him. "See? I'm just so happy that's all."

"So...you get extra quiet when you're happy? *That's* what all of this silence treatment has been about?" He turns, quirking a brow, like now he's trying to memorize...me. That or he wants to kill me?

"Yes. I guess." I nod, laughing a little. "You were probably right to check in and see if I was okay, because I also get extra quiet when I'm over the line pissed off or really sad, too. So..."

"All good things to know. I like finding out more about you."

"Me too. That's why we're doing this, right?"

"Right," he echoes pacing around the room a bit, then returns to sit beside me on the couch. "Damn-me, but you're the first girl I've even known that can make me feel this insecure."

"I am? I do?"

"That and more," he mutters so quietly I hardly hear him.

I'm hit with this unfamiliar twist of longing—but I don't know for *what*. It's so strong that it's making me feel jittery. To hide it, I lean back onto the soft velvet couch, faking a yawn while patting my stomach, forcing the conversation away from *us*, getting to know each other as quickly as possible.

I glance at the time on my phone. "It's after six."

"Maze time, you down to do that first? Get really lost in it?"

"Yes, but we'll need supplies." I reach for the old-fashioned looking telephone sitting on a very spindly looking table and dial '0'. The owner at the front desk answers: 'Hello.'

"I'm sorry to bother, but is there any chance you guys have flashlights for the maze, because what if it gets dark and we're still in there?"

I pause, raising one eyebrow up high to Royce and making my challenge-fun smile, as the woman takes over the conversation.

"Oh, yes dear. I forgot to tell you both about that while you checked in, but we call them *torches,* love. Only you yanks say flashlight, because in fact...it doesn't flash now does it?" She laughs at her own joke.

"Torches," I repeat. "And you're right flashlights don't flash." I laugh a little, too, drawing a smile from Royce.

The owner continues, "There's a mudroom just off the left of the kitchen where you'll be-havin' breakfast tomorrow. Come down the butler's staircase you two went up to find your room, pass by the very big landing, then take the *servants* stairs off the back straight down. It's obvious which is which. That same staircase will lead you to the mud room and the backdoor access to the mazes, but please remember your keys to get back inside because I'm off for home in a few. Only phone if there's an emergency, dear."

"Oh. Um. Okay. Yes, and thank you." I pull a face at Royce who's pacing around looking curious.

The woman continues, "As for the torches, we strongly encourage that you do bring them. Please, gather them on your way out. Wi-Fi and internet work inside the maze if you can't get out you can call us. Also down by the door you can find Macintoshes and—oh there's Wellies. All for your use, as well."

"Oh, thank you—we—uh already, ate and I don't think we'll need computers," I answer, with a little shrug.

Her response is another laugh, this time longer, as she adds, "You Americans. Always making jokes. So precious."

I hang up the phone, frowning a little. "All set. Flashlights in a mud room. As well as Macs and Wellies." I shrug. "I think she means snacks —and…guest laptops? Logging on right now while we're in hiding would be a bad idea, right?"

Royce cracks up, throwing his head back. "Robin. Macs are raincoats…and Wellies… are…"

"Not snacks?" I sigh, slightly frustrated at my inability to speak this UK English.

"Rain boots."

"At least they're not ducks," I mutter.

"What?"

"Nothing."

21

ROBIN

ROYCE HAS BEEN TRYING to have fun now that we've left our room, but he's failing miserably.

First we walked through this cool, modern water-squirting maze that was located by the entrance of the castle. The whole thing is wide open, and every time you went on a wrong turn, water would squirt out. Luckily, you could jump back before getting too wet.

After that he humored me, because I asked if I could walk around the entire castle because I wanted to look at it from all sides before it got dark. Halfway around, I realized I'd made the wrong request because from the look on his face I can tell that in his mind this activity has us too exposed.

Instead of admiring the amazing, *castley-castle* details of this place, he's been staring into windows for people who might be looking out at us.

(For the record, there's been no one.)

When not staring at windows, he's been whipping his head back and forth like a psycho to check behind us in case someone was watching, waiting in shadows or approaching.

(Again, thankfully, there's been absolutely no one.)

Finally, I gave up my idea of seeing the whole building and dragged Mr. Stress-freak-out across the grass, following the signs that led to the entrance of the maze. It's not until we've been inside the massive, *coolest-maze-ever* for about fifteen minutes (and not until we still haven't seen or heard anyone at all) that he seems to have finally relaxed.

He's started to smile, and to look around—actually look at the maze, and on the last few twists and turns, I've even caught him uttering the words, "Cool." And, "So very cool to be in here," a few times.

We both pause next to one of the spots where we have to choose if we're going right or going left. Instead of choosing, he reaches into the maze, pushing back branches and looking up into how it's growing into the next section while saying, "That modern maze with the squirting water out there doesn't count as a maze at all compared to this awesomeness."

He pulls his head back out, grinning at me while gathering up the small leaves that have stuck to his hair and his vintage shirt. "This Yew, or heck it's got to be so many Yew trees, right? It's got to be as old as the castle. Super impressive, because it's not easy to keep Yew trees alive for that long. Pretty sure there is no cooler tree." He blinks, eyes going over my face. "You know?"

When I only blink at him in return because I don't have anything to say, he tilts his head and asks, "Are you just being happy again and that's why you're all quiet all of a sudden? Or…you're pissed at me because you disagree about old Yew trees? Maybe you're having a maze allergy attack, or…what?"

"I'm happy, but…" I answer, laughing a little at his last guess, but I'm still avoiding his gaze while trying to shrug off the insecurity that comes over me at times like this.

Like he's reading my mind, he stops in his tracks and flip turns around to face me, blocking my path. "Robin…remember the purpose of this weekend? We're getting to know each other." He leans down. "What are you thinking right now? Tell me. You make this face a lot and I want to know what it means."

"What face," I bluff, forcing myself to look up at him.

"It's not really a face, it's more…you won't meet my eyes, your body goes all stiff, and suddenly it's awkward between us. What's *that* about? What do I do that brings that on, so I can simply stop doing it."

I chew my bottom lip nervously. "If I answer this question, then I get to ask you an awkward personal question, too. Deal?"

He crosses his arms, one side of his smile going up. "Yes. Of course.

Deal. But start with this exact moment. What just happened. Blow by blow, okay?"

"Okay." I copy his crossed arms and step back a bit so I can look all the way up at him, adding in a defensive glower. "First, I felt like I'm not as smart as you are, because I don't know what a Yew tree is. I've never even heard of that kind of tree. Second, I think I got slightly upset." I motion at the tall leaf-lined walls surrounding us. "I thought all of this was some sort of special, only grown in the UK, awesome species of green-maze-*bush*. Bushes. Not trees. So, the face I was making meant I was feeling twice-uneducated and twice-unsophisticated, which is how I always end up feeling when I'm hanging around you. So, in order for you to stop me from getting to that face, you'd have to be someone else. That or I'd have to be someone smarter. See?"

"No. Robin…don't say that. This was not the direction I wanted this conversation to go." His voice sounds sad. "Hey…look at me."

"Hey…" he says again when I shake my head, deliberately avoiding his gaze because now I can't control the butterfly-swarm that the concern lining his voice has brought about. It's swirling in my belly even faster because he's reached forward to tug on some of my escaped curls like he's trying to get me to look up and smile.

"There's more," I say, stepping back again, forcing my hair to slide out of his fingers. "I—think you're intimidating and it's probably good we have a fake marriage, because we're not at all a true match, are we?"

His brows have shot up really high. "What do you mean by that?" His voice sounds even sadder.

I shrug, trying not to react to him this time, and stick to what I'm trying to say. "Compared to army-brat me, I'll never be at your levels of sophistication or of worldliness or—whatever the proper word might be for someone who's very classy like you are. And of course I don't match your prettiness, because for a guy you are extraordinarily, freakishly pretty and handsome all at the same time—but I guess that helps with your success at a job, and all that. So…yeah."

"*That's* what you've been thinking when you make that face?" He shakes his head. "I'm sorry I asked."

"I'm not. I just want you to know that I'm very aware of all of the differences between us, as I'm sure you are, too. I also know I'm the weakest link in the success of our 'marriage'." I finally meet his eyes again. "And, in the future I will try to be better at hiding that face I make when I'm feeling completely clueless, because like you said in that limo—right before we got married—if *you* can see it on my face, then the press can probably see it. Which means I need to work on hiding that better, so it's good that you called me out about it, and please don't just be awkward and throw out compliments to me to cover the part where I'm being really honest with you. Okay? Let's just stay real."

He clears his throat when clearly I've finally run out of words and a too-long silence has stretched between us.

"Shit. Robin." His expression is now dark, troubled—maybe angry? "You're completely off base. You're the smart one that's headed to college with a scholarship, not me." He flings his arms wide, and looks up at the night sky. "I know *nothing*, and I'm not worldly or sophisticated so I don't know where you got *that* insane idea. I'm a raging, anxiety driven—*mess*—every single day. And if we're talking about pretty, then we do not match, yes it's true. But that's because you're so far out of my league that I don't deserve to stand next to you. And heck *yes*, I'll throw out compliments to you, because that part is just true. You're *so* beautiful." His voice drops to scratchy-sexy-low again. "Beyond beautiful. Swear."

I pull a face. "Dude. Do *not* patronize me right now. You asked me, I answered honestly. Now it's my turn to ask you one."

He rolls his eyes to the sky, then he paces around the closed off area of the maze like he's got more to say to me, but instead he breathes out a long, frustrated sounding sigh and returns to stand in front of me. "Fine. You go. Ask away."

I move some curls away from my eyes and fire up the flashlight because twilight is quickly turning to real live darkness. "If you aren't going to university yet, then how do you know all of the UK words and facts. Like Macs and Wellies? While we were eating fish and chips you were going on about the gorgeous *undercut cliffs of Scotland's highland coastline,* and—and—I point at the maze again. "And where did you hear about these *Yew* trees as well as—as know anything at all about maze *horticulture.* Were you secretly born in England or something? What's the deal?"

His silver-bright eyes have gone wide. "That's way more than one question."

I stamp one foot, smiling at how his cheeks have flushed slightly. "Oh come on. Answer *all* of them." I toss his words back at him. "For the sake of the weekend goals."

His eyes start twinkling teasing-bright. "I love UK history, always have. And…over these past few years I wound up obsessed with Victorian and also Edwardian times for a long while. Mostly because… uh…well…" He looks at the sky, groaning a little then looks back at me, shaking his head. "Crap…it sounds really bad now that I'm about to say it all out loud."

"Do it." I mock glower at him.

He's leveling his gaze into mine like he's about to trust me with spy information then clears his throat. "Uh. So…as you know, I hide out in hotel suites, never going outside in the real world much."

I nod as he continues, dropping his voice to a new sexy whisper that's full of laughter. "So…it's *possible* I've watched every episode of Sherlock, The Crown, Victoria, Downton Abbey, Outlander and Poldark." He re-closes the space between us to take up the edge of one of my curls again, this time he winds the tip of it around his finger. "And…I mean I've watched them all more than once, okay?"

My eyes have gone wide. "All seasons, all episodes? More than once?"

"*Huge* true confession of a guy who wastes a lot of time." I blink back, biting my lip so I don't laugh out loud all while deciding my crush on this guy has just doubled. Tripled. Bad-boy Royce Devlin is a home-body TV series whore. *BBC, series no less!*

He's nodding, face very serious. "If you want to know all of the UK words, just watch all of those shows. I only told you because I know my secret is safe with you.

"It is. Very. If this gets out… " I can't help it, that's when I laugh out loud.

He laughs, too. Tension between us erased, we both turn and re-start up our walk through the maze, choosing to go right at the end this time.

Once we round a corner we realize we've reached another dead-end. Instead of turning back, Royce motions to a grey, weather worn, wide wood bench at the end of the dead end we've found. We head toward it, sitting side by side. "Can we sit awhile?"

"Yes." I follow him to the bench, loving how the worn teak-wood looks like soft fabric under the flashlight's beam. "Do *you* want to go to university?" I ask him.

"I am going," he says, sitting, then crossing his legs in front of him while I sit, too, but tuck my legs crisscross under me, pulling the edge of the flowered dress skirt around my knees to stay warm. "I started some college classes online. It's been very little by little and not at all how I'd imagined it."

"Which is?" I ask, curious.

"I'd always had this idea the music career would slow and people would stop tracking my life. My mom and I thought I'd transfer into a regular university. I always dreamed I'd live in the dorms and somehow, blend in. I'd have a group of trouble-making bro-friends, and I'd go to all kinds of keg parties with them. You know…those kind of parties you regret going to with the kind of friends everyone *says* you'll find in college. The ones you'll keep forever, then meet up with at all of the reunions." He looks over at me, smiling. "I wanted all of that so bad."

"Me, too." I sigh out, nodding while looking up at the now dark sky and a few summer stars twinkling overhead. "I can't wait for my dorm. I'm so excited to meet some roommate I've never met yet. I want to decorate the place with cool posters and my own bits of furniture. I also hope for that same band of friends."

"Yeah. Well you'll get it. Maybe not this year, because you have to live with Sage inside our penthouse apartment while we end the *marriage of the century*," He makes quote marks, referring to the latest magazine article published about us. "But after Sage is used to my grandmother's place, and you two are settled into NYC, maybe *next year* you could swap to the dorms if…well…maybe…shit. It's so complicated, isn't it…" He trails off, and I'm thankful he's stopped himself before talking about more things I just do not want to talk about.

Quickly, I slap on a smile that matches his and say, "Yeah. It is. And, you never know. Maybe."

He nods. "I'm twenty-one now. I'd feel like an old man living in one of those dorms. Probably won't happen for me at this point. Can you imagine my bodyguards all lined up in a dorm? I'd probably have to pay to house them in rooms next door to mine, or pay the university extra to blow out a wall so we could have interconnected spaces." He shakes his head. "At this point, I'll still probably transfer into a big university, but then work with counselors and whatever online programs they've got, so I can finish the degree remotely."

"What degree will you get?"

"Do you have to ask? It's pretty obvious."

I quirk a brow? "Music?"

"Music Theory, actually."

"Cool, wow, right." I'm working really hard to mask my face extra hard so he doesn't see that I have no freaking clue what a Music Theory degree is, or that it was even possible to obtain one.

"I'm so lucky." He goes on. "I shouldn't even long for all of the regular stuff I didn't get to do in my life, right? I've got my bandmates to be those life-long friends."

"Exactly," I agree, keeping my voice light, because suddenly he doesn't sound lucky at all. Once again, I can see how the Guarderobe guys have given up so much just so they can live this dream of making music.

Trying to make him feel better, I add, "I also think you don't even need university. You already have a whole successful career, and that same career is what's teaching you more about the world and life than anyone or anything you could get out of books."

"Who knows if I will ever go." His brow furrows. "All that I know about life is disconnected and random. Plus I love to learn. Sadly, my current compilation of facts and ideas was formulated while on TV show backlots with tutors, and while traveling. Your knowledge seems consistent and stronger because it's from real teachers following organized curriculums. Real studies and real-life experiences. After you go to university you're going to grow all of that even more. You're already an amazing artist, but I predict, you'll be such a cool force when you're done with school."

"I hope so. Thanks." I feel my cheeks heating at his compliment. "But I would say your rockstar experiences are real. And consistent in their own way." I frown, considering all that he's said.

"Surreal, maybe. But I think my upbringing and education got me zero grit and even less substance, while you wound up with both of those things times-two." Yawning, he stretches both arms wide then clasps his hands behind his head, stargazing along with me. "I've seen first-hand your amazing perseverance. How you successfully, against-all-odds landed a job, got a place to live, made your own budget, all so you could selflessly parent your little brother. You did that at the same time you were dealing with the grief that goes with your dad's situation, and you did it all by yourself."

"You dealt with your own grief. So much." I sigh out, thinking of his mom.

"With my grandmother and uncle helping me through it." He blinks. "And with my best friends carrying all of the work weight for me." He shakes his head, glancing sideways at me. "I'm the inadequate one compared to you. I've never done anything by myself. *Anything.* Do you know the little train bathroom we used to change in earlier?"

I nod. "Yeah?"

"That was the first time I've been to a public restroom *alone* without a bodyguard in like ten years. And the only thing that kept me from panicking in there was that I knew you were in the hallway watching over me. How pathetic and unworldly is *that*?" He barks out a self-critical laugh. "You've only just graduated high school, yet you are so… damn…smart, clear eyed and possibly the bravest, coolest person I've ever met while…I can't even pee alone."

I shake my head again, looking away from how his eyes are glowing at me. "Again, thanks, and nice of you to say, but…I'm going to have to continue to disagree."

"*And*, you're so unfailingly polite. How do you to that?" He flings his arms wide. "You protect your little brother and all helpless *babies* like you did for Adam's little girl Apple like it's a natural state of being for you."

"It is." I blink. "I'm a soldier's kid. That's part of the code."

"Ah, *ha*," he cries out, startling me. "You just admitted you have a *code*! Boom! That's why your internal and moral compass is huge where mine is broken—if nonexistent. And, *damn-girl*, with that code, you're going to go so far past me in life. You'll look back at this year and laugh that you ever thought you couldn't be equal to a guy like me."

His bullshit is now starting to annoy me. "False. You protect people way more than I do. Protectiveness is why you can't ever relax. You're protecting me, Adam, Hunter, Vere and your grandmother non-stop. You also let yourself be thrown under the bus because of Adam's little baby." A breeze picks up so I cross my arms over my stomach, wishing we'd have taken the *Macintosh* jackets off the hooks back in the mudroom, as I go on, "You also go on stage and sing songs you've created out of the words and feelings that come from inside your own heart and share them with strangers. I'd never do that and you've done it for years. That's beyond brave. You married me after only one week—for the sole purpose of saving me and your friends. This marriage was not at all to save yourself, so you also are selfless."

"Damn. Damn!" He leans forward, burying his head in his hands and groaning. "I'd call you out right now and say—*boom again*—then make you admit that we are equals based on all that you just said, but…

since we're being all honest and real right now, I'm going to hold steady, grow some balls and tell you that on that last point—on the part where I married you to be all *selfless*—I can't agree."

"Please. Yes it was. Explain what you mean. Right now." I blink at him as he sits back up and meets my gaze. "Fine. Uh…we had other options we could have tried to save you and Sage, but each of those *other plans* meant you would have left us. More specifically, you would have left *my* life the very next day. And…I didn't want you to go away so suddenly, so I convinced everyone that marrying you was our *best* option." His eyes are burning into me.

"Seriously?" I whisper, feeling goose bumps go down my spine. "Why?"

"I—didn't know you well after that week. But I did know, that had you left, I would have missed knowing you *better*. I was curious about you. I liked how you made me laugh, made me think, how you challenged me. Loved your outlook on life and how you could see past people's masks and believe in them. How you encouraged everyone to just be—be better. First I wanted to know you better because I'd never met someone like you. Then, you were so refreshing and hilarious, I sort of couldn't wait to see what you'd do next, and then after I found out about how you were a runaway I was so humbled and overwhelmed that I'd realized you were this very deep well of…cool, see?" He chuckles, shaking his head as he notices my cheeks have flamed. "I guess meeting you made me realize that I needed a new awesome friend and I wanted it to be the funny, strong, deep-seeing girl—*you*."

"Aww." I smile, shaking my head, overwhelmed at what he's said. "And…wow…but like, Royce, you didn't have to marry me. I would have been your friend anyhow."

He grins. "How could I be sure of that? You'd have been taken back to the military base in North Carolina. And you know how my life is like this zig-zagging tornado that you may have never crossed paths with again." He shrugs. "Marrying you pretty much guaranteed my personal, very selfish goal, all while getting everyone else their goals, too." He turns even more towards me and his eyes start probing mine—in this way that I do to him to try to read his feelings. "See, Robin? I'm totally, shamelessly, utterly selfish. It was all for me. We aren't equals. You're better. I think you win."

"Was it a competition?" My brows have shot up so high I swear they're about to pop off my head.

He laughs. "I don't know. It sure felt like it there for a minute."

I shake my head and finally laugh at the cryptic, odd expressions crossing his face, because—he's got to be kidding, right? Only, when his gaze remains so intent on mine that it's making me feel all fluttery and uncomfortable and it's made the air between us nearly sizzle because he's staring at my lips and I can't stop staring at his.

"Well…uh," I shake my head, trying to clear it by forcing myself to stand up and walk a little way away from the bench. "Have you heard the expression be careful what you wish for?" I flash him my own cryptic look as I point down the maze pathway, motioning that I'm ready keep exploring the maze, when in fact all I want to do for the next, I don't know—the next forever—is stay hidden in this maze with him while he stares at my lips!

I'm pretty far in front of him now and I've reached a point in the maze where I think he can't see what I'm doing exactly, I place one hand over my thrumming-skipping heart—willing it to slow.

"Why be careful what I wish for?" He asks, finally catching up to me and surprising me because he's grabbed my hand up into his.

"Well," I shrug, walking side by side with him and loving how he always twines his fingers into mine. "Once the novelty of me nearly dry-heaving fancy foods while wearing my clothes backwards wears off, you'll realize you've made the biggest mistake of your life wishing to know me better."

"Never. And never try to change any of that, because it would be a tragedy if you somehow got that stuff right."

I unclasp my hand from his and punch him in the shoulder.

He laughs low-and long when he catches my glare. "Seriously. I'm counting down the minutes until your next social fail. I really love that about you."

"Shut. Up." I punch him again. "If I can't get things right, I'll eventually do something so terrible and damaging in public that you won't even be allowed to call me once I move out." I bump him hard with my shoulder, knocking him off balance a little as he cracks up again.

"Again. Never. But I'm pretty certain when *you* get to dump *me*, you'll be the one who never comes to visit me and this mad-life—because that's what I'd do. If I could get out, I think I'd never look back."

"Please. Don't say that. I'll always look back…and…don't say that because what about the music and the band. You'd look back."

"Maybe. But you shouldn't."

I shrug, hating the course this conversation has taken. Hating more that I don't have the words to fix it or solve any of it—solve us. So, I start running ahead instead. Right here and right now, full speed, and as fast as I can go.

"Wait. Robin! Don't leave me, you'll get lost." He sounds worried.

"No I won't," I shout, letting my legs lengthen and stretch under me as I pull the first full breath of cold night air into my lungs that I've taken in a long time. "This feels good. Come on. We're going to run until we find the center."

"Okay…but. You're the only one who's got a flashlight. Wait up, or I'll be the lost one," he calls out again, sounding even more worried—sounding so darn adorable.

I side step into the next area of the maze and wait, panting and grinning while I shine the light back behind me to show him the way. In my very best English accent, I shout out, "Do you know nothing, Sir? It's called a *torch* and…"

He rounds the corner, but he's not expecting me to be right there. He's been running lightning-speed so we almost collide.

Skidding to a halt, he flings his arms forward and grabs my shoulders, stopping himself from slamming into me. His worried expression morphs into sheer belly laughter. "And what?" he asks, breathless and grinning so wide, with his bright eyes and the planes of his face so highlighted under the rising moonlight, that I'm humbled by how beautifully this guy is made. Inside and out…

"And…catch me if you can!" I squirm out of his grasp, and we both run together into the darkness—both of us—still laughing.

22

ROYCE

IT TURNS out we couldn't share the same bed last night so I slept on the lumpy Victorian couch next to the bed.

That's because the Victorian version of a 'butler's bed' is only the size of a modern double bed, and…hell…I simply couldn't do it. Last night I'd decided that it didn't matter how high we built up the pillow fortress. There was no way I could share a bed with Robin after how close she and I became yesterday.

How close my heart feels to hers now, that is.

After running around the maze and sharing possibly too much information about how I feel about her—how she let me hold her hand—how we laughed, and actually played tag like we were little kids. How she got me to this point where it was just me, and her, and the whole outside world seemed erased? That was such a gift.

For hours last night, hell, maybe for the first time since I was about seven which was when I'd started working the TV shows at Newt TV. I had not a care in the world. Not other than the moments Robin and I were living and laughing together inside of that maze. It was like being in this perfect peaceful bubble.

It was humbling, moving and beautiful. And, somehow, yesterday changed me.

Found me.

Thankfully, Robin hadn't re-hashed the stuff I'd said to her about just 'why' I'd agreed to marry her. I think it's probably because she doesn't truly believe me, which now that I've had some sleep, I think is good. Very good, because had she pressed me on any details last night, I would have had to confirm all that I'd said was true.

Had she pressed me more after playing tag with me and while she was holding my hand, and smiling up at me in the moonlight? I might have fallen on my knees and told her how much I love her. Really, and truly love her.

I'm down with us getting to where we are today—we've crossed over into true trust. Into mutual admiration and being able to talk freely with each other. how I think she's the most amazing person I've ever met, and how I'm happy she's my friend—but anything further would be me, telling her, that I'm in love with her.

And as honest as we're being this weekend in this effort to get to know each other better, that honest statement won't serve my ultimate goal.

The goal of not hurting Robin ever again. Me, declaring my love, or whatever would do just that to her, because if she loves me back…and who wouldn't wish for that, then I will screw up the course of her future. She may try to stick around which means that dreamy excitement of her living in a dorm and going to art school could easily get derailed. Hell, based on my own life goals and the ones I'd never achieved—it's possible she'd wind up not going to school at all. Maybe years would pass…and maybe things would be okay, but even with the coolest people and the coolest couples, like my mom and dad were back when, they got divorced.

And after they got divorced, they weren't even friends anymore.

So for now, probably forever—because not being friends with Robin seems unacceptable to me, then…hell no, and no way are the I-love-you words ever going to tumble out of my mouth in front of her. She and I are now…well and truly, very-good friends. It's what I wanted, and that is where it stops.

If I can keep myself together—keep my selfishness in check—then I will, in my way, get to keep Robin with me long-term.

Keep her long term, while liking me *back*, that is.

For our second day of running away and being 'normal tourists' I've convinced Robin to go see this little church nearby called St. Peter's before we decide if we're going to go explore a few old villages or make our retreat back to the London Orb.

I've texted Adam to check in, and so far, he says our cover is holding and everyone thinks we've gone to Wales to see him. Hunter and Vere say they've acted *vague* as to our whereabouts with my grandmother and uncle, but they did say they *thought* we'd hopped a train to head to Adam's place yesterday afternoon.

So…I think we're good if we want to play this runaway game for another day. After last night, I'm hoping we can come back to our little butler's quarters for one more night, because this is the best fun I've had in a long, long time.

For today's costume, I'm back into the same pants from yesterday and same hat. I'd shaken out and put on the first shirt I'd worn for only an hour or so before we'd changed outfits on the train. It's the one with the stripes and the world's coolest abalone buttons. This morning, because it's cool outside, I've paired it all with the grey suit jacket I'd brought along.

I have to say the whole get up (minus the hat, of course) is so cool that I've already vowed to wear this all again.

To stay warm, because the morning is cool and foggy, Robin's got on the odd, oversized lumpy 'woolly-jumper' she'd grabbed last minute from the flea market. It's this massive navy blue cardigan with its own cool, little shiny buttons. The length is to her knees because it's a men's sweater. On her shorter frame, it's almost as long as the hem of the latest vintage floral dress she's wearing.

Like my shirt and pants, the dress is real vintage from times gone by. The waist has sewn in pleats and most probably it's got some sort of puffy slip underneath like yesterday's dress because the skirt is very 1950's full. To make the cardigan not look like a ridiculous bathrobe, she's left it completely unbuttoned, then she's belted both garments around her waist in this way that makes the cardigan and the dress appear to be one dress that's supposed to go together.

She's done her hair up in one loose bun at the nape of her neck, instead of the two she'd done yesterday, and with those wayward curls of hers popping out how they always do, and her face looks so fresh-washed and bright minus any makeup, she's all but taken my breath away.

It's amazing to me how this girl never obsesses over the mirror or makeup or blow-dryers. I swear she gets ready faster than I do. As she crosses in front of me I pull in a breath that's all lavender and her, and my fingers itch to twine into the riot of smaller curls already escaping that sexy bun. I analyze—stare-at—*love* the long, graceful line of her neck and adore how the old-fashioned dress has a wide oval neckline that allows me to see the upper curve of where her collar bones and neck come together. Girl's necks…are so sexy.

We lock our door, and head down the butler's steps, heading for the kitchen which is where the breakfast is to be served.

At the big landing where the servants of the past would have gone into to the main part of the house via the main stairs, or ducked into back staircases leading off to attics, the dining room or the mudroom from last night, I hear the low murmurs of the other guest's conversations drifting up, as well as the clanking of cutlery and plates. I panic slightly and grab her hand and pull her toward the ornate framed, floor to ceiling mirror that is built into the wall. Probably placed here for the masters of the castle to check their looks before making grand entrances to balls or whatever dinner parties were held in this place.

"We should check our disguises. Hold on." I try to keep the tension out of my voice and curb the wild look crossing my expression.

Thankfully she doesn't notice so quickly, I add, "Look at us in these cool outfits, huh?"

Our smiling gazes meet in the reflection. she's so darn cute, relaxed and happy—happy with *me* right now that I swear my heart just flipped upside down.

"Look at *you*, styling in that blazer." She pulls the glasses I've stuffed into my lapel pocket and slides them onto my face, nodding when she's completed the task. "There." She drops her voice to a very quiet whisper. "Now you're the handsome rockstar-gramps you were yesterday. How's my look?"

"Beautiful," I blurt out, tearing my eyes off of her and bending fast, pretending that I need to straighten a part of the hem on her dress.. "You're amazing at putting together outfits. This look—it all could be on any magazine's 'hottest-looks-for-fall' list. We need to wear these for a press conference and I'll tell everyone you're the genius behind it all."

'You think?" She shakes her head, putting a hand up and self-consciously trying to smooth the curls I love. "That's not what Clara and her mom tell me. To them, I'm an endless daily dress-up disaster. You've seen it and you've seen how the clothes on those racks are very cool, they just don't ever quite fit me."

I laugh, fixing the lapels on my jacket. "Well…if you're talking about that red skirt, and I know you are—the size was wrong, right? And they have to dress us in whatever the trends might be, even if those trends suck. I hate most of the stuff, too, but just know their choices are all about money and designers we've also promised we'd wear as part of paid deals."

She fixes the belt at her waist, turning to check if it's lined up okay in the back. "If only I *could* wear this kind of stuff daily and not be mocked for it. I *would* wear this to a press conference."

"You can." I blink at her, not understanding what she means. "We've talked about this before, but I'll say it again. Robin, you should wear whatever you want. It's a free world, you know?"

She blinks up at me. "Is it so free? What do you think the Instagram crowd would say about us right now? Clara and her mom would die of heart attacks if we got photographed together." She pulls on her granny glasses and scrunches up her face all funny. "Me with these and you in that hat? What if people noticed you didn't even have *lenses* in those glasses?" She cracks up. "Truly? Admit it, you're just being extra nice and optimistic." She wiggles her glasses up and down, then points at mine. "These babies will never be on any *hottest-looks-for fall* list."

"Maybe not the glasses," I agree, laughing at the funny faces she's pulling. "But." I turn her face back toward the mirror. "Look at us, Robin. They'd say we look great together." I drop my voice to lower. "They'd say you're absolutely charming and unique, and at least the old-school dresses and shirts with shiny buttons like mine would wind up in every clothing store in the world within a month."

"Not even—and no way. Even I think this outfit is strange. If people photographed me in it, I'd feel awkward—maybe I'd feel bad or regret it."

"I didn't take you as the type to care what anyone thinks or says about your clothes?"

"I'm not, but I've recently become someone who *does* care. And I care a lot."

"Why? Because of me?" My heart drops with sadness and what feels like remorse when she nods.

"Yes. I mean, not you directly, but, yes." Her eyes cloud over with confusion and doubt as I start glaring and I can't quite re-mask my emotions from how I want and I'm really bummed as she continues, "I care *because*...I don't want people to say bad things about you *because* of me. The stylists say I represent you and your brand now. And even more, I'm like a branch on the Guarderobe tree, representing them, as well. I also care because I want to do right by you to make up what you've done for me. If I mess up on things like outfits and makeup and hair, the three things I absolutely suck at, besides table manners and swallowing down the fancy-foods, that is." She laughs but it doesn't reach her eyes. "Then *all* of the people who are watching us will mock me, but more so, they will mock you for marrying me."

Her words have hit me like a rain of bullets. Worse, they confirm all of my worst fears—about how me, my life, my world—and all the crazy spotlight shit will change her. Have obviously already changed her, because damn…I don't want her to worry about this shit. And *damn* again, this eroding of her confidence—which happens to anyone who's flung under a microscope, makes me feel so guilty.

When I can't answer yet, and continue to glower, she shrugs and whispers, "It's bad enough people think I'm a gold digger and pregnant, right?"

Forget being hit with bullets, I've just had a knife in the heart. It's so bad, I groan out a strangled, "Yeah…I guess." While all I can think is: *Hell yes. Hell yes, it is bad enough that people think this amazing sweet girl is a gold digger and pregnant—and it's all because of me.*

My mouth is opening and closing like a fish out of water, but no other words are coming out yet, because Robin's gone on babbling, and she's slaying me permanently with her next sad lines of: "Clara says I don't want articles published with titles like: *Royce Devlin and his backwoods bride cause another scene.*" She points at us in the mirror. "These outfits and us…dressing up like this, it has been fun but, well, I can only imagine you're dead wrong about these looks being trend-setting. Instead of the *credit* you think I'd get, I'd take all kinds of blame for sucking at high fashion again."

"Okay. Um. No." Finally I'm able to hide the regrets that I've somehow changed her for the worse, and get my thoughts in order. So I'm sure she gets me, I pull the hat off so she can see my eyes. "I think, because you're an artist you have a better eye than any stylist as to what would look good together. I order you, immediately on our return to the hotel, to send away all racks of clothing sent up to you. From now on we delete Clara and her mom from our lives. We will dress ourselves."

She laughs and shakes her head, but instead of looking happy, the worry-clouded look crosses back into her expression again. "As tempting as that seems, because I do get annoyed when Clara flirts with you so endlessly, my response to your command is: *No way.* Not happening." She crosses her arms over her stomach. "Royce. After London we go to Paris. As in...*Paris.*" She puts a hand over her heart and I grin at her anxious frown. "There's going to be fancy dinners, and press appearances, *and* the red carpet music show, awards thing is happening there, right?"

"Oh crap. Yes. It is." I nod, loving how her face is so expressive.

"I've never been to one of those. And you will playing or lined up backstage right?"

"So?"

"So I'm going to need all of the advice I can get about what to wear...because..." She blinks wider. "Because it's *Paris!* Plus, you and I don't exactly have time to visit flea market after flea market to get our wardrobes filled with cool—vintage evening wear." She pauses to make quote marks before adding, 'And down-dated' stuff like *this*. We can wear these again, maybe. But...do not, I repeat, *do not* cut the stylists loose." She spins once, making the skirt on her dress go impressively wide before executing a cool curtsey while adding a very formal, "Please."

I sigh. "Fine. You're right. We will need you to be perfect for that awards show, I forgot about that. But it's not about me or any news articles anyone might write. It's because it is your first and the press is going to gobble you up like you're free Skittles left in a bowl. You'll need all of your fashion armor in place, as well as your confidence, so you're protected. But listen. If you showed up very late on the red carpet wearing only a cardboard box, you'd still look and be amazing inside of it. Got me?"

She laughs saying, "Okay. Yeah. Right. Sure."

"Yes. You would. Imagine it." I sweep her closer to the mirror. "You'd be late, because cardboard requires extra fitting."

She laughs again, this time rolling her eyes and nodding sarcastically. "Oh yes. Who isn't always late when they do cardboard."

I grin, nodding. "And so when you walk in, I stop my own interview smack in the middle, because everyone on the entire half-block long red carpet has literally gasped-and sigh and we've all turned to crane our necks to see who's causing the stir.

"Yes. Okay...and of course it's me." Her eyes are twinkling bright, imagining it with me.

"Hell yes. And I'd be very proud stalking towards you so I could walk along with you. All of this of course could be read by the paparazzi in my perfectly smoldering expression. We'd stop at the photo screen, and I'd point at you and say, *Damn…would you look at my beautiful wife over there wearing that exclusive gown, obviously done by the renowned designer: Card-and-Board*."

"Crystals are *Swarovski*, though." Robin calls out. "Earrings and necklace, Tiffany's!"

"Yes!" I crack up. Acting it out more, I mock my best amazed and adoring face to her in the mirror by making my eyes go all big—yet squinty at the same time. "I'd pull you up close like this." I turn us to the side so we can both act out my imagined scene in the mirror, then I pull her in, but only half-way. Pausing to do a huge fake smile and talk through my teeth, "Thought you'd never show, *honey*. Hold still, let them take some good shots of me gazing into your eyes because this cardboard-brown is really popping the summer-sky-blue in your eyes."

"How's this?" Her brows shoot up high and she slaps on her own extra giant fake smile as mirth plus laughter dances behind the blue I was just talking about, all while I turn us to face the fake paparazzi line. This time, I pretend to make room for the imaginary box as I put my hand up over her shoulder while I pause and wave at some more fake cameras.

I whisper through my teeth again, this time acting like the fake crowd is actually watching us and I truly don't want them to hear me, "This box leaves nothing to the imagination. You're driving me insane." Then I fake a paparazzi question: "Robin. Robin, can you answer a question. Is that…cardboard…some kind of special blend…like, is it cereal boxes or…shipping boxes, because it moves so well on you."

As she cracks up, she flutters her lashes like she's honored to answer the question and hams out her answer: "It's actually made up of Amazon boxes. Mr. Bezos—Geoff, is a big fan of the band so he donated them." She spins a little. "The trim is all made up of deconstructed Amazon Prime tape. See?" She does a little spin. "Royce just loves the brown-paper and bubble wrap under slip but only *he* gets to see that."

I step back one step, laughing along with her addressing the imaginary press line for myself. "It's a great look, but the box corners around her neck line are really sharp. Which means I have to…" I glance at her in the mirror.

She's grinning at me and shaking her head, while biting the left side of her lower lip. "I have to lean way over to kiss her…like this."

Suddenly I've got my lips on the part of her lip she'd been chewing. She gasps slightly but without resisting, she kisses me back.

Laughter and butterflies make up the sensations on my lips as I deepen the kiss, while galloping beats take over my heart. Imaginary boxes and press conferences fade away as I pull her up close.

I swear I can taste a mixture of lavender and her happiness on this kiss, and it's *so* addictive. I also note how it is intertwined with my own happiness. It's honey, it's sheer sweetness, it's heat and as she sighs into me it's suddenly the air I need to breathe in order to live.

I do that thing I've been trying not to do. I start to *long* for things, permanent things that do not belong to me. I try to pull back, but the way her face moves toward mine, and how she's opened her mouth and is pressing her tongue so tentatively into my mouth—like she's taking the lead but is terrified I'm going to reject her, almost brings me to my knees. How can I stop kissing her now?

Though she and I have logged hundreds of public pecks with people looking on, this kiss is something different. Equally as passionate as the one we shared in the closet the time I tricked her into kissing me back in Orlando—because the attraction we've always shared between us has always been real—but this is more than attraction and kissing and the white hot desire that always consumes me when we're doing this.

This is…everything.

It's friendship and respect. It's trembling and tentative. It's pressing and it's hot, and mostly it is me falling so far in love with this girl right now, that I'm sure this moment with her lips on mine, has got to feel like what the last seconds of dying might feel like. At least…if you are lucky enough to get to go to heaven, that is.

And heaven? Dying like this? It's perfect.

I want to call this kiss, our first *real* kiss because to me, now that I know her and she really knows me, it means so much more than any of the others.

Involuntarily, as she's pressing in again, I'm pressing back, and my lips coax her half open lips wide as my hands go around the narrowest part of her back. Her hands twine around my neck, and I love how her fingers go into the hair at the base of my neck, something I'm realizing she will always do when she kisses me.

I can feel her body completely relax next to mine, and I glance in the mirror sideways, loving how her curves melt against my chest and seem to fill up the space between us perfectly. This girl is so hot…

I slant my kiss deeper, admiring her flushed face as I take in how her long lashes create soft brush-shadows below her eyes.

When her bun comes undone, I'm struck again by our reflection in the mirror. Struck by how hot she looks with her head going back and her hair tangling between us as my hands are moving through it and up her spine.

I groan, because I'm unable to control how hard I'm throbbing against her lower belly. When she moans against my mouth and pushes into that hardness like she's fully aware of what's going on down there, it feels like the landing is suddenly spinning beneath my feet.

I want to scoop this girl up into my arms and take her back upstairs to our room. I want to make love to her in the amazing, carved, two-hundred-year-old bed. I want to burn her *sleep-hoodie* in the Victorian fireplace, and tell her straight up that I'm in love with her. And then I want to beg—*beg* her to love me back and throw away her whole life so she can stay with me.

Suddenly afraid of this speeding train that's become me, my heart, my thoughts and my suck-ass, selfish as hell impulses, I pull away from her fast.

Too fast, because she nearly stumbles.

I'm afraid to touch her again or help right her balance, so she has to catch herself by quickly gripping the edge of the wall next to the mirror.

"Shit. Shit. Shit. I suck," I'm panting, staring down at her and watching as her rosy cheeks flip to bright red. "I'm so sorry," I add, waiting for her to come to her senses. "I guess I got out of hand there." I force a chuckle. "That was an inappropriate and misplaced kiss with zero cameras rolling. Very sorry and wrong of me how that just happened…and yeah…I think I just took advantage of you, *and*. I'm an asshole, okay? That's what I am—to my core. Won't do it again. Don't hate me for crossing the line?"

"What? No." Like she doesn't recognize herself in the mirror or something, she simply stares at herself for a second before shaking her head. It's as though she's trying to clear it as she starts roughly dragging her fingers through her tangled hair.

I swallow, watching her…thinking: *hair I tangled.*

Then, as though she's shocked by how she looks in the mirror, she starts pressing her hands against her bright-red cheeks, then the back of one hand presses against her kiss-swollen lips.

This has me wondering: *Did I bruise those lips…do they hurt? Because…shit…they look like they might actually hurt…*

Of course I don't ask those questions, because my throbbing boner has got to hurt way more than whatever her lips are doing, and I need to stop looking at her mouth altogether while getting myself to calm the hell down, because there's no cold shower anywhere near this landing!

She steps back from the mirror and creates a larger distance to separate us like she understands the need to cool the heat that won't stop pulsing between us.

After some long breaths she says, "I could never hate you at this point. And don't say sorry for that kiss, considering I was participating fully… a-a-and yeah…it is fun to kiss you back. I guess maybe the line we've crossed is that we're now getting too comfortable with each other?"

"Yeah. Right. I guess," I bluff out some short laughter again, still pulling in deep breaths.

She nods again, unable to meet my gaze as her cheeks pile on a new layer of flushing. "That *was* really out of control, though, huh? *Oops* on my part, too. Okay?"

She tries to match my forced chuckle, but hers has come out as shaky as the backs of my knees still feel.

She turns her back to me and drags her hands back through her curls again, then deftly winds the entire mass back into the bun. When that's solid, she finally meets my gaze in the mirror. "We were simply swept away in your imaginary, paparazzi moment. That's all. Funny…" Her shrug and her smile are not at all convincing, but to her credit the next laugh she gets out does sound rather solid.

"Yes. Well. You in cardboard. Who knew the effect it would have on me?" Again, I'm unable to tear my eyes off those damn lips of hers—she needs to stop licking them like that.

And…all control below my waist is surging again! Crap. What this girl does to me. My body and soul—gone forever.

"Swept away," I parrot her words next, because I can't think of any of my own right now, managing another laugh through the throbbing that is my head, my temples and everything else.

I step really close to the mirror, pretending to comb my fingers through my own hair for a long moment, and then, needing more time, I mutter, "I uh…did my buttons wrong. Hang on," I lie, thus giving me the excuse to unbutton every single button on my shirt—and then slowly I re-button them. I then pause to tuck in the tails. This of course is a front for me to make careful adjustments to parts of me that are still throbbing and in the way. And, when I'm as ready as my frustrated self will ever be, I turn back, avoiding looking at her face completely while I point down the stairs, hoping I can at least walk and say, "Let's get some breakfast?"

"Okay. Yes." I can tell her eyes are flick over me, up and down, then down and up as she adds, "But…don't forget to put together your—stuff first."

I panic inside. *Hell. Did I fail at fixing the boner? Is that what she means?*

Can she see it? Sucks to be the guy.

Sucks!

Thankfully, she points at my head—the one attached to my neck. "Your glasses and hat?"

"Oh. Yeah. Thanks." I search around, finding that both of those things somehow had hit the floor during our kiss.

She nods stiffly, recovering her own glasses out of the tangle that's still on top of her head before adding her own garden hat over the golden mess. "I need—coffee. Don't you? But first I need the restroom."

"Me too."

"I'll take the one in the kitchen, you head back up to the one in the room"

"What?" I ask.

"Meet you in the dining area," She says, but this time her voice is cracking. Before I can even panic about her leaving me alone—and before I can panic about her being alone without me, she all but bolts down the steps away from me.

Still in a daze, I pause to glance in the mirror and note that I hardly recognize myself underneath an expression that is very much me…lost and in love. I note that my mouth might be just as swollen and as burning as hers looked, and that I do need to go clean myself up some. "Is that what she was staring at? Is that why she ran?" I mutter, laughing at myself, adding. "Damn, Dude. *Who are you right now?*"

23

ROYCE

WHEN I JOIN her at the breakfast table, the woman who'd checked us in comes quickly to greet me. "*Mr. Dash,* welcome to breakfast. I have your wife seated over here."

She walks me to where Robin is seated, reading a little printed menu. We gave her the name 'Dash' when we checked in and paid, but how she's just said it to me with this horrible *knowing* smile has made my heart sink. Hoping I'm wrong, I study the gleam in her expression and my heart sinks more because…yep she knows. Her eyes have that twinkling and over-excited—*wait until I tell all of my friends on Facebook who I met today,* hungry look. She's also suddenly trying to over-act her customer service. People always do that.

"I have some great news for you two."

"You do?" I answer, giving her a look that's begging her to keep pretending not to know who we are—begging her not to ask any crazy questions or blurt out crap while I start glancing quickly around the room to take stock of the other people in here. My heart goes from sinking to a full-stop when I note that at least two tables of guests are trying to hide that they're pointing cell phones at us.

Robin, still pinked cheeked from our kiss, has been pretending to stare at the menu this whole time so, thankfully, she hasn't caught on yet.

"I'm making *you two* special omelets. You aren't vegetarians, are you?" The owner lady holds up a steaming coffee pot as I sit in the chair across from Robin and answer tersely while directly glaring 'how-dare-you-eyes' at the people who think it's okay to film us like we're monkeys in a cage.

"Not vegetarians. And omelets sound great. Whatever you want to make we will eat. Thank you." I try to dismiss her with a cheery smile and even more eye-begging.

She doesn't budge. "Coffee for you both?"

"Yes, oh yes, and thank you." Robin finally looks up at her while the woman pours us steaming hot cups before she finally walks away.

Robin's eyes meet mine through her first sip of coffee and the smile drops from her face when she reads my expression.

One of her arched brows goes up in question, and before she can say a word, I answer her with a very small head shake. "We're outed. Be cool. Make no sudden moves. Sip your coffee and act like you don't know."

"What's going to happen?" She glances around, trying to act all casual, all while sloshing half of her cup of coffee off the side of the table, worse, some splashes on her lap.

"Oh…oops-*ow*." She glances up, quickly setting the cup down as though it's a dangerous weapon. "I've already failed. Don't ever order me to be cool. I'll never, ever be cool. We've discussed this—it makes me the opposite."

She's so cute I have to laugh, despite the stress and worry coursing through my body. I stop her hand from trying to mop up the sloshed coffee, and quickly drop our napkins onto the spill. In silence, we both watch the dark-brown seep into the bright white fabric napkins.

Again, I drop my voice to as low as it can possibly go. I lean in, brushing the side of her hot cheek, acting like we don't know we've been outed, and that we're just two people in love, about to have breakfast. "Well…*try* to at least sit very still." I smile into her big worry-frozen eyes. "We're fine so far. It's still early. Despite what information has leaked out of here, and despite what is currently being posted online by the few tables of people in this room—who *all* seem to know who we are—this castle is also not set to re-open to the public until 10AM."

"So what are we going to do?" She's said that with such perfectly stiff ventriloquist lips, that I almost laugh out loud.

"We're going to eat our breakfast, pose for a few selfies with the owner, do something similar with the intrusive, over-happy tourists and staff of this place." I nod at the tables around us and to the one waitress who is running plates to the tables. "And then, because we have no bodyguards, I'm going to call for a car and we'll hold steady up in our room until people arrive to escort us out."

She blinks, her shoulders visibly relaxing. "Right. Right. Easy. We're fine. Like I said yesterday, this is just people after all. People just like us. We're fine and safe, right?"

"Let's hope so. I mean, of course we are," I reply, not feeling safe at all. I reach for the phone I'd tucked into my back pocket and pull it out, just as the innkeeper brings us two steaming cheese and bacon omelets. "We may as well eat up. This could be a long morning for both of us."

Robin, also pulling out her phone to check it, gets distracted by hers going off two hundred beeps a minute.

Mine starts buzzing in my hand even worse than hers. "OH hell-yes, we are so outed," I mutter.

Her caller ID says: *Mrs. Felix*, while mine alerts me that my Uncle Gregory is trying to call me at the exact same time. We blink at each other helplessly but neither of us make a move to answer the calls.

Robin's phone then flashes text alerts from Vere while mine has alerts from Hunter and Adam.

"This can't be about us being spotted. It's literally everyone trying to get contact with us. Maybe…maybe something's happened to Sage?"

I shake my head. "I think, even though we're both grown adults, we're about to be chewed out by each and every person who loves us. We used to do this swarm-texting and calling to get Adam to return our calls when he ran away. Mass-group lecturing is about to happen to us."

"Oh. Aww. That's kind of sweet." She giggles a little.

"No, it's not."

My grandmother calls through on *my* phone next while Gregory's name and face light's up on Robin's phone.

Her brow furrows. "Which one of us should answer? We should, right? How bad could they lecture us for this stunt? They're all the way in New York City with Sage," she whispers out fast.

"I guess you're right. You take Gregory's next call. He's always so nice that you might get off without anyone shouting." I grin. "I'll keep watch over us in case someone tries to approach the table while you're on the phone. People always try to approach the table." Quickly I add, "No more spilled coffee. Okay?"

"Okay. Okay. No more spills. He's already calling." She flicks me a look while sliding her finger over the screen to answer the call. "Hello? Gregory? Hi. Hello. Yes, it's me. No. We're absolutely *fine.*" She rolls her eyes at me with a little knowing smile. "We know it was impulsive, and we're sorry. We've just made a plan to get back to the Orb London right now. Oh. You are?" She blinks, ducking her head lower. "Wait. What you're here in England? Already? Sage also? Wow. Yay this is great news. I can't wait to see you all."

She smiles at me, then frowns as my uncle Gregory says something more. "What? That's *good*, isn't it? We can get there very soon, yes," she whispers, as the smile she was making all but falls off of her face. "Royce was going to call for a car after we eat, but we can do it right now, yes. Yes, we will." She blinks again, then puts her hand over mine, pulling the phone away from her ear to tell me, "A car is here. Already outside." Back into the phone she says, "Oh, that's a relief. Thank you, because as I'm sure you may have heard, we've kind of been spotted and Royce just showed me there's a crowd forming outside and—oh what?" She pulls in a sharp breath. *"Excuse me? Please repeat that?"*

Her voice has changed to—tight—small—tremulous and she's using a tone I've *never* heard her use before.

My eyes go immediately off the people I'm watching and onto her just as her face goes bone white.

"What?" She nearly shouts this time, and before I can stop her she stands up and reels back like she's been shot. Her movement knocks over the wobbly antique breakfast table and crashes our plates plus both cups coffee to the floor, making glass scatter wide across the whole room.

Like she realizes too late she's just done exactly what I've directed her *not* to do, she backs away more, clutching the phone and says again. "I'm sorry. Gregory. Again. Say it again please, because I think I don't understand..."

Quickly, I stand up, right the table and apologize to the poor young server who's dashed over in a flurry to help. I fish in my pocket for my wallet, and pull out a huge pile of Euros, placing them on the righted table while telling the waitress, "This is to pay for any damages as well as extra tip for you. So sorry."

Without a backward glance at the girl, I approach Robin cautiously. She doesn't move as I gingerly put my arm around her stiff shoulders, turning her back to the people holding the cell phones. "Robin. What is it?" I whisper—this time it's loud and deliberate.

"Oh God. Oh God, *please*." Her eyes are frantic as they clash with mine as she ends the call and hands me the phone. My stomach drops with fear, and I think maybe her first guess was right. "Is it…Sage? Is it my grandmother. Is everyone okay," I ask softly.

She shakes her head. "No. Not Sage. Everyone's fine, but…" She's gulping for air. "There's a letter and it says…well…they think…they…think…"

She looks up at me, her big eyes look like hot-blown glass. Too shiny from unshed tears—too wide from unguarded vulnerability. *Fear?*

My heart drops again. If this were any other situation, any other person, I'd drag her out of here before more words were said. But because I know that all that's happened here is about to hit social media, like it or not, I can't budge. If we leave now, she's sunk for crashing plates and acting nearly insane right now. People are going to assume crazy stuff—like she's on drugs, or that we had a fight or both. Mad-rumors will spread it all over the internet. Hell, based on how two of the people having 'breakfast' in here with us haven't set down their phones this whole damn time, I figure these people are probably already filming us on Facebook Live or Instagram Live feeds right now.

"They think *what*?" I call out clearly, so everyone can hear me. "Honey. *Love*. Please, tell me what's wrong." I put my hands on her upper arms, and give her a little shake. "It's okay, Robin. Tell me. Please."

The owner has come in from the kitchen holding our omelets, as Robin blurts out: "Royce. Y-y-you—the people…that company you hired…they think they've found my *father*. People have him. That's what they say, they've been holding him *hostage*." Her face crumples and her expression is sheer broken-confusion. "It's Ivory poachers in…in… Uganda. And…my father, they don't…know…" She sobs out. "Only…. We need to go now. T-t-t0 verify photos. Only, they don't *know*, they can't tell—"

She places a hand over her mouth, her eyes boring into mine like she's fallen into a tunnel and I'm the only person she can see or hear while she speaks through her fingers. "They don't know if he's dead or alive."

I lock gazes with the owner. Her expression grows from nosy to kind and, thankfully very concerned as she sets down her load of plates. Quickly, I turn on the charm on to her, and send her out a look that I hope draws her into our team because—*damn*—I can't hold this face straight and I need do because I need this woman to be my ally.

I pull Robin deep into the circle of my arms, because I know she wants to hide her face, bury herself somehow, and once she's next to my heart, I turn and speak loud enough so everyone who's been photographing us or watching us like a circus side show, so they can hear every word. "I apologize for the terrible mess. My wife just got the happiest surprise of her life. See, her father has been missing. Missing in action—and—"

The owner lady butts in, "Missing in action. For over a year. We know all about your story. Everyone does, Mr. Devlin. What amazing news. Of course we now can all hope for the best, right?"

"Of course," I manage, noting that Robin is about to lose it. I quickly change the subject by pointing to the money I'd left on the table, repeating what I'd said to her staff member. "That is for your trouble. For damages. For the mess, of course, and for the chaos our sneaking away here to your beautiful castle for some private newlywed time might cause you today." I raise my voice to include everyone. "I apologize for everything, and I hope you all understand. We had wanted to take some photos with you all but now…" I motion toward Robin. "It seems we can't stay longer."

"We don't mind that, not at all, we all know what it's like to have a shock. I'm so happy her father has been located, and from the line that's forming outside the castle this morning, I must thank you for making our little tourist attraction be on international news. I think your visit will help my business very much, sir."

"Are we? Have we been on the news? Already?" My temples start to pound.

The woman nods. "Yes. Local last night, and national news this morning. Some big vans have been set up out front, hoping to catch your exit. My bookings are already up fifty percent for the summer, all in one day. Can I have this food packed up for you two?" She glances kindly at Robin and hands me some tissues for Robin's tears.

"No. That's not necessary, but we might need someone to dash up and grab our suitcase and the things we've left in the room."

"Of course." The woman signals to her helping girl who dashes off to complete the task.

I ask, "You wouldn't be able to help us get to our limo? Mostly I want to get my wife—out of the line of—cameras." I nod to the other guests, dropping my voice I add, "If we can do this quickly without the press out front being involved, I can have concert tickets sent over for you, for your staff and for a few of the people who've been inconvenienced today. Please. Can you help us?"

Her face grows bright with anticipation. "Yes. Certainly. I'll call the bellman and we will figure this out. Oh, thank you Mr. Devlin. This is above and beyond."

As we move Robin toward the back mudroom where we'd exited last night to go to the maze, Robin comes back into some sort of consciousness, she turns back and sees the mess on the floor and says, "I'm so sorry. I told you. I'm not. Ever. Cool." She starts openly sobbing.

I force a smile to every onlooker, and get my arm around her tighter as I lead her out of the kitchen.

ONCE WE'RE in the limo, Robin hugs our little vintage suitcase on her lap, clutching at it like it's some sort of odd floatation device that she will never relinquish.

And I, the entire way back to the hotel, simply keep my arm around her.

We don't utter one word, because…it's like we both understand that if we did, we'd have to talk about what finding Robin's father *dead or alive* could mean—to her…to Sage…to me, hell… to *us*.

So we hold tight. Lips pressed into thin lines of silence, because we both know speculating on shit that is going to hurt either her, or me, or both of us at the same time—well what's the point of that?

24

ROBIN

It's 3AM. My whole body aches from stress, from worry, from my pounding head, and after such a long day, all four limbs don't want to move anymore.

My throat is raw and dry, first from crying too much, and now from holding back my tears, something I've had to do because when Sage and I freaked out after getting our hands on copies of the ransom letter that was sent regarding our father, we'd lost it. So much so, that Mrs. Felix had started questioning if we needed a doctor to prescribe us Valium, or at the very least a team of therapists.

People didn't understand that Sage and I had bottled up our tears ever since our dad went missing. These were tears we'd been holding back for nearly two years. First, they were tears of relief, then heck-yes, once we realized that we still didn't have any concrete answers about our dad, even with the ransom note in hand, we shed more. More because of a new layer of fear that he may not be okay—or worse. Based on the crap photographs they'd shown to us, we then shed tears of utter desolation because we couldn't make out if what we were seeing was really our father or not. Interspersed inside of all of those horrible tears, there were also tears of gratitude for Royce, Gregory and Mrs. Felix, tears for the team that got this far—and for those who are still helping us find out more information.

Of course, they told us, that no matter how much things were pointing in the right direction, that we were not to get our hopes up.

"We need, proof of life," one guy had said.

Proof of life.

Words that made us cry even more. Words that have bounced around and around inside of my head, shredding up my heart, and words that and nearly scraped out the insides of my aching eyes.

Proof of life.

This is why I've not slept and why I've been hiding in the bathroom for the last two hours, because…I've been working so hard to tamp every emotion I finally released today about my father back down into the Pandora's box I'd had them shoved into.

Only, I haven't been successful, because once a box like that has been opened…well…I'm screwed. Despite what they've all advised us about hoping? Our hopes are sky-high. How could they not be?

Exhausted now, I've finally crept out of the bathroom and I creep into the main part of the room, going up on my tip-toes to confirm, that *yes—success.* Sage and Royce appear to be sound asleep.

I head toward the bed cautiously, longing for the softness waiting in my pillow and the down blanket, wanting the oblivion sleep can give me, that I'm now craving.

I check again on Sage who's tossing and turning under his own soft down blanket. He's on a roll away bed we'd had brought in to the room. He'd wanted to sleep in our room instead of sleeping in his own ever since he arrived in London.

It was a request I was happy he'd made, and happier to grant, because since we've had this news about our father, I've had this silly and irrational idea that I should be holding my little brother tucked up on my lap just like I used to do when he was small and very upset. The kid…that's all he's been…is very, very upset.

Only, he's hardly a kid anymore. Taller than I am now, as well as, Sage has had new levels of independence since I've been married. Under the watchful eye of this supportive new family that came with my marriage, he's had his own hotel rooms, his own quarters in Mrs. Felix's apartments in NYC, as well as quarters within the apartment Royce and Mrs. Felix set up for 'Mr. and Mrs. Devlin' one floor down from Mrs. Felix's apartment as well. He's been hanging with his rockstar idols and, unlike me, Sage has no problem spending the allowance Mrs. Felix has given to him.

So…yeah, I'm happy he still wants me, still leans on me when he needs me during this time. Maybe I can't squeeze him like he's a little stuffed animal anymore, but I'm happy to pull his blankets just right, and fuss over his hair when he's sound asleep and completely unaware of it. The feeling I have when I look at his handsome, flushed face right now, must be what my father had always felt when he used to tell me with this sappy look on his face how *bittersweet* it was that I was growing up so beautifully right in front of his eyes.

Making sure Sage's feet are tucked under the blanket, I head for the steady rhythm of Royce's deep breathing. The sound is like a balm to my ragged-feeling-soul. The guy has been hovering over me nonstop since we got the news—as is his way—heck as is his whole personality. Only, I think, after the last 40 hours or so, the only escape Royce has allowed himself away from worrying about me and Sage, happens while he's sleeping and so I'm very grateful that he's finally let himself go to a place where he can recharge some.

Before I crawl in, I take in his beautiful face and I bite my upper lip, watching as Royce smiles in his sleep, but then I wonder if he's dreaming about how his life used to be before his fake wife and her problems consumed his world. Like...what did this guy fret about before we showed up, took over his mind, his worries, his entire bank account, his private hotel rooms—heck even his very own bed?

I swallow, crawling into my side, pushing away those stupid words again.

Proof of life...

What if our dad is not alive. What if he's never coming back...what if he is alive but he comes back changed...or broken, and not at all how we'd imagined he'd come back?

I push back the attacking 'what ifs' and force my thoughts onto the facts I do know now. On the one solid thing--is that the investigators told us that the ransom note appears to be *real.*

Real is good news. Good news. Real is good.

As I scoot deep under the covers, I eye the pillow fortress Royce has built up between us tonight and for the first time, I decide I hate that we have it always between us. Royce has built it triple high tonight, out of respect to my little brother being in here with us. Sage even helped him make it by adding in some seat cushions off the two reading chairs that are in front of the fireplace.

Suddenly I'm freezing—with worry, with my stupid hopefulness, with utter fear, and I acknowledge that all I want right now is to be next to Royce's constant heat. To be in the arms of my new best friend and to listen to his very-steady breathing up close, place my hand over his loudly beating heart, because I feel like my own heart and lungs might not work by themselves anymore.

I eye the pillows, deciding I'm going to move them all, figuring I could explain why I needed to be held by Royce should Sage wake up and catch me wrapped in his arms, because...*heck yes*. I breathe out a long breath. *I'm doing it...who cares what society and propriety say, anyhow.*

Why can't I have his arms around me? Why...?

Because you will wake Royce, up, that's why. Because you need to do this on your own, that's why...

Just as I'm about to fling pillows right and left...I take a deep breath and hold my impulse, leaving all in place. I cross my arms over my stomach instead and roll onto my side, curling my legs up so I'm half in a ball—so I can make my own heat. Comfort myself.

I do need to be able to do this on my own.

It's my job to worry about my Dad, not Royce's. It's up to me, only me, to be awake late, thinking about 'what's next' for my little family.

Only weeks ago, I was strong enough to run away to Orlando with Sage and try to start a life for us all on my own. Two months ago, I was strong enough to steal food out of hotels to get us fed, and brave enough to accept an insane job offer to work for Royce. And then, on the fly, I had to be brave enough, all alone, to decide to leap into the abyss and marry this guy the very same day I found out he wasn't a jerk and that everyone was lying to me—all to save Sage from being sent to foster care.

As I feel my throat thicken and the tears start to creep into the edges of my eyes again, I sniffle into my pillow wondering where that brave-badass-girl who never cried has disappeared to? Is it so bad or wrong to want his arms around my body? Is me, relying on him so much, making me weak? I sniffle again, trying not to feel guilty about how much this guy has given to me.

We are friends, right? He's always saying that. Is it wrong to want his non-stop comfort when he so willingly gives it to me? And...after that kiss we shared on the landing back at the castle...is it wrong to wish we could kiss like that again?

And again?

So many people have the friends with benefits thing going on, and Royce kissing me a lot in public, that's one amazing benefit I've shared with him all along. But that last kiss we shared, well, that just upped all of my expectations of how I hope to kiss for the rest of my life.

And now, after how he held me so sweetly in the limo all the way back here to the London Orb Hotel, smoothing my hair and keeping me close. Is it…too much to want more?

More. More. More. More…what? If I want anything more, then I'm the one that's selfish in this relationship, not him. I must be losing my mind. I can't want more when he's given me everything…

I shake my head, trying to clear it, telling myself that I'm losing it, begging myself to just go to sleep. I stare into the dark room, watching how the lights from outside makes small stripes on the sheer curtains covering our window.

Royce Devlin has given me his time, his concern, his *name,* his family, loans—and after this weekend, his open and honest friendship. I'll never be able to repay this generous person—friend—husband—all that he is to me, whatever he is to me.

He'd even read the ransom letter out loud for me when I couldn't do it myself. That's when I'd found out Royce, or Guarderobe, or Mrs. Felix, or all of them collectively, have offered up ten million dollars for the safe return of my father.

My head spins every time I think of what they'd done. Of the amount they laid down to literally buy my father—even buy simple information about my father.

Ten. Million. Dollars. Cash.

According to the note, this money is supposed to be delivered as stacks of 1k each, wrapped in neat little rubber bands and stuffed inside an unassuming black duffle bag, just like what you'd see in the trunk of a car in a movie!

My head spins with the amount.

Ten. Million Dollars.

Proof of life.

Those last words make more white-hot fear crash through me. My skin is lost in a swarm of clammy goosebumps as I can't escape the memory of the attorney who was overseeing the transactions. He'd mentioned this *proof of life* to us with such a dry and clinical voice. Saying, that if the kidnappers couldn't provide that, with something tangible and recognizable, then we'd need some real, and valid *proof of death.*

Because… if this is all fraud—*fake*—like some horrible people pretending they've found my father so they can trick us into sending money. Then a second investigation will happen quickly. One where people will pay much less for…this…horrible *proof of death.*

Apparently, death proving is cheaper than life proving…

They'd said we'd have to be patient. That if we thought the worst had happened, they would ask for a delivery of our father's dog tags, or clear photographs where we could easily identify his body—at least *something* like that before one dollar exchanged hands.

It will take time to navigate this portion of the negotiations because Uganda is a place like no other. People have their own ways, it's all very corrupt there, and we will be moving very slowly to make sure everyone involved stays safe.

Dead. Or. Alive. Time. Takes time. Ten. Million. Dollars.

The letter from the kidnappers had come via email and had been very short. One sentence, to be exact that read: *We have the man you are seeking, officer Bradley Love, so please contact us again as to how you would like to make this exchange.*

Attached to the email were three random cell phone numbers, a photocopy of Dad's military ID, and two photographs. Those pictures are what I've been trying to get out of my head since the moment I saw them.

One was a shot where there was what looked like my father's passport, his military ID, and a blurry photograph of who they said was, Captain, Bradley Thomas Love. Next to that, in the same photo was what seemed to be the military issue Velcro patch that would have been placed on my father's shirt, and it did spell out the name: LOVE.

Unfortunately, it was so blurry we couldn't make out any features of his face. The second one, showed a man, knees up and back to the wall, leaning against what one of the investigators called a classic village 'mud hut'. Which meant, he was being held somewhere rural.

The man in *that* photo was so skinny, and the picture also *so* blurry, neither Sage or I could confirm if it was our dad or not. The investigators told us not to be excited about the presence of Dad's military ID, either, because those could be made, bought and sold on the black market—*a common practice over there*—the man had said.

At that point Sage had lost it more than I had—and his tears had flowed so hard they'd made nearly in the room everyone tear up, including the loud mouthed investigator.

Like Royce knew we both needed to be taken away from

conversations going around and around us, he'd hustled us both back to this suite. He'd announced to everyone that it was late, that we'd had a long day of touring, and that Sage most probably was starving. He also covered the part how Sage looked pale and was possibly in shock, by telling everyone it was obvious he was dead on his feet from jet lag.

Once he got us both alone, he'd said what I was thinking but was unable to utter to Sage, because I, also think I'd gone into in shock.

Royce told us both that we needed stay positive and to keep on living life. That Sage and I already *knew* how to get through this day and this information, because we'd been doing it all along—MIA is MIA, until it isn't, right?

But when I'd asked him in a whisper so Sage couldn't hear me, how I could go on living life if the skinny-sick looking man in the photo *was* actually our father? Or, how I'd go on if someone delivered *dog-tags* to me?

He'd wrapped me so deep into his warm embrace and told that *he didn't know how I'd do it*, but that he'd be there for me no matter what. That comment made me able to breathe again. Made it so I didn't melt down in front of Sage again, either.

Then he dragged my brother into the hug, too. He reminded Sage and I that our father would want us to carry on together, just how we'd been doing all along. Reminded us that nothing had really changed, that tomorrow we could still look at the world with our same bright blue eyes and continue to pray and hope for the best. That is what our Dad would wish. Crying and stopping our lives, no matter what the news, was not an option…because if our dad knew we were breaking down, dead or alive, it would crush our father.

And…he was right.

After a long half hour of trying to sleep, I've at least, calmed down my headache, and I've stopped the random shaking thing that had been going on ever since I crawled into bed. And though I'm upset that I'm not asleep—because I really want to just black out—I congratulate myself on how Royce is sleeping like a baby on the other side of the pillows tower we'd made, and Sage, who'd asked last minute, if he could sleep on a rollaway bed near us, is also sound asleep.

At least they're both getting what they need. Better, I'm relieved my ongoing distress hasn't disturbed either of them or set off Royce's worry-radars for once. He's actually sleeping so deeply I'm giving myself the bronze medal for being able to get my own shit together—all on my own, just like old times.

It's not perfect because I'm so happy they're both near me right now —so I don't deserve a silver or a gold, but I think I'm at least back on the podium for champion levels of *unassisted-self-control.*

And because I'm doing so well, because I haven't even snuck out one tear in hours, I decide to go further. Why should I wait to ask questions of the investigator guy tomorrow when I can find out stuff by myself?

I pull out my phone and Google phrases like: *US military involvement in Uganda.* Then: *What is the country of Uganda like?* And: *News stories about Ugandan rebels or Ugandan poachers,* and lastly: *Facts about the Ugandan/African ivory trade.*

With each search, I devour page after page of facts, thumb through hundreds of horrible heartbreaking images of dead rhinos and elephants guarded over by angry looking and defiant men and boys. Next, I search for other other hostage and or kidnapping stories that were written about happening Africa, past and present.

My next searches have me Googling articles so I can understand the complicated relationships the US Military has with Uganda, and then I give myself a crash study on how the US deals with other African countries. Though, truthfully, this is hard because I'm so ignorant on this topic, even more ignorant about the countries of Africa, but I settle on reading up on countries like Cameroon, Gabon, and Congo. Ones that also have ivory poaching and huge corrupt transit rings where the Ivory is run through. Countries, sadly, that I'd never even thought about once before today.

My had father once explained to me that main reasons our troops go into Africa, these days, is because new wars crop up in the middle of old treaties the US has promised to help honor—treaties from long ago. The old treaties aside, our military also goes there to try to stabilize governments and to help governments decide who will have control over things like oil, diamonds, water and coal. We try to work on human rights issues and on a smaller and tragic level, we get caught up in trying to help stop things like the ivory trade and to protect the environment where we can.

So far, I'm surmising from my research that our troops don't actively engage in battles there, but that we will give supplies and training to the governments of these countries, as well as defend ourselves if attacked, but we don't help with any of these 'wars' as far as I can tell. If my dad was in Uganda, I would suppose training people is what he was probably doing, because that's what he calls himself when he does talk about work. But, because he's Special Forces, I will probably never know the truth as to what his real mission was all about. They're often, not allowed to tell.

The investigators had told me I should be relieved that my father was picked up by ivory traders—that this was lucky—and if it's true, it's the best of all scenarios.

Apparently, the traders operate more like old fashioned mafia guys. They're business men, and all about gaining more cold-hard-cash any way they can and less about killing random foreigners like some groups do. They also use hostages to trade with. Like, to gain 'forgiveness from the law or to pay off corrupt government officials'. Ivory traders are known to hold civilians, missionaries, and even military soldiers from many countries in stockpiles for months, using prisoners like bargaining chips for when trouble arises.

Sage and I already knew that the US Military doesn't pay these kinds of people for hostages—not ever. We get in there and get our own men out when we can, and often, we do. That's because paying ransoms would just encourage more people to try to take hostages for themselves.

Should a civilian prove that they're rich, or the kidnappers discover that one of the prisoners they've been holding has someone far away that might send money, then these people will gladly trade the prisoner for lump sums.

Unfortunately, my internet research was making sleep feel even more impossible. I now had all of those images I'd just seen online in my head. And I couldn't get this one that was of these two kids who were not much older than Sage out of my mind. These boys—these kids—had been dressed in green army clothing and were squatting in front of a military Jeep.

The photographer had taken the photo at an such an odd, almost fisheye angle, that while they were holding their giant black machine guns—the guns seemed bigger than the boys' whole bodies. It was beautiful, riveting, horrible art.

Instead of looking scared or afraid, these teens looked fierce and proud to be holding those guns. Worse, their expressions were so determined. The photo editing that had been done—some kind of fade-filter—had made their eyes seem so black and shiny; it was like they didn't have pupils. Yet, I could tell by how they held the guns that they were very familiar with using them. It seemed obvious that they'd killed people with these guns. More, the photo showed that they would be okay—proud to kill more people, and possibly…without regrets.

I'd memorized the photos of the classic Ugandan village mud huts. Many of these would be clustered together to form a village. Each one was made with hand hewn, very long sticks, that were about the width of my arm. All laid beautifully on top of the round structures in an exact circle to form a roof. To me these structures seemed artistic and so beautiful. The people who'd created them were good at balance and composition. And it seems these straight laid sticks were used for everything. I'd even found a photo where they'd created these beautiful reclining stretchers out of the same sticks. Sadly, on the ones I'd found, they'd used them to lay their blood covered dead after a suicide bomb had decimated one of their villages. Though the caption under the photograph didn't mention it, I assumed, people had taken the blasted off hut roofs and collected the sticks to make these in order to carry their dead…but…I'm not sure.

I'd even wondered, as I looked at more and more photos of these huts and villages, if one of the ones I'd seen was were my father had been held. Wondered more if he was sitting inside of one of them, even now, waiting for the pay off.

Or, maybe like the photographs I'd seen of other 'prisoner' rescues —rescues that had ended in the hostage dying, that maybe my dad had been kept—knees bent and tied up in a dark a hole that was dug into the *floor* of one of these kinds of huts…because there were plenty of images like that, too.

To keep my mind off of that, I start chanting to myself the only positive thing that one of the photo captions of those last, terrible photos did tell me: *Those other hostages had died because no one came forward to pay the ransom…*

No one paid the ransom…

Royce swears they are paying.

Ten.

Million.

Dollars.

Dead…or alive…
Proof. Proof of life.

When I wake up, hours later—it's to the grey-light of early sunrise.

I'm shaking again, but I've been nestled safe in Royce's arms. He's got his chin against the top of my head and he's breathing deep, holding me tighter than ever as though he thinks he's going to stop the shaking for me.

And I love him. I love him so much.

25

ROYCE

"ROBIN. It's your last full day in London," the reporter from the London Entertainer calls out. "Will you be doing anything special?"

With still no word about her father, or if the cash drop the mercenary team did execute a couple of days ago worked or not, we've settled into this strange zombie routine of press interviews, interspersed with…plain old…waiting.

Combined with more waiting, all while smiling and remaining positive, which has, in fact…*sucked.*

Like she can read my mind, Robin leans into my shoulder as though she's looking for a little strength to help hold up her spine. I'm happy to tighten my arm around her because her gentle warmth next to me, and the way she's places her hand on my leg makes me calm, feeds my own depleted strength reserves.

Robin answers the reporter, "I think our sneak-away trip to Hever Castle was as special as it gets and, since the news of my father, we've all been in a blur, so…I don't know."

She tosses me a glance as a different reporter calls out, "Can you tell us about who made the outfits you wore on the trip to the castle? Instagram has gone insane with posts of people trying to replicate your looks."

"Everything we had was vintage. I love vintage floral dresses, and it turns out Royce has a thing for old shirts with shell buttons. But I actually don't know if any of what we wore had designer labels. It may have been hand made."

I'm so proud of the confidence in Robin's voice as she deals with these reporters that it makes me smile as I fill in some of the conversation. "We got them at a London flea market stall on the way to the castle. Greenwich Market, I think all of the ones I picked seemed completely hand sewn. Probably tailor made."

We're sitting on a love seat back in the London Orb's lobby for our final UK interview. It's a spot I chose on purpose, because I knew it would be tight quarters and, better, I knew that Robin and I would have to be sitting so close we'd be literally tumbling onto each other's laps.

And we are.

With Sage wanting to sleep in our room these last nights, I've had to sacrifice most of my sleepy-Robin-snuggling and settle for hugging her briefly at sunrise, then bolting out of the bed like none of that really happened should either she or Sage start to stir.

To make up for the lost body-contact hours, I've had one arm around Robin's shoulders for this entire interview. I've also had one hand deadlocked on hers with our fingers intertwined. She's holding on so tightly to me that I decide then and there, that I don't want our fingers to have to let go of each other for the rest of the whole day…

"And today?" The same woman asks Robin another question, jolting me out of my thoughts. "*Who* are you wearing."

"Today my shirt is Prada and…I forget who made these beautiful pants." She glances at me looking worried like somehow not knowing what pants she's wearing has failed me.

"The pants were Valentino, I think," I cover.

"I *do* know who made the shoes." She holds her sneakers out in front of here. "These are my oldest pair of Vans." She grins over at me because she's rebelled against the toe-pinching stilettos Clara keeps sending up for her, even though I did hear Robin tell Clara straight-up she would not be wearing heels again—ever.

Impulsively, I interject again, "If it's okay with my wife, I did make some surprise tour plans for her last day."

"You did?" She blinks up at me.

"Yes. Because there are sights on your bucket list that must be seen." I grin at the reporters asking them, "Would you all like to come along? Document the day?"

"Hell yes! I'm in," a man shouts out, popping his camera off of his tri-pod so his assistant can pack it up.

Robin's shaking her head, *'no'* so quickly I add, "Hear me out, *love*." I like how her cheeks go pink whenever I call her that, and sure enough —it's happened. "Ever since we returned from the castle and received the news that your father might be alive we've been holed up in this hotel. It's all been a lot like that analogy of watching a pot of water and waiting for it to boil. It's something everyone knows they shouldn't do, yet we wind up doing it, even though it's out of our control, right?"

Robin nods and clasps her arms across her stomach, while I've paused dramatically to remind the reporters to focus the story of Robin's dad. We want to gain publicity and public sympathy combined. Two things that will keep the story on the nightly news feeds. This kind of exposure will remind the animal murdering ivory poachers and kidnappers—whatever the hell they are— this will maybe hint to them that they can have more money if they want it. Hell they can have whatever it is they can come up with, as long as it serves to bring news of her father back. All I want is to end the utter torture Robin and Sage have been going through this week.

I toss Robin another small smile. "This summer is supposed to be one ongoing romantic honeymoon holiday, only now, with good reason, my wife and her little brother have been pacing holes in the Persian rug up in our suite while we all wait for the phone to ring."

"Can you blame her?" A man calls out. "It's got to be intense and nerve wracking waiting for news."

Robin nods as I add, "I agree, which is why I also thought it might be time to go out and have some major distractions. It's a beautiful, summer-sunny-day." I grin. "Let's get some fresh air. Make everyone's day and give the paparazzi some fun?" I motion to the press. "Make some fans smile, and make ourselves smile, too? What do you say, Robin?"

Not as convinced as the reporters who are now holding their breath —hoping and wishing this is going to happen—Robin raises one brow at me and as if to call my bluff. "What do you have in mind?"

"We kiss on top of that famous Ferris wheel? The London Eye?"

The pink in her cheeks deepens. "But…you're afraid of heights, and each car, or round riding-in…er…*thing*…they're mostly made of glass, right?"

"They're called *capsules*, mum," the concierge calls out, obviously charmed by Robin. "They're rather oval shaped, and it *is* Europe's tallest Ferris wheel, and yes, it's mostly made of glass and steel."

I grit my teeth and my smile turns from real to half-fake at that information, because *damn-me,* but, I *am* afraid of heights. "If you kiss me a ton while we're riding, I will close my eyes and not notice the height situation. Besides, I need to desensitize myself on heights. After London, I mean to take my wife up the Eiffel Tower for a kiss up there, too. I've promised her."

"Aww." The press crowd sighs and snaps a ton more photos, a few quickly typing notes into tablets and phones.

"Come on, what do you say. A kiss on the London Eye." Like a dork, I point at my eye.

She laughs. "Okay. But you get the kiss only *if* we're alone in that capsule." She ducks her head away from the reporters. "You know I'm shy about PDA."

"So that's a yes?" I wiggle my brows and wave my hand to signal one of my assistants to come over to me. "Oh, *we will* be alone. I'm working that out next."

I'm acting all confident like I'm some professional, romantic date planner, but I'm making our outing up on the fly. I step away from her to whisper in the assistant's ear, telling him I want them to try book up the entire London Eye, or at least part of it, so Robin and I *can* be alone in a capsule. He's whispered back that he doesn't know if he can pull this off, because we've never done anything like this, and I beg him to simply…try. Try hard. No matter what it costs.

My publicist and the bodyguards became agitated the minute I invited the press to come along, (I never done anything like that, either). Their faces nearly cracked off as they were motioning me to take it all back— and when I announced we were going on the Ferris wheel, because that's a very high profile and crowd-heavy attraction, I could swear some of them looked queasy.

My whole team, as well as my bandmates, and my grandmother and uncle, have started zooming around, acting like bees who've had their hive kicked—hard. I try not to feel bad for the bodyguards and our assistants, they're paid well, after all, to do this job. And I, more than the other guys, too often keep things easy on the entourage by choosing *safety first*—choosing to stay inside and to hide.

Smiling with the confidence I don't quite feel yet, I return to

Robin's side, recapture her hand in mine, and keep my grip tight while tugging her off the love seat so she has to stand up next to me.

"We also never got to see Big Ben. Can we see that too, maybe?" I blink at her innocently, then turn back to the concierge who's been taking notes and trying to help my staff pull this off. "Do you know the best, no, *fastest* way we could get to those two tourist attractions without causing a mob-like traffic jam?"

"Because we're so close to the docks, sir." The concierge points out toward the street. "I suggest a quick cab-ride down to the piers, then find a company that has speed boats who tour people up and down Thames. There's tons of those. Many of them pass Big Ben, even go under the bridge and then stop at the Eye. It's a classic tour. I quite recommend it."

I widen my eyes and pretend I don't notice my team shaking their heads even more at me. "I'm up for paying for a few extra speedboats to follow us along if anyone would like to film our last date in London. It could be a really romantic memory for Robin and I to have footage of us on Robin's first trip here."

The concierge takes in the group of about twenty reporters and camera men plus the entourage that are now shouting-out how much they'd love to tag along.

"All of this group will go?" The concierge asks, Royce. His eyes go double wide at the mob of thrilled reporters who now are all packing up their things.

I nod. "Looks like they're down for it! Will you text up to Hunter, Vere, and Sage to see if they want to go, as well?" My heart thrums with anticipation, and I feel myself grinning wider than I've grinned in a long time. "I know Hunter will love speedboats and Sage is going to love this. Hell, yeah. How do we get to the boats?" I blink at the concierge and add, "Hell. Dude. Do you want to go, too? I'll tell them I need you." I glance over at the grey-haired guy who appears to be this kid's boss."

"I'd be honored, sir. If they'll allow that, yes."

"Ask them, and see. I can be very persuasive."

"Yes, sir." The concierge colors a little and he smiles at me like he can't believe that he's now included. "I'll make a couple of quick phone calls to ready enough taxis and I will return straight-away to get us on our way."

Now Robin's grinning, too. "Can our taxi be one of those famous black cabs? Riding in one was on my bucket list."

"We can arrange that, too, Miss—I mean, ma'am." He dashes away to make phone calls and warn his staff what is about to happen.

Robin looks up at me with a little frown saying, "The only part I hate about being married to you, Royce is when people call me ma'am. It's the worst."

I laugh, as a reporter calls out, "The London cabbies will also appreciate this publicity. Right kind of you to think of them."

"I've been thinking about those cool, black cabs and London cabbies, and red phone booths, and Big Ben, and going to London for half of my life." Robin's eyes twinkle as the reporters laugh. I can tell she's pleased that she may have actually just done something *right* to charm the press, something that doesn't involve her personally messing up something for once. "I'll appreciate riding around in a piece of real history, as for the boat ride and the chance to get on the London Eye? I can't wait." She breathes out, her expression open, happy and nearly free of the worries and fears she's been carrying around with her for days.

As the reporters take notes and shout out a few more praises, I pass the concierge fifty euro for his suggestions, and when the man whispers our cab is ready, I signal our bodyguards to follow, then squeeze Robin's hand to signal her we're on the move. I urge her toward the spinning bronze doors at the center of the Lobby, and in seconds we're out, and into the waiting cab before anyone out on the street caught on to who we were.

As I look behind me, waiting for the bodyguards, the press and the happy concierge who was allowed to come along after all, to load up behind us, I also have to grin at how happy everyone (everyone besides my personal entourage) seems about this.

This is going to be fun, but our feeling of anonymity is instantly lost as Hunter and Vere exit the hotel with Sage in tow. The sounds of screaming and feet running creeps up around our cab, as the public realizes Guarderobe is filling up all of the cabs that are pulling into the parking area at the front of the hotel.

I try to share a glance with our cab driver, but he's now fumbling with his cell phone. His mouth is so agape, and his smile has gone so wide to have found me and Robin sitting in his cab, that I don't even wait for him to ask me. I smile back, and I motion to Robin so we can scoot up right behind the driver as we each lean to the side and ask the man, "Do you want to take some selfies with us?"

Then, because I know Robin will want this memory for herself, I pull out my phone and we ask the cabbie to turn in his seat so we can also have our own selfies with *him.*

26

ROBIN

THE BODYGUARDS PUSH Royce and I into the waiting London Eye capsule because the crowd of people who are now waiting in line has grown so big they're worrying someone might start a riot.

While we were on the speed boat, Royce tweeted once what we were up to, and when we arrived at the base of the London Eye, I couldn't believe how many people had beat us there.

As the thick glass doors on the capsule slide shut, we soak up the silence between us by both walking around the tiny oval shaped cab, admiring the long, low wooden bench (also oval) placed in the center of the cab is made. Instead of seats going all around the edge, making people face each other, this single seat can accommodate a lot of people and it's positioned so that people might sit all around it with back's facing backs, and all eyes pointed out to the view.

Royce, crossing his arms over his chest as usual, looks worried as he pauses to scan the ever increasing crowd. "This is all my fault. I shouldn't have posted there'd be rides for *any* fan who showed up, huh? I should have put a number on that. Sorry we have to wait here while they sort things out."

"I don't mind. It's kind of interesting, actually. Feels like we're real fish inside of a fish bowl."

He snorts, "Yeah…well. You call it that and I call it just another normal day." He glances up at the structure holding the capsules onto the wheel. "Did you know this thing moves so slowly it takes about thirty minutes to go around it once? It actually never stops to load and unload? Once they get it going the other people will simply walk-on and walk off sort of like a giant version of how some ski gondolas work."

"I've never been on a ski gondola, so I'll take your word for it, but I could sit in here all day checking it out, because it's designed so beautifully."

"Well, that's good because I have paid for us to go around three times. If the speed thing is true, we will be in here for an hour and a half. And if the crowd can't be contained somehow, we might stay in here forever." He waves at the crowd, and we can hear the cheering go twice as loud outside.

Laughing at his cynical expression, I glance back over my shoulder at the crush of smiling people and wave along with him. "Aww. It's going to be awesome. It's so much bigger than I thought it would be in here." I point to the bench. "The design of the bench, and the way they've framed in the glass makes is like…a tiny greenhouse. Do you have that sensation?"

"Yes. Yes I do." He's smiling, looking around at each thing I've pointed out. "Each capsule usually holds twenty-five people, and, at thirty bucks per person, that fact is going to really piss off my accountant."

"And it's going to make so many people out there happy."

"Always looking to the bright side, *you.*"

"Always worrying too much, *you*. The accountant won't be upset if it gets you the right kind of social media marketing." I grin, trying to distract him from the mob outside.

He nods, still looking worried. "I suppose you're right, and *damn,* those speedboats were a blast, huh?"

"So fun." I admire the boyish twinkle in his eyes. "Thank you for thinking up this day. It's really too much, but I'm loving the distraction."

"That's all I need to hear." The smile he's giving me is so genuine and so brilliant it takes my breath away. "Thank you for agreeing to do all of this with me. I've decided doing first-time adventures with you is the best fun I've had in my life." He motions around the cab. "Every day is like a challenge to me now. I wake up and think…what will make Robin smile."

"Why?" I blurt out, even though I know it's possibly rude.

"What?" He furrows his brow.

I shake my head, wondering at his expression. "I…I don't know. I mean, I get that perfect, romantic dates like these are all part of the mirage we're sending out to the world, but after the last few days when you haven't left my side, and how you've just been doing everything with me and for me. How you've patched me and Sage back together. How you have worked so hard to make us adjust to this new and endless level of *waiting* we're all now doing for news of our father, even though it appears we'll never hear anything more." I shrugs. "I guess…I can't help but wonder if you'd rather be doing other things. So…I just don't get, why? Why are you so kind and generous with me, Royce?"

"Because…because it's so easy? Because you're so considerate and nice to me back, and I'm talking *every* chance you get. Because you don't expect it, because you don't want anything from me other than for *me* to be myself." His brow furrows like he's surprised at my questions, and he's searching for better answers. "Because we're friends now, right? Real friends. Right? Amazing good friends, and you've had one hell of a shitty week so I'm just doing what feels right. And because I know you'd do exactly the same as I'm doing for you, and…*shit*, after all we've been through, Robin. I'll go so far as to say you're becoming one of the best friends I've ever had." His brow furrows and his lips turn down into a small frown as he flicks me a cautious look. "You don't feel the same way about me? Tell me the truth?"

My heart flips a little at his last request, but as much as I don't lie to people, I'm not going to admit the *truth* behind my feelings for him. What would I say? That somewhere in that castle after he kissed me, and then somewhere a couple of days ago when I woke up to find him holding me while I'd been asleep—that I've fallen head over heels, forever-in -love with him? No. No way. It would freak him out, so instead I answer, "Yeah. I mean. I guess I do feel the same. I guess…I just wanted us both to say it out loud." I tap the glass with my fingers, staring out at the view. "It's just hard to know what's real and what's not real with us sometimes. That's all, and so I'm really happy our friendship is so solid now. It feels great."

"Yeah. I guess you're right to ask, but understand, please that me, being nice to you, is real. Always and forever. As for our friendship? *Damn,* Robin, that's so fucking real to me." He shakes his head. "If *that* turned out to fake at this point, it would break my heart. So…please don't do that to me."

"I wouldn't. It's real. It's real for me, too. Very." I laugh, hating the forlorn expression that crossed his features. "Thank you for clarifying. But know, you don't have to do these huge epic things for me. Like taking me to castles and booking up whole Ferris wheels and… taking me on speedboats. The last few days of hanging out watching movies and doing nothing up in the hotel suite was also perfect."

He turns with a sigh and leans his back against the glass of the capsule and grabs my hands so he can pull me to face him. "I know that. I just…like doing it. Love…doing it. You make me realize that I missed a lot of fun and excitement as I toured cities like London the first time."

I keep my eyes lowered, watching as he turns my hands over in his, and runs his tanned thumbs across my palms in this way that makes the back of my neck get tingly. "Which was when?" I ask.

"Which was what? When—what?" His voice is catching in that sexy way that makes me afraid to look up at his face, because I know, if I do, I'll wish he would kiss me. I'll also wish that he were way more than just my *good friend.*

"*When* was your first time to London?" I press on, shoving my thoughts away.

"Oh." He laughs. "The first time to Europe was right after Guarderobe formed. Newt TV sent us on a mini-tour. We were sixteen. It was the year before Hunter got so depressed and had to go away to Colorado. I remember we were trying to be so damn *cool.* The band was skyrocketing to fame and we were more focused on stupid stuff like buying our first cars. Oh, and we were all really into sneaker collecting, if you can believe that. We didn't know how to be comfortable in our own skin let alone be comfortable as famous rockstars. We also had huge fan-screamer-mobs like these chasing us all around. We did think that was kind of cool because of…the girls… well. You know."

"Well, what about the girls?" He shrugs and glances outside, as I arch a brow asking again, "What?"

He sighs. "I'm not going to lie about it. We were *all* really into how our fame let us get any girl we wanted, and we were all pretty consumed with…the easy access to…everything." He shakes his head when I pull a face. "Those girls would do anything we asked them to do. It was…an insane and very…*educational* time." He chuckles at my grimace and continues, "Which means, we didn't take the time to understand the history and the beauty of what we were seeing, and no one ran away to any castles, that's for damn sure."

"But you came to Europe again on other tours. What happened then?"

"More of the same." He shrugs. "Things became habit. We worked so hard we were like hamsters running around on a wheel and we couldn't hop off. The time passed and I guess, that's when Adam started running away. We took city hopping for granted, but traveling with you gives me this chance to make it all new again. I don't think you take anything for granted."

I pull a sarcastic face. "Yes I do. Please." I point at the screaming crowd outside. "Like, here we are talking as though this is totally normal to have shut down the entire London Eye, and I hardly notice the people staring and screaming at us anymore. Is that not suddenly taking all of this…for granted?"

"Not what I mean." He shakes his head and tugs at a curl hanging over my shoulder until it pulls straight, then he lets it go, watching it curl back up again. "You made me see the architecture of this capsule. You always point out how you see your world—and to me, your world is simply breathtaking. It's because you're wonderful, and an artist, or maybe because those eyes of yours see more—connect to little details no one else would notice because they're so darn big." He grins, laughing at that as do I. "I don't know, Robin. You constantly make me wonder if I was blind or existing in an unconscious state before I met you."

"Aww," is all I can say, because my heart has swelled so much when I smile into his moon-beam eyes, I can't say what I'm really thinking: *that no one in my entire life has ever said anything so sweet to me before.* And now, just on the day I've vowed to not be in love with him one bit more, my heart is going to belong to Royce Devlin forever.

Suddenly, the air between us seems to crackle, and I'm staring at his lips so hard I'm relieved when the capsule jolts and swings, breaking the tension between us just as Royce's bodyguard knocks the glass, his voice hardly comes through the capsule as he shouts, "Are you two still a go? We're paid and approved now to fill it up with your fans. Last chance to get out."

Royce *thumbs-up* back, but when he realizes that motion means we're going up to the top, I can tell by the way his eyes are flicking around that he's nervous.

The capsule begins this almost slow-motion movement, and I

almost laugh out loud as Royce drops my hands to grip the sides the glass behind him like the thing's about to detach and drop us to the ground. Which is still only about two feet below us.

He breathes deep and I smile pretending he's not hilarious as we watch some of the press that's come along for the ride crowds into the first capsule below us. Some are already pointing cameras up at us. I try to catch my reflection in the glass because I can feel my hair starting to curl up, probably because it got damp from the speed boat ride as it zoomed up the fog laden river.

"Shit." Royce grips the glass again as we rotate higher, then laughs at himself and let's his arms drop to his sides and shrugs his shoulders. "I'm nervous. Can you tell?"

"Not as nervous as I am now," I blurt out, pulling my hair out of its bun and finger combing some of the thick-curl-locked mess.

"Why?" His eyes are going over my hair, and then going over it again.

"We should have had the stylists hop in here and help us clean up after the boat ride. And now about two billion photos of us are going to go to print. We're going to look like the Beverly Hillbillies go to London instead of how we're supposed to look."

I feel bad because the laughter's left his voice and he's shaking his head…probably because he agrees with me.

"Don't stare. I know it's a mess," I whisper, tugging the hair more. "The boat tangled it. I'll get it back in the bun and then—" I drop my hair band and it lands at his feet. When I look at him, he's still just there—gaping at me. "I said, don't stare."

"No, I wasn't staring like that." He bends to collect the hairband and he hands it back to me. "I was staring because it's…you're stunning. Honest. I think it's co cool when it curls up how it does. I was analyzing how it looks four inches shorter right now."

"Four inches shorter means five inches wider. It also means it's about to spring so huge it will fill up this capsule." I laugh, rolling my eyes. "From how dense it feels, I'm sure I look like a clown, but I have to leave it down to dry or I'll freeze all day long, because it will stay damp." I shrug. "And if that happens, I'll have a major cold for Paris."

"And we don't want that." His eyes do that shuttered-dark thing as he watches me take up the edges of hair that are around my face and twist them in my fingers a little, then pull only the twisted bits back behind my head and secure only them with the hairband. He adds, "I just realized that you never freak out about your hair like some girls I've met."

"Yes I do. I'm pretty sure this is *me*, freaking out, *duh*," I laugh again, making sure the band is secure and pulling on the length at the back, willing it to dry fast.

"Well if this is you, freaking out, it's amazing because you did all of that without a mirror. In two twists and a smile you made it look even more beautiful, and you do it all minus a blow-dryer or a straightener, and minus a whole purse full of stinky-sticky products—all the time." He crosses his arms over his chest. "It's one of the things I love about you. How you're not vain. I'll never forget how your hair looked the day we met."

"After I'd been running in one hundred degree Florida heat." I laugh, shaking my head. "When you have hair with a mind of its own you don't have a lot of options. I gave up the check-the-mirror fight years ago after I realized that I always look essentially the same no matter how hard I try."

I walk to stand next to him so we can peer out at the view together, because we're finally gaining some good height on the wheel. I think that because he's been focused on me, he hasn't noticed the slow rise of our capsule, but because I've been focused on him I want to keep him distracted so that tense look he's wearing goes away so, I babble on, "Although, this hair does look really cool straightened and I love getting it done. I just don't usually have the patience or the money it takes, because there's so much I need help." I nod when he doesn't respond only stares out the window, his shoulders and back ratcheting to extra straight. "And today, I wouldn't care at all what it looks like but, like..." I nudge him to distract him and point at the reporters in the capsule below us. "You told everyone you were *going* to kiss me, and so I get nervous if I *know* that's coming. Especially if there's going to be photos taken of us. It's the buildup getting to me, I guess." I breathe in a long breath and pick up his hand and place it over my heart and smile over at him as he grows still, pressing his hand against where my heart is beating.

He blinks, locking his eyes away from the view and onto mine. "Damn. I can feel that. It's like you're having a heart attack. The buildup to what?"

"To the...uh...*kiss*?" I feel the back of my neck growing hot as he widens and flattens his hand against my chest. "Every time, if I know one is coming up, it's like wild horses in there."

"Is it? Damn…I didn't know." He pulls his hand away and by his expression I get that he's misunderstood the reason for the fast heartbeats. "We don't have to kiss so much if you don't want to. Seriously. We do *not* have to." He sighs out a long sigh and his voice grows more tortured. "We've never talked about it—not since just before the wedding. I assumed it was…okay but we could totally adjust that if you need to? Have I been a total asshole? *Shit.*" He turns away slightly and lowers his head.

"Oh. I—*no.* I love—kissing you. Even though it's fake or… whatever…it's nice and," I feel my cheeks going hotter and hotter. "And, after that amazing kiss in the castle, I *want* to kiss you on this Ferris wheel because…"

"You just scared me so badly. You want to kiss me because why?"

He's picked up my hand and is now playing with it.

I shrug, trying to joke my way through this. "Because I'm like you were back when you were figuring stuff out. I'm looking for a little more…*education* and you're an excellent teacher."

"Christ. Don't say shit like that to me," He tilts his head in that cute way he does, and looks at me. *Into me...*

Heart racing more, because I swear I can suddenly feel the heat rising on his skin, and because I'm nearly blinded by the relief in his smile, I don't tell him that my heartbeats just doubled with the sad idea that he'd stop kissing me all together.

He goes on, "Well…then, I suppose I'm happy to oblige…"

But instead of going for it how I'd hoped the guy ruins the moment by grimacing and gripping his hands to fists as he realizes we are at the very top of the wheel. His voice gets all shaky as he adds, "But…maybe as soon as this thing is a little closer to the ground?"

Even though I'm slightly disappointed I have to laugh, because he's really cute all freaked out like this. I tear my gaze away from his lips and turn back to stare out at the Thames along with him.

Working to regain my equilibrium, too but for very different reasons, I breathe in deeply, working so I can talk without a catch in my voice, then add, "This *will* be a good one for the memory books, like you said. And…the press, as well as the fans who are riding along with us now… I'll bet everyone is having a blast on this thing."

"Right? Do you think they can see us in here? The tinting on the glass is darker than I expected." He glances around the cab. "Hmm… maybe for the kiss, I should pick you up shove your back up against glass—so they can really tell we are all about it in here." He laughs.

I swallow hard, but manage to laugh along with him because my stomach just dropped hard when butterflies shot down my spine so fast at his words.

Of course now that he's said that…it's hard to not imagine how a kiss like that would be. Feel. Worse, it's really hard not to want a kiss like that…

As much as I know he's joking right now, I want to say, *yes-let's do that,* but instead I keep it together and answer, "This is supposed to be a romantic public kiss. Not *Royce and Robin go wild in London* kind of kiss where the press types that I've probably wound up fake-pregnant all thanks to our time here on the London Eye. Remember we're trying to dissipate that rumor."

"Wow. You're right."He belly laughs, adding, "So right. There should be a progression before people think I've knocked you up. First we kiss here *romantically*, and then we up the stakes at the Eiffel Tower kiss." He scrunches his forehead, contemplating. "But wait…can I fake knock you up in Paris next week, then, or do I have to wait until we make it to Berlin?"

"Oh you're funny. You will not fake knock me up one bit, because at the last press conference you told people we were waiting until I finished university."

"Oh, yes, right. Lost my head there, imagining the fake pitter-patter of the little golden-curly-haired little babies we'd make. Anyone would be impatient for that."

"Right?" I swallow, as another surge of butterflies hits the back of my throat, because…holy cow, in addition to kissing this guy here in London, I'm going to also probably kiss him in Paris…and then Berlin? My head screams, *someone pinch me!*

When I don't answer any further, I could swear his cheeks get some color all the way to the tips of those amazing cheekbones of his. He looks sideways at me. "I'm talking like a crazy person." His laugh sounds tight, worried—cute. "It's not my fault. It's the nervous energy I've got from being afraid of heights, and like…who can think straight after you admitted to those wild horses? I guess I've got them going on too, so…" He shakes his head, looking sideways at me. "*Not me*, that's for sure. Not me."

I laugh too, but before I can say more, he scoops me away from the glass walls of the capsule and sits with me on the oval shaped bench. Then he drags my legs up and over his so I'm halfway on his lap. "The buildup has started doing the same thing to my heart."

This move reminds me of how he kissed me the night he asked me to marry him. *Fake* marry him. Even though I know this is all for show, just like it was then, I try not to care. Because, it's like I said, kissing him is nice. *So…very nice.*

Our tongues find each other and I tilt my head back, opening the kiss for him more. I'm lost in that mind-wiping-heat thing he does to my body as my limbs go limp and this fire starts up in my belly. I love the soapy-cologne scent that is always just *him* and, breathing it in, I work to match the intensity of his kisses.

When he rains kisses down my neck so we can both catch a breath, and I push my fingers deep into his thick, curling hair deciding to place a few kisses next to his ear.

Like he can read my mind, he whispers against my ear, "You always smell amazing. And now that you've told me about your adorable crazy heart beats, I swear I can't stop feeling them. It's so noticeable… so…*cute* that you do that." He's buried his face into the side of my hair.

Shivers go down my back and I copy the ear-kiss-nibble thing he just did to me.

His lips find mine again, and somehow my hands creep up under his shirt at the same time his hands have gone up mine. Way up. His fingers brush over my bra. I gasp and lean into that feeling because it's the first time he's ever done that, and because, *oh-my-wow, goosebumps and shivers* and…that's when I half notice that the capsule is all the way back to the top view point.

We've been making out for one whole rotation on this bench. But… didn't Royce tell me it takes thirty minutes to do a whole rotation?

Again, like the guy can read my mind, he pulls his face back from mine and yanks his hands off my body, nearly shoving me away from him on the bench as he stands and reels back from me. "How long have we been doing this? Shit. I'm sorry. I totally lost it."

I'd answer, but I can't. I feel frozen solid. My skin is ice cold from how quickly he let me go, and I'm simply longing for him to return to me and place his hands back to where they so obviously fit. Besides, I want to tell him that I think we didn't make out long enough. I know that's not the answer he's looking for, so to hide my desperate desire mixed with this strange desolate feeling that I can't quite understand, I simply try to regain my own breathing as I stare down at my knees.

"Christ." He says in that tone I know well—the tone that is him questioning if he's a horrible person for what we just did. "I also think we put on more of a show than I wanted to. I'm sorry."

"You know how you tell me not to apologize? Well, I don't want you to ever feel sorry about kissing me again. You need to stop doing that." I capture his gaze, still feeling all languid and dreamy as I try to rationalize him out of his worrying ways. "I'm pretty sure those were the best kisses so far. I don't want to ruin them with guilt. The world thinks we're married, we have a goal to achieve for the press, and we just did that and more. Why should we feel bad if we are getting really good at kissing each other? I see no point in feeling bad about this when it feels so darn good."

"Wow. Okay. You're right." He laughs low, and for a moment those sliver eyes of his go over me, and they feel so hot I have this feeling he's going to kiss me all over again, but he startles me by moving about as far away across the capsule that he can possibly get. "I—also—I also don't want you to miss the last view of London. Tomorrow everything changes and it's the Eiffel Tower we'll be looking at together."

Getting my bearings as the capsule finishes its second full circle, I try to ignore the burning on my lips as well as everywhere else, and I dutifully follow his lead, going to the opposite side of the capsule. I look out at the Thames river below us and wonder how, after a kiss like that, he and I can ever be the same with each other. Thankfully, I find my voice, and I manage to utter an inane response to him. "Yeah. Paris. I can't wait for Paris."

He doesn't say more.

Maybe, like me, he's just not capable. As the silence grows longer between us, I wish Royce Devlin could read my mind, because it's spinning out of control right now.

With possibilities. With possibilities of more kisses like the one he and I just shared. *Do* we have to go back to being the same together? He said he loves being part of my firsts. Maybe I need to simply ask him if he and I can go to the next…*level* after all of this amazing kissing. Because…why not?

27

ROYCE

WE'D ARRIVED to the Parisian Orb Hotel how we always do when entering big cities that are aware of Guarderobe's arrival dates: at night, around 2AM.

That's when most of the waiting, hopeful crowds have given up and left the area. But our tactics don't work on the Parisians. They're different. This is a city that opens for dinner at 9PM with dance clubs never opening doors before midnight. Two AM in Paris is prime-time here so the place is mobbed.

Once we make it through the throngs of people flooding the street in a full circle around the entire hotel, instead of going straight to our rooms, we've all been asked by my Uncle Gregory to have a quick meeting in the hotel conference room, because, it appears we need to adjust our plan or something.

Robin and I napped some in the plane while on the hour and a half flight over, and she even nodded off in the limo from the airport to here, but she's still not used to the *late-night-all-night* lifestyle like I am. The poor girl looks all puffy-eyed and out of it. She's also making this expression that has me wonder if she thinks she's dreaming that she's now standing inside a fancy hotel in Paris.

Meaning, she's so adorable and wide-eyed and leaning on me smiling, that I take advantage of the situation and I press a fast kiss on her lips, muttering, "There's paparazzi watching us right now, Robin. I think they're coming to this meeting with us. My uncle seems to have something up his sleeve. You going to make it through this without falling asleep on my arm?"

"Mm-hmh, thanks for the warning. Didn't see them trailing us. Do I look okay? I'm only wearing leggings and one of your concert t-shirts. I didn't think we'd have to see anyone who counted," she says, in this sleep-distressed-sexy-voice that has me regretting I'd only stolen one kiss. Because now I want two.

I grin at her. "You're so cute half awake right now. As for how hot you look in the Guarderobe world tour t-shirt? Let's just say I'm about to text the product manager to order more of this particular one, because once the press gets photos of you in it, we're about to sell millions of them. That ten-million dollars you're all worried about, will be paid back by next week. I don't know why I didn't think of this before."

She weakly punches my arm. "Shut up. You know that's not true."

"As true as our skyrocketing album sales." I bump her shoulder. "Maybe that's why Gregory called this meeting. Hunter said he'd heard this quadruple platinum sales rumor. Adam swears it's true. The introduction of *Roy-bin* into Guarderobe's year has sold us more tracks than all of our years combined."

"I'd heard some things about that, too." She bumps my shoulder back. "But I wasn't sure it was true, and like I always say, it's all your talent and has got nothing to do with our *marriage*."

Now I want to run for the damn shower because she's now smiling up at me like she wants another kiss, all while licking her lips while we follow the entourage down into a conference room.

Damn those lips!

She appears to wake up more when we take our seats at the long conference table. We're sitting along with Hunter and Vere. Evie and Adam, who've been in Wales this whole time, slide in across from us. Baby Apple, still buckled into her car seat carrier and sound asleep for now, has been placed in a dark corner right behind us.

Robin, fully awake now, has her big blue eyes sparkling her excitement into mine while she looks around the conference room and whispers, "This hotel is so very…*French*, isn't it?"

"Is it?" I raise a brow.

"Yes. Look at *those*." She grins, pointing at three antique, Victorian glass chandeliers hanging over the conference table that I hadn't even noticed. When the hotel staff arrives with snacks for us to eat and they place an entire plate of flaky, perfect croissants smack in front of Robin, she bumps my shoulder again, this time waggling her brows like crazy. Her eyes are now so sparkling-wide and happy, she takes my breath away.

I also know what she's thinking, and it's probably something like: *Yay. croissants! Real. French. Croissants!*

I want to taste one of those croissants at the same time she takes her first bite and then stare into her eyes to watch her reaction while we chew. I discard that thought immediately, because—forget biting into my *own* croissant at the same time and staring at her while she does the same—I want to taste her lips while she's tasting that croissant and smiling at me.

She's now staring holes through the tall antiqued, shimmering lead-framed windows as she takes in what she can of the buildings across the street. Each building looks like a work of art, many with scrolling columns, and little wrought-iron balconies boasting thick summer flowers, cascading in every direction.

Forcing my gaze away from Robin's delight, I catch my grandmother sharp stare and hold it. She gives me this worried, severe head shake that has me wondering if I may have been flashing to the whole room just how irrevocably and deeply in love I am with Robin. I smile back at my grandmother, then give a side nod towards the group of press in the corner—sending out fat lies back to my grandmother that hopefully are saying, *whatever* look I'd just had on my face was simply *all for show.*

She frowns more, and for now, I do not risk looking at Robin again. I do not risk tasting a croissant. Hell, I even consider holding my breath for the rest of this meeting to see if it would abate the expanded feeling I've got going on in my heart. I wonder if there is any way I could somehow punch my heart back down to normal size and order myself to make it feel, *back to normal.*

But I know that's impossible.

This feeling, the one I've had since the day I met Robin, is now my new normal. It's like a drug and I'm addicted. I also don't care if my heart explodes one of these days. I think, at this point I'd rather die than try to stop it. I like it.

Love it.

Love her.

Love…her….

As our attorneys, the entourage and even more press get into the room, we shove our chairs closer together to accommodate the crush. Robin takes up my hand into hers, and I squeeze back, smiling and hoping she can read my mind that I can't wait to show her Paris. When I release her hand, I also have to force my gaze away from her beautiful face again, because—*shit.*

I wasn't supposed to look at her or touch her again, but I just did it. And damn all croissants to hell, because the girl has her cheeks stuffed chipmunk-full of croissant, and she is licking flaky crumbs off of her sexy lips right now, just how I imagined she would, which *is* killing me.

And… damn my grandmother, she's still staring at me! Still reading every tangled-up thought in my head.

When I look up at my Uncle Gregory his face is like a mirror image of my grandmother's disapproving expression. Worse, when I look between Hunter and Adam, *my very best friends*, they're also firing out their: *dude-you-are-in-too-deep* expressions, right along with the waves of *don't-you-dare-hurt-our-Robin* glares.

As if they all own her, or something.

As if I would hurt her when I've sworn not to. Assholes, all of them.

I'd like to see them do what I've been doing while trying to stay sane.

Fuck them. Fuck all of them. Did they think I wouldn't fall in love with this girl when they all love her, too?

Suddenly everything feels too raw, too over-exposed—and insane. To make it all worse, Clara and her mother have slid into seats on the left side of me.

Vere, thankfully surprises us all by dashing in behind Robin, putting her index finger up to her lips so we all stay quiet. She distracts me from my dark thoughts by placing her hands over Robin's eyes, and then calling out, "Guess-who," before leaping onto Robin with a clumsy, whispered hug. "Just made it! So happy to be here!"

Robin beams at her like Vere's her long-lost sister. "I've missed you! Yay! Yay! Yay! Oh, you're here!"

Vere pulls away, pausing to tighten the rubber band on her bun and skips right into Hunter's lap, planting a distracted kiss on his lips while babble-whispering to Robin, "*Paris.* We have so much to see, to shop for, to eat!" She claps her hands. "We've also got the Paris Teen-Select Awards this week. I'll get to be there with you the whole time."

Robin shakes her head. "I was trying not to think about the awards show. The whole idea of me, on a red carpet, makes me feel really queasy."

"Well nerves be gone. I wouldn't leave my little friend alone to attend her first red-carpet awards show, all while Royce skips around being a *famous rockstar*." Vere giggles, making Robin giggle back, and for the first time since I've known my best friend's girlfriend, I envy her for the close friendship she has with Robin, because…is it horrible that I just don't want to share her?

"I don't skip, and she wouldn't be sitting *alone*," I grumble, feeling suddenly cranky. "Her seat is next to mine."

"Which will be empty nearly the whole time. What do think she'd be doing while you're interviewing and presenting the awards, and then performing your hit single with the guys? She'd be alone for half of the show all while those camera men walk by and shove those freaky lenses in her face; but not anymore." Vere beams. "Awards ceremonies are lonely-long nights for us *long-term-relationships* without best friends along."

Clara clears her throat, and I catch her rolling her eyes. "Vere, you'll need to make sure Robin holds steady during the camera-cuts to the commercial breaks. She's going to need to be trained in front of a mirror how to sit and how to hold her crazy expressions in check." Clara adds, laughing a little—but her laughter sounds sharp and unkind.

"Oh she'll be fine, we all love her beautiful-crazy expressions," Vere answers, tossing Clara a small frown like she also didn't like the way Clara had laughed.

"I didn't think about the cameras," I add. "Those do tend to freak people out. And fine. Vere, I guess I *am* happy you'll be there for her." I frown, tossing a grateful look at Vere for knowing she'd need to step in keep Robin company during the ceremony, but Clara has just made this little sarcastic-snorting-sound to go with her advice, so I feel like I need to put her in her place so I add quickly, "It's just that I've never had a real girlfriend attend these shows before. And of course never a *wife*, one whom I adore. So I'm going to want it all to be perfect for her," I add. "I'd always had movie stars or other performing artists as 'dates' to these things. Dates set up between my agent and publicists and theirs."

"Why?" Robin asks, seemingly oblivious to Clara's veiled insults. "Wait. All those girls you dated before me, they weren't *real* dates?"

"Duh." Clara rolls her eyes again. "They were business arrangements set up between agents. Stars often want to have maximum media exposures at these events. Pair one starlet to Royce Devlin for a night and the gossip magazines can't take enough photos. Talk shows invite those girls on to 'talk' while everyone else speculates for weeks if they'd hooked-up, or were truly an item or not. Honestly, Robin. It's like you really did just fall out diapers sometimes," she says, adding in a little laugh and making this face like Robin's this adorable little baby-pet we all found. This treatment adds to the ticked-off-cranky feeling I'm having, as Clara continues on, "*This* awards show is one that's going to require tons of work on your part." She scrunches her face, motioning to everyone at the table. "From Robin's hair, to her nails, to even how she *walks* slightly like a hunchback. We can't wow people with that, or with any sort of thrift store outfits like what you did in London. Not here in Paris, or you'll be crucified. Literally. Crucified."

I hate the way Clara's words have all but wiped the excited smile off of Robin's face and worse, have confirmed Robin's fears about needing a stylist here in Paris. I just don't agree with that idea, and for some reason I hate how Clara will be Robin's advisor, but instead of being able to formulate my thoughts, or say the right thing, I'm distracted when Clara leans way too close to me—giving me a view of her over-large-over-siliconed fake breasts in her low cut blouse. "Which is why you can just lean on me." It's all I can do not to grimace and lean as far away as *possible* while she smiles cloyingly up at me and adds, "And don't you worry about any of this, *Royce*. Mother and I have a huge plan in place for Robin. She won't mess it all up once we're done helping her."

I want to shut this girl down, but her mom pipes in before I can say anything—and as much as Clara is annoying as hell, Clara's mom has done such a good job for us, and for years, that I'm going to let this obnoxious, rude girl slide for now. "Clara's right, Royce. There is work to be done. I'm glad we had a moment to talk about it. We want you to know Robin will be booked solid on Friday from dawn to dusk before the awards show."

Clara smiles, acting all professional and bossy. "Yes. We have hairdressers and dress fitters coming. No coming in to distract her that day. Promise?"

In an attempt to get the twinkle back in Robin's eyes, I do manage to say clearly, "Do what you want with Robin's styling, but Robin couldn't mess anything up. And she doesn't need lots of work, or whatever you're planning. I'll give you Friday afternoon with her, and Friday afternoon only. The rest of the week is mine and just like in London we will be *picking* our own outfits this week. And I'm taking her—alone—FYI, to dinner and the Eiffel Tower as soon as I have the chance." I toss Vere a look. "And unlike the London Eye day, Robin and will be on a *date*, a really romantic perfect date, and no one will be invited along on that. It's been been a dream of my wife's to see it all lit up at night. And she wants to see a ton of art here, so I also want to be there when she goes to all of the museums, as well."

Vere's forehead has creased into worry lines. "You can have the Eiffel Tower, but Hunter and as well as Evie and Adam are coming along to the museums, too."

I sigh, happy my comments seem to have put Clara in her place, because she's now sitting back away from us all, pretending to ignore what I've said while chewing down her croissants.

Turning away from Clara completely, and wondering how Vere and Robin can stand this girl, I address Vere only. "Fine, but don't think I'm going to share Robin easily. I'll be holding her hand the whole time at every museum."

Robin has colored some and I breathe much better when she laughs. "You guys. Please. You're acting like I'm a kindergartener and it's my first day of school."

"This is more important than a first day of school." I place my arm around her shoulder and tangle a finger into her amazing hair. "It's your first days in Paris and I refuse to miss one second of you, experiencing all of the wonders this city has to offer."

Vere pulls a face. "Royce. You know this city means extra concerts and band appearances. Robin and I are going to go shopping here. Girl-bonding-shopping, and no offense, but you can't come. There's only 24 hours in a day. Last I heard you might also have to sleep."

I pull my arm tighter around Robin and wink. "It's hard to sleep with this one right next to me, because all I want to do is...*this*," I drop a quick kiss on the side of her face. This brings every color of a fiery sunset into her cheeks and she breathes out, *"Royce,"* laughing a little as though in protest, but I can tell Robin understands that I've done this to put Clara off a little.

Clara, as if on cue, nearly chokes on her croissant, drops it like a stone onto her plate and pushes back her chair. "Disgusting. Anyone want more fruit? I'm heading to the side table."

When she's gone, Robin squirms out from under my arm, and asks, "What extra concerts?"

I sigh. "Happily and sadly, thanks to our romantic love story, plus because of our antics around London, the fan base seems to have doubled here in Paris overnight. They love us more than ever right now, so we've agreed to two extra shows. Which *again*, is why you have to finally believe me that the money we've put up for your father is hardly a drop in the bucket you've made for us." I can't resist tugging at one of the curls framing her face.

She drops her voice. "Please. Royce. It can't possibly have made up anything near ten million dollars."

"Yes." I blink back. "That and more, so stop feeling guilty, because I know you have been ever since you found out that stupid, irrelevant number."

Her mouth turns down into a frown and her eyes flash with challenge.

I shake my head, deciding change the subject because I don't want to argue with her. "Anyhow, four out of the seven nights we have in Paris will be show nights now. One will be for the awards ceremony on Friday." I wink at her as Clara returns to the table and raise my voice to be certain the glowering girl overhears us. "But, *honey*, that leaves tonight, and tomorrow night for dates and fun and hanging out together just you and me. I only wish it could be more."

Robin shakes her head and smiles at me, biting into another croissant, pausing to close her eyes with what looks like sheer-food-joy, before she waves it in front of my face, talking with a full mouth she says, "You gotta taste this."

But I'm not looking at the pastry. I'm staring at her lips again as she beams, taking another huge bite, then she shoves a chunk of into my mouth and I think I should get a medal because I did not capture her wrist and hold her hand at my mouth so I could suck on her buttery fingers.

She's saying, "Royce, you don't have to take me anywhere. Honest. This, amazing French croissant alone, it's enough."

As I chew the bite of pastry she gave to me, it takes all of my strength to tamp down the desire that's flowing in my veins now. I also have to swallow this burst of happiness I get just watching her chew and grin at me, because, damn but I love this girl too much.

Thankfully, my uncle saves me from leaning over and kissing her hard in front of everyone, when he turns on a small microphone and clears his throat. Still love-drunk on Robin's sweet face, I'm half wondering why the guy has a microphone, and also why he's signaled some cameramen to start filming, but as Robin wipes her face and fingers with a napkin, then settles in next to me so close, I'm busy making sure my chair is closer to hers. And when she picks up my hand like it's fine and natural for her to do so, I'm all nearly rendered incapable of conscious thoughts because I'm just about her soft curls tickling the underside of my chin where her head is close to my face, and only into breathing in her lavender scent and become lost in the heat and too much damn *white-hot-want* to pay attention to anything beyond the bubble of energy that is simply *us* right now.

"People. People. Listen up. We have lots to discuss. Announcements that absolutely cannot wait will be first." I glance up again at my uncle and see he's waving a paper. "Robin. Robin where are you. Sage? Are you in here?"

"Here!" Sage calls out from the other side of the table where he's been entertaining Adam's little baby.

"Here." Robin, shifts a little against me so she can pull out her arm to wave.

Gregory spots her as well, locking eyes with her as he clears his throat again. "I don't know how to say this. We have news." At those words, Robin has gone stiff and simultaneously gripped my hand vice-tight, but as Gregory smiles at her she pulls in a half breath, and nearly chokes on it as he goes on, "Your father's been found. It was all real. The ransom's been paid. He's been extracted. Kids. He's alive. Your father. He's alive and well."

Robin shoots out of her seat and stands frozen like she's been hit with a bullet but doesn't know how to fall. My gaze is drawn to her other hand, the one that's not in mine. It flutters first toward her heart then, gets stuck frozen in mid-air halfway to her temple as Gregory nods encouragingly at her statue-still form. "He's on his way to a military base near Berlin, Germany. If all goes well, with debriefing, he can join us next week as we arrive in Berlin. We're going to need another press conference and fast." He shakes the paper toward her. "This last communication says he will call within the hour. Maybe sooner."

The room erupted into motion and noise then. Everyone moving, shifting, and talking. Everyone except Robin, that is, who still couldn't seem to move.

I can't recall what words I said to her exactly, or when I stood up next to her, as well; but I distinctly remember understanding why my Uncle Gregory had invited the press to witness this announcement—because now the world would witness this emotional reveal and re-visit the story so Robin, when she divorced me would have public sympathy and understanding. *Hell* it was all probably going off live, right along with all of us, which made my heart feel heavier and heavier because I wanted to shout for someone to turn off the cameras, but…at this point causing a scene in the middle of an unfolding scene wasn't going to change anything, or get anyone to turn off their cameras.

I also can't remember when this constant shuddering overtook Robin's whole body, but I think it was the same time the same kind of horrible shudders overtook mine.

I remember her face going from shock to relief, and how her breathing stopped momentarily as the whole room started cheering. Her eyes had met mine and had gone double-wide as we connected, and I could sense she could already imagine her father here in the room with us. Somehow in that blip of time her lashes had loaded so heavy with crystalline water droplets that with her first full breath, and her first blink, her lightly freckled cheeks were instantly soaked in tears, as her face crumpled into both cries of joy, body-wracking sobs, and amazed-laughter all at once.

I also remember how she couldn't hide one feeling crossing her face from any of us—how she made us all touch and taste—*feel* every bit of the incredible strength and bravery she'd been fronting these past months. Even more incredible, now that it had been suddenly stripped off, we all were face-punch reminded that underneath it all, Robin was only this girl made up of glass. One who, all along has been so breakable—too vulnerable—so frightened and so alone.

I remember that's when I pulled myself together and crossed gazes with my grandmother and Uncle Gregory, Adam and Evie, Hunter and Vere—and the looks we shared said we were warm and satisfied. Secure in the knowledge that we had stepped in and had managed to keep Robin and Sage safe and unbroken—despite all of this crazy we'd surrounded them with.

Which is why, when she'd choked out the words, "Thank you.

Everyone, thank you so much for helping us." We all teared up big-time, too.

But…above all, I'll always remember how empty my hand felt when Robin released it to run to her little brother who had crumpled onto his knees, as his own choking, gasping cries of relief had filled the room.

28

ROBIN

WHILE ROYCE and I pace back and forth, trading places in front of the windows Adam calls out, "Uh. Does anyone feel like the air is so tense in here the room's about to split in half while we all stare at this phone?"

He's sitting between Hunter and Gregory who've been squished on the couch in our suite, ever since the press conference ended. Evie and Apple left us after the press conference so the baby could sleep in her own little crib, but everyone else has been pacing the room along with me.

Adam groans again, this time stretching his back. "I swear the walls are cracking too, and if we keep staring at the same spot, I'm sure the table under this phone is going self combust."

"He's right. Dear, me." Mrs. Felix, laughs a little. We all pause to watch her while she zooms her wheelchair around in a small-nervous-circle and then she returns to the table to stare again—as do all of us—like even she can't take her eyes off the phone.

"Waiting is the most excruciating thing, isn't it? Gregory, please open a window?"

Gregory obliges, lifting the curtain and cracking one of the tall windows about four inches.

Sage, who's been perched on the edge of a chair, puffs out a frustrated sigh and pulls out his phone, checking the time. "It's been way more than an hour. Maybe because Dad hasn't called us yet, maybe…none of it's true?"

Hunter throws a wadded up napkin at my brother. "Dude. Don't even go there. Of course it's true. Your dad is fine, he's been recovered. He's all good. These things take time."

Gregory pulls a face, but it's more to hide what I think may be his own worries. "I would not have made such a serious announcement to you or to the press if the story were not true. They did say he was weak, and as we all know he had been under a lot of stress. Maybe he had information on the people who were holding him, and he's still in debriefing."

Mrs. Felix adds, "Or, maybe he needed some sort of minor medical treatments. It's very possible he was dehydrated and they had to hook him up to an IV, or maybe the poor man simply fell asleep?"

"My father would call us, even if he felt like falling asleep," I whisper. "I'm with Sage. Maybe something is wrong."

Royce pauses in his pacing right in front of me, examining my face in that over-analyzing way he always does, then he pulls me into a small version of his bear hug. "Well, whatever the reason, he's going to call eventually, but I've decided we don't all have to sit here like this. I think we should all return to normal activities. We're all on jet-lag here. We should try to sleep some, or tomorrow's tours of Paris will be wasted."

"I agree." I sigh. "It's so cool of you guys to want to be here for me, but we are all exhausted." Without thinking, or because it's become a habit, I take up Royce's hands and squeeze them both as I pull out of his comforting embrace, adding, "I think Sage will sleep in here on the chaise, or on a rollaway like he did back in London?" I turn to my brother, because after all that's gone down these past months, he hates when people make decisions for him. "I mean, if you want to do that again, Sage?"

Sage stands and stretches his arms over his head. "Hell yes, I do. I also want to move the furniture so my hand is resting on the phone while I sleep," he adds, suddenly sounding too old and like some low-voiced man instead of sounding like my little brother. "And…did we check the *damn* thing again to make sure it's working?"

For the first time ever, Mrs. Felix or I don't chastise him for cursing, but from the circles under her eyes, I get that maybe Mrs. Felix's slip means that she's more tired than all of us are.

"It's working," I say, picking up the receiver, hitting speaker so everyone can hear the dial tone, then hanging it up really fast again, just in case that one move has caused us the miss the call. "Everyone, thank you for your love, for your support. Go to bed," I add. "I promise to text a big group message a simple thumbs up when he calls and all is well. Okay? Because all will be well."

Gregory nods, agreeing, "Thank you. Yes. A good idea."

Vere gives me a quick hug, her big brown eyes are encouraging and smiling as always, while Gregory's already maneuvering his mom's wheelchair out the door.

Hunter and Adam exit next, with Vere trailing behind them.

"Text right away, dear." Mrs. Felix calls out. Vere turns and locks eyes with me one last time.

As the door closes, I call back, "Promise. Right away."

I return to the table to stare at the phone just how I vowed I wouldn't while Sage grabs an orange juice off of the fancy room-service cart we'd all been munching snacks off of this whole time, while Royce starts scooting furniture around. "Sage. I'll move this so you're close to Robin. I think I can stick the phone on to a side table and jam right between you two so you won't miss the call."

I smile my gratitude at Royce while Sage sets down his juice to help Royce shove the ornate chaise over to my side of the bed, all while I turn back and continue to stare at the phone.

I find that I'm doing it even more steadfastly than before, because now I'm the only one left responsible for it.

Once Sage is settled on his chaise with pillows and blankets, Royce comes to stand behind me, and he drops his hands onto my shoulders, pressing thumbs into the tight muscles of my back. His first movements nearly melt me with the instant relief he's brought me. "Breathe. Your father is okay." He trails his fingers under my hair and gently presses away the rods of steel that my thoughts and worries have made out of my neck. "Thank you," I breathe out, turning to face him, only to find him frowning and unable to meet my gaze.

"What?" I ask.

"I…uh, just wanted to tell you that I can leave you and Sage in here alone, if you want? Like to have it be just you two, together…you know for when the call comes in?" He shrugs.

"No!" Sage and I both reply at the exact same time.

Sage is sitting straight up on the chaise now. "Robin's going to be all blubbery and awkward afterwards. You have to stay, because I can't deal with that. You're the ones with matching wedding rings. That's your husband-job, right?"

"Right." Royce grimaces at that, and he gives me a look I don't understand as Sage goes into the bathroom to brush his teeth. "Robin, I'm serious? Am I making this awkward?" he whispers out quickly as Sage shuts the door.

"Do you *want* to leave, because if you don't want to be here that's understandable," I ask, tension shooting straight up my neck again as I pull on my oversized sleep hoodie. "But…I can't imagine going through that phone call without you by my side."

He looks over his shoulder to be sure the bathroom door is still closed. "Yeah, but remember? Sage doesn't know our marriage is fake. Do we tell him now? If you talk to your father, you're going to have to explain some things about *us* to him, and…*shit.* I don't want to let the kid down, but like, what if Sage gets upset about all of the lies? He's my bro now. The idea of disappointing him makes me sad."

The bathroom door swings open, and Sage stalks out holding his hands up. "Guys. I already know about how this has all been a '*marriage of convenience*' or whatever arrangement you have between you."

"How. Who told you?" Royce nearly chokes on his words, flushing suddenly bright red.

"Your grandmother is going deaf." Sage starts fluffing his pillows. "And when she talks to your uncle, she sort of shouts. That's how. I knew two days after you two got hitched."

"Why didn't you say anything? Talk about it with me?" I gasp out.

He shrugs. "What was there to say? Once the stars got out of my eyes, and once I was safe from being forced to go back to North Carolina, I didn't care if it was fake or not." Sage delivers a wide smile to both of us. "Because fake or not, it was…*is* totally awesome. Mrs. Felix and I have talked about it a few times, because she's always checking in like she's a real grandmother to me. She asks me all the time if she thinks I need a therapist from all of this. " He laughs and puts his hands up to his eyes, rubbing them and yawning some before continuing, "Which is why I didn't want to talk about it with you, Robin. Because I can't change it, and because the whole thing is so nice. What everyone's done for us, it makes me choke up and cry like a baby even if I *think* about it." He pulls in a loud sniffle. "See? It's happening even now." He shakes his head, blinking tears away. "Who wants to cry in front of your sister and the dudes from your very favorite band? Not me." He pulls in another long sniff and crosses his arms.

Royce walks over and pulls him into a half hug. "Dude. You're *so* cool, you know that?"

"Back at you." Sage says, voice slightly quaking as he's trying not to tear up again.

"Swear you're not mad?" Royce asks him.

Sage's next sniffle is longer and louder, but thankfully he doesn't let the tears he's trying to swallow flow. "How can I be mad? I like—love—Robin being married to you, Royce. It makes me feel so damn happy, because I know she's been *safe*. You've protected her in every way that I would want to do, and you've been building that pillow fort each night like a pro." He points at our bed. "And I know you are such a cool guy to do that—to respect my sister how you've done. And…like…every day Robin tells me about how much she admires you and that she loves the person that you are, so how could I be mad about any of this?"

Royce raises his brows and darts me a glance at what Sage has just said, because I'm not sure I've shared those exact sentiments with Royce quite yet; but I don't deny it. I simply nod as Sage continues, "And… shit, dude. You went all out and helped us find our father. If you hadn't married Robin, maybe our dad, maybe he would still be a hostage somewhere and…not okay."

My chest twists as a few tears escape and fall down his cheeks.

Royce draws the kid into another full hug and after a moment, Sage adds a muffled whisper, "Thank you, Royce. Just, thank you. I know that if our father had never been found, that you all were setting up something permanent to keep me in school and keep both of us housed and safe. Like…you'd meant to be with us for the long haul and that means everything."

"Hell yes, Dude. Of course we'd have been there—without question." Royce's answering voice is sandpaper-low as he looks over Sage's head and paints me with tears glistening in his silver-bright eyes.

"Yeah well," Sage goes on, shuddering out a long breath and pulling awkwardly away from Royce's hug. "I don't know where to put what you did, or hardly even how to think about it." He rubs a hand against his tear-wet cheeks, trying to get it together. "Because what you did, shit." He shakes his head. "And then, bringing us to Europe and *everything*? It is so huge, that it's easier to not think about or talk about it with you guys, you know? I should have said something sooner, or tried to say thanks more. Just wanted you to know now, that's all."

I nod, completely choked up. Luckily, Royce saves me from

answering with, "Dude. I totally understand. As long as you and I are good, and you're good with how we pulled off all of this lying, that's all I care about."

"Cool." Sage shakes his head and moves away to sit on the couch. "I probably would have pitched a fit during the wedding had I figured it out earlier."

Finally able to talk, I laugh and agree with him. "I knew that to my core. It's why I didn't want you to know. Because you'd feel guilty and you would have tried to stop it."

"Yeah…I would have. Because I wanted it to be *me* fixing everything for Robin and I, but I couldn't. But when I get older—grow up, I'm going to figure out a way to pay you back. Both of you."

I smile at my little brother and join him on the couch, hugging him way too hard. "Sage. It's possible you've already grown up because of all you've just said. And you never, ever have to pay us back. Never."

"Yeah." Royce crosses his arms over his chest, smiling at Sage. "Whatever happens, and wherever your father takes you after this, we're going to be part of your family now. It's not like we can go back from this or forget, right? I messed up your lives then *married* your sister to make it right. We care so much about you two now that it's…gone deep. I mean…shit…we're going to be friends forever after this, aren't we?" His eyes skate to mine, and then away, and for some reason the look he'd shot at me had made me sense he's holding back, and that there's a whole bunch of words he is not saying right now.

Makes my tummy hurt, makes my heart ache, makes me feel like all of the air is going out of me. Because…like what my brother just said. What is there to talk about right now that's not going to hurt between the three of us?

He's Royce Devlin. And despite the name I've got on my driver's license right now, I'm still—always and forever going to be —Robin Love.

He wants to be *friends* forever, when he's got no clue that he and I being *just friends* passed by me so long ago, that I can't hardly remember if he and I ever *were* just friends.

How's that for admitting that things have gone…*deep*? Deep is an understatement about the extra two-million-feels I'm going to have for him for the rest of *my personal forever*—whether he loves me back the same or not.

Looking at his tortured expression now, I figure that it's possible the guy has some extra feelings floating around about me right now, too. Simply because we've grown so accustomed to each other that…well, now that everything is going to change between us, he's probably feeling weird about it, too.

His feelings will fade, mine probably will, too. I would also assume his will fade much easier than mine. His life moves Air Force fighter jet fast. He'll simply zoom ahead to the next cool city, to the next show he's got to preform, that when he comes up for air to wonder about us—to remember this month we've shared? He will be planets away, probably cutting album number ten.

I will be living my life, too. Hopefully, I'll be in NYC, starting art school if all is well with my dad. But for my extra-big-fun, I'll only just be downloading the Uber app for the first time, because I heard you need Uber in NYC, and buying new paints and… socks or…yeah… normal stuff like that.

I figure Royce gets how we're about to split apart like one of those rockets to the moon, one part going all the way up, while the other bits fall back to earth. So, of course, just like whatever it is he's *not* saying to me right now, I'm not saying my stupid lines of what is completely obvious, right back to him.

I'm pasting on my own small smile while trying to live *this* moment, because here and now, he is still our friend. He did help my find my father, so he's also our hero and he will always be that to me. And, better, it's not quite over yet, is it?

Royce and I are going to spend some days seeing Paris together.

So…yeah. Whatever becomes of us a month from now…or ten years from now, I need to just realize that all of what he and I have shared has been more than enough. I can't expect or even want more when I've already had so much. Besides, none of this was ever supposed to be real.

Like my brother's somehow psychic, and because the kid is too young to process all that I've just swallowed down, Sage suddenly blabs it all out loud: "Do you really mean we'll be friends *forever*, dude? Because." Sage glances at me, then back to Royce. "I have this weird feeling, like…maybe we'll never see you again once my dad comes back. Or, I'm wondering if all of this will become some sort of a strange memory. Or…" He blinks. "Wait. It will all feel like we dreamed this whole thing. Hell, it kind of already does, right, Robin?"

"Oh. Well. It's silly to speculate, right? And don't cuss." I snap out.

"I mean, like Dad hasn't even called us yet, so let's just don't play it too far forward yet, okay? I don't want to jinx anything."

Sage shrugs and lets his shoulders droop. "Yeah. Right. Sorry." He points at the horrible, endlessly-silent telephone. "I…uh…don't know what I'm trying to say anyhow, except maybe that I'm really tired?" Sage looks away from both of us and toward the window, which highlights the very dark circles under his eyes.

I hate that I don't have the courage to meet Royce's gaze right now, so I also stare out the window. "Me, too."

Royce's voice is clear and unwavering as he steps up and places a hand on my shoulder. "Then, let's just all try to get some sleep, okay?"

"It's all going to be fine," I whisper out the words I always used to say to Sage when things were not fine—when we were runaways. I regret that I've said them now, because they've somehow made Sage look even more deflated. Quickly, I add, "Royce is right. Let's all snuggle up to our pillows, okay?"

I finally risk looking at Royce, watching as he stalks away to the couch to gather up some more pillows and seat cushions for the pillow fortress, acting as though this is any other normal night for us.

Breathing in again, I take stock of my lungs, surprised that they feel normal, that I'm able to simply breathe in and breathe out just fine right now.

As for my heart beating okay?

Well…it's not doing as well, because I think it's cracked right in half.

29

ROYCE

THE CALL COMES HOURS LATER.

I know this because I haven't been able to sleep. When the phone rings, Robin rockets off the bed, voice full of breathless hope and audible heartbeats as she answers with a quiet, shaking whisper: "Hello?"

I hold myself still. Keep my breathing quiet, not letting on that I'm listening.

"Hello?" she says again, this time a little louder. "*Yes. This is Robin Love.* Daughter of Captain Love. Yes, Sir. That's me." Her voice starts shaking more. "I can wait for the connection. I won't hang up. Thank you, Sir."

Sage, ever the solid sleeper, hasn't budged from the chaise. Instead of waking, Robin's activity has him rolling over, and he actually snores a few times.

Because I want Robin to have this call be as private as possible, I also roll over, facing away from her, breathing in deeply then out, acting like I, too, didn't wake up.

"Dad? *Daddy. It's you?* Really you."

Each word she's uttered has undone me. I feel like I can taste her tears at the back of *my* throat, and my chest has grown so tight at the *sad-happy* sound of her wavering voice I can hardly breathe.

"I love you too," she's whispering. "Let me catch my breath. Yes. Yes. I'm fine. Sage is fine. I'll wake him up, hang on. He's knocked out sound asleep." She starts to move then stops. "Okay. Yes. Sure. You know how it's hard to wake him anyhow. Let's just talk then, you and me. Sure."

A long, shuddering sniffle emerges from her—and I know she's crying, only it's a cry I've never heard—she sounds desperate, like she's been holding this all back—like she's a wounded animal. "Dad…don't you cry, too. I don't know what to say…I don't know what to ask you, but please don't cry, Dad." Another round of sniffles as she listens. "Okay. Well, I can tell you it's amazing to hear your voice. I can tell you that I'm so happy right now. How about that? Is it enough for now?"

Whatever he's saying on the other side of the line is serving to help her to gain some control. "You're right, so much time ahead of us now —and maybe if you don't want to talk about it, maybe we don't need to now? We can wait for that and like…we can talk about now. Why did you have to wait so long to call us? You just woke up? Why did they sedate you?" She sighs out. "Wow. Okay. So you are kind of sick? Or… Dad, what's wrong with you. Please tell me at least those details. I want to know."

"Oh. Good." It sounds getting some control over her emotions. "Just tired. Okay…well that makes sense. Sage and I…we're very tired, too. We've been running all round Europe. We've got jet lag and sometimes we're awake at odd hours to travel, and so an irregular sleep schedule is part of our lives now. No. Dad. We're used to it, honest."

I wince at that, feeling guilty.

"You know we're in Paris." She pulls in a deep breath. "And, you're in Berlin? Right? That's what they told us and that is where we go next. Think, we're so close to being in your arms. We're so close, and everyone is okay. We're okay. You're okay and we're going to be together."

Her voice dissolves to tears again. "I prayed so hard, and every day. And—no. No. We were fine—even before Guarderobe helped us out, we were *fine*. You know me. You raised me right, and even if Guarderobe and Mrs. Felix hadn't helped us, you *know* I would have handled it somehow." She moves around some, I think fixing her pillow, before going on, "Though I can't lie, Dad. It's been great. They've been great. Stop switching the topic back to me. We're so happy. We've been so safe this whole time. How do *you* feel? You haven't answered the questions about you beyond telling me you're tired. You're not…hurt are you? You don't have anything…permanent?"

She pauses again, I hear her shifting, scooting around more, maybe heading toward Sage?

I turn just a bit and catch her using the bedcovers she dragged off the bed with her to wipe away some of her tears, and the only reason I can finally breathe is because she laughs suddenly. The sound fills the dark room with its brightness, adding oxygen into our shared dark space.

"Dehydrated and skinny, is good. Right? Dehydrated and skinny is *awesome*, Dad. If that's all, then you're better than okay. I can't *wait* to see you. How long will they observe you…or debrief you or re-hydrate you, or whatever?"

She pulls in a breath. "Okay. Well that's not bad. It's perfect actually because we need a few days to get to you. There's some concerts for the guys to get through, and also this awards ceremony which I think will be kind of fun. And right after that, we will come straight to you at the hospital. I'm sure they will make a good plan, they're experts at that. Either way you will have rooms booked at the same hotel where we will be staying."

She laughs again and I can tell she's going to be okay. That she's processed some of this and she's coming to terms with all of this being true, with her worst fears being *erased*—with her dad coming back to her.

With her life returning to normal.

She pulls in a deep breath. "Dehydrated is *not* better than married to a rockstar. *Dad*, Don't even joke. Royce is amazing and wonderful. He's been a perfect gentleman and now one of the two people Sage and I hold in highest regard—right next to you, Dad. I swear. He's at your level."

Her words fill me up---all while the words I can't hear her father shouting are tearing me apart, because even without meeting me, it's possible this guy knows me way better than his daughter does. I'm pretty sure I've heard the word, 'asshole-player-manipulated you into marrying him.'

"Dad. No!" She pulls her covers over her head as she keeps talking. "Those kisses are for the press conferences only. What you saw of us on the London Eye was all for show. We had no clue someone had a video camera trained on us or that any of it would be posted online. So what? It was a kiss—and it was staged for a reaction. And…so we're great actors. Dad. Please. We are all good and this is in name only and you need to stop going on the internet and reading insane stuff and just believe me." She laughs again. "Please. Dad I'm not talking about kissing with you. I'm eighteen. Yes. Dad. Eighteen. And even though you're misunderstanding everything you've seen, you should know that I can kiss who I want how I want, when I want. Dad…why are you shouting? Don't. Dad. Please. Save your strength and believe me."

She scrunches down into the covers a little more, and her voice grows tight like they're back to the teen-to-parent relationship already. "Fine. We will talk about it once. But we're doing it here and now, because when I see you in person and when you meet *him* in person, as well as his grandmother and uncle, I don't want these thoughts you're having, clouding things up between all of the good that has happened here. Royce—every single person in this band, as well as Mrs. Felix and Gregory deserve your respect, your thanks—and none of this cynicism."

I wince, biting my lower lip, wondering what her dad is saying. I think of how she says I'm at his level, and then I think of the kiss he was referring to on the London Eye, and hell he's right. I was *no*t being a gentleman, not one bit. I don't deserve her defending me.

She's going on, "It's been a marriage in name only, despite what you saw online and in magazines. *Dad.* Those shots were all staged. As for the photos you saw of the honeymoon, the outfits were a huge oversight, but how it played out, was also very staged. Everyone was so freaked out after the wedding, we didn't have clothes sent in to the honeymoon suite." She laughs a little. "Dad calm down. It wasn't a real honeymoon suite in any, way, shape or form. The entourage was 'leaving us alone' to have our special honeymoon time but and we slept in a hammock, no one used the bed once, and we wrapped up in tightly-tied togas. I swear."

She laughs again, this time her voice tinged with warning. "Take my word for it, because any more conversations in that direction ruins how awesome Royce has been with me, and it wrecks all the beauty of how I feel about him. And, Dad. It takes away from the awesomeness of what he and his whole family and friends did for me and Sage. You'll love him, because I love him so much, Dad. Period. End of conversation and please trust me?"

MY CHEST CONSTRICTS. That or my heart has grown three times as huge.

She said she *loves* me to her father. Said it like she means it, said that and more and…hell. And I know she does mean it, because she's Robin. This girl doesn't lie, would never say what she doesn't mean—not to her father, that's for damn sure.

"Say what you want, Dad. But you'll soon discover he's exactly like *you*. Honorable and caring, kind and good, worries about everyone first before himself, and he works so hard to do the right thing in all situations. He's so very good to me and Sage. *No.* I won't hear another word. Again, wait until you meet him. All of them. Don't say that—the first articles about me being a prostitute and all that happened in Orlando—that was my fault as much as it was his fault. He made it all safe and right by *marrying* me. Dad! No-Dad. I am not pregnant. Dad." Her voice drops to a whispering-hiss. "Please, I'm not. You know *I wouldn't be. Our relationship is not like that.*"

I'm wincing now. Imagining Robin's father going online to try to trace the trajectory of our relationship. *Nanny, for one week—prostitute for one day, teen runaway whose father is MIA marries world's most notorious womanizing rockstar! Royce Devlin and his eighteen year old child-bride run away to an English castle for a second honeymoon and get caught kissing. Newlyweds Royce and Robin can't keep their hands off of each other on the London Eye…*

I wince again.

Shit…the last article I read just today was something about how Royce and Robin's—'*Roybin's*' nine month 'countdown to baby' has to be on—and did Robin have a baby bump. If he saw even one of the articles—and hell now I know he's seen the video feed of me making out with Robin, well…of course, Robin's father must hate me--big-time.

"Dad…and this is not fair. Please, I don't want to fight about this. You're piecing together all of this information based on magazines and internet posts and what you've been told by others. I want you to listen to me. To me and Sage. We are the ones who count. Don't make assumptions, stay off the internet until you see us in person."

She sighs out, sounding desolate as she continues, "You don't know how crazy this life is. Wait until we're face to face and believe in me. I'm still your daughter and nothing has changed inside of me. Okay? All of those other people don't know what's really happening here inside the inner circle. Please understand—all of it. I know it's a shock and a stretch, but you don't know what we went through. I was so afraid Sage was going to be taken away from me. They offered to help get me out of a situation I put myself into the first time I kissed Royce. That was my fault as much as his. Maybe more. They offered to search for you. Dad. It's been terrible to miss you, but you have to understand that these people have taken the last few months of mine and Sage's life and they've turned our nightmare into something that felt like a fairytale. *They* brought you home to us. This marriage was a kindness and a huge show of pure generosity. It's become a friendship and they're our family now."

She pauses, listening. I can only hope the man has calmed down because, at least I don't hear any more shouting through the receiver.

"Yes. It's just like you going missing. We couldn't control it, change any of it, even if we tried. You'll have to absorb this and adapt. You'll see. They paid for the investigators, and they are the ones who hired people. They paid off those people ten million dollars to let you go—"

"No. Dad. No." She sits up even more, voice growing still. "There was no *price*. There's no payback. Dad. I swear. Again, take my word—my word of honor that every bit of this has been legit. Dad. *Please*, just wait until we see each other. Please."

Sage rolls over, finally hearing his sister and like a half-asleep puppy who's heard a knock at the door he shoots toward her and the phone, but his legs aren't awake yet. Nor does his body know he's about to move so the kid literally lands on the floor in a thump and a tangle of long legs and blankets. "Robin. Is it him? Is it Dad? Holy shit…it's Dad. *Dad. Robin hand me the phone. Dad!*"

Unable to stay quiet pretend I'm sleeping anymore because Sage has knocked over every bit of furniture around him including a large chair, I finally sit up and face them both, only to find them both now crumpled onto the floor.

Robin's face is sheet-white and the phone is clutched so tightly in her hand it's gone white, too. She's also somehow tangled herself up in the bedding while trying to get to the collapsed form of her brother and his smaller form is curled up onto her lap.

If the sound of Robin's voice cracking and saying she loved me to her father did me in, the sound of Sage breaking down with his relief that their father has finally called—watching Sage the smiling kid who's kept it together this whole damn time like a champ crumple—has aged me ten years. One hundred years. Shit. That has to explain why my whole damn body hurts right now.

Phone nearly forgotten for now, Sage is simply shaking his head at Robin like he can't…like it's all too much. This is not a simple choked-up tearing up either, but full-on curled-up bawling. It looks like his whole body hurts, like he can't face the phone in case this is all some sort of messed-up nightmare, or, like he's grown so reliant on Robin, he's staring at her like he's in shock. "Dad…he's okay?" He gasps out finally, the sound of his voice, raw like he's eaten rocks. "He's okay? Tell me he—that *every bit* of him—is okay. Tell me that they're letting him come to us. Why isn't he here already?"

"Hang on, Dad. I'm putting you on speaker," Robin says, reaching to where the base of the hotel phone has fallen onto the floor next to them and pushes a button.

"Robin?" their father's voice comes through the phone receiver. "Guys." I hear him pull in a breath as he pauses to listen and then says, "Hey…hey…guys…*Sage*?"

I take in the scratchy-low, and very intense voice of a man who sounds very much like his son. Sounds like he wants to crawl through the phone line to get here, saying over and over again, "What's wrong? What's going on. Sage, talk to me, son. I'm here. I'm okay. I'm coming —or rather you're coming to me. Sage. Talk to me, son."

"Dad…hang on. He's crying too hard. Hang on…Dad. We're just so happy…please hang on a second."

My throat closes up some as I take in Robin—handling things how she does. Her wild hair is flowing around her pinched, determined and ever beautiful face. She's not shedding one tear because she's on big-sister mode, taking care of her little brother.

Fierce. Warrior. Angel…

Their father commands over Sage's cries, "Robin, it's what I've been doing every day. Hanging on. Tell him I don't care if he's crying. I *want* to talk to him. Need to. Now. Sage. Sage. It's me and I'm here and I'm okay." His voice cracks as he's obviously registering the extent of Sage's sobs. "Sage I love you little dude. I'm okay. Talk to me, son."

Robin's voice encourages Sage, as she pulls him up into a tight hug, fixing the blankets around them while wiping the tears from Sage's face. "Did you hear him? It's him. He's fine. He's in Berlin, still. We're allowed to go there, and he'll be finished with his debriefing in a couple of days—right when we arrive there. Come on Sage. Nothing is hurt—he's tired, he's dehydrated and he's whole. Say something to him."

I get the courage to move only when Robin glances up at me, and instead of giving me a look that says I'm intruding, she simply smiles at me and beckons me over. Her saucer-round eyes so wide open that I can read that her happiness and feel how her relief—her belief that all of this is real and that she has her family back—is settling in. I pad over to her side and sit on the floor next to them, smiling as she—despite everything that's going on—distractedly makes sure my legs are snuggled under some of the bed coverings as her brother takes the phone from her hands.

Sage, white-knuckling the phone just how Robin had been doing, starts choke-talking with only, "Hi Dad."

Robin, breathes out an audible sigh and she leans into me. Accepts my arms around her like she's using me to hold her up which I love. I pull her into a big-bear-side hug, breathing her in, wishing she would relax against me, but her whole body is still leaning toward her brother's sobs. Leaning toward the man on the other side of the phone who's still on speaker and who hasn't responded to his son yet….

Because…his breathing has grown so harsh that I get this man has started bawling now, too.

———

ROBIN and I share a glance of horrible understanding, and I let my arms drop off of her like she's on fire. Feeling completely awkward, I quickly stand up because I've got this urge to…fucking run.

Robin scoots away from me quickly, giving me this apologetic, half guilty looking backwards glance—and from the panicked look on her face and the way that she's covering her mouth with a hand, the way her eyes have gone nearly wild with horror mixed with worry, I understand that Robin's dad, may have never cried in front his kids before.

Crap. Does Robin's expression hint that I should walk out of here?

Is she pleading with me to go?

Should I just…go?

"Dad. *Dad*," Sage calls out again, his voice is destroyed as his father's, while his back heaves from the effort of pulling in simple breaths.

"Sage," their dad finally whispers over the crackling-popping line. "This is not how I wanted this call to unfold. Kids…I'm so sorry."

"There's nothing to be sorry about, Dad," Robin calls out over their father choking out the words, "I love you…kids. I love you so much."

Hell, I think as I start backing away. This man thinks he's alone with his *family*. This man…Robin and Sage's father…I know enough about the way that he is, and I've learned some about Special Forces dudes, to know he would never cry in front of a stranger.

And that's what I am to this man.

A stranger.

Nobody.

Some dude he currently hates because I made out with his daughter all over Europe. I'm not part of this—of them.

I quickly tip-toe around the room gathering up things I'll need for tomorrow, and head for the door as I hear Sage utter out, "I--love you so much, too, Dad. So happy you're back. You're okay. Safe." The kid pulls in a shuddering weighted breath that is so heavy it nearly crumbles me. Sage goes on, "I'm sorry I flipped out I just—I couldn't believe it and then I was so happy to hear your voice and…sorry."

A loud, long breath comes out of the speaker phone. "There's no shame in crying, son. None. In case you didn't notice me losing my shit all over you two." He crackles out a harsh chuckle and pulls in another long breath. "I'm going to get the hell out of this hospital bed as soon as I can. Apparently when you get as skinny and dehydrated as I was when they found me, you need to move slowly. I'm taking their advice which is why I'm not already standing in front of you two, but they're trying my patience." His voice grows quiet. "Your rescue company…the people you hired, they saved my life. Thank you kids…thank you for not giving up on me after—all this time. Will I even recognize you kids when I see you? Will you even recognize me? "

Acting like I'm heading to the restroom, I duck the opposite direction and edge into the suite's small entryway before Robin and Sage notice that I mean to duck out. But, because I'm *me*—the guy who's always searching out that bit of information so I can maybe help fix stuff, I'm unable to walk out of earshot yet.

"Dad. It wasn't that long," Sage says, getting some of his bravado back. "And, we look exactly the same."

"He's lying," Robin calls out. "He's taller than me now, Dad. Maybe as tall as you are."

Their dad laughs. "I suppose I should be warning you ahead of time. I might still look like hell in a few days. Lost the rest of my hair, and I know I'm skinnier. I've seen photos of you two. Online, in magazines, and hell....you're both so sophisticated...so grown up. Beautiful. I missed so much of your lives."

"Well...we're not so different. Despite the altitude Sage has gained, I swear we're exactly the same, aren't we Sage?" Robin asks that like she's trying to convince herself.

Sage pipes in, "And we don't care how you look, as long as we get to go back to being a family again. I've missed that so much."

"Me too. We'll recover what we can. Soon." He chokes out, suddenly his voice goes all rough again as he tries to cover it with a cough as he adds, "And once I'm done squeezing the hell out of you two, the three of us are finally going to go home. *Home.* Home where we can get our lives back, make up for lost time. Can we try to do that?"

They both answer "Yes," so quickly and without hesitation, that the affirmation has knocked the remaining air out of me.

Quickly I step out into the hallway. After I've made my way to the elevators that will take me down one floor to Hunter and Vere's suite, I have to pause and lean against the wall. Because...damn-me. I'm the now the one who can't hold myself up.

I've known all along Robin's going to leave me. Hell, it's been part of the grand plan since the day I proposed to her. So why do I feel so fucking sorry for myself suddenly, when I'm supposed to be *happy* that this is all over way sooner than anyone expected it would be?

Robin's father is alive, her dreams have come true. As planned. We did the impossible. But I can't help think that... if Robin's father is taking her *home, well shit...what home, where will that be?* And if she's going back to be this family again, then were does that leave me when...she and Sage have been part of our family...

I shake my head, and push myself off of the wall, jabbing my finger into the 'down' button. Watching it light up, I force away my next wave of self-pity as I answer my own damn selfish question: *It leaves me just where I started, that's where. Just where I want to be. Single, without attachments, without responsibilities. Free.* I know where I'm going and it doesn't really matter where Sage, Robin and her father wind up as long as Robin is ultimately happy.

I need to just look at today—and today I think I'm going to the

Eiffel Tower. And then I'll breathe and look a bit ahead to where I'm going next. To Berlin, then to Barcelona, to Stockholm…that's where *I'm* going, with or without Robin, that plan is set. And, I'm going there all while doing the job I love.

I've made a great friend, one I hope to keep and for the next few days and the rest will sort itself out. It's not like I've had to rip-a-Band-Aid off fast. She and I still have a few days. She still gets to be my wife for a little bit more. She will sleep in my hotel room, and I will make a few more memories with her and then we will say goodbye and it will be…sweet.

I step onto the elevator, watching the doors slide closed and press the button for one floor below me, thinking…*Hell yes, I'll even get kiss her a few more times because—because even with the possibility of her father looking on his certain disapproval, I won't be able to resist th*at.

And none of this is sad. None of it. Before she leaves me for good, I'll get to show Robin the Paris of her dreams.

For the next few days, it will still be only me and her. Us. Making a memory that we do get to keep, forever. Which is why I mean to make it perfect.

30

ROBIN

"I'm sorry Robin. This sucks."

Royce throws his buzzing cellphone to the seat where it hits with a solid *thunk.* "All I wanted was to show you the Eiffel Tower. And now it looks like we won't even be able to exit this limo. This is not what I had in mind for our last days together. *Crap. So sorry.*"

Royce looks more than upset, he looks positively tortured as he motions to the phone, acting like he now finds it offensive. "And before you say your bright-sided comments about how it's *cool* and how you *don't care,* let me just tell you that Gregory's just nixed our outing to the Louvre tomorrow." He glowers over at me. "So, your dream trip to Paris stops now." He flings his arms wide. "Here we are in the most romantic city in the world, with some of the best art in the world that you *need* to see, that you've *dreamed* to see, and thanks to someone leaking our whole damn schedule—we're now prisoners."

Though he just told me not to say this, I blurt out, "It really is okay, Royce."

I paste on a smile as his glower darkens, all while my heart sinks with my own disappointment because—I really wanted to see all of my dream things with him—because these are our last days together—because I'd heard we were going to have a *photo-opportunity-kiss* on top of the Eiffel Tower.

And because I really wanted that darn kiss.

When he doesn't answer, only looks *more* distraught, I blab on hoping I can make him feel better. "Look. Paris is not going anywhere, and like I've said all along, I'm happy just hanging around with you. Besides, now that my father is truly okay I have new perspective on life and patience. Everything is amazing. Perfect. My life-long-goals of checking to see if the paint on the Eiffel tower is really a gradient brown paint that's darker on the bottom and lighter on the top?" I shrug. "That now seems so trite and silly. I'll just take the Internet's word for that."

His stony expression lightens some as he recovers his phone, glancing sideways at me. "I love your odd, *artist-girl* meets *city-tour* goals." He laughs, shaking his head at me. "*That's* why you wanted to see the tower? Is it really gradient paint?"

I waggle my brows as I point out the window at the Eiffel Tower's top which is visible in the distance. "It could be urban myth. Who knows. And of course that's not the only reason I wanted to see it." I evade his gaze—avoid looking down at the sexy lip twisty smile he's giving me. "Someday, I will come back and climb those metal steps and see the sparkle-lights and eat crepes while staring up at it, and buy some horrible souvenirs, because those are other good reasons to see it, as well." I pull a face. "Maybe during my years at art school I'll come back. Yeah, like when I've studied the history of it more. That's when it will be much more meaningful. People say, Paris is lost on today's young people, because we don't study history enough."

"They do? Who says that?" His brow furrows.

I shrug. "You know—those—people who say all of the *stuff*." We both laugh then, as I go on, "Heck, maybe I'll get to come here a lot. I heard my art school has a year exchange program where you can go to art school in Paris. Maybe I'll do that and then I can pace myself. See everything when I'm not…"

I stop because his face has frozen on this wounded expression. The laughter he'd found just a second ago is gone, and now he looks… haunted? Depressed?

What?

Before I can ask him, he finishes my sentence for me. "When you're *not married*? When you're *not attached to the Guarderobe noose*? When you can actually see monuments without being screamed at and chased away by strangers? Maybe it's for the best, then." He leans back and groans, running both hands through the hair on top of his head. "I hope you *do* come back, Robin. I really hope you do." His sigh is so heavy I could swear he's taken every ounce of air that's inside the limo cab and sucked it into his lungs.

He seems to get himself together some, and glances up at me again, adding, "Sorry. I know I'm acting crazy. It's the first time you have taken the '*we*' out of our future. I—guess it sort of caught me off guard." He sighs again. "I was wondering if, or when, you were ever going to bring up what happens to your life after...this. After *us*." He winces and looks away. "After your father takes you home. Have you thought about it? About where you will go? What home base will be yours? I've been patiently waiting but as you know, I'm not very good at patience. Do you have a...*p-plan*?"

I shake my head a little, because I *haven't* thought about it.

I've *refused* to think about it.

How can I tell Royce that every time I try imagining this '*life after us*' it all seems completely unthinkable.

Should I bring up how I don't want to be without him?

Should I mention that I'm so in love with him right now that I can't picture this 'equation' as he called it without both of us inside of it? Should I tell him that his verbalization of my father taking me 'home' plus me imagining touring the Eiffel Tower '*some other year*' and without my favorite tour guide, has made my chest hurt like someone threw a sand-bag into it, which is why I've got no answer for him right now?

Like before, I somehow manage to paste on a smile and add in a little laugh. "I guess you're probably looking forward to be getting rid of me. Old ball and chain—I'm so high maintenance. Now you won't have to see all the sights in each city all over again. And just...imagine all of the free time you will suddenly have."

He shakes his head, 'no' but doesn't say more, only squints up past the driver as though he's checking the unmoving traffic through the front window.

When the silence stretches from awkward to painful between us, and the limo still can't get out of the gridlock, I finally add quietly, "Mrs. Felix says you and I need to stay married for a year or so at least. She has offered for the three of us—me, Dad and Sage, to stay next year in the apartment you and I set up in NYC."

"I'd heard that." He's grown completely still and I can't tell if he likes or hates this idea. "Will you?"

"Well, your grandmother thinks that would be a good basecamp for the year while we let the rumor mill start up. Should you need to go *home,* while we're staying in our newlywed-apartment, your grandmother would keep smaller apartment next to her penthouse, just as it was before we were married. Then you could pretend to," I pause to make quote marks. 'visit me at *our* place' but then simply live upstairs when you're in New York. You know—so you won't be bothered by our mundane day-to-day stuff that will go on—like. Sage will be just hanging around doing homework and like I think Dad will have to be going to a therapist and doing some physical therapy nearby VA hospital for a while. I would assume he can't go back work right away, and of course I'll just be busy with my own school work, too."

"What about the dorms? Won't you live in the dorms how you wanted?"

"Well." I wink at him. "*Our* place has the amazing art studio you made for me and, it's just right near the school, so it would be wasted…and…so…"

He nods, those electric eyes of his are shuttered in that way that I hate as he's painting me with thoughts I can't read.

"So….yeah. If it's okay with you…I'd try to convince Dad to stay there until Sage was done with at least one year high school and until our divorce goes through. He will insist on paying your grandmother rent, though." I sigh out. "As for the dorms, I guess I won't feel comfortable about moving into any dorms until I'm sure my dad is… really and truly okay. I'm sort of worried he's going to have some sort of PTSD or need me." I shrug, keeping my voice cool and steady, my eyes trained on his sculpted, unmoving profile. "Gregory and Adam think it's pretty cut and dry. They say time will pass quickly, and Vere says there's tons of ways to start the rumor mill about our breakup that could speed things along, if we want it to all go faster."

One of his brows goes high. "Does Vere have it all planned out then?"

"Not planned, but she and I chatted through some plausible scenarios. Like…you could suddenly *stop* visiting. Start partying, going out every night to fancy, high-profile night clubs and—and, then… you'd wind up staying in your place in Los Angeles too much—going to events without me. Appearing on red carpets and in restaurants with other 'beautiful, notable stars."

"You mean, bring back the Royce Devlin bad-boy, rockstar image?"

"Yeah." I shrug again. "Like what happened with Katy Perry's ex-husband. Remember that jerk? You could drop a couple of lines to the press—about how I don't fit in with your crazy life, how we are in love but it's often not a match to be married to a quiet painter who should be living in the college dorms. One who is pretty young and immature compared to you, because all of that is pretty darn true right?" He nods almost curtly, then looks away from me, analyzing the traffic jam again. "And…yeah…somewhere in the middle of all of that you will eventually land a girlfriend somewhere, and make your affair all public and yeah."

"While you do *what*, exactly? Did you and Vere think up the other side of this scenario?"

I sigh, and decide it will be easier to tell him the truth than make up fake smiles and bullshit about what I will be doing when our relationship is over. "While I smile through my tears of course. Because I can't pretend letting go of Royce Devlin, my first husband…is going to be easy."

He frowns, looking over at me finally. "But you aren't going to really cry, are you? I mean, you should be happy, right?"

Now it's my turn to look away and stare at the traffic, because I really am probably going to cry, but I'm not going to tell him that. Instead I say, "Royce. All of this and you, has made me the luckiest, happiest person in the world. I will be having my cake—and eating it too. Going to school, being around my dad while he recuperates, all while Sage gets to go to one of the best college prep schools in the nation? What's to cry about, right? And, maybe it sounds selfish for me to admit this, but I'll be missing…I'll miss…"

"What?"

My chest tightens, as his beautiful gaze locks onto mine and that's where I start lying again—because I don't want to tell him that I'll be missing him.

Him!

Instead, I start babbling, "I will miss this crazy summer. Limos… and…yeah." I motion around the limo. "You get to live like this all the time but I'm still not used to any of this. I can imagine it's going to be really hard to go back to driving my old Subaru around, that's for darn sure. Sage won't know how to use a microwave anymore, and he'll be staring at the door expecting room service to just appear with fancy cold cuts."

I force out a laugh continuing on, "Although…one bright spot in all of this break-up stuff is that it will be nice to be able to visit the Perino family in Orlando so soon. Mrs. Perino is beside herself happy about this break up as is Angel completely relieved all went so well. I want my dad to meet them in person as quickly as possible, so I'm already planning how me, Sage and my dad will fly there to collect my car and then we will drive it back to New York. Maybe we will make a week-long trip there around Labor Day. I was kind of planning and thinking, if my dad retires or can't work anymore, that he'd feel at home in one of the small towns around Orlando. Either way, I will finally get to take Sage to Universal Studios and into Disney World like I've always promised him." I blink up at him, wondering what in the heck I just said.

"That will be nice."

His eyes skate off of mine and when he sighs it seems twice as heavy as his last sigh. "Gregory misses Mrs. Perino so much. I think we will all be paying some visits to Orlando in the near future. I can't imagine Mrs. Perino without her farm, can you?"

I think of the wonderful older woman who sheltered Sage and I when we ran away. Think of her gorgeous little mini-farm, and the cottages in the back that hold her family's whole heart. "You're right. There's no way she'd leave that farm, but as long as he doesn't expect her to sell it, I also think she'd be happy to travel around with him how you and I did this summer. She's from Italy. It would be so great for Gregory go there with her."

I suddenly feel sad because Royce doesn't even know the deeper parts of the Perino's sad story. Doesn't know how amazing Angel and Mrs. Perino truly are…but it's not my story to tell. Besides, if his uncle Gregory is really going to marry Mrs. Perino, which is the way I think things are going to go between those two, then eventually, Royce will know everything. Most probably, as time passes, Royce and Adam will wind up better friends than Royce is with me right now.

And if I can convince my father to go down there and stay…then maybe…just maybe…I can still…somehow…be part of…

Royce leans over and tugs at one of my curls, and I could swear he's reading my mind as he continues, "And…maybe…once everything is sorted…maybe we will cross paths down there quite a bit? I'm pretty sure my uncle is going to propose to her. And of course if that's the case, you will all go to the wedding, right? So I'll see you then, at the very least, right?"

I nod, and his face is suddenly so closed off I wonder at the expression he's trying to hide from me.

Suddenly he's dropped my curl and he's staring around the room at every single thing that's as far away from where I'm sitting as possible.

"Hey." I put my hand out and squeeze his forearm. "Are you okay? Did I say something wrong, because I'm just trying to make it sound easy…and fun, so if I popped off in the wrong direction and somehow hurt your feelings by discussing all of these possible scenarios with you then, I'm sorry. We can do how I exit here in million other ways." I squeeze his arm tighter when, still he won't look at me and I whisper, "Whatever we pick, I'm afraid that what's ahead for our breakup might be way harder than we're planning."

"Shit. Robin…I don't even want to think about it because…I'm afraid, too…"

"Afraid of what?"

"I'm afraid of what your brother said to me the other night. That we will wake up and it will seem as though we dreamed all of this."

"But that's how passing time works. Right? Like…sometimes I try to remember my life before our mom took off, and I can't remember any of it. Not even how her faced looked, you know?"

"I do know, because that has started happening to me with how I remember my mom, and it's only been six months. Which is why…yell yes, I *am* afraid. Do you know that book, the one where the monster says, 'there's a monster at the end of this book' and then he begs everyone not to turn the page?"

"I love that book."

"Well, I want to scream for the page not to turn, and I hate that it's turning anyhow." He leans back throwing his head against the seat. "We *will* be friends forever after this, won't we? Say it, because all of the plans we'd come up with involved at least *two year*s, but in less than one week, your father is going to take you home and…shit, I don't know how to deal with idea that it will all suddenly be *over*. Because, it has been so… fun, right?"

"Yes. And don't worry about that. You and I…we're bonded forever." I smile at him. "We will," I insist, but I know I'm trying to convince myself way more than I'm trying to convince him.

He shakes his head like he's trying to clear it. "I'm glad we talked about it some without Sage in the room, though. *Not* talking about it was killing me."

"Me, too."

I also lean back against the seat, trying to hold with my idea that this conversation is not a big deal. Only, now that he's said it all out loud, the image of me, walking away from him forever is about to swallow me up, so I change the subject. "Well, going forward, let's try to keep it in the moment—how we've always done," I suggest. "Like…I wanted to see Paris with you, and maybe we can still do that a little. We can stay in this limo and drive around all night. How about that for *not turning the page*?"

"How about great idea!" He looks over at me, eyes going from sad and unreadable to mischievous. His smile is so beautiful I just soak it in, because it's just for me.

31

ROBIN

Royce scoots forward and taps the glass between us and the chauffeur and the one bodyguard that rode up front with us.

"Guys. Okay. Let's re-adjust. Can we do some sort of drive-by-Parisian-tour? How about we drive the entire Champs-Elysées both directions, then we hit all the famous roundabouts beginning with the Arc de Triumph. Oh, and just go around and around that one for a while—like ten times? Oh, and because we've had success with boats before, could one of you *please* call PR and see if it would be possible to rent out one of the entire tour boats that go up and down the Seine for tomorrow. Maybe if we can't *walk* through the streets of Paris like we planned, we can at least float past Notre Dame and all see of the famous bridges, right?"

He glances back at me and I grin, wider and wider.

The bodyguard nods. "I'll tell your PA crew of the change in plans for tonight. But, Sir." The guy glances back. "Please know we're currently being tailed by at least five paparazzi in different vehicles. Also, I'm sorry to be the bearer of bad news, but it's very doubtful you'd be allowed to rent one of those floating tour boats, because once word got out you and the guys from the band were floating under the bridges, all of Paris would be in a traffic shut down while people flocked to each bridge, trying to get a glimpse of you. Even without vetting this, I can imagine fans trying to jump onto the boat or some such nonsense. I will check, but in my honest opinion, it's not advised, Sir. We've already been fined big-time for causing traffic mayhem by the City of Paris. Because of that, Gregory and your grandmother are going to suggest you and Robin hole up in the hotel for the next two days until the red-carpet awards ceremony. "

"What? Seriously?" Royce frowns at that news, then turns and surveys the cars tailing the limo. "Fine." He sighs out. "What's your advice on the paparazzi for tonight? Can we at least have tonight?"

"If no one exits the car and we drive a steady pace, we're good to go," he answers. "Will keep you posted if anything changes. Hunter and Vere have volunteered to go out on the town nearby the hotel, so maybe this crew will lose interest and head over there."

"Thank you. And please tell them, thank you, too." Royce nods, and the privacy window zooms back up.

"Damn. Robin…I'm so sorry. No museums. No Boat…it would probably be dangerous for you, so…just…sorry."

It's suddenly too quiet in the limo again, but this time it's my fault. I can't quite think of anything to say because I'm having a hard time hiding just how much I love Royce's protectiveness, sweetness and utter thoughtfulness.

Because I'd never had any sort of boyfriend before marrying Royce, I've started wondering if this kind, endless consideration is what it might feel like if someone truly fell in love with me?

"If it helps at all, Royce. I…uh, love the idea of hanging in the hotel, *and* I'm pretty sure I get really sick on boats," I lie, because I've never been on any kind of boat, but I'm trying to make him feel better. "It was a cool idea, though."

His sigh is half frustrated half agonized as he says, "Come to this side." He taps the seat next to him and I swap from facing him to sitting side by side with him on the back bench.

"At the very least, I did manage to stash one bucket-list surprise in here this limo for you. I was saving it to take up to the top of the Eiffel Tower, but we can…open it here."

"What is it?" My smile returns. "Oh my gosh, if you got me a present—well—I've got nothing to give back to you."

"It's not exactly a present. It's an…experience." He leans forward and pushes a button on the limo's center table. A silent hydraulic lift eases up a hidden compartment. Inside of it, a half-sized, opaque green bottle with gold wrap on the top is sitting in a mini ice container is revealed. Though small, it's on this very fancy silver platter, and resting inside what looks like giant flakes of hand crushed ice. It's also been paired with two amazing clear crystal flutes. Even better, there's dainty plate of massive, chocolate dipped strawberries, also set on gorgeous chipped ice.

"Champagne?" I gasp out. "Wow. And Wow. *Real Champagne.*"

His answering smile looks so happy it warms my heart. "I nabbed it from the mini-bar in our room and had the chauffeur set it up for us in advance." He whispers. "It's maybe enough for a glass for each of us, but I wanted to be the one who got to taste Champagne with you the first time."

He blinks, then pulls this face like for some reason he regrets what he just said. "I mean, I wanted you to taste it with me. First. First because…uh… we will have to drink a bunch more of this stuff on the night of the Paris Teen Select awards on our last night here."

"We will? Why?"

"The entire French region of Champagne is sponsoring us to be at the entire event and sponsoring the event itself. Champagne where they grow the grapes to make it. There is some national marketing push to make Champagne cool for younger people right now." He shrugs. "It's a huge deal and all Guarderobe people will be expected to be holding a glass of this stuff the whole night all while making it look exciting and delicious. *Le-drink-to-drink!*" He winks. "Considering you're one of the group's most watched stars right now, you have to be able to handle yourself."

"Does this have anything to do with your grandmother telling you how I freaked when she tried to get me to eat a whole bunch of caviar?"

"Yes." He laughs.

"To be fair, that was the same day she made me taste those snails. I could only take so much, you know?" I add, trying to slow down how fast I'm talking. "It's my first champagne, *in a limo, in Paris.* This is even better than the Eiffel Tower. I'm sure of it."

"Robin…you're always letting me off the hook. Why are you so damn nice about that?" He bumps shoulders with me.

"Because it's never directly your fault."

"Isn't *me*, being me, my fault?"

I don't answer that as he leans forward and pulls the Champagne out of the ice, because…I'm not sure, and because I don't want to argue with him.

I momentarily panic, holding back the comment that I've never had anything alcoholic to drink in my life past a couple sips of my dad's beer once, because I don't want to ruin the moment. But…what if I mess this up somehow? What if I spit it out and it sucks way worse than caviar sucks?

He's draped a white cloth over his forearm and he shows me the bottle, pretending to be a waiter now. "Does the lady approve of the vintage?"

"Yes, as long as it's real *Champagne*." I laugh, admiring the label while pointing at the top of the bottle. "And it must be, because it even has the little twisty thing up top as well as one of those extra-fat corks."

"Did you know you can only get Champagne from France? It has to be from the Champagne region? All the other bubbling wines have different names like…*Prosecco*. That's the bubbling wine of Italy. *Cava*, that's from Spain. They aren't allowed to call it Champagne unless, it is —" He pauses to points at the scrolling word on the label and reads, "*Champagne.*" He wiggles his brows. "Do you want me to open it?"

"*Yes,*" I say, feeling my stomach flutter with anticipation. He starts to work through the thick gold foil hiding the cork and I poke at the fancy ice chips, accidentally knocking some of them onto the silver platter. "But…Royce…uh…"

"What?" He pauses, his fingers poised on this little twisty wire thing that's sticking off the cork.

"I'm only eighteen. Won't we be severely judged about this on social media should anyone snap a pic?"

"Now you sound like me. Haven't you learned yet that we're severely judged for simple breathing? Has my worrying rubbed off on you that much?"

"Yes?"

"It's okay." He bites his lower lip, and shakes his head at me. "I double checked, *and* our PR group also double checked because I asked them to. If someone does get a photo of us having a sip of this stuff, it will be okay. The legal drinking age for wine products in France is sixteen. Eighteen for the hard stuff. You're good to go and completely legal. If anything it's expected you drink gallons of this stuff while you're here, especially at the awards ceremony coming up."

"Okay. Yay! I'm *of legal drinking* age. Feels nice to have grown up so fast here in Europe." I add wiggling my own brows back at him, laughing. "A sip or two tonight, and then…long as this tastes okay, I will try *gallons* of the at the awards ceremony.

"Please note that gallons of anything will give you a horrible hangover, and you will be vomiting all over Paris should you try more than three glasses so…pace yourself, yes?"

"Fine. Yes. Of course." I clap my hands, relaxing finally. "And can we please note that this *Champagne-info-night* is so much more fun already than the itty bitty pickles lesson you gave me off of the room service cart yesterday."

His brows shoot up and he laughs. "They were called, *petit cornichons*," he adds in his sexy very perfect French accent that always sends goosebumps down my spine.

"Peter and Cornish-hens. Got it," I joke, because I've long since given up on ever having any sort of decent French accent. I've also learned that if you are as terrible as I am at French, then it's offensive to even try. So I don't. "Despite what they're called, though. Some of those baby pickle jars will be packed in my suitcase when I go home."

He laughs again. "They sell them in every market in the states."

"Not where I shop." I mutter out distractedly watching intently as he slowly begins to untwist the basket covering the cork. "I can't believe Champagne, even tiny Champagne, has to be literally tied down into the bottle. So cool." My anticipation butterflies double as the thing loosens. "I hope it goes *pop,* like it does in the movies. It will, won't it?"

His silver eyes glint with amusement as they flick to me, then back to the bottle. "Shh. I'm supposed to be very careful."

THE LIMO GOES from stuck in traffic to creeping along the street. It gains speed as it moves us through some side streets that take us further from the Eiffel Tower. We both pause and stare out the window as we turn onto the famous, double-wide Champs-Elysées.

Unable to contain my excitement, I blurt out. "Holy cow, this is same street that I know from history class. Our classroom had this famous photograph of when German tanks to rolled down her during WWII, and here it is, exactly the same as the photo, minus any soldiers and tanks, and all lit up with twinkle lights, on shop windows and in tress and…it's freaking perfect."

The limo gains speed and we zoom along heading directly the famous Arch De Triumph which is still very far ahead of us. For a moment, when I glance over at the beautiful guy who's watching me watch Paris fly by the window with the strangest expression on his face, and I shake my head at him, asking, "Why do you always stare at me?"

"Because…uh…because for…two million reasons I can't say," is his cryptic answer. "And, because you're beautiful when you're soaking up the world."

"Oh, uh. Okay…well thank you, and stop that, would you?" I point at the bottle. "Open the rest of that bottle so we can have our first sips when we're zooming past the arch!"

Suddenly Royce is acting like I've embarrassed him, when in fact I should be the one that's embarrassed, he turns back to the Champagne. Wire basket off now, he makes sure to tilt the bottle so the cork is facing away from both of us before taking the white napkin off of his forearm, then places that over the top of the cork.

"What are you doing?"

"I had to watch a YouTube video on how to open it just right. I talk like I know shit, but everything I learned was off my phone about an hour ago. Also, I've already had one black eye while hanging out with you in a limo, and I don't need another." He winks, calling up the first day we met when I'd back-elbowed him in the face. "Ready? Listen." He points the top of the bottle away from us and does this concentrated half twist until it the cork makes a perfect Champagne-popping sound."

"*Yes!*" I call out.

He pulls the bottle out from under the cloth and hands me the cork which I quickly tuck into my purse to save, and we both watch in wonder as what looks like magical steam and a few bubbles rises out of the top of the bottle. When it clearly isn't going to blow up or spill over, he gingerly pours us each a glass.

"Cheers," he says, handing me mine. I hardly notice him clinking my glass with his, because I've been struck motionless, watching multiple lines of micro-bubbles floating up and up on what appear to be endless, self-replenishing streams.

"Beautiful. Champagne is utterly *beautiful*," I whisper.

"Very beautiful." He traps my eyes with his over the glasses like he's waiting for us to both have our sips at the same time.

Scrunching up my nose, I pause to sniff at the top of my glass, flicking him a glance. "I'm afraid to taste it. What if it's terrible and then forever I'll have ruined this perfect memory." I point out the window. "Because look, we're into the round-about, and…*ahh,* the Arc de Triumph is right out there!" I almost spill the entire contents of the glass getting closer to the window. "It's huge." I lean sideways and stare up, trying to get a better glimpse of the amazing monument as the limo starts going around the multi-lane round-about. "My heart is beating so fast right now. Is yours?"

Royce laughs. "Very, but it's more about the dangerous traffic zooming all around us."

"How many times did you tell him to go around this?" I sigh out, scooting back over to sit beside him again. "We should up whatever you said to two million times."

"I told him only ten, because truly we'd get car sick if he does too many. So you ready?" He raises his glass high again and quirks one brow. "Cheers?"

"No, wait!" I scoot forward a little too fast and he flinches back like he thinks I'm a fangirl that's going to attack him or something, which makes me feel bad.

"What?" he asks, trying to cover the flinch with a little shoulder shrug.

"This is my cliché Champagne moment. We must intertwine our arms. Can we?" I hold out my arm try to get our arms linked together without spilling, but to manage what I'm picturing, I have to sit up on my knees because he's too tall.

That move nearly topples me off the seat. Worse, he's had to pull me back upright to save me, and worse? I've spilled half of my glass all over myself, and he's now laughing at me.

"Oh, man…" I frown down and wipe the wasted Champagne off of my lap. "I've already ruined it, haven't I? Ugh. I'm so awkward. Can you try to forget that I just did that?" I try to pull my arm away, but he gently tightens his bicep and stiffens his arm to hold me fast so I can't twist away.

"Never." His voice is silk. Expression all easy-kindness plus heat, a combination that wipes away any mortification I was feeling. "The memory's set in stone, and it's perfect because you're so damn adorable."

"Well now who is letting who off the hook?" I laugh, breathing in until I'm able to return his easy smile.

He nods at my glass, and I realize my antics have brought him so close to me I can feel the minty-warmth of his breath hitting my cheeks. "You're going to like it, Robin. I promise."

I show him the remainder of my fancy flute. "One taste is all I have left." I tip the glass back mouth and let it swirl around my tongue, then too quickly I've swallowed it. "Hmm." I frown, wishing for another taste.

He takes a small sip of his own glass. "Hmm. What?"

Frowning I motion to his glass. "I'm not sure because I didn't have that much to go on, but already, I think it should not be called Champagne. What does that even mean, *Champagne*?" I scoff out, shaking my head.

"Remember? Named after the region where the grapes grow. Here finish mine and then we'll refill." He hands over his glass, laughing as I down half of his in two big gulps. "Go easy now."

"I would, but before each swallow, those cool bubbles start dancing on my tongue." I finish two more gulps, then hand his empty glass back which is when I notice he's staring at my lips. I lick them, worried that I've drooled champagne all over my face. Instead of helping, he stares at them even more as I add, "I think it…uh…should be called… something like, golden-bubble-dream-drink?"

"*You* should be called golden-bubble dream drink."

"What? Uh…are you *flirting* with me? *Bad* flirting?" As the Champagne goes to my head, I start giggling.

He laughs too, then places both hands gently on the sides of my face. "Robin. What you do to me. Can I kiss you right now? One kiss, even though no one from the press is watching?" His voice is so whisper-gravelly-low it speeds up my heart just as the smell of his cologne floats over me like a wave, sending a twist of firing heat through my belly.

"Sure. If you want to?"

"Christ. I always want to."

The laughter dies on my lips, as he pulls me onto his lap. The champagne, or his words, or that voice, or the way he's pulling me deep into his silver gaze, or how his thumbs are going up past my temples and roughly into my hair makes me feel like something has changed between us. Or at least inside of me.

"We probably shouldn't be…doing this…" he's whispering.

"But it's Paris…and it's my first Champagne and I just said, *yes.*"

His lips are already on mine, or maybe mine were already on his.

I lean toward the pull of his hands, sink into that spot where his heart beats hard and loud, and his kiss he plants on me is so sweet…so gentle, despite the roughness that had been in his voice, it melts my spine. My heart. My soul.

The way I think he's trembling as much as I am right now makes me I forget who I am, and for a moment I feel completely desolate because…how could what we have between us, even this beautiful-perfect-kiss—how could this not be something lasting or even…real? *How?*

When, in this moment in time it feels real, and because how his lips fit onto mine, and mine onto his feels like this guy's soul is mine, really mine, just as much as mine feels like it belongs to him?

When he twines his arms around my waist to pull me next to him so my body puzzle-pieces so perfectly into him that I could swear my heart and his heart are beating simultaneously, I push away my thoughts and simply kiss him back.

But always, when the kiss is over and we pull away from each other the cool currents of air that rushes between us takes away everything I'd just imagined. And all of the good, the connection…the things I guess I can't help but wish for, suddenly feel like a punch. A punch, that today…actually hurts.

My head is spinning, probably from that Champagne. And my heart aches how it always does while my lips throb like they want to say, that this kissing—it's not enough, while my body thrums with absolute hunger and curiosity, because…

I don't care if it's real or not. I want more.

More. More. More.

And maybe…just maybe, after that awards show, after my allocated third glass of champagne that surely will give me courage to get to this kind of kissing with him again. I might just ask *my-husband* for more.

And I'm talking…so much more.

32

ROBIN

"I've now agreed to slather on this horrible purple metallic nail polish, but what more do I have to do to please you, Clara?" I ask the glowering stylist.

"It's not *purple.*" She grits out her response. "It's *black* with ground up purple glitter to accent it, and how can you not like it?"

"Fine, sorry. It's not horrible, it's fine, but I'm only wearing it, because the stylists told me that Royce picked it himself. To match is tie or something, right?"

"Yes. It. Does. *Tie. Socks. And pants.* Which brings us to the part where you need to pair your outfit with the proper matching footwear," She holds out a box. "Then you're done—er—finished." She laughs to herself.

I glance down at these strapped, shiny torturous looking things she's holding out for me to see, and, though I'm trying to have a better attitude, I can't hide my grimace as I poke at them. "What are these things? Are you sure they're even shoes?"

Clara's entire forehead furrows. "Why are you being so disagreeable?"

"I'm not. You are." I blink at her. "I've *agreed* to the severe gown with the slit going up the leg and almost to my *waist.* The same dress that has almost no front—like I've never seen on any dress. I've agreed to put it on, despite the part where it's exposing my entire chest for the world to see. I've *agreed* to walk around in in this, even though it's made up of all lace and netting and not much else. I've *agreed* to wearing weird, awkward, and uncomfortable flat *stickers* over my *nipples* so when it gets cold or the stupid dress rips or falls off of me, I won't embarrass my husband. But…" I point to the shoes she's set near my feet. "But those shoes, are not shoes. I won't wear them."

"Stop calling one of a kind, designer high heels—heels that are worth thirty thousand dollars, you ungrateful brat, *shoes*." Clara picks up one of the offending objects and holds it high so it twinkles in the lights. "Look at these beauties. These were made by Pierre DeLune. The heels are subtle, artistic *replicas* of the Champagne glasses. To go with how the Champagne region has sponsored these awards. Didn't Royce tell you about that?"

"He did." I swallow, feeling guilty now.

"This is not a shoe, it's modern art and *you* of all people should appreciate it."

I eye the shoe again, finally making out the lines of how, the heel is, in fact, an insane looking, fused glass Champagne flute with little bubbles going up the stiletto. It's so darn high it's insane. It's also very dangerous looking—like it could be a weapon because you could whack someone with this 'work of art' and kill them. Or, for that matter it could be a murder weapon, because if I wear these Clara will have finally won in her passive aggressive attempts to kill me.

"I do appreciate the art and the creation time involved," I say, trying to remain calm. "I will appreciate them…in a museum where they belong. Not on my feet. Can't you please find me other *shoes*," I can't help bud add, because now that I know that word makes her mad, I have to use it. After all, she's the one who wouldn't let me eat dinner for fear my stomach would 'pop out' so…this is only fair.

"It's Haute Couture at its finest. And this time, my answer to you is, *no*! If you don't wear them you will insult the sponsor as well as the designer. And if you *do* wear them you will wind up in every fashion magazine for months! You will make every TV network, and you will be reblogged on Instagram more than any other person tonight. You will also be invited to wear them on every single talk show that can book you, because despite how boring and bumbling you might be personally, people will want to take a closer look at these magnificently beautiful heels." She gingerly places the shoe back in its silk lined box.

I try another tactic to change her mind. "Yeah, but I'm going to fall on my face wearing them. And… didn't someone famous already do that falling-down thing at an awards ceremony? You said yourself I shouldn't copy what other stars do."

Clara shoots me a look. "Robin. My mother told me to say this to you. She and I have babied you like crazy. You managed to get photographed with designer shirts on backwards while on your honeymoon, and then you ran out and bought hideous, stupid looking, worse-than thrift store outfits from that flea-market place, and both times you survived the mistakes. But this is your first, *red-carpet* awards ceremony. Pardon my *French* here, but you're the world's real-life Cinderella, and Cinderella needs awesome-fucking-shoes and we've found them for you, and they're *perfect* to the event. So stop whining and start thanking me for knowing what I'm doing for once. Royce needs you to step up. This is a very big deal."

"Fine." I sigh. "I'll wear them. What are you planning with my hair? To shave it off?"

She shrugs. "Not shave it, but we are sending in a stylist to cut some of it. He's French and he doesn't speak any English, which is lucky because now if you say stupid stuff you hopefully can't insult him. I've told him exactly what to do, so you won't be, as usual, a complete embarrassment to Royce and the franchise that is Guarderobe. With your father being located, and the whole world now watching you, you need more than great tonight. You need to be glorious."

"Glorious. Check." I nod.

"The Champagne deal they made with the French government is huge, so you also need to look older, sophisticated, and like you actually fit in with the rest of the inner circle for once. Can you handle that? Because I need to go help dress everyone else now. I'm not going to be able to stay in here to hold your hand and feed you lollipops while your hair gets trimmed."

I purse my lips and cross my hands over my chest, hating how she's opened up my worst fears—that despite the progress I've made and the successes Royce and I have shared, I'm still not sophisticated enough to be married to Royce Devlin and represent his brand. She's also right that I do complain a lot…and I do need to stop being such a baby.

"I've got this. Please. Go," I spit out.

Clara adds, "If it helps, you could pretend it's all a *costume*, because that's what we're going for here. Can you at least do that?" She glances at her buzzing phone. "Hair will be here in five. Make up in thirty.

Don't waste their time. See you in the hallway for last checks before you and Royce head down the elevator. Deal?"

"Yep. Okay. Deal. And thank you…Clara…for all of the hard work. I'm sorry if I haven't appreciated you."

She rolls her eyes at me, my compliment falling on deaf ears and she slams the door without responding. I look back at the dress giving myself a pep talk.

Costume. It's a costume.

But after a long moment of my eyes darting between the horrible shoes, I switch to thinking: *It's a costume…a horrible hellish… vampire costume…*

My only solace is found in the idea that if Royce is going to match me somehow, then *he's* going to be some kind of sexy, vampire-looking-husband in *his* red-carpet, costume outfit, too.

Which could be…hot, because… maybe I read the books a long time ago, but I'm totally unashamed to note that I'm a die-hard Twilight fan.

If this costume brings out Royce Devlin, crossed with my secret-fan-Edward Cullen crush...then this will all be worth it.

33

ROYCE

Just as I'm about to head over to see how Robin's doing, my assigned stylist makes me pull off my shirt, and my tuxedo jacket. I can't understand what they're going on about. Worse, now I'm wondering if something is wrong.

With a flurry of an intelligible *French-language-WTF*, they've returned me into the styling chair and I realize they're trying to do something with my hair. They've put me under the hair-cut sheet thing they put over your shoulders and torso when you get a haircut. I listen carefully and through his thick accent I think he says I need a *sharper, more lined and edged haircut. Parce-que, there izz something with Robin's new look that's happening right now across zee-hallway.*

I sigh, and submit to what they're doing, because I've learned on red-carpet nights it's much easier to submit than to argue, but when one of the hair dudes pulls out the clippers and pulls off the guard that keeps the length of the hair in the back long and looks like he's going to shave my head, I put my hands on my head and jump out of the chair. "Hold up. Dude."

"Monsieur Royce. Do not panic." The stylist smiles, turning off the buzzing clippers. "I thought—*la mademoiselle Clara* told me that you were aware of what we are doing."

"Clara?" I frown. "She hasn't spoken to me all day."

The man looks confused and pulls out his phone. "But that is impossible. She told me *zisss-isss* your idea. You and your beautiful wife wanted a different look. One zat-matches zee clothing? Non? This-short-hair-cutting is what you are both going to do for zee-awards ceremony?" He flourishes his hands in to the air. "To be *dramatic*, and make *the-big-splash, non*? *Ça-va, être très-fashionable?* It will take but a moment for you to cut zee-hair shorter for you, but for your wife, it will be extreme. And, we have time because it will take longer to cut Robin's hair off. Oh, how *zee-effect-will* turn out *jolie*. I told Clara we must be careful with Robin because she such *zee-curls of zee hair*, so we must be careful or it could not be beautiful. I told Clara this look works best with *le-straight* hair." He holds out his phone and shows me a photo of a man with a head that's nearly shaved, and then he scrolls his thumb to a high-fashion model girl with her eyes closed.

She's got more smudged smoky-makeup on her eyes than I've ever seen, and her eyes have been paired with bright pink painted-on eye liner slashes, as well as some old-school David Bowie pink rouge on her cheeks. But…holy-hell-no her hair is cut down to one inch long, and it's all over and spiked!

"Oh *f-heck-no*. No. This is not right. You're doing that to Robin's hair?" I start tugging at the cape around my neck.

"*Zat*-is-*zee*-directions we've been given. *Oui. Oui.*" He points to the door. "They are working on *zee*-transformation de-Robin now. Maybe he izz-already finished. *Oui*?"

"Well stop him!"

Panicking, I push past the guy, throwing the haircutting cape to the ground, but before I'm even out the door, I'm shouting in the direction of the room where Robin's been getting ready, "Robin! Robin! Don't let *them*—open-up. *Robin!*"

Not even caring that people from the entourage are peeking out of their suites, I skid to a halt and pound on door to our hotel suite. *"Robin! Christ. Robin. Open the door."*

"Royce. Are you okay? *What?*" The door swings open and she's there, standing in this dress that blows my mind because it's more skin than dress. I'm momentarily stunned because I'm registering how she's all legs and soft-skinned—*skin—skin—skin*! That I forget that I've come here for because, *legs—legs—what the heck is that slit going all the way to her waist and how does the front of it cut down her middle like that, and what kind of undergarment is covering her—her— holy shit! This dress…*

I'm searching for words but as I get my bearings my eyes go to her furrowed brow and up to the top of her head and like a moron, I shout out only, "*Hair,*" like my mind remembers my damn goal of saving her hair just as I'm letting myself breathe because…holy shit again, *Her hair!* It's all there. And it's fine.

The slay-me beautiful curls I love haven't been cut off like I'd feared.

Instead, all has all been straightened and it's so long now, that it's halfway down her backside, which is….*wow*. That's because the backside of the dress is the only place where there is actual fabric on the gown—so all eyes go there. And that's because it's so tight that it seems as though someone painted the dress onto her!

But I hardly have time to register that either, because she's turned back to me, and I can't take my eyes off of her belly button. Because I don't think I've ever seen her belly button before…like not *once*, and… I…holy shit.

It's adorable and hot and...fuck my life! Is this is the same Robin who wears the hoodie to bed?

My…wife.

Not my wife.

Not even my girlfriend.

But I want her to be both. Girlfriend Wife. Everything.

My eyes travel over her form again blood the blood have rushed to where it shouldn't—where it kills—where I hope it kills me dead right now—and, forever. Please.

I want her. Want her to be my girlfriend. Wish she could be my real wife despite all of the obstacles between us, and holy-shit right now I want to do everything…with her…that body, hell what I could do with that belly button alone…and someone help me—that dress. It would take two tugs to get it to pop right off of her.

Calm. The. Fuck. Down.

"Don't you like the hair?" Her brow furrows more and her shoulders droop. "I can go right back in and do your original plan of cutting it. I just thought—I'd try this, because…I…"

"Holy shit. Holy shit. Robin. Holy shit…no," are the only words I'm able to say at first because, yep. I'm pretty sure I'm hyperventilating in front of her. And I swear my knees are buckling. That or the very devil himself has slammed the back of my legs with a crowbar, and now he is tugging me down through the floor straight into hell and laughing his ass off because he and I both know that's where I belong after where my thoughts just went.

For my next attempt at coherent thoughts, I manage to stutter out, "I-I thought they were going to cut your hair and I was so scared. And…holy shit, Robin," I say again. "You're so beautiful right how I can't—*even* process. I don't know what I'm trying to say at all, because I can't seem to find a place to settle my eyes that's not inappropriate."

Not understanding my extreme torment, she laughs and answers, "Right? I'm *literally* naked."

Making things worse, the damn girl pulls in a huge breath of what sounds like relief, which literally makes all of her curves move and stretch the dress in impossible, horrible wonderful ways across her breasts and the whole time I'm staring and thinking and I suck, but yes, I'm hoping that—it's going to fall off all the way, but it doesn't, and then, damn her again, she spins to show me the back! The deep cut V in the back matches the deep cut in the front, meaning it also goes way-too-far down, which is why I have to grip the sides of the door frame to hold myself up while I stare at it. "They had to put little sticky things on my skin so it won't move and reveal things like the top of my butt crack and…" She turns back places her hands directly over her breasts which nearly brings me to my knees, and she winks as she adds in a laughing whisper, "I've even got these insane things stuck on these babies." She makes her fingers do flash-pointing over her nipples and wiggles her brows at me like this is all funny, normal and okay to talk about with me! "You know, so in case…it gets cold and they go…*pop*." She flushes, then and suddenly her eyes are on my bare chest like she's realized I'm only half dressed.

When I don't answer she adds, "What? Too much info? I…" her eyes skim my chest again and she points at my nipples. "I see you don't have to wear them…I'd heard about stars wearing them, I guess I just never thought it would ever be…uh…me…so…did you know about them? Sorry to ruin the mystery of all female red-carpet beauty… or…whatever."

"Yes. I knew about them." I'm choking. Swallowing my heart down hard so it can go all the way back where it belongs. But to pull it off, I think I've just damaged half of my esophagus.

"They're funny that's all, huh?" She adds, suddenly sounding as awkward and as cute as hell. "Um…" Her eyes meet mine and flood with doubt. "Yeah. So. Sorry for the info dump about my body—parts. I'm…nervous."

"No. Not at all," is all I manage to get out, as my throat goes too dry to find any more words, while my heartbeat betrays me by coming right back up and nearly explodes my temples. Forget waiting for the devil to finish me off. I'm dead. I'm dead. Dead, because I swear I'm about to bust a nut in my pants like an out-of-control eighth grader. At least my tuxedo pants are loose and pleated. And black.

Robin points at my bare chest again. "Is..is…t-t-that what you're wearing? Only pants with no shirt? Wow. Okay. So at least I'm not alone in my nudity. This is going to be one insane red carpet." Suddenly I get that Robin is very much pretending *not* to look at my abs, my chest and my shoulder muscles, just how I'm working so damn hard to keep my eyes only on her face, because that is all I can handle. But her, checking me out, kills me dead a second time, because I love that she's looking…I love *how* she's looking, and then staring, and licking her lips, then not looking again, and of course she's blushing some…

"I should…go back and finish getting dressed, huh?" I blurt out. *Because I should go back and get the hell out of here.* "I had my stuff off because I think the stylist was about to shave my damn head, all while he'd implied that they were smack in the middle of cutting your hair short to *match* me."

"They *were* going to cut it, and I was *going* to do it, but…" She frowns. "Didn't *you* tell them to do it? Clara said you had this idea that we were going to make a splash and that we had to match."

"Splash is the same word my stylist used. Make-zee-splash." I shake my head.

"Well, Clara said this was a very big deal and it was time for me to finally do things right. It is true that I needed to stop being a whiner, but when the hair stylist brought out the big scissors, I freaked. Even worse. I actually cried on the guy."

I breathe out a huge sigh, and add, "Had he done it, I would have cried on the guy, too. Then killed him."

She smiles up at me, adding, "Luckily the guy felt bad about my tears, and we called up someone who spoke English *and* French which really helped. Together they helped me come up with a better plan for my hair that would keep it long and still have an equally wow-effect." She flips her hair to the side, making it cascade all around her shoulders. "I'm pretty thrilled with the result, because it hides the dress some. And the press has never seen it straightened so I thought it might be enough?"

Thankfully the images of Robin crying over this has cooled my jets and turned me back into a nice-guy instead of a half-brained, penis driven idiot.

"Robin. Again…you're just…breathtaking." I say. "Please excuse me stuttering there when I first slammed in here, but I was not prepared for you to look like *this*. Not one bit. And I think they've finally succeeded in making you look older. Or at least finally old enough to be married."

"Really?"

"Hell yes, really." Her smile widens with pleasure as I step back a little, working to keep my eyes trained on hers only and away from that extra skin as I add in a little head shake. "I only need to get used to this look, if it is at all possible so hold while I pause to thank God that I didn't have to see you with the cameras rolling first, because I would have lost it."

Smiling like she's pleased at my comments, she turns and pulls at the dress so the slit up the side cracks open. "Well, in that case, you will need to prepare to hold me up all night because I've been ordered to wear these Champagne-glass heels. Look at these things. You're going to also have to hold my arm every time I move in them. You might even have to walk for me. Luckily, the base is not a pointy stiletto, rather it has this round wine-glass bottom, which helps, but one wrong move and I topple sideways." She holds one foot up so I can see what she's talking about.

"Shit." Is all that I mutter, because I'm not seeing any heels…I'm only seeing straps going over sexy feet, and one narrow strap that's around her ankle, which is really sexy, because it's made me notice how slim her ankles are, as well as…every curve of those…*legs, legs legs!*

Suddenly my mind is spinning-splintering with whacked thoughts like…where in the hell did she get those legs? Has she has them the whole time? Oh wait. I know where they came from—the fucking new-sexy-belly-button store. That's probably where.

"What? You don't like them?" She asks, and I realize I've been shaking my head over and over again, and possibly I've been frowning. "Well too bad. I've got no other choices thanks to the Champagne sponsorship, and FYI, these are supposed to be works of *art* so do not call then *shoes*. Call them art or you'll insult the most famous shoe-designer in the world and Clara will yell at you."

"Art." I parrot out.

"You're making me more nervous, because you're staring too long. I know I look insane…but Clara said, to just pretend it's all a *costume*. So, try to do that, would you? This is a *costume*."

"Yes. Yes. I will, but Robin. You don't look insane. You're going to blow this awards ceremony away, and you're going to be listed as best-dressed all over the place."

"Well, that's the goal, right?" She grimaces, clearly not believing me as I go on. "As for my costume, they've given me a cape to wear over the tux stuff. It's very French, and sadly for me, very in fashion this year which is why I have to wear it. But, as soon as the red-carpet photographs are finished, you can pretend to be cold, and I will swirl it around and onto your shoulders very dramatically, all while telling everyone it's to keep you warm. Something about my *wife always being cold*, and then you can hide in it. It exactly matches the dress, so I think it will look great for the remainder of the night. Do you want that? "

"Oh. You and a cape. Yes… I want…that." She smiles, and I can tell she's nearly about to laugh or something. Her eyes have gone down my chest again and then creep back up, very slowly. When finally her gaze meets mine, suddenly her cheeks burn bright red. "Uh…could you please go get some clothes because um…" She blinks. "Because I probably need to get used to you…in your costume too, in case it's as jaw dropping as mine was for you…so…yeah. Go. And stuff." She rubs her temples. "I'm feeling a little light headed or something because I didn't eat dinner. Maybe while you're doing that I'll just go have a little snack."

She points distractedly to her dressing room door, but once again, I'd swear her eyes are locked onto my abs—or worse—maybe she's noticing that her staring at me is making the blood rush all over again, and this time the effect of that is popping the plant pleats.

Thankfully I don't have to turn away like a freak, because right then —like I've embarrassed her—or like she thinks she's just embarrassed herself, she turns away first, saying, "See you soon. Doing the finishing touches, meet me back here?"

"YEAH…" I call out, but she's moved so quickly away from me that her newly straightened hair flashes like a frozen waterfall in the light. A mass of the bone-straight cascade, flows over the ass that I'd promised myself to not look at again, but now that she's not facing me, *how in the hell can I not look?* And worse? Some of the shorter tips of that glistening hair settle at her bare waist…and they are skimming just where I want my hands to be right now.

Thankfully the door to the suite closes between us, because I'd almost reached out let my hands go where they I shouldn't. And when Robin and I are alone, and I do shit like that, things get out of control. But once we're in public and the cameras are rolling so I'll be forced to check myself, I'm going to examine every inch of how that dress is staying on her body. I'm going to trail my fingers all over every bit of the skin that I've never seen or touched before, too. I'm realizing this is probably my only and *last* chance to do that. We're down to the last days here, and I think this will be our last major public appearance that won't have her father in tow. Soon she probably won't be sharing hotel suites with me anymore, and that skin won't be near me or available to touch, the smile not mine to steal kisses off of whenever I want either. And that hair…that hair…*damn-me*, how I will miss the feel of her hair curling around my finger whenever I want…

Why in the hell did Clara think she could direct Robin to cut off her hair?

Pissed off now, I stalk back into my suite managing to feign a calm expression for the waiting stylists and say, "We are good. All is fine."

They return to finishing the final trims at the edges of my hair, then help me put my shirt and cufflinks back on. While they run around trying to do my tie just right and quickly stitch some seams at the back of tux jacket I've been getting angrier and angrier thinking about Clara's styling plan.

Thinking about Clara and how she sucks—wondering how this damn girl that none of us really like, gets to be stuck inside of our inner circle for this whole summer. Wondering if I should fire her ass, but then knowing I can't, because of how much we all love her mother. It's only a few more weeks and then, thankfully the damn girl will be back to her university. And then we can make sure she never works for us again.

I know for a fact that Clara understood just how much I *love* Robin's hair. I'd talked to her about those beautiful, long curls with her just yesterday. And, hell, I think I'd even mentioned them to her the day before that. Did she try to chop it on purpose—for malicious reasons? I start to remember all of the crappy, ugly, slightly trashy and badly fitting outfits she's sent up to Robin. Ones Robin had 'edited' in her way, by adding in her own pieces, or toning down some of the 'looks' before we'd decided to dress ourselves. And then I remember all of the snide comments Clara's made to Robin while dressing her—about how she's kind of low class, and that she's ignorant and needs to fit in with us *better*. Maybe Clara wanted to cut Robin's hair so Robin would wake up tomorrow and feel less beautiful and less confident. Shit…maybe this delusional, jealous girl had this idea I would wake up and not think Robin is beautiful anymore.

My chest constricts. I worry and wonder that if some of Robin's self-doubt is partially centered around all of these snide things Clara has said to her. And shit…what does she say to Robin when I'm not around? Could it be worse than what I've heard her say to Robin's face?

Probably. Yes. I'm sure of it. I should throw her out of this hotel on her ass right now. But we're late to the event, and it's possible half of this mind-spinning I'm having is just me, over worrying and over analyzing. Either way, Clara will never be left alone with Robin again, and she's about to be reassigned to style Hunter and Vere, because she is Vere's college roommate, after all.

Besides, I learned long ago nothing good comes from making an enemy of a *mean-girl-psycho* like Clara. If I dump her out of our inner circle without warning how I want to, then I won't be able to keep an eye on her bullshit, and it's possible later on we can use her crazy to our advantage…

I decide to at least out Clara to Vere and tell her my thoughts. Then we will tell Clara's mother how we want her to move to another couple, and from there we will all, at least be on high-alert and everyone will work hard to deflect her away from Robin. I will also make sure Clara *knows* that I'm pissed as hell before we leave for the show tonight. That girl deserves, at least, to lose some sleep over this, as I'm sure Robin has lost sleep wondering if she's good enough.

When they're done dressing me, I spin making the cape flare and then I practice my 'place the cape' on my wife move in the mirror, getting some advice from the stylist how to look like a champ as to how to settle it on to Robin without messing up her look.

When I'm all set I almost laugh at myself in the mirror. The purple black velvet backed cape is gorgeously made, and it's cool, but it's ridiculous. It's also so long that it goes nearly to my ankles. Which means on Robin it's going to drag along the red carpet like a black-bridal train once I get it onto her.

I grin in the mirror again, thinking: *the photos of her in this…with that hair… this night will be epic.*

Epic.

34

ROYCE

If I thought Robin was cute *before* she'd tasted her first Champagne in the limo a couple of days ago, watching her finish off third glass then lean back and get the giggles for about three minutes straight *after* the stressful awards show night we've all survived, has permanently robbed me of my heart.

Despite the Champagne region's sponsorship, during the show, we'd decided last minute she'd only *pretend* to drink it, because I was worried about how quickly this stuff had gone to her head the other day.

With the long hours of waiting during the banquet meal we'd had to sit through—and then waiting more while the awards were televised —and then waiting *more* as an entire show was performed by the various artists who'd been honored at the awards (including Guarderobe) — I was afraid Robin would wind up either falling asleep and snoring in her chair, or she'd get tipsy and do something unexpected.

Mostly, because if the last option, I didn't want to miss one second of any antics she might pull.

To compensate, I'd personally dragged a bottle from the sponsor stand on our way out of the ceremony. I'd made a big show of holding the bottle up high with one arm, while my other arm was draped heavily around Robin's shoulders.

It was a fake pose I used to execute all the time before I got married.

Half-drunk bad-boy rockstar, dragging a bottle and a beautiful woman to a limo and 'home to bed' is just what the paparazzi loves.

Of course back then, it was just acting. After much waving and provocative public kissing, we'd drive away as quickly as possible. Once out of camera range, I'd have dumped my date straight back at whichever hotel or home she'd been staying in, while I'd apologized to her for suddenly having a horrible headache.

Watching Robin now, as she's staring at the bubbles in her *third* glass I can't even pretend that I want to dump her off anywhere. Ever. I also can't pretend that I'm not in love with her. She's been stream-of-consciousness babbling to me non-stop to me about things like: *how amazing it was to see us perform in such a small setting, because we are all really so very talented.* And, *how cool it was that I got to hand out the Best New Artist award.* And, *how awesome my stage presence is—and did I know that I have this cool power to lift people's spirits up just with a smile and a twinkle of my beautiful silver eyes?* And, *did I know my eyes were beautiful, or did I just take them for granted, because pretty much all of me top to bottom, inside and out is made so beautifully?*

After that last one, I'm to the point where she's going to *my* head as much as the Champagne is going to *her* head. I've had compliments from girls before, but I've never believed them, or hell, I don't know, I guess I've never accepted them as any sort of 'truth'. But, the other people who gush crap at me like Robin is doing now always want something—expect something from me in return for those compliments. There's always this underlying…motive. Only, I know this very uninhibited Champagne filled version of Robin doesn't want anything at all but to make me happy as she's chattering away. Because even when she's not lit, that's her ultimate goal. With me, with everyone.

And hell-there she goes again calling my eyes beautiful all over again. Something about moon-beam-comets. To which I've replied, "You're the one with the combo ocean-sky pretty eyes." I realize that analogy kind of sucks for a guy who's a songwriter, but it's the best I can do right now, and it did the trick of making those cheeks of hers go pink.

She's so great—and kind.. and utterly *happy* right now, that I might lose my mind from how badly I want to kiss—*touch*—*consume* her and that happiness. If only I could swallow down that smile of hers, and somehow keep how that grin—beaming back at me—makes me feel—keep at least that, forever.

She's skyrocketing the *chronic-want-feeling* I always have, and she's taking my heart all the way to the top of the moon. And I'm calling out all of those 'to the moon and back' sayings. *To the moon* is where I want to stay—because who in the hell would ever want to come back from the moon, if the moon is where you felt like *this*.

I laugh a little at my thoughts, and lean back into the seat, trying to stretch tension from my neck while wishing for a tall glass of ice water. Unlike Robin, who only just started drinking, I've been participating on the Champagne all night long. Every time I was handed a glass of the stuff I drank it down. And who could blame me? After being near Robin in that damn dress, with that damn sexy-straight-waterfall-hair—I needed a drink or two to calm myself down. And then I needed a drink or two more to just…keep myself mellow, because going back to my dressing room and placing ice on the back of my neck didn't help one damn bit, just how yelling at Clara for being part of trying to cut Robin's hair before the show didn't help, either.

The Champagne helped while I was drinking as we were surrounded by people and my bandmates. Only now, watching Robin lean across the seat towards me and gravity takes over, making the soft, half exposed rounded skin of her breasts swell in my direction while she asks, "Hello? *Earth to Royce*? Are you okay?" That…plus how I'm half drunk, and how she's always wondering if I'm okay… has just wrecked me.

"Yes. Totally okay," I answer, removing her full glass from her hand just as she tips it up for another sip.

"Hey…you…*why*?" She lick-giggles the few golden droplets that made it out of the glass off of her pouty-bottom lip, then leans even closer, like her body's gone all limp, and warm and languid and she's eyeing my lap like she'd like to sit on it!

It's all I can do not to groan out loud and adjust what's happening in my pants right in front of her. "Maybe you've had enough?" I ask, leaning away from her some for self-perseverance, but as her brow creases into a small frown, one I can read too much doubt in, I lighten my tone, careful to add, "You will thank me later, okay? This sugary stuff gives massive headaches on the flip side, that's all."

"Oh." She smiles, looking relieved. "Then, I'm *goin'-to-thank-you-how-'bout now*?" She hiccups, wrecking me a second time because oh man—that sound—this girl—is so damn surprising. Cute. Hilarious. "Thankss-Royce." She closes her eyes, wobbling some like she's trying to get her balance against the seat. "This was-sush-fun-speshhial-times-tonight."

"It was," I agree, trying not to laugh, and to force my gaze away from her face I place my lips on the exact spot where her lip-gloss has darkened the crystal glass, then I drain the remainder of the Champagne, hoping she will forget to ask me for *jus-one-more-lil-taste*, which is how she got this last glass out of the bottle.

Who could deny her right now? Not me, and not tonight—that's for damn sure. Because I can't seem to say 'no' to this girl ever. Whatever she wants, I want to get it for her. If it weren't way past midnight right now I'd be trying to piggy-back her up the Eiffel Tower like King Kong, just to make that last dream of hers about Paris happen. It still kills me she didn't get to go to the top of that with me.

"How about, I ask you a *srri—eeeous—thing*?" She blinks, making her lips scrunch up. "Wait. Serrr-his-ishhh." She holds up one finger. "I *can* say this word. Holll—on. Seeer-is-ishh. Quesshton. There. Can I?" She giggles again then looks over at me as the limo pulls into the Parisian Orb Hotel driveway, the bright lights of the portico suddenly distracting me.

I take her hand and give it a squeeze. "How about you wait to ask me questions until we get up into our suite? We're home."

"Home." Her eyes dart to the window, then she sends me a lopsided smile and ramps into singing, "*Home is whenever I'm with you.*" She grins like she's proud of herself with that one and leans her body weight half onto my knees, that or she's toppled, I'm not that sure. "Thass-not *your* hit-song. I know. That's how I feel. Home with you is great." Her eyes grow wide as she hiccups again. "Royce. What is happening to my head? It's spinning some. This is probably me being-drunk, huh?" She whispers, glancing around. "If I'm drunk, does that mean I can't have the rest of that?" She points to the bottle. "Delishhhious. Stuff. Probbbly-I-need-jusss-one-more-sip up in the room. One more time?"

I shake my head, trying not to laugh out loud at her again. "You're tipsy, not drunk. As for any more Champagne, the bottle is empty, which is for the best. We're both switching to water upstairs."

"Okay. But water plus cookies because we need a snnnack." Her brow creases. "Or…wait. Pizza could be also delishhhious?" Her eyelids droop heavily. "Let's make a plan. One of the plan-plans. A *new* plan," she jokes.

"Fine. The plan is water, and we'll get you *any* snack you want. Also, based on how you just broke out singing and you just botched the word delicious twice, I *am* going to have to ask that you staple on a smile and stay *very quie*t while we cross the hotel lobby. I've already tracked how many paparazzi are waiting for us outside, and it's fucking way, too many. Got me?"

"Okay. Check. No singing-songs." She leans her weight onto my side. "Do you know? When you're stressed you *all-alla-always* drop f-bombs?"

"Yes. I know that."

Her head bobs heavily, and her smile says she's maybe already forgotten what she's just said.

As the chauffeur opens the door, a nervous giggle escapes her. Then, as though that was a complete accident for her, she purses her lips extra tight and she bites down hard on the bottom one, rolling her eyes a little like she's holding back more giggles.

I step out, and turn to guide her out then tilt my head raise a brow, wanting to ask if she's with me, just as she moves forward me and says with a glower, "*What? I know. Be. Quiet. Your eyes is ruining my concentration. Stop the beaming silver color.*"

"I'll try." I grin, laughing some and placing my arm loosely around her waist as she stands right next to me.

The crowd that's been waiting outside the hotel ever since we left for the awards ceremony cheers as we pause to wave. Everything goes great until we try to head up the steps into the hotel.

It seems Robin's forgotten that she's wearing the Champagne-glass heels.

I'd also forgotten.

"Damn." I utter, feeling her careen away from me like a train heading off a track. I dive in and scoop her up into my arms, then spin her around to face the crowd who cheers even more at my rescue.

Instead of being mortified, how she usually is about public mess-ups, she simply wraps one arm around my neck and crosses her legs in front of her so everyone can see the shoe that almost killed her while she points at them saying, "These things are dangerous." After the crowd cheers more and the paparazzi has gotten more than their fair share of shots of Robin's shoes, legs, and how she's wrapped up in my arms, she tugs at my lapels to get my attention asking, "Royce? Is it time?"

"Time for what?" I frown down at her.

"Time for you to kiss me? It's my favorite part." She sighs up at me, her big blue eyes drawing me in in this way that makes the noise, and the people and the whole damn world around us fade.

"Kissing." She goes on. "Happens each time we go out and people are watching." She waggles her brows. "If iss-time, I'm ready."

She licks her bottom lip and like a starving man, I bend in to capture the tip of that tongue of hers before it makes it back to her mouth.

I know full well this move of scooping her into my arms would have been sufficient to get two days of social media posts. And because of the 'look at my shoes' talk Robin shouted out we probably don't need to do this kiss.

But…fine…we're doing it… it's not a big deal, right?

Only, instead of pulling away like I normally do at just the right moment, I press my kiss a little longer telling myself it's because the lingering taste of champagne resting on the curves of her kiss-and-smile lips is like an amazing drug that I didn't know. And…when she says, "Mmm," against my lips and makes her arms twine around my neck, trying to deepen the kiss, well…I kiss her more.

Fuck. I think cannons have shot off behind my eyes.

The sound of the crowd's cheering slams into my very out of control body, and it's so loud I feel like someone's poured a bucket of ice water on me.

I pull back and spin both of our faces away from the cameras who have surely caught on to just how badly I want this girl right now. I'm hardly able to keep my expression in check, muttering, "You trying to kill me?"

"That was *the best* kiss." She's nodding, cheeks flushed, lips swollen —every smiling "Kissed-me-right-out-of-my-shoes. So you need-to-help-fix-this. If they drop, we're in big trouble." She's smiling up at me, totally oblivious to my pain, the crowd, to the paparazzi which is when I realize her insane shoes are now dangling by their very thin straps off of her ankles like they're cowbells something.

"How in the hell did that happen?" Laughing, and happy for this distraction, I reach down and slide them off her pointed feet. This makes the crowd go crazy again, because maybe they can't see our faces, but they've still got a prime view of Robin's bare legs hanging over my arm, and now it looks like I'm undressing her in front of them, but instead of shouting, "It's just *shoes*, can't you idiots see they're falling off?" I play it up and turn back to wink at all of them like, *hell-yes-I'm–undressing-my-sexy-wife*, because at this point, and after how we just kissed for so long in front of all of them? What else can I do before I carry her into the hotel.

I GENTLY SET her down in front of the elevator, and push the button, but keep one hand firmly around her waist in case the Champagne has gone too far to her head and she winds up toppling around again.

My fingers brush against the skin on the waistline of her backless dress and I realize it's searing hot. As hot as my hand that refuses to do anything but stroke the length of her back up and down, up and down because, again…what else am I supposed to do here? I've got to keep the flow of this natural.

Quickly, when the doors slide open I lead her into the elevator.

Too late, or—*again fuck-my-insane-life*! But, before she turns to stand shoulder to shoulder to shoulder with me, I realize the jostling of her out of the limo and into my arms, then all the way across this lobby to here, has caused that sticky tape the stylists had placed around her chest to come loose. If I let her turn, Robin will boob-flash every reporter that still has a straight shot into this elevator!

As the doors stutter, trying to close while the bodyguards are deciding who will ride up with us, I signal them both to step out, and ask if they'd leave the two of us *alone* and then I drag her up to my chest and hold her there tight.

This draws a little "*oof*" out of Robin, and more cheers from the crowd. Grins fire at me from Hunter and Vere who just exited their limo and came up into the lobby, and frowns from my entire entourage as well as my grandmother and uncle.

Knowing Robin would be mortified should she realize *why* I'm holding her like this—exactly how I shouldn't as in— smashing her too tight against my chest—with my arms locked so tight around her that should she suddenly get mad, or try to pull back and ask me. '*what the fuck I'm doing?*'— which is what she should be asking, then at least her chest will stay covered.

But…damn her, she doesn't resist. Not one bit.

Aside from her surprised little sound, she's now nestling in, and sighs happily like she'd been hoping for me to do this. She beams up at me, presses into me harder, and twines her arms around my neck. That damn sexy hair of hers tangles between us and the smell of it, all lavender mixed with some new expensive perfume she's never worn before tonight is making me insane.

When the elevator doors close us off away from the world, and she looks at me and smiles like she and I have zero walls between us, like she knows me better than I know myself, I don't step away how I should.

I lean in and kiss her like I've never kissed her before.

And she leans up and kisses me like she's completely mine—when she's not allowed to be mine.

So I kiss her back, like it's the last time I'm going to kiss her, because maybe it will be. Tomorrow we go to Berlin and her father is coming to take her away…and so, I kiss her again, like I don't fucking care about anything other than how soft her skin feels and I work hard to erase all space between our bodies.

Hell yes, I kiss her and kiss her and she's kissing me back like she can read my mind.

I let my hands go everywhere and I melt into her as she melts back into me. I turn and push her against the elevator wall so I can get some better leverage and I'm thankful for the slit up the side of the dress because it allows her to wrap her legs up and around me as I lift her up some.

I know I should stop. I know this, but I'm too weak to resist wanting her like this, because *I love… I love…I love…Christ…how much I love her ways, her smiles, the feel of her lips under mine, the way she just lets me do whatever I want the way she seems to want me back. Because…I love… I love…her.*

Love her far, too much.

35

ROYCE

We're both silent when we get to our suite. Robin's managed to wrap herself up in the cape and has creatively tied it over the failed top portion of her dress.

I glance at the tangle that has become her clothes and hand over her shoes, wondering if I should apologize for what I just did, or make an excuse to explain away how I just bruised her lips, tangled her hair, possibly tore that designer dress some while I put my hands all over her body in places they should not have been; but—I say nothing. I can't. I simply turn toward the bathroom because I'm heading straight into the shower.

Hell, yes. That's the plan. I'm going in, clothes and all.

I avoid looking at her sexy-flushed face for more than a second while I mutter something intelligible involving the words, "Gotta—uh—yeah," and then, "I'll just be a minute."

But Robin halts my steps because she's almost shouted, "Stop! No. Wait."

My whole body tenses and I have the urge to run and slam the door between us, but then she ruins it by adding a whispered, "Royce. Please."

Fuck. Me. Doesn't she know what she does to me when she calls out my name plus the word 'please' like that?

"I have something to ask you. Before I lose my courage because that kiss sobered me up way too much." She's said that last line with a raspy, self-depreciating laugh on the end of it. I've also heard a little catch in her throat. It's made her sound suddenly too trusting and too vulnerable.

"What?" I ask, slowly risking a turn in her direction.

"I was wondering." Her pink cheeks flush pinker, but she keeps her eyes locked on mine. "Would you consider, since it's probably our last days together, um." Her voice drops to a whisper. "Would you consider being my first time. Tonight? Now? If—if you want to, that is?"

"Why?" is the only word I allow to escape my lips, because all other words crashing around between the pounding that makes up the inside of my head are simply me screaming: *Yes. Yes. Fuck yes. Please, yes. Yes. Yes. Yes. Take off that dress, hell yes.*

"Why?" She's echoed, unaware of the madness that's taken over my mind.

Her brows have shot up like my question has caught her off guard. "Because of that kiss we just shared in the elevator? Because every bit of my skin is pulsing for another one, and I think you feel the same? Because the last few times we've kissed I haven't wanted you to stop. Because…losing my virginity with you is all I can think about these days? Oh, and," She pauses to tighten the cape that has started slipping down. "And because I trust you not to hurt me or to scare me while we're doing it. That's why."

She shrugs. Her obvious, small attempt of 'playing it cool' fades away when I can only shake my head once.

I can tell she thinks I'm denying her, but I'm just trying to clear the buzzing from my head. It's not that I don't want to say anything back to her sweet offer, but before I do, I want to memorize the look on her face, the flush against her cheeks and how her eyes have no masks over them right now.

She's so open and beautiful right now, and… she's offering me…*everything.*

God help me right now because…how I love…I love…I love…this girl, too much.

"Look," she goes on when I can't find words yet. "I'm the last living virgin among anyone I know. I was too nervous to go all the way when I was around the guys I kissed before you. I also did this thing in high school where I told myself I couldn't be with anyone while I took care of Sage, but… I think that was just a convenient excuse. Now that I've had this relationship with you, that I pushed them away because maybe

I wasn't ready. I was afraid to trust myself and to trust someone else with my heart—and my whole body."

Holy shit. Her body? Are we talking about her whole body right now?

I force my gaze away from her, and somehow make my legs walk to the mini-bar, because I know that inside the waiting sterling silver wine cooling tub, I will find cold-cold ice waiting for me. Ice I mean to pair with cold-cold water.

Worst case, I can spill a whole bunch of it on me should I need to.

I risk glancing at her once I'm done flinging ice-cubes all over the floor because of my shaking hands, and only *after* I've finally managed to fill two glasses to the brim.

Her cheeks go one shade brighter as I walk over and hand her one of the glasses asking, "Why now…why at all? Seriously Robin? Come on…" I front, praying silently that she will throw it all into my face, or quickly laugh and save us by saying, '*Just joking, Royce. I only wanted to hear what you would say if I asked you.*'

But instead, she takes a small sip, then carries on, eyes searching mine for a way in. But as open as she is—I'm closed off. I have to be, or I'll die right in front of her.

She goes on, "Well, I've spent this whole summer married to *you*… and…" she pauses…looking a little lost.

"And…so what does that mean?" I urge her on, actually curious now, as my mind screams: *What the hell does that have to do with you, trusting me with your body right now?*

"Our marriage means I've had zero chance at meeting any *other* single guys who might take me up on this kind of an offer."

"What?" The walls feel like they're closing in.

"Hear me out. I'm already halfway to nineteen with zero experience. I thought, considering our friendship that you would do me this…*favor.* Like…a—uh—friends with benefits. Or married people with benefits kind of thing? No one would talk, because we're already married and everyone already thinks we're doing it." A desperate sounding laugh escapes her and her sweet mask of calm-practicality starts to slip. "And see…I also don't even know about blow jobs or *anything* aside from stuff I've seen on the internet and, I'm feeling really behind."

I spit out the entire gulp of water and start backing away from her as she relentlessly keeps talking.

"Before you cut me loose, you could show me what to do, give me a list of skills to work on, maybe show me some quality tips and tricks." She shrugs. "Fast track me, before you send me back out into the world?"

From very far away, I hear my own voice, utter, "*No.*"

And as I shake my head, 'no' at her more than once, she's stepping toward me like a little beautiful devil, saying, "Yes! *Royce*, it's going to be a whole year before we're divorced. And maybe even another year will pass by before I can even get out of the paparazzi's radar. Think how long it will be for me before I can get to the point where I might find the courage to simply *talk* to another guy about going out. Which by the way is awkward—because like I'm not going to advertise to potential future-boyfriends that you and I weren't really married. See how problematic this is?" She blinks. "Which means I could easily still be a virgin when I'm pushing twenty-one. Walk in my shoes a moment. What if I finally do meet a guy I trust enough to reveal how lame and inexperienced I am, and we get to the point were we discuss having sex, and then *that guy* discovers I'm still a virgin after being *married to you*. When I'm supposed to probably be a pro! I will either have to lie to him, or fake it until I make it, which will suck because for the first time, everyone knows you're supposed to go all slow and be careful and how will the next guy know to do that, if I can't even tell him the truth. And worse—say I manage to figure it all out, well it won't possibly be any *good,* right? And my lack of skills will probably make *that* guy think there's something wrong with me. He will then dump me, assuming our divorce was caused by me, being horrible in bed." She crosses her arms, nodding emphatically. "I know you can see my logic. I need this. I want this." She crinkles up her brow and shrugs. "Please?"

I'm backed up against the wall, holding my glass of water between us with both hands like it's some sort of broken lightsaber that won't activate. I've gone from choking while holding my breath, to wishing I could choke some nameless, faceless guy who exists in Robin's future—a loser who would dare break up with her for *lack of skills!* What the fuck. This guy she just called the 'next guy' is a guy that I totally hate even more than I hate being forced to imagine a future—a naked-having-sex kind of future, without Robin in it.

Fuck every thought in my head.

Because before all of that crazy she just uttered, did she say blow job and tips and tricks to me? Really?

Girl has just murdered me so many times, I'm going to need an entire graveyard to bury all the shredded up bits of me six feet under properly.

When I don't answer more, only crease my forehead at her and clutch my water glass for dear life, she puffs out a frustrated breath.

Mercifully, she steps back while frowning. "What is wrong with you? Royce. Say something. We aren't living in Medieval times here. Is this such a horrible idea? If you think I'm drunk and making bad requests, I'm *not* anymore. Saying all of that to you sobered me right up —just so you know..."

She's now wiggling her brows, trying to joke her through this. That, plus the flood of white hot desire that's exploding between my ears and throbbing painfully in my pants even more, because she's so damn hot with that hair of hers cascading to her waist, and her eyes all twinkling and openly honest, and the part where I know her dress underneath that cape-wrap would fall off of her completely with the touch of one of my fingers, have made me imagine her naked, and smiling up at me while my hands finally get to touch every inch of her—

"Christ." I think I've been holding my breath because talking is hurting my lungs. "Hell no. Just hell *no*, Robin. I can't do that with you, not now just... *No*." Too late, I realize I've said those thoughts out loud, and I think I sounded really harsh. I try to cover how my mind is spinning and spinning and zero words are coming up now by drinking the water I'm holding as though I just took a million-mile walk in a desert.

She sighs, coming back way, too close to me again. "But...you can. You *can*. We should. Listen." She folds her arms over her stomach—*over that belly button*—which makes me start quickly shaking my head at her again.

This time I'm shaking it for myself though—to help me keep my resolve.

NO-no-no!

She's saying, "Statistically, so many girls have a *terrible* first time experience. Maybe it's a selfish request, but if you agree to this, I'm certain I won't have to be one of them. My skin lights on fire after you kiss me, and after that elevator ride, I'm surprised my legs are holding me up right now. Like..my spine...it's still tingling." She points to the bed and whispers, "Is it too much to ask for us to...just...keep on kissing, but...over there?"

"No. Robin. *No!*" My voice is still too loud, and worse, it sounds like I'm half-insane, but I can't change it. "I mean, yes," I go on, "It's too much to ask. Too, damn much." I jump to the side before she can fence me in again, and before I make a fool of myself.

She's dropped her gaze to the floor and that sweet cajoling smile has been replaced with sadness. "Oh. Okay. Right. Never mind." Her voice is all shame and humiliation. It seems like she can't return her gaze all the way to my eyes, so she's settled on a spot somewhere between my knees and the floor. When I don't answer again, she colors even more.

"Please understand, Robin," I gasp out.

"Oh. Oh, man. I get it. You're just not into me. In *that* way." She slaps a hand on her head. "I'm so sorry. I'm so embarrassed." She flinch-winces under her hand and gives me this quick grimace, and this time her voice comes out rough and sounds despondent. "I uh…think I just sounded like that groupie who wanted five minutes in the closet with you—or at least who wanted five minutes with your—junk." Her laugh is brittle. Her shoulders droop more as she runs on with this new, horrible chatter. "I didn't realize that what I'm feeling is *not* what you're feeling. You don't want to do it?" She shakes her head, locking gazes with me. "You don't have *same* feelings for me that I have for you after we kiss?" She places the back of one of her hands against her lips, before going on. "Well, of course it probably isn't. You're just a really good actor. And nice, right? Shit."

I shake my head, digging deep to find my voice as she turns away, placing a hand on her forehead and walks to lean on the window so she can look out at the night sky. "Again…so embarrassing. I don't suppose you could forget all that I just said?"

Stepping up behind her, I pull in the biggest, most painful breath I've ever experienced, but because I'm scared to death to touch her because I think one brush against her skin will break my resolve, I keep my hands locked around my waist and start out very quietly with, "Robin. I'll never forget what you just said."

She turns to face me and I quickly add in a shaking voice, "Please. Hear me out."

"Okay," she whispers looking down at our feet. "But don't patronize me. Deal?"

"Deal." My voice is all sandpaper as I tilt her chin up to me with my index finger so she's forced to meet my eyes. "I'm going to be completely honest with you, because I feel like if I'm not, you will take this moment and twist my denial of your beautiful—offer—into being something about you, not being good enough for me. When this time, it's all on me."

The pulse in my temple is warring with the pulse that won't quit in my pants as I rip my gaze off of how she's chewing her lips. "Robin. When we kiss, I feel *more* than what you feel. I've always felt it. I want to trash that slip of a dress into shreds and rip my shirt off, all while pushing you on your back on that bed where I'd give you everything you don't even know that you want yet," I say, jerking a thumb towards the bed, watching her eyes go wide with surprise—with her own flash of desire, and with this adorable curiosity that nearly shatters me.

I start trembling, because now I've said the words out loud and visualized what could be—I'm having a difficult time holding to the honor that she deserves, but I forge on, "I've felt this for you—*hell,* I've wanted to sleep with you since the day I met you. Since before I knew you. Since before we were truly real friends. Since before I stopped wanting to *sleep* with you and started wanting to *make love* to you, since before…I…"

I stop myself short. It would only do harm for me to finish that sentence with the truth: *Since before I fell in love with you.*

Regrouping, I add lamely, "Since before everything. You know?" I take my hand off her chin and shove it through my hair. "These past weeks, and the connection we've formed? Damn…girl, don't think you're not the sexiest the most attractive girl, inside and out, I have ever met in my entire life. If this were just about sex or friends with benefits we'd have done this weeks ago."

"So okay, then. If all that's true, I don't understand why you say *no* now? Now that it's all about to be over."

The vice grip on my lungs releases some because I'm happy that I've managed to erase the flickers of self-doubt from her eyes.

"Robin, it's like what I've said all along. I have this terrible feeling that I will somehow hurt you. If we do what you think you want us to do, I would try to keep you, and when it was all over there'd be nothing left of *you, especially* when I, and the press, and the machine that is Guarderobe is finished with you."

"What about how I feel, because I feel that you won't hurt me," she insists. "It—you—haven't hurt me so far." She places both hands over her heart. "I'm right here—being me. And you're you, being you— and we truly see and know each other so well now. Bringing us closer would change nothing between us. Nothing."

"Are you really being you? Have you been yourself all summer?" I challenge. "Robin, I have already changed everything about you and I'm not going to destroy you."

"What? Now you sound crazy."

I shake my head, willing her to believe me. "You can't be sure of how you feel right now. You can't. You've been completely reliant on me and the Guarderobe machine this whole relationship. Being married to me has made you doubt even the shoes you choose to wear on your feet. It has changed you inside and out and you know it has."

"That's because--" Her brow furrows. I can tell by her expression she stopped talking because she's wondering if I'm right.

Quickly I press on, "You have this misplaced gratitude because of all we did for you and your little brother. Now that we've found your father, you think you owe us because of the money we paid to get your father found. You're so emotionally raw right now that your heart has been flayed wide open in front of me daily—and that is scary. That leaves you open to serious pain."

"So? What's the big deal about my heart? All you've done is care for my heart. Protect it. Protect me. Make my heart feel good." She sighs out. "And I think you'll keep doing that while we're in bed. Which is exactly why I want you, *only you*, to be my first."

When she bites her bottom lip and stares up at me all matter-of-fact, I almost give in to her request, but as she flips her bone straight hair back over her shoulders, and my eyes fall to the perfectly manicured hand she's laid over her heart I hold steady and say, "You need to go home and recover your normal life. Find that girl who's an artist, the one who wants to take sculpting classes, and recover the path that literally disappeared out from under your feet because you had the misfortune to meet me. At least admit that creating art is your essence and you haven't even been able to pick up a paintbrush since you got on the plane to come to Europe."

"But that's because we're touring cities, and because we're newlyweds and because—"

"It's because I've stolen all of that away from you, Robin. I've even stolen you from yourself. Think about it. As my wife, you haven't had time to follow your dreams and worse you've been a prisoner these months."

"It's been fun." She glowers.

"I will not, take more from you. I can't. Especially not take away your first time! Because if I did that…shit, I'd be taking advantage of you in every way." I step forward and move some strands of her beautiful hair away from her brow and tuck some strands behind her ear. "Friends with benefits would never do justice to how things should be for you."

"But."

I place a finger on her lips. "One day, whenever that *next guy* you spoke about comes along, the one who is worthy of building your trust so you can have this same conversation with him. The one who will be awesome. The one that you will easily be able to tell the truth to, about how and *why* we were once married—and how you and I never had sex but are still *good friends*? That guy." I think morbidly: *the guy who is not me.* "He's not going to judge you, or break up with you. He's going to keep you, forever, because he's going to be really in love with you. How could he not be, Robin? Your first time deserves *forever*. You and I… we're not supposed to be that."

I lock gazes with her wide blue eyes, and as she starts in with one of her little head shakes, and makes that face she always makes before protesting something, I hold up my hands again. "Please Robin." I whisper. "I understand why you asked me, but please tell me you understand some of what I'm saying. Tell me that you know I'm right, or I'm going to have to stay away from you. As in…go sleep in Hunter's room tonight and for our last days together which would be really sad."

"No. Don't do that. Please." She says, but she's still shaking her head and making this face like she's still going to try to convince me.

"Robin." I pull her into a giant bear hug so I don't have to look into her pleading eyes anymore. My voice—hell my whole soul—is shaking as I put the last nail into my side of the argument. "I want to look your father in the eye when I meet him. I want to be able to shake his hand, and thank him for his service before he takes you home. If I sleep with you I will not be able to do that. I also will have ceased to be that honorable guy you wished I could become be when we first met, and I think…I think I am becoming him." I lay my chin against the top of her head and breather her in.

"Fine. Okay. You're right. I wasn't thinking about my father."

"Obviously." I chuckle, relieved that she and I seem calm—and that we're both breathing together again.

She breathes a warm resigned sigh into my neck. "Does this mean no more elevator kisses?"

"Probably. And definitely no more Champagne. We both lose a little control on that stuff, huh?"

"Right?"

I laugh along with her as I step away from our embrace. "Can I take that ice-cold shower now?"

"Okay. As long as when you come back out there's no more dumb…faking stuff between us when we're alone. Like, can we stop pretending the pillow fortress is helpful? Because if we only have a few days left, I'd like to get right to the part where you hold me in your arms *sooner*, because I'm going to miss that so much when it's all over. And maybe, since you don't even want to sleep with me when I *beg* you to do it, then can I feel safe not wearing the giant hoodie anymore? It's getting so hot."

My eyes go wide realization that she's known all along what I've been doing, but damn…she's right, with only a few days left why waste that extra time when soon I won't have the chance. My eyes skate to how the spot on the dress that shows me her bellybutton, and I answer stiffly, "No more pillow fortress. But the hoodie —it has to stay on."

"Fine."

36

ROBIN

"BERLIN, Robin. Tomorrow we get to see Dad in *Berlin!*" Sage's smile is contagious the next day when he leans down to give me a quick hug before joining me at the breakfast table in mine and Royce's room. After the call from our father, he'd finally returned to some semblance of what was 'normal' for him on this tour. Meaning, hanging with Hunter Kennedy, Adam, and the roadies. Playing video games non-stop, and loving his private, room service filled private suite down the hall from ours.

Sage plops some pineapple in to his mouth, talking while chewing. "Remember the video-swag Royce gave me as a gift when we first met? It was his entire concert, *Live in Berlin*, from his first world tour. And now we're going to *be there.* We will get to see the same stadium, and the see nearly the same concert, *live*! And for frosting on the cake, our Dad is supposed to be there at the end of it all." His beaming smile grows wider as his eyes catch on mine. "Like I've said all along, Sis. Do not pinch me to wake me up. I want to keep on dreaming this dream."

"Hey team," Vere comes tearing into the room, holding a pile of magazines and newspapers, along with her iPad and laptop balanced on top. "Mrs. Felix is going crazy. Says we need to do a social media check, and maybe post some distraction posts fast. What the heck did you and Royce *do* last night to make the world sit up and notice, the feeds are blowing up and I've got questions. So many questions."

I get cranky at that question, thinking: *What didn't we do? That's one of my questions. How long will I be the last living virgin on earth? That's another question.* But instead, I stare at the latest, delicious still-warm French baguette in front of me, and answer only, "There is no Nutella. Should I call and see if we can get some."

Sage, pops out of his chair. "I'll just go down to the kitchen area. I've made friends with the concierge at this place. The guy will hook me up."

Vere has moved to a longer side table to spread out the newspapers and plug in her iPad and laptop. "Headache from too much Champagne, Robin?" As Sage leaves, her eyes trap mine and she lowers her voice. "What's wrong? What happened last night. I saw some photos of you in and Royce in that elevator and what the heck happened?"

I pick at the table cloth, and decide to tell her the truth. "I tried to drop my *v-card* last night, but Royce denied me."

"*What?*" Here big-brown eyes go wider than ever. "Why? Holy cow. No wonder this morning he was stomping around, acting different."

"How different?" I ask.

"Answer my question first *Why*?"

"Why did I ask him to do it with me, or why did he blow me off?"

"Both. Of course. *Both!*" She giggles, then clamps a hand over her mouth, because she gets by my expression that I do not find any of this funny.

I furrow my brow and decide to be completely honest with her. "I asked him because… he's beautiful and kind to me, and because of how he treats me with such consideration, I thought he'd be the most wonderful guy in the world to be my first time you know…because…"

She finishes my sentence for me. "Because…he probably would be, and because you're in *love* with him?"

"What does that have to do with anything?" I evade her question. "I feel like, we're more than friends after all that we've been through in this short time—that's for sure—and he's even said the same to me. I figured we were married and we love kissing each other, and so…*why not*."

"Shit. So…you *are* in love with him?"

I blush, glancing at the door to make sure Sage is nowhere near, and I whisper. "Who could blame me? He's amazing. Inside and out, amazing, right? How else am I supposed to feel about Royce after all of this fake marriage stuff. I'm not a piece of plywood, I'm a real human girl and I've been sharing a bed with him on and off for months and he's…so…great." I shake my head.

She nods. "Yeah. He is. All that and more." Leaning in she also starts whispering. "So, why did he say no? Why?"

"Bullshit excuses so my feelings won't be hurt." I mimic his voice. "*Because my dad is coming to take me home. Because it would mess with my head, and because his life will ruin my life. Because I need to get back to the real world. Because he needs to be able to look my dad in the eye and shake his hand—because I deserve forever.*"

"Aww. Oh that's really sweet. Do you believe him?"

"Whatever. I don't know." I huff out a breath. "I'm not an idiot. It's because he probably wants to get back to *his* real life, dating models and movie stars, and he doesn't want to have my broken heart on his conscience—because I think he does care about me. He probably knows I'm stupidly head over heels in love with him, and me, having sex with him *would* make that worse, which is true, damn him." I shrug, feeling even more desolate now that I've said it out loud. "I don't know. Why does *any* guy say they don't want to have sex with you after you ask. Because they don't think you're hot. It could some of that, too."

"Oh, Robin. It's not any of that—yet—it's probably all of that stuff —not counting the line where you think he doesn't find you attractive, as we all know he does."

"Vere. I was nearly naked because that stupid dress was falling off. I was begging him to do it…begging him…" I crack into the baguette and take a bite, frowning.

Her brows shoot up as I nod talking with my mouth full, "And like it could have been so easy…yet *no*. We didn't." I put a hand on my heart because it's twisting so bad it hurts as I go on, "I guess I'm like a casualty of war, huh?" I try to joke my way out of this feeling. "He was firing fake love-bullets all around me for the press—holding my hand and gazing into my eyes, and kissing me all the time—and of course being so nice and so handsome. I think each one of those moments became a direct hit to my unsuspecting heart." I rip into another bite of bread. "And, even worse, going by the way this heart of mine wouldn't stop flutter-beating all summer whenever he was around me—and no— after how awkward I made it between us last night, it's all but cracking in half?" I drop the bread onto a plate. "Vere…after last night, I'm bleeding out." I drop my voice lower. "And…I can't stand how painful it all is." I shake my head. "Because…yeah. This has to be love…and it really sucks."

"Oh. Robin. Oh…I'm sorry." Vere comes to put an arm around me.

"I've never been in love before, so don't have a comparison, but I'm pretty sure this is the real thing. I'm so stupid, huh?" I laugh, acting like it's not a big deal. "Because, now that I'm finally going to get to see my Dad—which was the only thing in the whole world I thought I wanted. Which is the only thing I do want, right? And…I'm supposed to be happy. I'm supposed to feel excited for what's next, but all I feel is this terrible sadness." I look up at her. "It's like I'm stuck on some steep snowfield and I'm scrambling around but I'm slipping in place. Unable to go up or down, and worse," I pull my brows down. "I feel like I'm going to die on that snowfield."

"You sound like that TV show, where they're all alone and naked and— do you know that show?"

"Yes. It's exactly like that." I manage a smile for her. "I've done the whole mission and all I have to do is walk out and there will be food and some helicopter waiting to transport me to the shelter and the prize money. But instead, I'm just lying there and I don't care that I won. I can't move and maybe there's wolves lurking around, and I probably have hypothermia —oh and I've been eating only snow for days so my stomach endlessly hurts, and I actually am staring at the snowflakes pelting me and wishing to just die to end this pain and I don't care about anything else." I pull out a shuddering breath and blink at her, coming back into focus. "Does that make any sense or have I simply just lost my mind?"

"Heck *yes*, it makes sense." Vere's shaking her head. "That's love all right, and you've got it so…so bad."

Sage skips back into the room with a massive jar of brand new Nutella just as I'm whispering, "I'm afraid. Really afraid. Of…of…"

Sage has already cracked the thin gold foil that comes sealed over the top of the jar and he's eating a cake-pop sized spoonful of the stuff. "Afraid of what?"

Turning my back on Vere, and hoping she will understand the topic of Royce is closed, I flip the conversation away from Royce and onto other things I'm afraid of. Quickly I answer, "I'm afraid to go back to our old life. That things won't be the same. That we will have all changed too much. Including…Dad."

Sage shrugs like my fears are unfounded. "But we aren't going back to our old life. We're going to New York City to live in the awesome apartment under Mrs. Felix. It's going to be a whole *new life,* at least until I'm out of high school and you're out of art school." He grins that irrepressible grin of his. "No going back, Robin. The Love family is back together and we will be better than ever, starting a great *new* life. Robin! Just think, we will hang out with the Perinos again. I spoke to Angel, he's *dying* to see us."

"And I'm dying to see him," I say, ruffling the too-long curls on top of his head. "Ana and Julia, too. All of them." It's not hard to pace on a sincere smile at Sage about seeing the Perino family again. Despite all that I just said to Vere, thinking of Angel's little cousins and of my good friend Angel and of his mother waiting to see us again has been like a balm to my tortured thoughts about Royce.

Sage swipes a second Nutella-gob onto a croissant. "Aren't you ready to go back to the good old USA? It was fun to see some of Europe, but I'm done. I want Domino's Pizza. I want Taco Bell so bad that the craving hurts. I need the crunchy round ice from Sonic. For that matter I need every single drink to be super-sized with double ice. I'm also excited to start the new school. I thought I'd never say this about hanging out with Guarderobe—because, Hunter, Adam and Royce are awesome brothers to me. I want to be with kids my own age again. Ones who aren't stuck in long term relationships, or worse, *married.* No offense to Adam, Evie and that baby, but let's just say, their disgusting mush-relationship and all of the diaper changing and worrying about how much baby Apple eats has put me off babies for life."

I laugh a little at that, as does Vere. "Well, I hope Hunter and I added to your disgust."

Sage nods to her solemnly. "Yes. You did. You both wrote the book on sappy and disgusting, I'm terrified for you two to have a baby."

Vere grins at him, clearly not offended. "You'll fall in love just how we have, one day, Sage. And you'll probably be sappier than all of us.

"Never. Well…maybe. But I can't do that while on tour here with all of you." His eyes capture mine. "Robin, don't you feel the same? Like it was all fun, but you're ready to get back to being un-married. Back to regular life? I'm going to get a girlfriend, I guess…but I'll pick very carefully. Pick a girl who plays video games, too."

Vere laughs and so do I. "Good plan."

He nods to me. "Robin, you also should get a boyfriend."

"Heck yes…and…I will. I will," I say, trying to match the bravado in my little brother's voice while not thinking of the humiliating talk I had with Royce last night on this very same topic. It's made my heart twist so hard again the corners of my eyes are threatening to water. "I'll be very picky like you. Shop around and get a guy who really wants me…for me." I dart a glance at Vere. "Get an…artist guy like me…or…yeah, just a…a nice…guy. Very nice," I finish, feeling stupid and forlorn and very sorry for myself because Royce Devlin is a nice guy.

Sage smiles, still not understanding any of the layers of hurt and confusion going through me right now. "How long will it take for the divorce to get ramped up and over." He puts the lid back on the Nutella, frowning up at me.

"I—it depends on when…Royce, uh…publicly, you know." I swallow, hating how my heart is twisting and buckling more, so I drop my voice to extra quiet. "Cheats on me."

"Shit. *That's* what's going to happen?"

I can't answer, only nod, because it feels like there's now a bus sitting somewhere on my chest.

Vere, like she can sense it's upsetting me even more to talk about this, answers quickly, "Heck yes. Cheating will bring on the most public sympathy because people always feel sorry for the one who got cheated on. He will probably get some photos taken of himself with his arm around some girl, which will start off the gossip train about how the marriage may not be doing so well. Knowing Royce, he will want to do it quickly and thoroughly."

"Thoroughly…" I whisper out, choking on that word as my thoughts spiral out of control. *Will he thoroughly kiss someone else? Thoroughly get a new girlfriend? Thoroughly sleep with her when he wouldn't touch me after I begged him like a fool? Thoroughly publicly dump me—which shouldn't matter considering—none of this is real, right?*

Vere goes on, "If the photos are solid and the rumors hit fast, Robin should be free to date. Back to being…." She pauses to make finger quotes. "*A single, normal college freshman* somewhere around Thanksgiving break. Maybe sooner. I heard Royce saying we might invite Clara to do be the girl who breaks you up. Gregory thinks it would be easy to get her in on the scheme since she literally stalks Royce. If we use her, we won't have to explain anything to her because she thinks the relationship between you two is completely legit. She also thinks she's a way better choice than you to be with Royce—meaning she seems the type who would love being your personal home wrecker. I think it's a perfect idea, actually."

I haven't been able to breathe in or out since she uttered the word Clara, but finally I manage to shout out, "No!"

Only…my voice has come out raw and unclear and it sounds like I'm talking through cardboard, or sandpaper or dirt. "Not her. Anyone but her. Please." I close my eyes, and bark out a laugh so Vere can't peer into them anymore. "I—I just mean that I think it would be *easier* if it could be someone I *don't* know. If I have a say in it, that is, and I hope that I do."

When she doesn't answer, I open my eyes and shoot her a look, hoping to God I've got my 'could-care-less' mask locked back in place. "Vere. What I'm saying is, Royce doesn't even like Clara that much. Maybe for once the guy could try to have a *real* relationship, since I don't think he's ever done that in his entire life. *Naturally* meet a girl under *normal* circumstances and be *himself.* I would be happy to know that he was going to walk away from this to start a nice—new life, too. *But a real one.* I mean, is it that hard for a guy who looks like him to meet a girl and flirt with her, call her on the phone, follow some sort of normal relationship progression all the way to honest butterflies and a sincere love story? Does it all have to be so fake and orchestrated for him? Does it?"

"Oh. Wow. Now that you mention it, I guess not." Vere blinks. "You know? We've been all so caught up in the scheming, that I think none of us ever thought of that for him." Vere's rubbing her chin, thinking hard. "I'll mention it because, yeah…you're right. He needs to move on from this just how you will, and why not move out of the lies and back to something real. Why not?"

"Thank you." I shrug. "The guy acts like he's not able to forge connections, when in fact, he seems to be able to get any dumb girl like me to fall for him in seconds flat. Half of his work is done with just one smile, right? And well, the world is full of millions of dumb girls like me, right? Millions…he can have his pick." Another too-harsh sounding laugh escapes, and somewhere from inside the hurting, my voice has turned sarcastic…heck, maybe even bitter as I add, "Please mention he'd have to do something called *being himself* to make it solidify. All he has to do is twinkle those electric eyes, or quirk one side of his smile up how he does, or brush his hand against her cheek, because that always buckled my knees since day one—but he needs to *mean it* instead of *act it* how he was doing with me." I shudder out an angry breath. "Again…not so difficult…right?"

Vere's shaking her head at me, and making this expression that looks way too much like pity, but I don't deserve that, nor do I want that.

I just have to remember that my cup is so full it's spilling over right now, and I'm not going to feel sorry for myself or have anyone else feel that for me either. I got everything I wanted. Sage is safe, my father is home, people here truly care about me, and I've made so many memories and friends. Longing for a 'more' that was never really there seems just…rude or ungrateful or…something.

I force a deep breath into my lungs and the ache of it expanding has nearly cracked my ribs as I turn away from Vere to stare out of the window as I add in a couple last lies, "It's all going to be fine. Just, tell Royce whomever he picks, to please make it quick. Rip off the Band-Aid—be thorough or whatever you said. I…truly, don't care."

"I'll tell him."

37

ROYCE

It's two AM, and we leave for Berlin in only a few hours. I know I shouldn't be in here, watching Robin sleep, searching her face in the moonlight for signs of crying or stress.

Because…of course, I've found them.

I can see the faint salty-tear tracks under her eyes, and if that's not enough, it appears the girl has taken a whole box of tissues to bed with her. Worse, she's clutching it to her heart like it's a long-lost pet, and *damn-me-to-hell*, but I know I'm the cause of those tears.

See, I'd made up some lame excuse as to why I had to sleep in Hunter's room, and why I was too busy to come in here tonight, but it was all lies. I was avoiding her. As the day went on, I'd become more and more worried that she'd do something off the wall like ask me to *sleep* with her again. Or worse, beg me. And despite how I truly do want to shake her father's hand and all that crap I'd spewed the other night. But, if Robin asked me again, I know I will not be able to tell her 'no' twice.

Not be able to tell myself 'no' either.

Which is why, I'm happy as hell this is our last night in Paris and that all of this will be over in a few days. Thankfully, far as I can tell—and as Vere had reported to me, both she and Sage have bought in to our exit plan. The cheating idea. Though I was surprised to find out Robin had balked on the Clara idea—I was even more surprised that Robin asked Vere to encourage me to go for a real relationship. Vere told me of Robin's bossy, a step-by-step plan to my-future-romance. A plan that Vere thought was actually a good idea, while I thought it was ridiculous.

I haven't ever had a 'real' relationship and after how this last 'fake' relationship nearly killed me, I feel like I should remain alone for the rest of my fucking life.

That, or maybe I'll get a dog after all of this…

I know it took a lot—and I mean *a lot* to convince Vere to say all that she said to them both this morning. She'd been tasked with saying how I'd cheat on Robin so that both Sage and Robin will be ready for it when it happens—because I mean for it to happen as quickly as possible. I also swore to Vere that I'd leave Robin alone from that point forward. That I'd keep our 'together time' to a minimum so she and I could get used to how that feels, but…I also can't stay away from her now. Vere told me straight up that Robin told her she really, truly and deeply in love with me. In love. With me. How I'm in love with her.

Like she knows I'm there—pondering love and our impossible future, she rolls toward my empty side of the bed, calling out, "Royce? I didn't think you'd come. Or that you were mad at me. Is everything okay between us after what I asked you last night? We're still friends, right? Don't sleep in Hunter's room. Please…come in here with me. I'm cold." She sounds…so sad, my breath catches.

"All is okay," I answer, unable not to crawl into the bed once I notice she's truly shivering. I eject her tissue box onto the floor, and pull her in so I can nestle her spine against my chest, but as I place my chin on the top of her head, I feel anvils of guilt striking into me that I'm doing this after I'd resolved not to be here.

More so, I feel shame that I can't *stop* myself from doing this—that I'm so damn weak where she's concerned that I can't stay away. I tense some as she whispers, "Thank you," to me, I hold my breath.

Thankfully she doesn't repeat the requests of last night, doesn't do anything provocative, only sighs and breathes in deep like she needed me to be here, my arms lock around her waist and this wave of love I have for her takes over. It's so huge and feels so desolate because I wonder if this is truly our last night together like this, that the magnitude of that idea nearly stops my heart. "Go back to sleep," I whisper, my breathing settling in to matching hers. "Everything is okay. We've been the best of friends all along, and we will stay the best of friends," I lie, because—*shit…I don't know what we are anymore, don't feel confident in what we will be in the future, either. I also don't want to think about it, only want to hold her…and wish away the relentless clock.*

"Thanks for not holding it against me. I thought you had and…I guess…thanks for saying 'no' because…I was a fool and you were right. Also, thanks for finally coming to bed with me. I'm…really sorry… about all of it."

Her words kill me all over again. Too late I realize she's not wearing the hoodie. Worse, she's wearing what feels like short pajama shorts and a tank top.

"If we're to get one thing straight between us, Robin Love," I deliberately, slowly drawl out the name she had *before* she agreed to marry me to remind myself to keep my hands still. "It's that I'm the one who is sorry. I'm forever going to be the fool."

She shakes her head, but thankfully doesn't say more.

I memorize this moment, taking snapshots of what I'm allowed to keep like, how her spine highlights the slight curve in her back, the way she melts into me as she warms up and grows sleepier and sleepier, the smell of her lavender lotion, the curls springing under my chin, smelling like lavender….

When I think she's asleep, I whisper very quietly, "Robin Love…" again. And then, again. "Robin….love."

I know I'm saying it simply because it is the only way I can say her name plus the word 'love' all together.

She surprises me with a sleep-heavy-protest of, "Hey. I'm still *Robin Devlin*. Today. Robin Devlin." She nestles deeper into my embrace, adding, "Hard to believe… tomorrow is Berlin…"

"Right?" I answer the obvious, but add nothing more, because… there's just nothing left to say that won't hurt us both all over again.

And…I think she and I combined…are at our limits.

38

ROYCE

Two hours later, I wake to the sound of pounding on our door, and I hear Sage's voice calling out, "Robin. Royce. Open up! Robin, are you in there? Guys wake up." Then Sage's voice is shouting, "Dad. I swear. It's okay. Honest. They're together in there, but they're not. You'll see."

Robin half sits up, blinking. "Did you hear—him say, *Dad?* Is my dad here in Paris? Is this a dream? *Dad?*" Her last word is called out to directly the door as she scrambles up from the covers.

"Yes. Robin. It's me. Open up," a man's voice comes through.

Robin and I leap out of the bed at the same time. She's running to the door and yanking it open while I lurch around with my legs still asleep, slamming into shit as I try to hit a light switch.

"Dad? Dad! It's really you. You're here!" When I look over, Robin's laughing as she nearly knocks a tall, slender man wearing a beige fatigue jacket and balancing on crutches into the door jam.

"There's my girl," the man says, voice heavy with emotion. I catch a glimpse of a his shadowed face as he envelopes Robin into his embrace, dropping one of his crutches in the process.

Sage hugs the man from behind and in seconds the three of them are intertwined and falling into our suite in one big a mess of noise, tears, hugs and crutches. It feels like within moments, each of them have said: *I'm okay-I'm okay, we're okay. Everything is okay, you're okay*, hundreds of times.

By the time they come up for air, my grandmother has wheeled herself into the room in her wheelchair, Uncle Gregory has appeared along with Royce, Hunter, Adam, Evie, as well as Vere. Right about then, I've realized Robin is truly only half dressed in her shorts and a nearly see-through camisole, so I've collected a throw blanket and her hoodie and I return and place it over her shoulders. She leans into me and smiles up at me in that way that warms my heart, and tugs on the hoodie. But when I meet Mr. Love's gaze, the look he's got for me is stone-cold-furious. So much so that I can't even hold the guy's gaze. I also have this sinking sensation—because shit, he knows Robin and I were sleeping together.

"The whole family is here," Sage cries out. "This is the best moment of my life. Dad, please meet Mrs. Felix, Mr. Gregory." He starts pointing around the room continuing his introductions. "This is Adam, and Hunter, Vere, and Evie, and that little squirmy bug, is baby Apple. The one who started everything. Who got us into this family."

Adam laughs, "Right? And the one who got all of us into a lot of trouble."

Mr. Love's eyes look wild and exhausted as he takes us all in, saying only, "I called Mrs. Felix and Gregory to give them warning. They told me that if I could get a plane to Paris, then I was invited, so I hope that is still true, even in these tiny hours of the morning."

"Of course it's still true," Gregory answers, "We never thought you'd make it, but we're honored to meet you."

Mr. Love grabs Robin's shoulders and gives her a little shake like he can't believe she's real. "I never thought I'd make it either, but then… I couldn't wait. I had to come. There were no flights, so I took a train, and then another train until Paris, then for the first time in my life I downloaded the app and took an Uber to get the rest of the way here, so I hope you understand." His voice turns rough. "None of me, getting rescued and being found alive was going to feel real or right until I could touch my kids."

"You don't need to explain." Robin's beaming at him. "We have so much catching up to do, and had you been anywhere but in debriefing where I knew we couldn't have access to you, Sage and I would have been pounding down the hospital doors for the same reasons."

Robin's father's eyes cloud up as he answers, "Ever since I've been allowed internet, I've been on YouTube trying to piece together what happened to you kids while I was gone. I know you told me not to track the press and the stuff I found online, but how could I not? I know you two ran away and the Perino family sheltered you, and then this rock band…" He flicks a glance at me and my bandmates. "This rock band bunch of people saved you two, but only after one of them had ruined Robin's reputation in the first place, right? Am I piecing it together correctly?" He shoots me another dark glare.

"After I ruined *his* reputation, too," Robin defends me. "I totally messed up. I take full responsibility—I almost lost Sage because of my part in it." Suddenly she's blushing beet red. "Dad…so…we—" She points between herself and me. "We saved each other."

"Yes, well. *Yes.*" The man looks positively tortured, and it's not lost on any of us how pale he is, how exhausted he seems and how skinny he seems compared to me, Royce and Hunter. "I saw the wedding online, the honeymoon photos, and all of how you went around New York City, then London, then Paris…and I was all good, especially after I spoke to you on the phone that first night Robin." His gaze darkens as he flicks it between me and Robin again. "But you told me that it was all fake."

"Dad. It is. It is," Robin insists, not meeting my gaze. "We spoke about this on the phone and you said you were okay with all of it…" She trails off, frowning.

Robin's father's glower darkens as he shakes his head at his daughter. "Maybe I was just too relieved to be out of that hole in Uganda. Maybe I was just happy to find out my kids who'd ran away from their guardian's house had landed on their feet. But the whole damn base seems invested in your story. Everyone in the whole world seems up in my—our—your—business, and I'm not okay with that."

"Mr. Love," Vere interjects. "That's all part of our crazy life. It can't be helped. It's always a shock at first, but you will get used to it."

Again, the man shakes his head. "The other night my staff sergeant told me to turn on the TV to see if I could spot you on the Teen Select awards he'd heard that you all were attending. Hell. I spotted you all right, Robin, wearing a bunch of tissue paper. I spotted you and the entire military base spotted you…and then saw how you were nearly naked."

"Dad. That was a costume. A costume for the red carpet," she insists.

He fists his hands into balls and his voice turns to ice. "Honey, I was prepared to suck it up. Prepared to be grateful and gracious for *all of it*, despite the mad circus you'd been sucked into, and despite the last minute surgery they'd put me into to fix this damn leg that some asshole broke a year ago by kicking it until it snapped."

At that news, Sage gasps, putting his hands over his mouth, and I can tell Mr. Love regrets letting that bit of information slip as he waves one crutch slightly at everyone. "And," he flushes and glances at Mrs. Felix. "I thank you all. I do. From the bottom of my heart, thank you. For the sacrifices you all seem to have made and for the safety you offered my children. Also, don't get me wrong, I thank you for the money you put up for ransom for me as well."

Mrs. Felix wheels forward. "There is no thanks needed for any of what we did. It was and is an honor to know your two children and help them how we did."

Mr. Love colors a little at that, and he backs away from my Grandmother a little as he adds in a shaking voice, "I've already got my team raising money to pay you back. And I will." He holds up a hand when Gregory and Mrs. Felix open their mouths to protest again, and goes on, "Because we SF don't like owing anyone *anything*. So, again I also thank you for the *loan*, but it will be treated as such."

I wonder then, if his voice is getting colder and colder—mostly because he's staring at me and Robin with this hard and assessing look—or, maybe I'm just imagining that?

"Sir. That's not necessary," Gregory starts out finally when no one seems to know what to say. "We're honored you showed up when you could and that you're here despite the hardships you faced in arriving here. It's very late and—you seem—tired. So…we will get you settled in your rooms because you must be tired, as I know we all are the same."

I send Gregory a quick glance and by my uncle's expression it's obvious he's noticed how Robin's father won't stop glaring at me, either.

My grandmother breaks into the tense silence next. "Yes, why don't we all re-group retire to our rooms and go over more details together tomorrow. We are preparing your rooms right now, and it is obvious you are distracted and that the leg is paining you some, yes or… something? We did get a call from the German Military base that you we're not *quite* released yet. Not medically released, that is. Maybe you need to rest?"

Mr. Love chuckles, then. "Well, like I said I didn't feel like waiting around anymore, so…it's possible I left without signing all of the papers how they'd wanted."

"Dad!" Robin calls out. "You're supposed to still be in the hospital?"

She starts to tug on a chair and drag it in the direction of her father. "If that's true, then you need to go to bed. You need to at least go and…lie down! Let's get him to his room."

She starts glancing between all of us when her father's voice turns even more icy, "You want me to lie down while you lie down in here with your fake *husband*? In the same bed? Forgive me, Robin, but is that what you want? Everyone just 'return to their beds' and you send me to my *room*? Has the whole world flipped upside down in my absence?" His laugh splinters and catches. "Damn…missing two years is much harder than I thought…because I'm looking at you, and I'm looking Royce and I'm wondering where in the hell has my little girl gone?"

Robin's face crumples and her eyes go wide. "No. No. Dad. It's not what you think."

Mr. Love leans heavily on his crutches. "It is what I think. It's my worst fucking nightmare, and forgive me if I'm having a difficult time digesting that you and he have been sharing a bed!" This tirade causes my grandmother to pull in a huge gasp of air as Mr. Love motions to her, and adds, "And you oh-so-proper people have been allowing it."

"Dad. Please. I'm eighteen. He has been sleeping with me but—Dad we don't—you don't understand."

"Sir. She's right, we need a chance to explain," I add.

Mrs. Felix pipes in next, "They've been chaperoned and they're under our vow of trust. They stay in here together to keep the press and the hotel staff from starting rumors about their relationship, but it's all been purely platonic."

Sage steps up to his father. "They build a pillow fortress-wall between them each night and it's always really big," Sage points to the rumpled bed and everyone in the room grows quiet and stiff-lipped when it is obvious that there is not one pillow that was separating Robin and I tonight.

Mr. Love slowly crutches over to me, and as he gets closer I note that his eyes are as clear and as blue as Robin and Sage's eyes. "Young man. *Royce Devlin.*" He barks a cynical laugh up to me. "I mean no disrespect for all that you and your family, and your band has done for my kids. I also realize you've done a great amount of good, but I'm not the kind of man who likes being lied to, nor am I an idiot. I was also a twenty-one year old boy once, and I don't think I could have shared a bed with a girl as pretty as my girl is, without going insane, so you better tell me right now. Are you gay, are you broken down there?" He points to my crotch, or. "Are you not all right in the head? Which is it, young man?"

I blink at him, and I finally utter…"Uh…I'll pick…the last one," I try to joke and it's an honest answer, after all. When the man doesn't even flinch or move or breathe, I add quickly, "My grandmother is right. It's been a wedding in name only." I hold his gaze. I hold it steady, just how I wanted to when I met him; but as he stares back his gaze does that thing to me that Robin does. It goes too far. It goes too damn deep and suddenly it's like he can read my fucking mind, so I break the stare. Put up the shutters.

But…damn-me…I think he saw…

"Dad. Please. Please. Believe us."

"Dad. No one has lied to you, all the shit they're telling you is fucking true," Sage calls out, sounding emotional, desperate, worried.

Mr. Love's eyes go wide at how Sage has just cussed twice in front of him as Sage continues, "We've just been living in a surreal world, that's all. We grew up some…and we had to do a lot of weird shit but I swear we're better for it."

"Are you?" Robin's dad has winced at that, and by the way his shoulders slump I get that he thinks all of this is somehow his 'fault' as he sighs loud and long. "Let me tell you all the world I've been living in. When I left for deployment, my *kids,* my sweet little kids—Robin was a high school junior and Sage was finishing sixth grade—I never thought I'd be gone for so long." He pulls in a shaking breath and I see that his hands are white-knuckling on his crutches from the apparent effort he's burning up by standing for so long. "I never thought I'd return to find my son looking like a man, taller than me and cursing like a sailor. Or should I say cursing like a mother-fucking *rockstar*?"

He's said the last word like it's poison. Hunter, Adam and I all flinch hard as he passes hard eyes over us. The whole room goes completely still as he reaches into his back pocket, and brings forth one of the photographs that was taken last night. Specifically, the one where I'm mauling Robin in the elevator. "If all that you've said to me is true, then maybe in addition to why you two are sharing the same bed, you can explain the look on my daughter's face in this *world-wide-news* story?" He shoves a finger at the photograph.

"Dad. I—I'd had a whole bunch of Champagne, and so that photo…I was just…"

"Champagne? You'd been *drinking*? Sage is cussing and now you're so all-grown up enough to *drink?* I wasn't gone that long. You're only eighteen!"

"It's legal in Europe," Robin pipes up again, but this time, her voice sounds small and unconvincing—even, suddenly—*kindergarten-young*. "And yes…Dad, it's not a big deal. The whole awards ceremony was sponsored by Champagne—uh—the region, you know." She does this funny little shrug. "And it was expected we all have some so…I did."

"Expected. *Expected!*" Her father's shouting more. *"Expected?"*

I make the mistake of nodding, how everyone else is nodding, and lock my gaze with Mr. Love's, as I step up to him, hoping to somehow calm him down, but when I try, nothing solid comes out of my mouth. "It's all part of it—things—the job—the relationship. Uh, our marriage —Sir."

While I continue to flail and stutter, I get freaked out when no more words will come out of my mouth. I also hardly register how Mr. Love's face goes from pale and tired looking to bright red, just how Robin's does when she's pissed off. And when his fist cracks me in the chin, the word *expected* is still clanging through my head, which is why I don't even try to avoid the hit, because I think I...

Expected it…

And when he hits me again, well…that's expected, too. But I am surprised to find I've fallen back and hit the floor so hard my head kills, and that my ears are ringing way too loud. The last thing I see are tears coursing down Robin's cheeks and all I hear is garbled shouting on the part of everyone in the room, while Robin's voice comes out clearly with, "*Dad!* Please, stop."

I try to stand—to get to her, but I can't. And when the width of the room fades into one bright pin-point, and the black crashes in along with utter silence, I'm only relieved that I can't see or hear Robin crying any more.

39

ROYCE

When I come-to, I find out I'm in the Paris *Hospital Saint-Louis*. Worse, I discover that I've been *sedated* here for nearly a day and a half. The blow to my head had been a concussion—*a grave worry*, said my grandmother who was seated at my bedside when my eyes had first opened. I'd been kept under so I wouldn't get myself worked up while the swelling went down.

And, that's because *apparently* there were tons of reasons for me to be worked up.

Like: Robin, being upset.

Like: Robin's father, being twice as upset.

Like: Me, personally, being upset because the guy nearly beat the shit out of me. And my grandmother was also upset because I'd *let* him beat the shit out of me without fighting back. Which, in turn, has made all my family and best friends…also very upset.

The most upsetting thing of all? The main reason everyone left me here to sleep it off and rest while in a drug induced stupor for way, too long?

Because there's one more reason for me to be upset: Robin and Sage have left Paris with their father. As in, they've gone back to the states!

My grandmother has just whispered to me that we've told the press the reason Robin has not been by my bedside, is because she's left get her father settled into the VA hospital in New York City right away. I'm to go with it. Tell everyone the bump on the head and the bruises on my face happened when I got tangled up in some stage cables while rehearsing and I bashed my head onto an amp. A plausible story, to be sure—for both Robin and I, that leaves her father off the nightly news feeds.

One I'm sure no one will question, either, because the whole world has been waiting for Robin's father to return home. Of course people will think that Robin will want to be with her father, to help get him well—and of course I'm the dumb ass who falls into—amps.

God help us all with this last round of lies.

When my eyes can focus and the sleep drugs are wearing off more, I sit up some and look around. There seems to be a crush of people—paparazzi mostly, and my bodyguards who look really cranky—are all stuffed in the hallway. I work to clear the cobwebs from my head—and my gaze travels to my best friends gathered around the bed.

I can tell form the expressions in Adam, Hunter's and most of all Vere's faces, even without asking, that they're as broken hearted as I am about Robin's sudden exit.

Apparently they'd boarded a plane to New York only an hour ago. My grandmother's leaning in, voice full of pity as she's whispering some junk about how: *It's all worked out for the best. That it was right and time for them to go…that it's possible this surprise mess has actually made things easier.*

I don't disagree. I don't speak or make one sound. That's because I'm locking down my heart again. Shoveling the pain into one pile how it was before it exploded out of me as I hit the ground back in that hotel.

I tell myself I'm *relieved* that the way it all played out so fast.

This all means I didn't have to tell her goodbye. I'd been trying to come up for just the right things to say to her for days—but nothing had sounded right—nothing…

My grandmother's words reach me again. "It's easiest. It's for the best…it's time for her to go. You'll see her eventually," she adds. "Royce, honey…say something. Are you okay?" She zooms her chair back a little and glances at my bandmates. "Maybe he's *not* ready to travel to Berlin. They said you'd be rested, darling. Are you not—rested?"

"No. I am. Sorry. Just trying to get my bearings, here. I feel fine, Grandmother. Foggy-headed but fine." Somehow, I muster up a decent masked expression—and I staple it on while I manage to smile at everyone else and whisper out, "We did it, guys. Goal accomplished saving the girl, and…now….*onward*, right?" I force out a small smile, while staring down at my blanket so I don't have to meet their gazes. "And yes, Gran is right. It's easiest, it's for the best and it was time." I reach over and pick up my grandmother's hand and give it a squeeze as she zooms back to my side. "Don't worry, it's weird as hell what all went down, but it was bound to be weird, right? The whole thing was… weird." She nods, smiling sadly as I forge ahead with more lies, "We did the right thing and Robin's father *should* have punched me how he did —because it's what I would have done if some asshole rockstar was found sleeping with my daughter in a Paris hotel—so we all need to forgive the guy for losing it."

"We already have. He did apologize before he left, and he means to call you next week," Uncle Gregory says.

"Good to know." I make the smile I'm faking go wider, but suddenly my head is spinning and I swear to God, I feel like crying for some damn reason—or hell, fine. I *know* the reason. I need to lie to all of them, but i don't need to lie to myself anymore, right?

Quickly, I swallow that shit down and sit up even more, making a show of flinging off the covers like I'm all full of energy, adding, "Did I hear we're going straight from here to Berlin? There's a jet waiting?"

Hunter nods as does Vere. "Dude, if you're up to it. This is as close to the wire we've ever been before a concert. We could cancel, but the damn stadium is seating right now. Our opening band is going to play some extra songs to stretch out the time, and we're going to pass out some cool swag as well to distract people should we have a delay going through customs, but if we leave now, and you're up to it, we can pull it off."

I try to breathe, but it hurts like hell so I stop mid breath, and say tightly, "I'm up to it. I think the faster we leave Paris the better. Crazy memories…and shit," I look at the doctor who'd just stepped in the room. "If I promise I not to jump up and down while playing the guitar tonight, will you let me out of here?"

The doctor, who turns out to be American, nods and says, "You will not jump. You will not do the crowd surfing thing, and you will not even dance. Should you try, you'll wind up with a massive headache."

"Of course not. Dude. I *never* dance."

Luckily everyone laughs, and they all seem to have bought into my act. The smiles of my friends go from stiff to easy. The only one who is not buying my bullshit is Vere…but she won't out me. As her wide brown eyes meet mine I get that she knows I'm not okay—deeply not okay—but what is wrong inside of me has got nothing at all to do with the lump on my head, and everything to do with the irreparable scars that are forming all over my heart.

Luckily, Vere, like me…is a practical person. She knows there's nothing I, or any of them, can give me to fix what's truly hurting. Besides, I already know this feeling because it's very similar to how I felt when my mom passed away. Which means I also know how to deal with it.

Ignore it, dive into work, and give it time.

Hunter's talking, and I realize I can't hear his voice as another wave of *WTF-is-this-my-life? Or am I in hell right now?* devastation washes over me. But I read his lips I nod like I'm hearing every word.

But of course I'm not. I'm counting up hours and imagining Robin stepping off the plane she's on right now. She should be doing that at about the same time we are to arrive in Berlin. I picture myself hitting the stage just as she's going to be walking into the amazing apartment my grandmother had set up for *us* to live in after the tour. She will be showing her Dad the studio space I'd had built for her. Knowing her how I do, I can imagine she's sad about this, too. Her smiles will be as fake as mine are right now—

We both were always so good at that…

We…us…the two things Robin and I are not going to be anymore…

By the time I'll be singing our new single to our fans in Berlin, and she will be calling in Chinese food from the place I'd showed her on the corner. Or pointing out the guest quarters to her father, then helping Sage and her father unpack suitcases.

We will do encores and pile into the limo so we can unpack into the Berlin Orb hotel, and Sage will be in his room setting up the video games probably. Robin's father will be exhausted and head to his room, and Robin will be in her bed alone, no hoodie necessary, of course. And I won't have to drag any couch cushions onto my bed…

I stop thinking about that—her—all of it then, because my thoughts had suddenly grown too dark. Too terrible. Selfish again. Because…that's me.

The lump on the back of my head has started throbbing, and what I think is a big black eye that I hadn't even noticed until now, starts to ache. I don't complain or ask if there's any pain medicines I could ramp up on, either. I don't even let myself wince because that would get me sympathy when I don't deserve any. Because every single lingering thread of thought I'd just let drift through my mind might have been me, wishing that Robin's father had not been found quite yet…

Which makes every punch that man hit me with seem right.

Which makes me more of a devil than Robin's father ever imagined.

I vow to not think about Robin again. Like when my mom passed, I have to acknowledge that this is a very final thing. There is no going back—the plan was executed and we only need to tie up the loose ends as quickly as possible.

I check the time on my phone and stand, "It's a 1.5 hour flight. If we head out now, we won't even be late."

Hunter smiles, but it doesn't quite reach his eyes. "That's the spirit, Dude. Stylists are going to fly with us. We're going to exit the plane and go directly to stage."

"Cool. Awesome."

As if on cue, Clara and her mother arrive in a flurry, bearing bagged outfits for everyone to put on and when Clara hands me mine, instead of glaring at her, how I've done ever since the awards show, I do what I've never done.

I smile at her. Then, I say, "Thanks, Clara."

First she blinks like she's shocked that I've spoken to her. Then, I see her wheels turning as she analyzes my face saying, finally, "Sure. How's the head injury? Looks bad." She's staring, too hard.

"Painful."

"Poor you. I'll have to put extra makeup on that bruising." She points at my eye.

"That's what I was hoping you'd say." I add, "I also hope it's not too terrible looking."

"Actually." When she beams back at me, I know I've got her on the hook. "The black eye makes *your* silver eye-color even more beautiful. Only you, *Royce*, *only you* could pull that off, and you should just know, that it also, *totally*, makes you look absolutely, way-way, and completely sexier,"

My heart shifts and drops—and every injury I have hurts more because it's like my whole damn body knows this is so very wrong to talk with Clara like this. But, I force my smile to go bigger and add in a little wink for Clara, using the good eye. "Thanks. That's really totally absolutely, sweet of you to say." And then because Vere's glaring at me, I add, "Maybe, because Robin had to go back to NYC so fast, and I won't have anyone to help me out…maybe later, after the show… you can help me ice…stuff." I force a grin.

When she stutters, then giggle-answers, "S-sure. Yes. I'd love to," before dashing away doing a fluttery-eye hair flip thing that turns my stomach, I feel so queasy that I actually have to sit back down on my bed for a second.

Vere, glaring bullets—knives—ice, stalks over to me and whispers, "Royce. Robin begged us. *Not Clara.* I *told* you that. Robin's request is that you find someone—something real. It doesn't have to be so fast, and it doesn't need to start happening today."

"Yes. It does."

"Not Clara. It's going to hurt Robin, you know it will," she insists.

"Vere, it's going to hurt all of us, and you also know how stubborn Robin is. Clara will send the clearest message to Robin that things are truly over, and show her that the world has—hell that I have—flipped back to the way it was before she and I had met. I'm still an asshole, and maybe Robin should remember that sooner than later. And…I choose Clara because—shit." My eyes flash to hers and hold her gaze, as my voice cracks. "You *know* why. After Robin…after my mom…" I put a hand over the leaden-thumping that's breaking down what's left of my heart inside my chest. "I'm fucking done with real. Done. I can't—won't—ever seek out anything real again because my heart can't take it. Clara is perfect, because she won't even care when I dump her."

Vere's shaking her head, and her damn, big-brown eyes have flooded with what looks like tears. "I'm going to blame this temporary bout of insanity on your head injury."

"It's for Robin. I don't want her just thinking about me…and wondering." I reach up and touch the parts under my eye that are swollen and puffy. Then I press them until they hurt more, because the pain, somehow is keeping me focused into this room and away from where I want to be right now. The pain…it's keeping me alive. "I'm pulling off the Band-Aid, Vere. I'm not going to communicate with Robin after this. It's the best, fastest way for all of us to cross back into our normal lives. Trust me on this. Okay?"

She doesn't answer. Just turns and stalks away.

40

ROBIN

TWO MONTHS LATER…

"When are you going to take the rings off your left hand?"

I point at the view of the Hudson River and hide my wedding and engagement rings behind my back. He's been pestering me about the rings since day one. "Dad. I thought we were watching the sunset together. I thought we were done talking about the wedding, and the rings. And I *thought* we were finally moving on from the topic of my soon to be *ex-husband.* Why can't you please leave it be?"

"So done." He doesn't hide the sarcasm in his voice as he picks up the glass of iced tea I'd made for him and takes a sip. His voice sounds extra forced as he adds, "New York City is not *ever* a place I planned to live, but it's been amazing so far. It's also nice that your school is so close to this apartment that you can walk back and forth."

"That's why Manhattan is so cool. Everyone walks, everywhere." We share a small smile—but we both know we're forcing this conversation as well as the cheerful tones. It's how my father and have been with each other ever since we left Paris. "It's also great your new physical therapy guy is only a few blocks away, too. You will get the extra exercise you need now that your cast is off, and if we're all lucky, you can get some sun on your limb, too."

"Right? The leg is still alien-pale." Dad nods, and we both pause to stare at the leg that's a bit skinner, and way-too white from being cast these past two months. "It seems to have healed whole, and despite some weakness, I think it's not at all so very worse for wear. Kind of like me, huh?" Not one to fall for my subject-change-bait and switch, Dad points at my wedding rings again. "Robin, if keep wearing those to school, people are going to think—that—"

"Dad—" I cut him off and he frowns. "People already think pretty much *everything*. Everyone knows who I am, everyone knows my whole life story, and everyone thinks I'm currently married to Royce Devlin, because that is what is true. So, yes, the whole world also knows that he hasn't been back to see me once since you brought me home." I shrug. "It's a daily internet gossip and it's going very well. It's what is supposed to happen and it does not bother me that I'm about to head into the world's most publicized divorce."

He winces slightly at that, so I lower my voice, adding. "It's all cool, Dad."

"Is it? I hate it when you and Sage say that all the time."

I shake my head, smiling at him. "I know the extra exposure that I'm getting upsets you, because the 'break-up' seems to have started, and all that, but I'm pretty much used to it by now. It's also not a big deal that I'm still wearing these rings. I probably *need* to wear them for now until they tell me to hire the divorce lawyer. Gregory promised me that by Thanksgiving we will be in full marriage falling apart mode—maybe even ready to sign some papers. Gregory wants to reconnect with his girlfriend—you know, Mrs. Perino, as quickly as possible. And Sage and I finally want you to meet the family that rescued us from that parking garage—so he says he might come meet up with us when we're down in Orlando. We'll draw up the play-by-play on the divorce stuff together. Like I can have a say in some stuff, because so far—I haven't. And… how Royce is dating that horrible Clara girl does kind of—hurt—I mean, suck."

I feel bad when my dad winces again and says, "I'm sorry. This is all my fault. All of it."

I wish he would realize that his children, being homeless and in that parking garage that started all of this mess, was *my* fault, not at all his fault. I also want to tell him that this *mess* was actually the best thing that could have happened to us, because it gave us such a safety bubble, one that my father gets to stay in while he recuperates.

My therapist—because we're all in therapy now—told me that my father thinks he failed us by getting kidnapped. So, it might be a long while before he can work through that and understand how Sage and I have no regrets when we look back at everything. We learned so much, saw so much—made so many friends, and luckily we'd managed to stay safe. That's what's most important, right?

"I can't wait to meet the Perinos," Dad says quietly, drawing both of our thoughts out of the past and into the trip we're waiting to go on down to Orlando next week. "Mrs. Felix told me she's not sure if Gregory will make it for the first few nights. Apparently, the tour is adding shows right and left. The guys have been too busy, they're sleep deprived and everyone is falling apart some."

'Oh. Really?" I nod absently, layering that insider information into my heart like a balm. "Well that explains why not even Vere has contacted me as much as I'd expected she would," I say, shaking my head—and silently adding that maybe just maybe it explains why Royce hasn't contacted me at all after the first day we arrived here when he'd texted from Berlin only: *You okay?* And I'd responded: *Yes. Okay.*

And then he hadn't texted or called once since, nor had he responded to my attempts to text him. Which hurt way more than him deciding to date Clara during this time.

"What are they like?" Dad asks.

"Who? The Perinos?" I smile, thinking of them. "When you meet them—you'll realize—you'll see. They're simply part of our family now. It's going to take you about one second to understand how wonderful they are, and how Sage and I fit in there. And it will take only one meal for you to realize that you're deep in the middle of heaven. The art studio in the cottage we're sleeping in is as amazing as the one Royce and Mrs. Felix built for me here—but in very different ways. Once NYC is over, they've invited us to stay there and start a real life."

"And do you think that's possible after all you've been through? Does Gregory think it's possible to do the same with this Mrs. Perino woman?"

"Gregory is so careful, he wouldn't risk hurting that family if he was not certain it would be okay. And, as for me, the end of my marriage to Royce will be a complete, successful slam dunk. It's not me the public wants to look at—it's silver-eyed, electric guitar playing, amazing Royce. I will be just fine anywhere once the public gets bored of me and my divorce. Although, it will be odd to be so young and divorced… because I'd never thought…." I pause, then shrug, trying to breathe in then out, trying to be okay as I add, "You know, because getting divorced is something I swore I'd never do in this lifetime. Ever."

"I wish I could solve it for you, honey. Hell. I wish I could be the one carrying that divorce."

I sigh, and force myself to stare at him. "You're still trying to be the 'man-in-charge' kind of Dad. But like I've said, I'm trying to live my own life now. I can handle my own problems. And I can easily do what's in front of me. I know eighteen seems young to you, and maybe it is, but I grew up when you went missing, and no matter how you want to protect me or get our old life back, it's not coming back. At least not how any of us imagined it would be. I'm an adult now and we all need to move on. We've all changed."

"I know that, and that's why I pester you about the rings. The fairytale is over. Take them off—you don't need to wait for a lawyer. It's time for you to start a new frame of *mind*, honey. Rings—they do bind. But to me…it seems you can't move on until you get rid of them."

I shrug, looking at my iced tea glass so I don't have to look into his eyes while I only give him half answers to what he's said. "Soon. I've learned this business is all about patience. I don't want to be responsible for messing it all up, either. They make the carefully laid plans—I execute them along with the other players."

"Ahh. I guess that makes sense."

I stare at the twinkle inside the diamonds on my ring finger. "I think it's going to be soon because he—Royce, posted a whole bunch of photos of him with Clara on his social media pages just yesterday. The day you arrived in Paris, we'd already been talking about my 'exit' plan. How it was going to feel, what they might do to fast-track it all. They'd mentioned Royce would be publicly *cheating* on me with someone and so…I guess, considering the buzz and the photos—it's in play."

"Sage told me that girl is a complete psycho."

I smile, pushing the lumps out of my throat so I can talk. "Sage and I didn't like her that much. Don't you love my brother, though? Always ready to kick butt for me." I pause searching my head for something true to say about Clara that won't make me sound like I'm all jealous, or sour-grapes. "She's very…beautiful. Matches Royce's look perfectly. She knows all about how to act in front of cameras, she knows the right Sushi to order, and which forks to use at fancy dinners. Oh, and she never teeters around when wearing heels. So…yeah. She's a good choice. Her mom is the lead stylist for the band, so Clara also wouldn't betray the inner circle if they let her in on the secret by now."

He takes another sip of tea and darts me a glance. "Again, I'd fix it for you, Robin. If you'd let me."

"Fix what?" I sigh, feeling my heart settle back into a place that only half aches. "There's nothing to fix. None of it was real—so it's kind of hard to fix intangible things, right?"

"Mrs. Felix told me that the friendship you'd formed with Royce was real, yet from what you've told me he hasn't communicated. I can't help but think that his utter disconnect from you is my fault. I could try to talk to him and ask him why? Personally tell him how sad you are?"

"No!" I protest. "I'm sure Royce needs time. And knowing him he probably thinks he's protecting me or helping me by not contacting me. Maybe he thinks if he doesn't interact at all, doesn't like any of my social media posts, doesn't talk about how he misses me, that the press will eventually start to take notice of that. See, it could be all part of the break-up. He also knows me well enough to understand that when all of this hits, I will probably need to cry in a very realistic way in front of a whole bunch of reporters—and so the way he's ignored me and seems to have plans to continue to do so, is giving me that feeling of utter desolation and sadness big-time. It hurts—it does, and I'm going to need to show that pain for the cameras, and then when it's all over I'll be fine."

"Well that's the saddest thing I've ever heard." Dad starts pacing the line of the railing.

I wrinkle my brow, ignoring his comment. "Maybe I should post photos of *me* going out with another guy on my Instagram, too? Like a social media sign to him that I'm all good over here. This is why I need to talk to Gregory." I lock my gaze onto my dad's. "Because I am, okay, Dad. I am. It has to be this way. It has to look and feel real. Don't worry. I signed up to do this and it's all going to be fine. Eventually."

"I heard Sage talking to Royce only this afternoon. As I walked up on him, I overheard the kid tell him you're not doing well. Then, Sage caught Royce up on all that you've been doing. Or *not* doing here in New York City. He told him how you've hardly left this apartment and that as the days pass you seem sadder and sadder."

My mouth drops open. First, because…what the hell. How dare Royce call Sage and not me! And second, because…how dare Sage just out me to Royce like that? He's supposed to be my brother. My brother!

"I've been painting." I stutter out. "I'm rusty on my skills and with the European tour gobbling up half of the summer while I didn't get the chance to paint I feel really behind compared to the other students who *did* paint all summer. I'm not hiding out. I'm doing what I want to do, which is live and breathe my studio time while completing assignments for my classes. I promise. I am living my dreams."

"I even said a quick, hello to him. And Robin," Dad's eyes turn double serious. "I apologized to him a second time. He did say how I decked him was all forgiven."

"Wait." I wrinkle my brow more. "*You* talked to him? For how long?" I blink, hardly able to believe it. "A few minutes. Sage was pretty upset after the call. He said he thought the call was sort of a warning from Royce for all of us to get ready for a storm. Royce is worried about how your marriage break-up is going to go down and that you might get a ton of hate pointed at you because of it." Dad waves his hand in the air. "Sage says the *SnapWebStoryChats* or whatever it is you all call it —he says the damn Internet is already going crazy with speculations and mean rumors about you not having what it takes to keep a guy like Royce happy."

"Well. I don't." I roll my eyes to the sky. "I'm a proud-hick-army-brat from North Carolina, and I'm not going to be ashamed of that, ever. Girls like me don't marry guys like him. The Internet gossip is right." I swallow hard, imagining a long snap-story unfolding where Royce goes from laughing to having his hand around sophisticated, beautiful Clara's waist like what he'd posted yesterday, to—to—what? To him in a night club, moving her hair off of her face? A couple of shots of him leaning in while everyone sips colored drinks in fancy odd shaped glasses, or whatever is in fashion in wherever the heck the band is traveling now. Shaking my head to clear it, I count through the dates and places Guarderobe had gone after Berlin. After Berlin was Rome, Madrid, then, if they didn't add Barcelona shows, they were supposed to do Norway, Finland and Sweden. Maybe they're heading for St. Petersburg, Russia.

If so, then maybe my breakup will all happen over shots of Vodka going down, which is just fine, because then Royce can mention to the press how I'm not even old enough to drink. How I'm just this boring baby who's never even tasted Vodka.

I picture Royce laughing more than he was laughing in the shot I saw online. He'll be close to Clara. Face next to her neck, eyes probably locked on her lips. I know when I see whatever photos I'm going to see--because I'm sure I will see them eventually--they will shred me up completely. I'm actually happy they chose Clara because now I don't have to hate some innocent girl I've never met. It's easy with Clara. I can simply carry on with my bad attitude about a girl who was never nice to me, no matter how much I tried to be nice to her.

Thinking about that has made my heart feel like it's a balloon and I have added far too much air to it. Like each time I've breathed, more air has gone into me, but it doesn't come out. It's pretty close to popping, and when it does, I swear it's going to be a relief to cry this all out, but that's not for today. Not yet.

Because Dad is studying me—me, as in this *new formed adult* I want him to think I've become—I shrug casually, and sigh adding, "Who knows how it will all settle out. And, I'm cool if Royce doesn't want to continue our friendship. I get it. It's going to be strange to try to keep that going, anyhow. As for how he's ignoring me and the social media posts with Clara that he's posting now…Royce is just really… really," my voice cracks as I think: *Stupid. The worst person alive. Having dinner with Clara while probably texting my own brother selfies—and emoticons right now—he's breaking my heart more than ever right now.*

I sigh again, finishing with, "He's really…*careful* about social media. I'm sure he's doing it all for a reason, but please know, I do still trust him. He doesn't want to hurt me. Won't. Not without a reason. When we meet Gregory down in Orlando, he will shed some light on all of this."

"That means a lot, coming from you." My dad says, his eyes piercing mine as though he's searching them to see if this time I'm lying about trusting Royce. But I'm not.

"Above all of this hurt and confusion, Dad, it's like I said all along. Royce, he's like you—very honest. Very trustworthy. I'll always trust him. I only need time to get over—him. That's all. Some of my feelings were so real, and there's a few holes in my heart I can't figure out how fill up yet. And…because of the whole experience—it felt like he and I grew so close. So, it's to be expected that I miss where he used to fit in there, right?" I sigh at my father's doubtful looking nod. "I can't lie to you about him—don't want to. Just know I'm probably acting all off because, maybe it was fake, and maybe Royce doesn't feel the same, but…I miss him. I miss our friendship and talking to him, and even how his hand felt in mine. I also worry about him non-stop. I Wonder if he's okay. I wish he would call me and tell me that he misses me, too. Which is silly because I know he doesn't. Not how I do, anyhow. It's stupid stuff—feelings and memories that I'm lingering over, because I know full well it was all fiction. But you know how I get attached to kind people—and Dad, he's so very kind. That attachment happened with him. It simply hurts to de-attach. I feel lucky I got to know him up close."

"That kid was lucky to know you up close." My dad's glowering now.

"He's not a kid, Dad. He's an adult. Just like me," I insist. "And I'll bet he's hurting some about this, too."

"Right. Right. And you're a very loyal young woman. Even now I get the feeling you're defending him when maybe you should hate him."

"He needs someone to protect him. Even if it's only me—and even he never knows I'm doing it, I won't stop defending him. He's awesome. Again, he's so much like you."

Dad runs a hand through the bright-white shock of short hair on his head. "I can't lie to you either honey, and I still don't know if I'll ever regret the awesome feeling that punch gave me when my hand connected to Royce's face after he'd crawled out of that bed you'd been sharing. I'd just watched YouTube video after YouTube video of that guy kissing you—first at the wedding, and then on those European dates, and then in that London Eye Ferris wheel—nearly thirty minutes, with the whole world looking on? Damn him. He's so lucky you and Sage have proved to me that he's not an absolute bastard-player like how he looked to me on all of those videos."

I laugh a little. "If it helps at all, I also whacked his face when I first met him, too. I didn't knock him out like you did, but I messed him up pretty good with your elbow move. Gave him a week long shiner—but what you've seen of him, it's only a mask and he's very good at that mask. It's not the real him."

Dad laughs, and pulls me into a hug. "Well. I'll take your word for it, Robin. And haven't officially said it *to you*, nor am I going to be good at saying it—and don't expect me to say this again to you but… I was wrong. You're all grown up now and as much as I didn't want to admit it, I understand why you've been so mad at me since we came home, because I've been treating you like a baby. Very undeserved."

"Thank you. But…I haven't been mad, and I don't blame you or anything, and…just thanks for agreeing with me." My grin matches his. "Let's don't look back or second guess anything anymore, okay? Can we try that?" I ask him and he nods in agreement. "We're only happy that you're back, and that you're okay and that our family is still a real family with you in it."

"God." He shakes his head, voice growing shaky. "I haven't even come to terms with the fact that I didn't get myself out. That *you*, Robin. My little daughter. *You* got me out of that hole. You found me when no one else could. Where would I be without you?"

"I didn't get you out, Dad. They did. Royce kept his promise to search, and he and Gregory and Mrs. Felix hired the extractor company. They had the money. They had the pull, the reach, and the connections. Not me."

"But you had yourself. You were simply you. They all met you, then couldn't let you go without helping you. I think everything fell into place because you're the most wonderful person I've ever known. Don't underestimate the power of how you love people, Robin. It's as special as you are, honey. Since the day you were born you've been magic to all who know you. I swear, it's all you—you're pure love."

I don't answer because if I do, sobbing on my Dad is going to ruin any of the *'I'm an adult now'* speeches I've been trying to make him believe.

"I'm so proud of you. So proud. That's all," he adds after the silence between us grows awkward.

I pull in a long, shaky breath and take up both of his hands as the feeling I'd had to cry fades away again. "I'm very proud of you, too. Thanks."

He nods, and the tension in the air that's been hanging between us since I left Paris is now gone. Something huge has shifted between us. He's standing in the same space I've been standing in since I first ran away with Sage. Instead of trying to pull me back into the past we missed, he's just let me grow up. Just like that. Here and now, he's treating me like I'm his equal.

His approval, his thanks—the way I can see myself shining back at me in his over-bright eyes, has somehow allowed me to *believe* what I wasn't sure of before—that I *am*, in fact, all grown up.

Like my dad needs a pause in the conversation so he can think on what to say next, or because now his throat probably hurts as much as mine, he gulps down what's left of his tea while I do the same.

We smile at each other over our glasses while we swallow down the last of it.

Yep. We're so much alike.

He starts up again with, "I'll stop being such a helicopter parent, and I'll let you decide your own things—life—choices—everything." He swallows again. "And I'll stop calling you a kid—more so, I'll stop *thinking* of you as a kid, okay?"

I nod, truly elated. "Thanks, Dad. This means everything."

He lets out a long sigh. "Just be patient with me though. Because, I did something that might piss you off."

"What?"

His face flushes a little, rushing on, "I—I booked special VIP tour tickets to Universal Studios for when we go down to visit your Perino friends. I—uh—never had the chance to take you two to see that Harry Potter, Wizarding World stuff. And, we'd all wanted to go see it before I deployed. While I was being held hostage, I used to pass hours imagining that I'd take you both there straightaway to celebrate my release when I got home. But if you don't want to go, or if you feel that my idea is silly and immature, now that you're all grown up, I'll understand."

Our eyes tangle and I leap into his arms. "Dad! I'm all in. Yes. Oh-my-God. *Yes.* It's *all* I want to do. Honest and yay!"

His relieved smile and bear-hug, makes my chest swell with just how much I love my Dad's heart, and face, and thoughtfulness. Just *everything* about him is so great. I'm also so excited that Sage and I will get to have this 'dream-come-true' moment with our father. But what my father has just said, has also triggered the memory from the day I rode my first real train in the UK with Royce. When he and I had talked on and on about our shared love of Harry Potter.

Royce had promised to take me there, too. Suddenly underneath my elation, I feel sad and confused. Angry that my heart hurts so darn much right now—when I'm supposed to be happy, when I've got everything I want, and more.

I'm disappointed that I'm lonely. That I can't stop missing Royce or missing our friendship. I try to shake the feeling off, but just like every single day that's passed since I last saw him, I can't. I just…can't.

Suddenly the smile I'm holding on my face for my dad hurts as much as my heart hurts. Worse, despite how hard I'm trying to play it down, I think my dad has caught on to the fact that something is still missing—even though Dad and I are now, finally okay. Quickly I tug on his arm and lower my eye-lids so he has to stop staring at me, and say, "Come on. Let's go tell Sage."

41

ROBIN

MRS. PERINO, the woman Sage and I had lived with when we were homeless and before I wound up marrying Royce, sets a steaming deep, rectangular dish of baked rigatoni with sausage down in front of us. I breathe in the salty, cheese scented steam rising off the top of it before smiling over it at my amazing new combined *family*: Angel, Mrs. Perino, Ana, Julia, my father and Sage. In typical Perino style my father's presence in this home fell right into place like he was some sort of a missing puzzle piece.

"After two days of my cooking, dear Robin. I'm happy to see the color back on your face." Mrs. Perino hands me a dish of freshly grated Parmesan cheese and flips her ink-black bobbed hair out of her face. "You seem too skinny."

"What? After two days of your cooking, my shorts hardly fit," I laugh, shamelessly sprinkling the cheese on top of…all of the other cheese. "Thank God we've only begun to tour the Orlando parks, because I'm going to need to walk all of this off over the next few days."

"Do you and Robin have a plan?" Mrs. Perino asks me. "I'd like to know.I'll be juggling schedules a bit in case Gregory really does manage to catch a flight here. Do you mind?"

I smile, watching as her cheeks have gone pink because she'd mentioned Gregory. "We're doing Disney World again tomorrow, Epcot the next day, then Animal Kingdom with Ana and Julia on Saturday as we planned."

"Which is the day I mean to tell Gregory to arrive," Mrs. Felix smiles, coloring more, "Because the girls will be out all day and with you on baby-sitting duty, and Angel at work, he and I will have some alone-time to catch up first."

"Yay for Animal Kingdom! But we should get to go to all of the parks with you," Ana shouts out. "Why can't we?"

"Because we can't miss the first week of second grade." Julia pulls a face.

"That's right, young lady. No. Missing. School." Mrs. Perino rolls her eyes at the both of the girls' pouting faces.

I smile at them both, and finish telling Mrs. Perino our plans, "After the weekend, the Love family has saved our best, most favorite park, for last. We will do two days at Universal Studios." I look at my dad and brother, for approval, adding. "Of course depending on weather, all of that could change, but that's what we're trying for, anyhow."

"I can't wait—it's been so wonderful already. I also can't thank you enough for hosting us here—for taking Robin and Sage into your home that first night you met them." My father flicks a glance at Angel, then takes the grated Parmesan cheese from me and rains tons of it down onto his baked penne pasta. I can tell he's gone all awkward, because it feels like it's his fault that Sage and I ran away and ended up down in Orlando. He takes a big bite of his dinner then, and adds, "Mrs. Perino, if you weren't already in love with Gregory—who by the way is a very good man—I'd get down on my knees and beg you to marry me instead right now. Hell. I may as well try. Will you? Marry me instead?"

Everyone laughs as Mrs. Perino shakes her head, spooning small piles of the baked pasta onto small plates for Ana and Julia while blowing on it to cool it off. "If I weren't so very much in love, I would definitely consider it, because then I could truly adopt Sage and Robin for myself and keep them forever."

She winks at Sage which makes him smile wider and wider and Sage answers that with his mouth full. "You *are* keeping us forever, because I'm not letting you go again. And from now on, Mrs. Perino? Is it's okay if I please call you *Zia*? The girls told me it means *aunt* in Italian."

"Can I call you that, too? *Zia*?" I ask, testing the sound of that Italian word, and loving the happy peaceful look on Sage's face.

Mrs. Perino—*Zia*—nods, obviously pleased with our request. "You would make me so happy if you called me that. So happy."

"This means we will all be cousins!" Julia and Ana shout out, as they leap onto Sage and hug him from both sides, nearly making him plop an entire forkful of steaming pasta onto the floor.

"Okay. Okay. Yes. That's what it means, now sit back down, you two."

As the girls regain their seats, my dad pulls a face and says, "Don't expect me to call you that. You will never be my aunt, and I'm going to give that Gregory a run for his money all the way until he puts a ring on your finger," Dad jokes, laughing.

"You're too late." Mrs. Perino laughs more as she pulls out a pale blue box containing a diamond ring that is bigger than the rock Royce Devlin put on my finger to seal our fake marriage. "That's what I wanted to tell you all. Gregory and I have been dating over since the day you left, Robin. We do it by *video-chatting* app on our phones each day."

"I kind-of knew figured," I say. "But wow, you're the first online relationship I've ever heard of that wound up with a *ring* so quickly!"

Her high cheekbones flash with color and her accent has ramped-in as she continues, "My Gregory, he *insisted on it.* He had the little box sent by a special courier just last night, and he proposed to me he while sitting in a dark garden where he was staying in Spain. I was sitting out back in our courtyard. It was not perfect but we both had lit candles, and it was very romantic." She points to the window with a view of the beautiful little piazza-type courtyard that makes up the space between her home and the three cottages out back. One, the largest, Mrs. Perino calls the '*piccolo Love cottage*' named after our last name, Love. It used to be her daughter's—Cara's—art studio. Before I ran off to marry Royce, Sage and I were supposed to move into it, and we had hoped to stay. Thankfully, since we've been back, Mrs. Perino has made it clear the cottage is going to be ours collectively forever. When we're done staying in New York City, Sage and I, as well as our father, now now our family has a real space to visit here inside of her family's heart forever.

I hop up to hug her and ask for a closer look at the ring. I'm nearly blinded by the square cut diamond, set in the center of a circle of alternating tiny sapphires and more diamonds. "It's gorgeous. Why aren't you wearing it."

"Did you say, yes to the dude?" Sage asks, also looking at the ring.

"I've accepted him, of course." She nods. "He's promised to ask me again in person, but that he wanted to make things more permanent between us. He says it's so people will know that I'm taken." She puts the ring away, adding, "I've decided that only *he* will place it on my finger when I see him again."

"Isn't it sparkly?" Ana sighs out. "I just love it."

"Damn." My dad laughs. "That Gregory, he's a smart man."

"But she won't let me wear it." Julia pouts again. "Gregory told me that when we have the wedding, that Ana and I will have our own little rings from him, too. Because he's not just marrying her, you know that? He's marrying our whole family. After the wedding, if we want, we can call Gregory 'daddy'—*if we want.*" Julia gives me a look, like she's still not sure about that idea.

Ana adds, "We've never had a daddy before, so…I'm thinking about it a lot. Thinking about saying, yes, too."

"Aww. That is so cute." I share a glance with Sage, and then with the smiling Mrs. Perino. Because I know the girls came from a broken and very sad, dysfunctional home, before Mrs. Perino adopted them, I can see a mixture of hope and excitement in their eyes as they look at me to see what I think about all of this, but also, there's wariness crossing their expressions as well.

I try to speak carefully, worried that I'll say the wrong thing. "I'm so happy that Mrs. Perino—I mean—*Zia,* will have Gregory to be her husband." I dart Mrs. Perino another look before turning to Julia and Ana adding, "It's also… so wonderful to grow your family, isn't it? Today you got me and Sage to be your official *cousins.*" I beam at them, "And I'll just bet, after you are used to Gregory being part of your family, you will want to call him your daddy, too. He's really going to be lucky to have you two girls in his life, that's for sure."

"Gregory's a smart man to send the ring. After last night's Tiramisu and homemade gelato desert, I was all set to break you up, too. Sage was almost talked into helping me, too. But if Gregory is going to get Ana and Julia matching rings, well I can't interfere. Besides, you ladies seem to be a very expensive bunch—with all of your fancy jewelry." He winks, making the girls crack up.

Mrs. Perino pulls the plates into a stack in front of her. "The ring he sent is so big that I wonder if it will make my hand feel heavy, and the dough I make for my pastries will stick to it.

"If the dough sticks to it, we all know diamonds and gold are washable. Once it's on, I say, never take it off." Angel, her twenty-four-year-old son, and probably the best friend I've ever had in my life, because he's the one who originally saved me and Sage from sleeping in our car when we were runaways, leans back in his seat.

His kind face is a mirror of my happy feelings for his mom.

"Maybe you are right." Mrs. Perino turns back to us all, smiling. "Robin, I'm so grateful for you and Sage, because—you two are the reason I met Gregory." She shakes her head, eyes wide with wonder. "You two, how can I ever repay this happiness you gave to me? This gift. What if I had never met you, and what if *Angelino* had never brought you home for dinner—and what if you had never taken that job with Guarderobe? I sometimes think, this kitchen…this place…it is so magic for us all. It's how Cara always said to us, everything happens for a reason."

"I think that, too." I agree, thinking of how Angel invited us home that night, only because I reminded Angel of his sister, Cara. "There is so much…fate between us all."

"Angelino, what do you think it is?"

"I say I don't like speculating on it, but whatever it is, it's very good." Angel shakes his head. "And, mamma, what if you stopped calling me *Angelino* in front of people. Please?

"It means a lot, a ring like that." Mrs. Perino nods. "A true symbol of love."

"What about you and your ring, Robin?" Sage points at the ring on my hand. "Why do you still wear yours if you aren't going to stay with Royce?"

I pull a face and glance at my father, answering, "That's what Dad asked me last week. So, before you all ask me about it, please know I'm still under contract until our—uh *situation* becomes official."

"What's a *situation*?" little Julia asks, frowning. "Why did Sage say you are not going to stay with Royce anymore? Isn't he still your prince?"

"Yes. He is, for now." I answer honestly, flicking Sage a *'thanks-a-lot-for-blabbing-in-front-of-the-girls'* glare. "And a *situation* is…something that's not quite figured out yet." I lean down and kiss them each, "Like how your mamma has made me too fat this weekend, so my ring is feeling as tight. Maybe I'll have to take it off one of these days if she keeps feeding me like this!"

"Mamma. Tomorrow, make salad for Robin. I like her ring where it is." Ana reaches over and places the tip of one small finger on top of the large center diamond on my ring. "I want *all* of us girls in the Perino family have a ring. So *don't* take it off, Robin. Not until Gregory comes here with ours and we can take a picture together."

"What a cool idea. I hope I'm here for that," I evade, but over their heads I shake my head so Sage and my father get the signal to end this conversation.

"A picture is a beautiful idea," agrees Mrs. Perino smiling, but this time it doesn't reach her eyes and she looks worried.

It's obvious Ana and Julia still think I've married the 'handsome-prince' who drove me away in a black stretch limo while wearing a bride's veil to marry me the last time we saw them,. Of course Gregory proposing to Mrs. Perino and promising them rings, and the wedding chatter that is going on now has made this whole Cinderella complex the girls have even worse. No need to frost up their rose colored glasses about 'love and marriage' by explaining how they're getting the *legit-dream-family*, while I'm getting a sad divorce. I'll explain it all to them one day, but it will be long after they've stopped believing in Santa Claus.

Like Mrs. Perino can read my mind she's quickly sent the girls off to the backyard with oversized bowls of gelato. As the back door slams shut, I quickly catch Angel, my brother and Mrs. Perino up on the same conversation I had with my dad before coming back to Orlando.

"Why *do* you still wear it?" Angel points at my hand, his obsidian eyes glaring at the ring.

"If I take my ring off people will talk. It's going to happen soon. The Guarderobe's Instagram posts have been consistently showing Royce with…" I pause, hating to say her name—hating more that I wince every time I have to say it, like now, as I add, "Showing Royce with *Clara*. There's been a lot of laughing with their arms around each other but not a kiss yet. The rumors are really simmering now, because it's been a whole week of this. Right? One kiss between Royce and that girl should start the boulder rolling down the mountain." I glance at Sage, who is really up on what Guarderobe has posted. "Do you think I'm right?"

"I have seen the posts with Clara," Sage gives me a little shrug. "But, Robin— they're not a big deal. It's them sitting side by side having dinner with the entire backstage group. Someone—probably Clara herself, zoomed in on the shot and cropped it to look like it's only the two of them on some sort of a date. But to me it's obvious they're backstage somewhere, and that there's a crowd around them. That's one the photo that went viral last week. I've really been tracking it. That Clara girl made some comments in her own Instagram about how *cute* she and Royce look together. There was also some bullshit about how she's been in love with Royce forever, and that she *has been for her whole life*. So now that *she's* posed that crap, people are making up things online, but so far Royce hasn't liked or commented or posted anything that matches Clara's posts."

"Yeah but you said yourself that people are making up…*things*? Lots of things, so…there you go."

Sage nods. "True, and I would recommend you stay offline, because it's going to make you feel sad."

"I know. I won't go look." I laugh a little. "I guess it's sort of a relief to hear it's finally spiraling though." I look up, watching as Mrs. Perino's happy smile turns to a dark frown that matches Angel's, and now my father and Sage are doing it, too.

I press on, "Guys, don't be all protective of me. That's what we wanted. Part of plan number 3,987, right?" I force a grin. "We have to get people to *talk* so there's a good amount of buzz before we split up. I've emailed Vere so I could ask her how I should proceed with my own social media posts, but she, like all of them, never wrote me back. *That's* making me way sadder than random strangers talking garbage about me."

"What did you ask her?" Angel asks.

"Stuff like, should I be all cryptic and depressed sounding on my posts? Should I make comments about how Royce doesn't ever come home to his *wife*? Or, should I like…post photos of me having fun with…other random guys just how he's doing over there?" I flick a glance at Angel. "I could post a couple of me, with you, because you're the only guy I know personally that could compete with Royce's handsomeness. And with the millions of social media followers I have now, you would wind up hired as a model or something, Angel. Say the word and I'll change your life," I joke.

Angel shakes his head, grimacing and laughing. "Thanks, Robin… but…*hell-no*. I'm good."

I laugh, too. "But…wait, if Gregory proposed from a garden in *Spain* yesterday, then I'm not sure where they are on the travel schedule. I'd thought Russia, but now I'm not so sure. Maybe she didn't answer because they're in transit to Russia and it's really far…." I frown, wondering if I memorized the end of the tour out of order. I look at

Sage for an answer because he usually knows more than I do but he simply shrugs. From the distressed look on his face I wonder if he's worrying about me and the break-up still.

"This is last storm we will have to survive—and we've survived so many. Guys. Please stop frowning and looking all worried. All of you." I stand holding my plate and bring it over to Mrs. Perino. "They've promised it's going to be big and fast and final. And…and if Vere Royce don't check in soon—then that's because they know Gregory is coming and that he will tell us everything we need to know and do. I've got no doubts—and I'm fine," I layer on the whopping lies. "And they said the break-up will be very quick and very… thorough. So, that's all good."

Suddenly everyone at the table looks like the conversation makes them as unhappy as it makes me. As I dry my hands with the kitchen towel, I pause to twist the rings on my ring finger, around and around. Then I test how it feels if I push them up against my knuckle like I *might* take them off. But…even though, maybe I really should just do it, I still don't have the heart to pull them off.

Not yet. Not today…

Like she's trying to change the subject and doesn't care that she's being obvious, my new, awesome, *Auntie-Zia Perino* clears her throat. "Robin. Tomorrow after you return from taking Sage to Disney World, you will have the birthday party that was taken away from you." She blinks when I don't seem to comprehend what she's saying. "Is it okay? I know you have many days to see the parks, but it would mean you and Sage have to come home early. Around six? Ana and Julia have been pestering me to do this, and after all of this sad conversation, I think it's a good idea. We still have many wrapped presents for you in the closet that were never opened that crazy night of your birthday months ago. And, I say, why not? But only if you're willing to let us sing to you and put out the candles and string up the piñata again?"

"Yes. An awesome idea." Sage leaps up from the table. "As long as we don't have to put on stupid prince and princess costumes this time." Sage is grinning now. "Dad never got to see you turn eighteen, and we never blew out candles on a cake, which means, Robin you never made a wish that night. Angel and I also never had the chance to show you the home-made slip and slide that we duct taped together out of tarps, either. It was supposed to be your big surprise. We can set it *all* back up out in the yard, and have a fresh-start do-over party. Say yes? I've got a present for you, too." His big blue eyes have grown so wide and earnest I have to laugh at him.

"Dad? You down for it, Dad? Even though I said we couldn't turn back the clock, maybe on this one thing, we can." I ask, locking eyes with my dad who's eyes still seem shrouded with doubt. "And…Mrs. Perino makes the most amazing cake."

"I'd be honored to have the chance to go back and share the milestone of you turning eighteen. But if we do it—well…" He shakes his head. "I just…hope it will be perfect for you, honey, that's all," he whispers, suddenly looking older and sort of worried.

I shake my head. "Dad. I've learned a long time ago that perfect isn't worth shooting for, because that could make you insane. It will be fun and memorable, and very…*great.*It will be all about celebrating our new, awesomely re-formed families. Which…is all that matters, right? Family?"

"Right." Dad's shoulders seem to relax some with that. He pauses to send a look and a little smile out to Sage and Mrs. Perino. "Great, it is, then. One great *family* party."

42

ROBIN

SAGE and I arrive home from our second day at Disney World in time for dinner and my party, as promised. Our father decided not to do the second day with us, because his leg had been bumped around too much on the coasters yesterday, and he'd wanted to rest it before the next park.

He, Angel, Ana and Julia have met us on the front porch. The girls are extra excited, because they've decked themselves out in their finest princess gowns, tiaras and what looks like buckets of their horrible blue-eyeshadow. Sage, obviously rebelling the costumes this time, rolls his eyes and mutters so they can't hear him, "I will not be tricked into wearing prince-shit or one damn cape. No matter how much they beg me."

"Good luck with that," I answer, while we all pause to admire them spinning-and-spinning in the yard. When they fall onto the grass giggling, I help them stand, then gush over their new sparkling, silver-glitter nail polish, saying, "Too bad I don't have a princess dress that fits me this time."

Ana flutters her lashes. "It's okay if you don't have a dress. You can be *the princess that's in hiding*. Sometimes there's that kind of princess and no one even knows." She gazes adoringly up at my face. "But usually you can tell because of their hair, and you have really good princess hair." She points. "If you take it out of that ponytail you will be nearly matching us, almost. And you will feel like a princess, too, which is the most important."

I laugh, reaching up to pull out my hairband and run fingers through my tangled hair so it drapes around my shoulders. "Okay. I can at least do that. How's this?"

"Great," Julia nods approvingly.

Sage rolls his eyes and laughs as Angel points around to the back yard. "They're all set up in the garden like before. If you don't mind coming around this way, it would help."

"Help with the *surprises*." Ana wiggles her little brows up and down.

"Ana." Angel's voice is all warning.

"Wait until you see the *cake*," Julia pipes in, skipping around me in a circle.

"Julia!" Angel's voice turns murderous. "You girls promised if I let you wait out here with us you would not blab any of our secrets." Angel grabs one of each of their hands and drags them away from me as if that could make them stop talking.

"But she *knows* there's going to be a cake and she *knows* that the piñata is going to be full of candy and toys and—" Julia wrinkles her brow, frowning. "It's a *birthday* party, but I won't tell her about the *sparkler candles* and I won't tell her about how the slip-and-slide thing is very—"

"Shh!" Angel shakes his head at both of them. "I knew they'd they ruin everything. Sage why did you make me involve them."

"Because, they have to be involved." My brother turns to Ana and Julia. "Remember. You two promised. No more talking."

They both nod, acting very serious as I ask, "Wait. Sage knows the secrets?"

Sage nods, his smile going from big to huge. "Of course."

"And I know about them, too." My dad laughs. "I actually had to approve each and every one of them. And Robin?" He pulls himself up tall and crosses his arms. "I do approve each and every one of them."

"How. Why? And…thanks," I add, laughing out loud at how now everyone's acting so very serious.

"Because *Dad and I* are part of the surprise, duh. So no more questions or you'll mess us all up," Sage glances at Angel. "Are we supposed to change or something?"

My father grins stepping away from me. "Yeah do we have to?"

"Change into swimsuits?" I ask, looking down at the shorts and t-shirt I'd worn today. "If we're going to play on that dangerous tarp thing you guys made, I want to do that first, because I'm sweaty and tired from running around rides all day, so I'll have to change, too. I'm sure Mrs. Perino—I mean Zia—is going to stuff us with too much amazing, food and I don't want to be slip and sliding with one of her food babies in tow."

My brother laughs at that and Angel evades my gaze. "Probably no changing, yet. Sage and Mr. Love, Sir." Angel flicks a glance at my father. "You stay here with Robin and I will go back into the yard with the girls, and you two wait a bit for us all to get into position and then you come in. Okay?"

My father nods. "Okay."

"If you're going to pelt me with water balloons or silly string, I think someone should warn me," I joke. "Ana? Julia? Now's the time to tell me…should I run? Put on my sunglasses?"

Ana starts giggling along with Julia and they both start to say something just as Angel clamps his hands over their mouths, muffling anything that was about to come out, into giggling squeals of protest. My heart swells with just how much I love this family.

"Robin, you will do what we say, exactly, or else you'll ruin the party," my father says again in that fake-stern-father voice he'd used before.

"Oh God. Now I'm scared. Is there a *mechanical bull* or something? The anticipation is killing me." I lock gazes with Ana and Julia who are working hard to squirm away from Angel's grip. "Am I getting a pet unicorn? A puppy?"

Julia gets away from Angel and dashes up the steps to the porch to grab a long flat box and hands it to me while Ana bounces up next to us. "We won't tell but we made you a magic wand, Robin. If you carry it with you won't have to get wet right away because it's really fancy and everyone knows about how hard we worked on this and they won't ruin it." Ana, also now released from Angel, runs to join her sister so they can both hand me the box at the same time.

Kneeling down to be at their same height, I open the box and gingerly and they help me pull out a long bumpy stick that's been wrapped over and over again in pastel ribbons and glued haphazardly with crystals. A few long ribbons hang down past the handle and a tiny star has been glued onto the very tip of it. It's so sweet and beautiful—so very *Ana and Julia*, all wrapped up for me to hold that I pause to hug them in close to me. "This is the best present I've ever had in my whole life. Thank you."

They beam up at me. Julia says, "Sage told us you will choose a real wizard wand at Universal Studios, but we told him that you also like more magical fairy tale princess wands like these, too. Right?"

"Right. I love *all* wands." I agree with them, working to keep my face solemn instead of about to crack up. "And this one is going to be my forever-favorite. It also has to be more powerful than any wand you could buy in a wand shop."

I hold what they've made up high for Angel, my father, and Sage to admire.

Ana clasps her hands to her chest and sighs. "It will make *all* of your dreams and wishes come true, Robin. That's why we made it for you."

"It really will." Julia nods confidently up at the wand. "Just go ahead and wish something you'll see, it *will* happen. Just go ahead and try."

"Okay. Enough of this disgusting, boring princess stuff," Sage interrupts. "Let's go start the party. Who's ready for candy?" Sage motions to Angel, and steers Ana and Julia toward the back gate.

Angel enters the gate behind the girls and Sage, turning back once to give me a wink. "Don't worry *piccolo-new-cousin*." He's using that low voice of his. "You're going to love this party. Promise. But just in case, the girls are right. Keep the wand handy." He nods to my dad. "Give us at least five minutes."

When the gate closes, Dad and I listen intently as we hear things being moved. Tons of whispering and door slamming happens, all followed with the girls giggling like someone is tickling them. Then there's more shushing than what you'd hear from a pack of angry librarians, leaving only the wind and crickets to make noise after that.

As I cross my arms and lean back against the Perino's front steps, I look at the wand again and catch my dad eyeing me and it, intently. He points at the wand. "Did you make a wish yet, honey?"

"Can't think of one. Maybe when we do the cake, but it doesn't really matter." I shrug and place the lovely little wand back in the box. "I don't believe in that kind of stuff anymore."

43

ROYCE

I'M REGRETTING the hell out of this plan. I've never been more afraid.

Adam and I were just joking moments ago, that this was the *new-new Robin Love plan*, number 4,356. Sage had protested that we were easily up into the 5,000 numbers. I'd laughed along with them, because it was kind-of true, but right now I can't even crack a smile. Whichever plan it is, it's the *last* plan.

I'm personally executing it here and now. All while my family and friends—*plus* Robin's family *and* the Perinos—some of whom are staring at me with worried half-glares on their faces, watch me take center stage.

If this were a normal situation I'd worry more about them, but I just can't. This the most important *plan* I've ever schemed up in my entire life. It's last minute, it's crazy and like most of our plans, I'm still making it up as I go. Anyone can watch me, as long as this works.

As the gate swings open and Robin enters the Perino back garden, I hold my breath. Her dad takes up her arm, leading her along, just how he should of held her arm, but couldn't, during our fake wedding.

Robin hasn't seen me yet so the irony is lost on her, but not on me.

She freezes her steps when she sees me standing at the far side of the garden.

I—we all watch and wait.

Thankfully, after her mouth drops open like she's gasped, and after she's glanced around the entire set-up garden. After she's taken in all of us standing around inside the circle of little white lights. After she's stared at the tables set up with linens and lit candles—with white ribbons hung on the trees. After she sees all of it. Set up exactly how it had been set up on the night I asked her to marry me, after she does all of that; she sucks in a huge breath, and looks at her father.

We all tense more, and no one moves as Mr. Love nods to Robin—one short, curt nod.

Unfortunately, that's when Robin locks down her expression to one I can't read, but after another long moment, I observe that at least she's started breathing, in-and-then out.

I was tracking that most of all. Tracking her face, her reactions to all of this—just in case she freaked out and went in the wrong direction. Like saw me here and immediately started shouting for me to *get-the-hell-out-of-here*. Or, like demanding Angel beat the crap out of me—or something worse.

Like… what if she'd cried?

Had that happened, I would have called out, 'stop' and taken a different approach (though, truthfully I have no clue what that would have been). And, holy-shit I thought for a minute there when she was holding her breath she was actually going to pass out—which was something I hadn't even considered her doing, but so far…so good. Everyone's still alive…including me.

I glance quickly at Mr. Love's wound-tight expression. He's slowly matching Robin's small steps to his. And as they both head definitively in my direction again, I can't help but have a moment of PTSD as I look the man in the eye and wonder if this time, they're *both* going to punch the shit out of me?

I swallow hard, knowing that thought is insane—because it was Mr. Love who helped me plan this moment. Who gave me his *blessing*. His word. Not mine.

As they get closer, I work to shove all of my doubts away. I can't choke right now. I need to be confident, steady and serene. Mr. Love may not like me yet, but he knows I love his daughter, and he *did* officially apologize, more than once for sending me to the hospital. All while I apologized back—hundreds of times for getting his daughter into the troubles she shouldn't have been in, while he was away.

He and I, after multiple phone calls, we're good now. We both also have the same goals tonight. He's an ally, not an enemy. Not anymore.

Because Robin's all about family, we—he and I, and Mrs. Perino as well as Angel, had come up with this re-do birthday party idea just yesterday morning. We'd also planned that everyone would be surrounding us in a big circle during this time, and so far, even the wiggle-twins, Ana and Julia have held their positions beautifully.

As Robin is brought closer, I let my eyes travel over her whole form, realizing what Sage told me on the phone was true. That she's lost some weight, that she somehow looks older—that maybe all of that has happened because she's been really sad since leaving Europe. Me. The hurt all of this has caused her is radiating out from her faltering steps, from her too-stiff shoulders. Her eyes are closed off from me in this way that's very sad and unfamiliar, and as she gets even closer, I see she's steeling herself away from me somehow. Protecting herself because she thinks I won't anymore. This undoes me, because glimpses of what look like white-hot fear—fear that I'm here to hurt her more, are cracking through her stony expression. Cracking my soul.

It was Vere's idea to keep our outfits kept to simple shorts and t-shirts for this afternoon. We're all dressed to match what she and Sage had worn to the amusement parks, and Robin's tattered, baggy jean shorts plus a plain t-shirt and flip-flops, remind me of how she looked the first day she came to work for Guarderobe. Robin's hair is glorious, hanging down around her shoulders, wild as usual. The blonde curls I love are swirling out in every direction thanks to the evening breeze and Orlando's epic humidity. She's not wearing one bit of makeup—which I also love—and oh, how I missed her fresh, pretty face and those rounded cheeks. After not seeing her for so long, not talking to her—she's so beautiful, so *precious* to me right now, that I can hardly hold still and stick to the plan.

When her father brings her to my side, my legs begin to shake some, because her carefully placed mask is slipping again. More flickers of fear cross her face. That hurt lances into me as she lets her eyes lock onto mine, before she quickly looks away.

But, because she's Robin, and she's brave, as well as the girl who always thinks everything is going to turn out fine, she straightens her back and finds my eyes again. I'm nearly brought to my knees when I see the last emotions she's trying to hide from me. Because—*oh-thank-you-God*—there's also love hiding behind that sky-blue gaze, and…I think…some shreds of Robin's unfailing hope was in her expression, too.

Before I can say anything, her mask goes right back on and she asks,

"Why—why are you here? Are—are you here to end it?" She glances over at Vere, my grandmother and Hunter. "To start the breakup?" She shakes her head, as though she's trying to clear it." Because that would be so like you, Royce Devlin. To ruin my birthday party all over again with one of your schemes." She glances around again, frowning. "Wait. There's no paparazzi. When does the press show up?"

The sound of her voice has taken my breath away all over again, because I missed it—her—so much. Worse, the faint scent of lavender coming off of her hair plus my own fear, is making me unable to respond.

When I don't answer, she steps forward, a little glare crossing her features as she hiss-whispering so only I can hear hear, "*Tell me fast. Is that what you're doing? I need to know how to act, damn you.*" Louder, she adds, "Why didn't you just text me a warning that today was going to be the day we end it?"

I FLICK a helpless glance at her father who quickly says, "No, honey. That's not what they're doing. Your young man here. Royce. He's come to ask if he can formally go out with you. He's asked my permission in advance, and Sage's, and Angel's, *and Mrs. Perino's permission, too.*" Mr. Love coughs.

"He even asked me," Angel adds, shaking his head. "I wanted to say no…but… fine, I also want you to be happy so…"

"W*hat*?" Her eyes are going around the circle.

"We've *all* given him our most sincere blessings," my grandmother calls out next. "And it took quite a bit to get us all here."

Mr. Love crosses his arms over his chest. "The rest is up to him. And you."

Her next whispers are strangled as her eyes circle back to me. "Aren't you supposed to be on tour? And…aren't you supposed to ask *my blessings* to date *me*?"

"I—yes—I, that's why I came here in person," I stutter out, working for control. "It's our second, week-long break. We're supposed to be heading out of Europe, and on the way to St. Petersburg. And, yes. Today was supposed to begin the official break-up by me, posting some horrible shit online. But yesterday, I just couldn't do it anymore. And I broke down. Then, I bawled in front of all of them." I point to my family and friends. "Which is when I convinced everyone to take a red-eye flight to come here instead, because they'd never seen me cry before. Because, *yes*. Robin. I—want your blessing. I want—you—your—permission. I want you and I to…do everything. Forever. Us." I shake my head, feeling my face flush. "Damn. I suck at this."

"And we were all very much in support of this marvelous, *new* plan," my grandmother calls out again as though she knows I need some back-up while I recover. "We miss you, dear Robin, and we hope you can forgive us as well as forgive Royce for trying to do what was best—when in fact, that last plan that let you leave Paris so quickly, was a horrible plan. Please hear what Royce has to say. He's been a terrible mess without you. We all have."

Robin starts shaking her head like she wants to protest or something, so before she can speak—or worse—shut me down, I rush in with, "I don't want to break up with you. At all. Ever. And I think —*God, do I hope*—that you might not want to break up with me. It's why I used Clara in the first photos—because I still had all of those concert commitments to uphold—and because I wanted you to have time to really think it over. To really know for sure if you missed me how I was missing you. See, I also thought if you saw me with Clara, you might understand that I was not moving on how you'd told Vere you wanted. Also, because you *know* I can't stand that girl. I'd thought about calling you, or giving you a warning that we were coming here; but then I could never figure out how to make it sound right. So, then I realized that it was important I say all of this in person so you could see my face at the same time. Because, at the very least, when I screw up talking about this—that when you look into my eyes—you can see more. Understand me and find me, and know that I'm sincere. God. Robin. I'm so sorry. Am I making any sense?"

"Yes." She nods, then shakes her head. "And…no. Why did you take so long?"

I flick a glance at Mr. Love, forging on—hoping this is all okay with him, as well. "Work…that's one reason. And, I also had some things to sort out with your father that took up some of the time. He, like me, had wanted you to have your space. To have time to just think about your future, and what you wanted without me butting in. I had to respect his wishes on that. And when he and Sage called me to say you were sad, that they needed me to at least come here and talk to you in Orlando—I was all in, of course. Because shit, I had way too much time to think about my own future without you in it and….damn, I'm still sucking at explaining stuff to you but," I shrug—pointing at everyone. "This is as quickly as we could all come. When your father said this weekend you'd be here, in Orlando, where it all started, I thought it would be perfect. I had this idea that we could go full circle and maybe start over?"

Robin's got creases forming deep in her forehead and she's looking between me and her father. "And what did you two come up with—without asking me? Without involving me." She shakes her head, obviously starting to get angry.

"We didn't—I came up with this idea and—well." I shrug, feeling helpless and way too vulnerable as I just say what I need to say: "I—I came up with—I love you, and I hope you love me back, and I'd like us to stay married while we figure it out, if at all possible. Please—let's not get divorced. We can hold steady without alerting any press to us. And I can be your best friend and then your boyfriend. And, even though it's all backwards, I just wanted to ask you to go out with me—for real."

I take up her trembling hands and drop to my knees in front of her. "If you'll have me. If you can stand to live a life where everyone stares at you, gossips about you, trash-talks you and adores you all at the same time. If you don't mind that all of these people—" I motion to the circle of people standing around us. "That they will come on every vacation we ever have. If you don't care that we will have a whole bunch of bodyguards for the foreseeable future, and a crazy life ahead, with very little private time or even privacy? Will you—would you—say yes to me, yet?" My heart starts thrumming in my temples and when she still doesn't answer I get so scared I have to ask again, "Robin? Do you love me, too? Do you?"

"Yes." She's nodding, grinning—eyes sparkling with unshed tears. "Yes, I love you so much, but…"

"But what?"

Like she can't hold herself up, she sinks down to her knees in front of me while she wipes some at her eyes. "But…how…like *how* will we *do* this? *Can* we do this—I'm still only eighteen and you're still only twenty-one, and…how can we do this for real?"

"How we were doing it before, only…better?" I shrug. "You will still go to school, and I will go back to finish the tour without you. And even though the schedule is impossible and horrible, we'll get through it. Then we'll hang out in *our* apartment as much as we possibly can hang out together. And when we can't—because of work or life or whatever your school and career is doing for you…well when we can't…" I shrug, unable not to pause and run a finger down one of her beautiful flushed cheeks.

She answers for me. "When we can't, we won't die inside like both of us just died these past weeks, because we will know—*know* for real—that we're waiting for each other?"

"Yes! *Yes.*" I breathe out, so relieved by what she's said I nearly crumple again. "See? You get me." I smile at her nodding, and choke out a rough sandpaper whisper, adding, "I've missed you so much. Love you even more." I reach my palm up to cover the few tears that have escaped her glistening blue-eyes.

She turns her face into the heat of my palm. "And if I try to call you or text, you'll answer as soon as possible? And you'll *never* say that you're too busy or refuse to video chat ever, ever again?"

"Never."

She's glowering through her smile now, which has me smiling back at her. "B-b-because that really sucked, and I think I'll never get over how it felt."

"I'm sorry. That was pure torture. I thought it was for the best."

She leans back then—really glaring at me now. "And if I agree, you and my father, and even you, Mrs. Felix?" She motions to my grandmother. "You never get to decide what is for the best for me and Royce, from now on? Deal? He and I decide together."

"Okay. Yes. I think I can agree to that."

"I also, will endeavor to try, Robin, but you know that will be hard for me." My grandmother smiles.

"I've already made that promise to Robin," Mr. Love says.

Robin nods to her father, leveling him with a serious gaze. "And, Dad. You will be okay with me, living with Royce. Because I'm not doing this if he and I can't live together. Because I don't want to start over. We've already done that and I don't want to go back to just—level one dating, or whatever. I want it back the way it was before, only like he said—better." She glances through her lashes at me then, and her cheeks fire bright red.

Mr. Love's shoulders go plywood-straight, like he does not want to answer this, and as we all hold our breath again, he answers, "Fine. I'm going to *make* myself be okay with it, because it is what it is. As long as you're happy." To me he adds, "But if she's not happy? The SF code is one ounce of your blood for every tear she sheds."

Everyone but me laughs at that, and I only shake my head at the guy. Because—even underweight and still limping from the messed-up leg, Robin's father still intimidates the hell out me. "I have no intention of ever making her sad, Sir. Robin's happiness has been my intent all along."

Robin's Dad manages a smile, adding, "I know that, son. And that's why we're all here today. I really, truly know that, and…thank-you."

"Thank you, Sir," I say, completely choked up. Humbled.

"Thanks, Dad." Robin grins at her father, and then everyone in the circle. "Thanks—everyone." When she turns her gaze back to me, I pull in my first full breath, and then I pull *her* into a hug that ends with her on my lap. Not even caring that now she and I are sitting on the grass, cry-hugging in the middle of everyone we know.

I pause to wipe at my eyes, and then nestle her more comfortably on my lap, saying finally, "And when you're old enough, or when you ask *me*—or when your dad stops looking at me like he might want to kill me despite the support he's given me to get here today—*hell, I actually don't know."* I laugh, flushing a little as I lock eyes with Mr. Love again. "Maybe when you've graduated from art school with a real degree and have a job? Then I can propose to you again. Have a real wedding? We will do it with these all of these same people staring at us and smiling like idiots just how they're doing now."

She shakes her head, 'no' and curls herself into my chest as closely as she possibly can, using my shirt front to dry up some of her tears. "No."

"What? Why not?" I ask. "Next time *you* can pick the dress, and the venue, and the decorations, and it will be the wedding of your dreams. Because—did you hear me? I love you, Robin. I love you so much and I'm so sorry I didn't think I could just tell you how I felt. Please. Forgive me for not knowing how to tell you I loved you."

She laughs and her smile is like ten million stars sparkling just for me. "It's not about that. And…I also wanted to tell you that I loved you long ago. But then, I thought, that even though we got along, that we were friends, that maybe you didn't want me. So I believed what you all told me. That I needed to get a normal life back, and above all I thought maybe…you needed *you*r old life back. I thought leaving quickly with Dad would help."

"My old life sucked. I was wrong. But it all got real clear when you went away." My voice cracks again and I whisper quietly so hopefully only she can hear. "I swear, Robin, I nearly died."

"It was the same for me," she whispers back. "I've never been so depressed. I tried to just make it all work, tried to *soldier-on* how I do, but nothing felt right. I was failing at it."

"I know. I'm so-so sorry." I hug her in tighter. "I was ready to swim across the damn ocean to get to you. First, I had to come clean to your father. Sage, of course knew everything. He even knew that you and I were in love."

"He did? That kid." She laughs.

"Your father admitted he'd talked to you and had realized that he couldn't just rewind the clock how he'd wanted. Not when you'd changed so much. Not when you were so sad all the time. I'm sorry for that, and later I'm sure he will tell you that he's sorry, too, for making you wait. I didn't understand that love, real love hurts the most—hurts when you can't be together, because I've never been in love before."

"I haven't been in love before, either, so it's not like I knew where to put my feelings." She presses her forehead into my chest. "Is this some sort of dream I'm having?" She blinks, looking back up worriedly. "It's not, right? Maybe you should pinch me. Do it very hard."

I laugh. "It's not. Robin, I never want to feel that brokenhearted over you ever again. I never want to miss you like I've been missing you, not ever again, and I never want to feel anything but happy when I think of you. Can you forgive me for not knowing what was happening? Forgive me for being afraid of what was happening to us? Forgive me for hurting you?"

"I feel the same…and yes…yes. But, *what was* happening to us?"

I smile at her flushed face. "Forever. Our forever was happening to us, we just didn't know."

"Aww." She grins. "Aww…that's the sweetest thing you've ever said."

"So…what do you think?" I give her a little shake and untangle my arms from hers so I can sit back and see her face. "Do you…could we do this? Can you agree to this next…amazing and poorly thought out plan?" I point at the circle, noting that my grandmother and Mrs. Perino are now also both teared-up. "All of these insane people here, plus me, they're all in, and we're just waiting for your vote."

"I—vote, yes. And I *love* this new-newest-plan."

We both stand together, and everyone's tears dry up as they laugh and congratulate each other.

The shaking goes out of her hands as she looks up into my eyes in that way she's done since day one—like she can see all the way through me, and too deep into my heart. She says loud enough for everyone to hear, "I never want to miss you again either, but I have one thing I need to change in the plan."

"Okay. What?"

She steps forward. "I don't want to get remarried."

"Why?" I ask, sharing a worried glance with her father.

"Considering how awesome the first wedding was, I don't see the point of doing all of that again. My dad hates wearing fancy suits, and he also hates having photographs taken of himself, so… I think, as long as we're all happy, this is good enough for him, right Dad?"

Mr. Love nods and smiles as Robin scrunches up that pert nose of hers and holds up the combined wedding and engagement rings so we can all see it, adding, "I'm also never taking these rings off, *ever*. I'm not sure how we'd re-marry each other anyhow, because we'd have to do the ring part again, right?"

Ana shouts out, oblivious to the deeper layers in the conversation, "That's what I told Robin. When Mr. Gregory gives us *our rings*, then we all need to keep our rings, and take a picture with them. No one is going to take the rings off, that's so silly. And the *next wedding* is going to be *our* wedding. When Mr. Gregory is going to marry Mamma and then he will be our Papa. That's the next wedding anyway."

Not to be left out, Julia adds, "Yeah. It's *our* turn."

"Thank God," I laugh out along with everyone else.

Robin's smile widens while everyone standing in the circle laughs and starts applauding at what Ana and Julia have shouted.

"You've just made me so damn happy," I say and tug at one of her long stray curls, winding my finger into it so I can tug her closer to me.

"I told you all of your wishes would come true. You didn't even need the wand," little Julia calls out again.

Robin replies, looking at everyone and adds in another quiet, flushed-faced whispered, "Thank-you," to everyone.

I waggle my brows at Robin and whisper, "My grandmother has agreed that your father will also have a small apartment inside the Orb NYC until his PT is completed." I grin. "On a different floor, though. And on the other side of the building from where ours is. He insists on paying his own rent, though."

"Perfect. He wouldn't have it any other way." Robin nods approvingly

"And to *seal* this new awesomeness." I say, tugging her curl again, so she has to step even closer. "I get to do the parks with you guys. Most importantly, I get to go with your family to Universal Studios in a couple of days. Chocolate Frogs—until our stomachs hurt. All of the rides. We're doing all of it while holding hands to make up for lost time, too. I'll even get on every single coaster without complaining."

"Do you mean that?" Those big-blue eyes of hers have gone wide.

I frown at her amazement. "Yes. I promised you back in the UK while riding that train. Did you forget?"

"No." She's shaking her head. "I did not forget, I just never thought it would happen."

"If you'll let me, I mean to keep all of my promises to you. Which means there will be chaos when we're together, running through the amusement parks. So much chaos. And one day, sooner than later, and even if we get arrested for creating a public disturbance, I will get you up the Eiffel Tower." I frown, trying to squelch one last wave of doubt. "Are you okay with that—with a lifetime of utter-and-extreme, inescapable madness, just to do the normal little things we want to do?"

Now she's the one frowning. "What have I always told you, Royce? That I'm okay with just hanging out with you, no matter what we do." Her frown turns to a beaming smile. "I'm more than okay with that, and even better?"

"What?"

Her eyes return to twinkling so clear, so bright and so happy that she's taken my breath away once more, as she adds, "I now absolutely can't wait for tomorrow."

"And I can't wait for all of the tomorrows after that," I say, matching my grin to hers. "Whatever happens."

She nods, grinning. "Whatever happens."

And, even though Robin's dad is standing only a few feet away from me with his fists all clenched by his sides like he still wishes he could throw some last punches at me, and even though Sage's expression is so happy, too, that it looks like the kid is going to cry right along with my grandmother and Vere right now, I turn away from them all and pull Robin in close. Then closer, and closer still, until it's just me and Robin. Face to face—breath to breath, and heartbeats to heartbeats. I pause to place a hand over hers—grinning when she tilts her head to the side and does the same to my chest.

"It's like wild horses in there…"

We've both blurted that out at the exact same time.

"*Every time,*" she finishes. Her giggle tangles up into my responding laughter as I sweep *my girl—my wife—my love* into my arms.

I spin her around and around because I can't hold her close enough…and, of course, I start to kiss the laughter off those beautiful lips.

With everyone looking on and applauding more, I kiss her again, and then kiss her until she and I can no longer hear the cheers around us. Until the whole world fades away and the only thing she and I can feel connecting us, is our runaway hearts, beating together.

THE END

Thanks for reading.
It means everything.

ABOUT THE AUTHOR

A quick note about me! I'm Anne Eliot. Hi.

My other bestselling books are:

***Almost**

***How I Fall**

***How I Fly**

***Unmaking Hunter Kennedy** (prequel to the Runaway Rockstar Series—How Hunter met Vere, way back in high school.)

The Runaway Rockstar Series

***Runaway Girl**

***Runaway Heart**

***Runaway Star**

Most of my books are in audio book on Audible or iTunes (or in production). (My narrators are so sweet—they're a guy and a girl and they read it together like it's a play—and even better? They're in love and *now married.* Oh, and they were falling for each other when they did my first books. How cute is that? Makes the first kisses so much sweeter.)

Being an author is a dream I've had since childhood, and one I thought could never come true. I want to tell you that if you also have a wild-big-impossible-dream, or a dream where people around you might not believe that you can do it, or worse, *discourage* you from doing it, or downplay it as 'a nice hobby' or 'cute' please do not listen to them. My parents didn't understand my desire to be an author, but often people who are close to you may not be able to see what you can see. Find a tribe that shares your same dream and hang out with them. Also… while we're on this topic, please ignore the voices in your head that can tear you down even more than unsupportive families and friends. Kill those voices—they can't get into your heart.

You got this. You do! I swear to you that if you don't give up, finally, one day all of the energy you've put out there will come together and fly you to exactly where you imagined. So imagine big. Very big. And... (((HUG))) message me to join my Annie Fannies Facebook page where I'll try to encourage you more there.

Some more about me. I'm also a dyslexic author, a situation that has driven me crazy for my entire life, because it is an unchangeable, inescapable, frustrating thing. Now that I'm wiser, I try to own it—love it and overall love myself anyhow and I hope you can, too.

I live in Colorado and my husband and I run a mad-circus made of up family, and teens, some cool exchange students and two very naughty, food-stealing, spoiled dogs. (Pico—he's the squishy-looking Chihuahua mix, and Blue, the very handsome, yet rather goofy, giant German Shephard).

I'm so honored that you know me a bit better now, and I hope I can one day know you some, too. I'm so happy that you support indie and indie/hybrid authors and that you love reading. (If you didn't you would not still be reading this, right?)

Anyhow...the last thing I'll share about me:

I kind of...talk too much.

Obviously. ;) or this *last* note wouldn't be so darn long.

Love and be love,

Anne Eliot

www.AnneEliot.com

For more information please go to:

www.anneEliot.com

Made in the USA
San Bernardino, CA
24 September 2018